EVERY
MAN'S HAND

EVERY
MAN'S HAND

A NOVEL

JAKE MOSHER

THE LYONS PRESS
GUILFORD, CONNECTICUT
AN IMPRINT OF THE GLOBE PEQUOT PRESS

The Lyons Press is an imprint of The Globe Pequot Press.

Printed in the United States of America

2 4 6 8 10 9 7 5 3 1

Design by Compset, Inc.

The Library of Congress Cataloging-in-Publication Data is available on file.

ISBN 1-58574-458-1

To my sister, Annie

· 1 ·

Here comes Billy Bristol. The great man labored up Main Street, a wad of loose papers clutched in his right hand, his left pumping hard, his face flushed, his stained Mariners sweatshirt beginning to cling to his chest. There was no traffic on the street yet, only feral cats that slipped in and out of narrow alleys, watching closely. Too closely. Billy turned his eyes to the sidewalk and pushed on, his breath heavy, his shoes scraping over bits of broken glass and cracked concrete.

The sun was within striking distance of the East Ridge but had not risen high enough to give the granite cliffs or the enormous statue of the Virgin Mary perched on them more than a dim, gray hint of the day to come. The floodlights at Mary's feet had not yet shut off, and as the drifting July mist passed through their beams, slipping over the west side of the ridge, retreating from the sun as silently as the cats, it appeared she was rising, ascending toward heaven, the airplane light near her head flashing to signal her approach.

Billy stared at her. She was watching him, too, it seemed, not impressed by the way he pushed the sleeve of his sweatshirt into his nose searching for the aroma of fermented hops, a little pick-me-up he didn't think she should begrudge him. He studied her, floating in the mist, and wondered if perhaps Our Lady of the Rockies had grown sufficiently disgusted with Butte to seek a better view. Perhaps she would cast a more approving eye down on Bozeman from atop the Bridgers or, like the Cardiff Giant, that bizarre hoax—or not, Billy wasn't sure—choose to materialize in a cornfield outside Billings. He stood at the corner of Main and Washoe thinking about it longer than he realized, his elbow tight to his face. When he finally decided he would not be afforded the pleasure of so much as the faint scent of last night's beer, an understanding that distressed but certainly did not surprise him, the sun was shining down on the city, dispelling his thoughts on the Virgin as rapidly as it did the mist on the ridge. It was going to be hot, and he wanted to get home and in bed before the brick apartment building heated up. It was easier to sleep when it was cool and easier to write when he was rested.

As Billy heaved along Washoe, he fished through his pockets and came up with one dollar and seventeen cents. Not bad. If he woke up by two, he could write until three, then catch the free spaghetti dinner at the Knights of Columbus, where draft beer was fifty cents a glass. He was confident that a thorough search of his apartment would produce at least another thirty-three cents. Billy ran a thick tongue over his lips, remembering the quarter that had slipped away from him and slid under his couch a week ago, thinking what a marvelous thing memory was. He only needed eight more cents now, no more than an average haul from the Harrison Avenue laundromat's washing machines. Below average really. Then there were the pay phones on Montana Street, with change-return levers like handles on Vegas slot machines. Billy remembered the time he'd pulled one, rubbing the smooth, plastic receiver for luck, and watched as four dollars' worth of change spilled out. As he turned up the steps to his apartment building, he was sure the spaghetti dinner would go down with three glasses of beer.

The apartment's new pressed-board double doors were easier to open than their heavy oak predecessors. It was all Billy had been able to do to get the hardwood monstrosities off their hinges, down the steps, and into the back of his mother's pickup without being crushed. Especially in the dark. The man at the pawnshop in Anaconda hadn't been much use when it came to unloading them, either. He'd dropped his end twice, then griped about "nicks and divots" as he tapped his diminutive pencil against a book of receipts during the appraising process. Forty-seven dollars was as high as he would go, and he gave the quote so ruefully that anyone unschooled in the miserly ways of pawnbrokers would have believed it a great injustice to take so much from him. Billy knew better, and he smiled thinking of how he'd jockeyed the brass knocker—worth at least another twenty or thirty dollars—loose with his pocket knife right under the man's nose, then rubbed his back wondering what permanent damage he'd done himself lifting the doors.

Back injuries were good. That nebulous mass of muscles, tendons, and disks seemed beyond even the doctors' complete comprehension. Billy figured there were enough things in there, and that they were sufficiently interwoven so a doctor more or less had to take his word for it when he said something hurt. Even if it hurt so much he couldn't work. And if the doctor wouldn't, if for some reason he was unwilling to assist in the quest for compensation—or better yet, long term—then a chiropractor would.

"God bless chiropractors," Billy muttered as he tucked the back injury away in his mind for future use and began climbing the cramped stairs toward his fifth-floor apartment. The stairs, curved and wooded, each step cut from a single slab of fir before the turn of the century, squalled as he began the slow ascent. A rusty nail had worked itself a couple of inches out of one board, and Billy wondered what it would do to him if it punctured his tennis shoe. He stared at the worn plastic tread, then at the nail. This was the sort of thing he should deal with the moment he woke up, he decided. A raging case of tetanus, while it might keep the employment agency at bay, wasn't something that appealed to him. He'd seen a special about tetanus victims on the Discovery Channel not long ago, and the very thought of that program caused his jaw to tighten. He worked his teeth, opening his mouth to its fullest extent, reassuring himself he did not have tetanus. He'd hammer home the nail later on and be sure to bill his landlady for it. In that context, despite the serious risk of illness it posed, it was almost a good thing.

Billy's breathing increased as he passed the hole in the plaster wall that looked like a buffalo standing on a Volkswagen near the fourth floor. Was it trying to tell him something? An idea for an essay, perhaps? He deposited that thought near the one about his back injury. Pull them out of the vault later.

There were eleven steps between floors, and the ones between the fourth and fifth were Billy's least favorite. To his way of thinking, he already lived a mile above sea level, and anything more than that was uncalled for. He climbed the stairs one at a time, drawing his size-twelve sneakers together at the top of each plateau, resting a full minute before lifting first one leg and then the other, which he did with the aid of his right hand wrapped in a loose fold of jeans just above the knee. The final three steps—Jesus, Mary, and Joseph—he called out each time he conquered them. This time he said their names forcefully in his best James Earl Jones voice. Standing at last on Joseph, his chest billowing in and out, his head beginning to swim from the beer and onset of hypoxia, he reached for the door, imagining its handle the blue-ribbon finish line of the Boston Marathon. He touched the cool steel, smiled, then lifted his eyes to the stained-glass porthole he'd installed at head level the week before. He hadn't billed his landlady for that nice addition yet, either.

This morning, there was something different about the kaleidoscope of colors. Something new. There in the lower left-hand corner, where the teal and olive swirls ran together, just inside their duct-tape border, a light was blinking. Three red blinks, a short pause, then three more. Billy's hand jumped from the doorknob as though someone had run a high-voltage electric current through it, and he sank to his knees in the hallway, tipping his head toward his lap, not bothering to brush from his eyes the long strands of hair that fell from his forehead. Inside his chest, his heart had assumed the rhythm of the blinking light: three beats, a pause, then three more.

His mother must have found the answering machine while rooting around his apartment. Perhaps one of its cords had spilled out of the boot closet where he'd flung it, or maybe she'd systematically searched for it, sweeping the living room in concentric circles. Had she found the quarter under the couch, too? Billy balled his knees into his chest and watched a bead of sweat tumble from his nose. His stomach was turning somersaults, and no matter where he tried to focus his eyes, everything spun. Answering machines were one of the great evils of modern society, he thought. A cop-out. A good opportunity for editors to reject his work without telling him personally, which he was sure they did because they could not justify their decision to turn down the masterful pieces he sent them. He stared at the papers still in his hand, proof that publishing houses would turn him down with or without answering machines, but at least this way they were forced to write something themselves. See what it's like, if only for a fraction of a second, to put pen to paper the way he so often did.

Answering machines were also the tools of people like his mother. People who always wanted something from him. People happy to bark their commands onto those awful miniature cassette tapes and expect prompt responses. Yes, the possibilities of who had called were infinite and terrible. His mother was unreasonably disagreeable about his failure to pay her the fifty dollars she'd lent him for rent, and one of the messages would be hers. That fiendish bartender from Chuck's who'd chased him halfway up Main Street a few nights ago, screaming threats involving the police if his tab wasn't paid in full. There might be something nice waiting from her.

What about the third message? The final blink? It would be an editor or, god forbid, that woman from Job Services whose looks were her only redemption and whose main purpose in life seemed to be keeping Billy from the ranks of the unemployed. Muff or Bush—he could never remember more than that it was close to slang for that heavenly part of a woman. If the third message was from Bug, or whatever the hell her name was, she'd want to know why he'd applied for those hospital openings instead of something he could realistically expect to get. She had no idea, as virtually no one did, of what writing was all about. How critical unemployment stipends could be, and how almost all jobs cut him off from his material and rightful work. She didn't understand anything about being cut off. Could not begin to fathom the necessity to run out the benefits he'd earned working—slaving—at his winter filing/folding job. Puss would rather he go to work at McDonald's than push ahead a writing project. Yes, Snatch would be upset. She would be upset unless—and the thought of this new and worst possibility was more than Billy could bear—unless she had found him a job herself.

A terrible throbbing began in Billy's head, a Chinese devil beating a monstrous gong, mimicking the tempo of the light on the answering machine. And when at last he could no longer crouch outside his door, as the gong mutated to a giant jackhammer, pounding against his skull in combinations of three pneumatic punches unequaled in force by any of the heavyweights he watched from time to time on HBO, he rose to his feet and groped for the key on top of his door—heavy, trembling fingers anticipating the awful feel of cool brass. Perhaps a black widow spider had set up shop on top of the door and would spare him the torture of the messages by delivering a vicious bite. He swished his hand around, hoping to get the attention of any poisonous spiders.

Instead of arachnids or cold metal, Billy found paper. Folded paper, which, although chilly from the brass inside, was far more pleasant than the naked key itself would have been. As he unfolded the note, relieved to see his mother had used only a half sheet of paper, his eyes focused sufficiently to read.

"Honey—I came by hoping you'd be here. Maybe that nice girl at Job Services has found you a job so you won't lie around watching the Discovery Channel all day anymore."

Billy's mother obviously had no idea how much material that program contained. Never having watched it herself, she could be forgiven her ignorance, but Billy could not forgive her hoping that Twat had found him a job. His mother knew nothing about being cut off. Besides, it wasn't as if he hadn't tried to find employment. What would she rather have, a son who washed dishes at the Wild Mustang Supper Club or one who worked in the hospital? She needed to adjust her expectations and start supporting his writing. She could easily be left by the wayside when the book signings began. He continued reading, even as the jackhammer in his head changed to a modern, as-of-yet-uninvented battering ram.

"I thought you might appreciate me cleaning your apartment. I know I taught you appreciation, so it won't hurt to thank Mommy. It ain't healthy to live like you are.

"I bet you could never guess what I found in your closet."

The three blinking lights inside the door had provided a clue.

"I plugged it in by your phone for a surprise. I found some money lying around, too."

Billy put his hand to his face. Please tell me she didn't take it.

"There was a quarter under your couch, some pennies in the kitchen soap dish, and a dollar under the *TV Guide* on your coffee table. I have no doubt you have a job now and are well on your way to being respectable, so I kept the money. You only owe your mommy forty-eight dollars and seventy cents."

A dollar? Billy was stunned. How had he overlooked it?

"A dollar," he whispered sadly, as the battering ram turned to a giant South American wasp and delivered the first of a trio of stings. "Oh god, oh god," he moaned. "No more. Please, no more."

Billy rolled onto his back, letting the beer, altitude, and disappointment come for him all at once, and with a plaintive whimper, an unintelligible prayer for mercy, he passed into sleep.

· 2 ·

Billy woke some hours later from a dream of unspeakable frightfulness. Something about his stint in college that chilled him to the bone and caused him to carefully scan every inch of exposed skin, searching for the hives such dreams invariably caused. He was mildly disappointed to find himself free of them.

The beer had more or less run its course through his system, settling in his bladder where it distended that reservoir painfully, giving rise to the question of whether it was more dignified to piss oneself on the way to the bathroom or placidly allow nature her way while lying on the floor. Billy believed he might make the toilet, though unlocking his door would slow him down. On the other hand, it would be easier to clean up if it was all in one place. If something burst on the run, that could be messy. He peered under the crack of his door at the pea-green living room carpet, careful not to move more than his pupils lest a body tremor prematurely decide the issue for him. The worn fibers would not make much of a sponge, and although there was something to be said in favor of taking care of business where he was—something fitting about a writer soiling himself outside his own door—he decided he would go for the bathroom.

This took some planning. Not rested sufficiently from last night, and worn out from climbing the stairs, Billy knew making the bathroom would be no small accomplishment. Once up, he might be able to get it out of his pants while he unlocked the door, and he was confident that enough pressure had built up so he wouldn't really need to make it all the way to the toilet. Seven or eight feet away should be good enough. Perhaps he should undo his fly while lying down. He slid his left hand to his groin. Nothing. Biting his lip, breathing hard and fast, he touched the zipper. At this prompt, he felt a tidal wave move inside him, realizing that before he had the key turned in the lock he'd have to pinch it off. He imagined it dammed up behind his hand and prayed it would not blow out some weak point. With a butt from his head, the door flew open, and five long strides took him to the bathroom, within range. A yellow stream arced out toward the toilet. Billy leaned his hips back for more altitude, closing his eyes when he heard the splashdown. Thank god his mother had not closed the cover. He sighed with pleasure, enjoying the moment, fully aware that making the toilet might be the best thing to happen to him for a long time.

Finished relieving himself, Billy knew now was the time to retreat to the living room and listen to his messages. Better to hear them immediately after something good had happened than to brood about them until misfortune played him a different hand. Touching the play button in a state of depression would be more than he could handle. He had to hear the messages, but first he needed to analyze his dream. Dreams, in particular bad ones, had a nasty habit of coming true and needed to be fully dissected, prevented if at all possible from leaving his head for a place in the real world. He dropped the plug into the center of his cast-iron tub and climbed in while hot water splashed down over his feet, mindful not to put them too near the drain. If fungus had bloomed in there, it could easily migrate under his toenails and cause all manner of troubles. As the tub filled, Billy leaned back, thinking of how his dream had begun, how peaceful sleep had been violently overthrown with the first image: a giant house of stone that he knew was a place of higher education.

It had that smell about it. Cleaning detergents, copying ink, new paper, and fear. It smelled strongest of fear. Unable to protest, Billy had been drawn deep inside, much further really than an ordinary building would have permitted: through rooms full of desks, past rows of little blue exam booklets, and toward the inner chamber—the room of polished hardwood and high bookcases where a man whose title he had vowed long ago would never again cross his lips sat waiting. Something led him to the chamber door, the shiny nameplate inches from his face, a cold draft seeping under the sill, and he could hear fingers tapping a fancy desk inside. *Ta-ta-ta-tap. Ta-ta-ta-tap.* Thank god he woke up when he did. If the door had opened and he'd been forced to see—to see what he couldn't bring himself to *say*—the damage done might have been permanent.

Billy bounced in the tub, letting the water slosh over his legs. What did this dream mean? Why was this traumatic event from his past cropping up again? A sign of things to come, no doubt. He must watch for any connection to this dream and be on his guard at all times.

"Brave and alert," he mumbled to himself as he climbed out of the tub, though he felt neither, unconvinced he'd solved much by examining the dream. At any rate, the answering machine could be put off no longer. Seated naked in front of it, one hand on the sofa to steady himself, Billy found it difficult to press *play*. It took three false starts for his finger to find the button and set the machine—the machine and Fate—in motion.

"Surprise!"

It was his mother. Her voice boomed out of the speaker with amplified gusto.

"You like where I put it, honey?"

Billy bit his lip. Compared with a kick in the nuts, where she put it was fine.

"Now, I know you've probably had a long day—out working— work, work, work, that's my boy, but if you get a chance, drop in and say hello to Mommy, okay?"

Ho-hum, when's she going to bring up money? Billy debated advancing the tape but decided against it. Things would only get worse, he feared.

"Billy, I've been thinking what you need is a nice lady friend. A county or state worker maybe. Someone who can cook you a hot meal after working all day."

Billy figured his odds of finding such a woman were only slightly greater than those that he would work all day. Writing wasn't like that. It came and went as it pleased. Nothing he'd expect his mother to understand, however.

"Baby . . ."

Here it was. His own mother was about to whine for money. No consideration for artists such as himself. And hadn't she just cleaned him out? What if the dollar she took was destined for postage on a proposal for a novel that would be snapped up by the first house he sent it to? How would that make her feel? Why not simply crush my hand so that it will never again put pen to paper? he thought.

"I know better times are just around the corner for you."

Billy stared across the living room to the window that looked out onto Washoe. It seemed that this was a very, very long corner. His mother should leave such clairvoyant insights to those who have a better handle on reality. One more unemployment check, then he would be destitute.

"And then you won't think anything of paying back the forty-eight dollars and seventy cents. Mommy loves you."

Static crackled through the speaker as the machine advanced to the second message. A blowfly the size of a quarter, perhaps attracted by the buzzing, kamikazed down from the ceiling and lit in the middle of Billy's forehead, where it began probing his skin with its suction-cup-tipped proboscis. He'd seen an enlarged picture of the tool on the Discovery Channel, and the thought of what now was taking place on his head made him ill. He swatted at the fly and poked himself in the eye.

"Mr. Bristol?"

Billy recognized the voice of his landlady, Mrs. Helmsley. It echoed off the wall behind him in an odd way that made him suddenly aware he was naked. Just like Eve's apple, he thought, unable to decide who was more devious, the serpent or Helmsley. He covered his groin with both hands, dismayed to see that one would have done the job easily.

"Mr. Bristol? Are you there? Hello?"

Mr. Bristol. It was almost as foreboding as *sir*.

"Hello? Hello?"

Hadn't she ever used an answering machine before? It would speak well of her if she hadn't, but that was very unlikely. Maybe she suspected him of being in the building.

"Yes, well . . . this is Louise Helmsley. Sorry to have missed you, sir."

Ah, there it was. With formalities out of the way, she could move right along to griping about money.

"I shall be coming by tomorrow afternoon and expect you will have the remainder of June's rent. My records indicate that you are in arrears for half the month. A day late on your July rent, as well. Also . . ."

There was more? Kick me while I'm down, Billy thought. Go ahead, it will make you feel a great deal better. And *tomorrow*?

That was today. Jesus, what if she came to the door now, master key in hand?

"Also, I'm going to have to insist that you pay in full at the beginning of each month from now on."

Quick, something to block the door. The couch. For the first time since his fifth beer the night before, Billy's mind was clear. The sofa scraped along the carpet and bumped hard into the door. Good, let her shove that out of the way.

"Yes, well, at any rate, sir, we will discuss these things tomorrow. Good-bye."

Billy flopped onto the couch, exhausted. The adrenalin surge that had enabled him to move it now left him feeling nauseated. He believed that before the end of the final message he might be forced to make another dash to the bathroom, this time to expel the contents of his stomach.

As the answering machine prepared to deliver the death sentence, he found himself thinking about what was in his stomach. Strange, he thought, but then he'd heard that the minds of condemned men often wander into odd realms in their final moments. A guard against reality, perhaps. Billy had backtracked everything he'd consumed the day before, just reaching the Polish sausage he'd had for lunch, when Buff's voice, similar to the women who answer the one-nine-hundred calls, oozed out of the speaker.

"Hi, Billy."

Hi, Billy. What are you wearing? Where are your hands? Oh, you don't have any clothes on? Well . . . let me tell you a little secret. You like secrets, Billy? I don't have any clothes on, either. And I'm touching myself. Would you like to touch yourself, Billy?

Billy didn't think this was the route Buff would take, though she sounded perfectly cut out for it. And he didn't like the fact that he remembered her name.

"I've got some really good news, Billy." She smacked her lips. "I need you to stop by the employment office as soon as you get this message."

Suddenly, Billy believed her seductive tone was indeed intended. She knew damn well how he loathed the idea of being cut off, and she was enjoying it. Getting off on it.

"We've got something that's perfect for you, Billy."

A million-dollar advance for my novel? A new Ferrari? Did the CEO of the Ranier Beer Company resign?

"See you soon," she said, exhaling so much with each word that Billy figured she either had the largest lungs in the world or was turning blue.

See you soon, big boy. Just me and you and a room full of desks. Oh, Billy, I bought us a new toy. Look, it plugs in.

Buff Austin splayed out on a metal-topped desk was a far more appealing fantasy than the more likely scenario that even as he lay curled up and naked in front of his door she was canceling his final unemployment check. That one stung.

Soft, deliberate footsteps on the stairs jarred Billy to attention. The greatest evil is always the one closest at hand. His impending visit to the unemployment agency, Job Services, was not set in stone. That was the glorious thing about the future. Never set in stone. He could be struck and killed by an automobile on his way there. But the present, that was a different matter. Much harder to change. He put his ear to the door and listened to the thick, padded shoes touching the wooden steps. They sounded like globs of mercury dropped from head level. Oh no. Mrs. Helmsley. Her goddamned special shoes for the corns on her feet. She probably had a whole field of them. Where was she? In the narrow stairwell, noises echoed deceptively. How close was she to the holy family?

Billy low-crawled, military-style, across his living room, taking care to keep his member off the carpet. The skin on his elbows would grow back more readily. Where the room goosenecked, the bathroom on his right, his bedroom on the left, he stood and leapt sideways for his bed. A pair of jeans, ones his mother had found on the floor, lay folded awkwardly on the bedspread. He jerked them on, not bothering with underwear, and threw his arms into the sleeves of a BUTTE sweatshirt missing the *e*. It was too hot for long sleeves, but now was a time of action first, prudence second.

Mrs. Helmsley worked quickly up Jesus, Mary, and Joseph. Lucky for Billy, she carried her key in that big, bulky purse. He could gain a few seconds on her while she dug it out. His feet slid into a pair of laceless Hawthorns, he snatched his Pegasus Gold hat from the bedroom door handle, and he broke for the kitchen just as his landlady began working the lock.

Right foot on the sink, left foot on the sill, window up, left hand on the sill, right hand on the faucet . . . push, jump, no time to be scared of heights. Billy exited onto the fire escape perfectly. Professionally, he thought. As he clanged down the iron rungs, he heard Mrs. Helmsley above him.

"Billy? Billy, what's the meaning of this barricade? Let me in this instant!"

Before he knew it, his feet were on concrete, and Helmsley's voice had faded into the sounds of traffic on Washoe. He bowed, saluted the open kitchen window, and bounced up the street whistling the theme from *Rocky*, jabbing at the air in front of him.

The shadowboxing didn't last long. The thrill of thwarting Helmsley ran out almost as quickly as Billy's breath, and by the time he reached Main Street, puffing hard in the thin air, all he could think about was the employment agency and having to face his nemesis: the little energetic blonde who couldn't wait to put him to work and cut him off. True, he hadn't entered the building yet, hadn't been assaulted by the clattering of keyboards as more eager job hunters than he took their typing tests, hadn't spewed out his social security number half a dozen times, hadn't shuffled to Buff's cubicle and seen her beaming face, but Billy felt that by dawdling he was only putting off the inevitable. When the future held unpleasantries, it was much harder to change.

Billy looked down Main Street, praying he would see something to divert him. Legitimately take him off course. The broad street sloped away before him, off the hill, out toward the flats at the base of the Highlands, where modern Butte was trying to distance itself from her dilapidated uptown sections. Crawling away from her cocoon. Heat waves rose from the tar and from the sidewalk as well, scurrying along the brick buildings, thrusting their tentacles into the sky. Sweat began running down Billy's back, gluing the fuzzy inside of his sweatshirt to him, and he shifted his shoulders, pulling the heavy fabric away from this throat, blowing onto his chest to cool himself.

Chuck's Corner Bar was just visible six blocks down from him, and Billy figured that he could find something in that oasis of tall stools and keno machines that would cool him better than his breath. He turned his Hawthorns south and began plodding down the hill. The richest hill on earth, he reminded himself.

Honeycombed with hundreds of miles of desolate mine tunnels, some clogged with enough wire to wrap around the world six times, others caving in from time to time, trying, it seemed, to pull Butte into the giant stomach beneath her, the richest hill on earth was about played out. It continued to cling to the title given it when millions of pounds of copper were dredged from its depths—a title that now seemed more like an epitaph. Perhaps there was a poem in it somewhere.

In the middle of the third stanza, "So went the buffalo, so went Butte," Billy drew even with Chuck's. Going down was so much easier than coming up. Five steps from the steel-strapped door, its painting of the underground miner and bold proclamation that all engaged in that line of work were forever welcome inside, the composition process came to a halt as the bartender, a beefy woman with the look of grizzly bear crossed with Angus bull, burst into the street.

"Bristol!" she bellowed.

Billy began edging back up the hill, wishing he'd taken the time to get his sneakers. Leslie Booth was a big woman, but she was quick, too. A combination that could prove fatal for him if she charged.

"You got your money?" She pointed a thick finger at him and Billy imagined its deformed nail digging in under his chin. "You ain't come to pay your tab, and you'll pay the piper."

She came for him fast, thighs rubbing sickly against each other. Her hands drew into fists and her nostrils, prodigious orifices to begin with, expanded to something in the neighborhood of a humpback whale's blowhole. Maybe she could seal them off and stay under water the way they could—almost an hour, according to the Discovery Channel.

"Didn't figure I'd be working today, did you?" she said. "That's what some of us do for a living, Billy. Ain't that bad luck for you?"

Billy figured this was his punishment for not going directly to the employment agency. He hadn't realized that the Fates considered it so egregious an offense, and in the back of his mind images from his dream, images he now feared foretold things yet to come, swirled with cyclonic speed. Evidently, he and the powers that be were at odds over the severity of shirking tasks. One eye trailed questioningly upward, as if to ask if sending this obese denizen was truly necessary. A voice all around him replying, "Vengeance is mine."

Billy remembered the National Geographic special on Kodiak Island brown bears. Until the bartender came for him, he had figured those overgrown grizzlies were the most formidable creatures on earth. Standing on Main Street in the clutches of more than three hundred pounds of vexed woman, he would have given a great deal to be off the coast of Alaska, ready to receive a healthy mauling. At least then he could play dead and maybe the bear would go away. Going that route with Booth would further infuriate her. She liked to make things slow, and if he didn't scream with pain, she would figure she needed to step up the attack. He wondered if she would bite him.

In less than two seconds, the distance between them closed to ten feet. Booth came on hard, her upper body oddly still in comparison with her whirling legs. If those monstrous limbs of propulsion ever wrapped around him, he'd be done for. It was this thought, the idea of Leslie Booth getting him in some sort of professional wrestler's leg hold, rubbing his face god only knows where, that spurred Billy into action. He knew he wasn't as quick off the block as she was, but he believed that if he could keep out of reach for forty or fifty yards, she'd run out of steam.

The Hawthorns clapped off the sidewalk, their loose tongues lolling out over his toes as Billy tried to run the forty in four. He threw himself up the hill with everything he had, cursing it and all its riches with every step, began to pull away, then tripped.

Vanquished.

Booth looked even bigger standing over him. She blotted out a good portion of the Montana sky, no small accomplishment in Billy's estimation. And to make matters worse, he had fallen in front of the R&R, Main Street's diner, home to a large crowd of professional drunks, some of whom were already filing out to see what was going on.

"Give him the boots," one man encouraged.

"Stomp his guts," another yelled.

Billy had not come to rest near a bastion of sympathy. He closed his eyes, preferring the darkness of their lids to Booth's boxerlike fists, which were sure to begin raining blows upon him any instant.

"Kill him," a squeaky voice called from the crowd. "Kick him in the balls."

Instinctively, Billy curled up. But what he felt was not a size-thirteen shoe searching out a testicle but a tongue, quite possibly the largest human tongue on earth, hot on his chin. It ran to his lips, lingered, cruised to his right eye where it licked open the lid, then zipped up the bridge of his nose, wetting a path more than two inches wide. Jesus, why was it so rough? Was she part cat? What if she could lick all the same places as a cat?

Billy began coughing, flipping around on the pavement, searching with his own little tongue for anything—dirt, glass, a bit of salt left from winter—to wash the taste of Leslie Booth from his mouth.

As she rose above him, flexing her arms to cheers of, "You bet, darling," and headed back toward Chuck's, Billy's relief was minimal. He hugged the sidewalk, wishing one of the mine tunnels would open and take him away from this new low he had reached. His fingernails bit into a seam in the cement, pulling and prying, all to no avail. He would not be granted a quick drop into the bowels of Butte. Three minutes later, when he pushed himself up, his feet shuffling as slowly as they ever had, on his way to cutting himself off, Billy found himself wondering again if Booth could really lick herself in a feline way. The thought made him sick, but try as he might he could not drive it from his head, and not until he found himself in front of the Job Services building on Granite Street could he imagine more than the brutish woman sitting on her haunches, her big tongue wandering over every inch of herself.

One of the more modern buildings in uptown Butte, the employment agency sat low to the ground in the traditional one-story western style. A small American flag hung limply from its post, a splash of red against the white stucco.

Billy drew his arms into his sides so that the ever-widening circles of sweat would be somewhat less visible, folded the tongues of his Hawthorns over on themselves to conceal his bare and blistered feet, patted his hair down tight against the back of his neck, and walked in.

Air conditioning. An empty chair with a thick cushion. Not too many keyboards going. Hell had an acceptable waiting room.

Vagina woman—Billy had forgotten her name again, but because he was in a government building he figured he should exercise enough restraint to keep his mind off the more vulgar terms—was conducting an interview. He could see her over the long front counter, hair laden with enough conditioner so that it hung as motionless as the flag outside. Her *client,* everyone at Job Services insisted on using that word, was a woman, and they seemed to be engaged in a serious conversation.

Billy sank into the yellow cushion on his chair and closed his eyes. He had not yet attended to the rejection letters he'd received the day before, and thinking about them made him mad all over.

"Dear Mr. Bristol," one had begun. "Please do not continue to use us as a sounding board for your ideas. We simply do not have the time to consider such folly. Your latest proposal, 'A Day on Main Street,' defies explanation. What Main Street? Where? What about it? For several weeks you have regaled us with similar nonsense, and I am begging you for the sake of everyone involved to move on."

There had been no signature, just a short P.S.: "Do you really think a comprehensive list of expenses, along with a demand for excessive payment, is the best way to get an assignment? Please, no more."

Good, Billy thought. I'm wearing them down. Take that feeling and multiply it by ten thousand and you might have an inkling of what writing is all about. That's what happens when you cut yourself off. You lose your imagination. What Main Street did he—he or she or staff (staff seemed to reply most often)—think he meant?

"Whoever wrote that letter should lose his job," Billy said loudly.

A slight woman, some sort of receptionist, looked up when he spoke. She should lose her job, too, Billy thought.

Then there had been a letter from *The New Yorker.* Very generic. Impersonal, thoughtless, patronizing, and, by god—Billy sat up straight, the blood rushing to his head—it was flat-out wrong. His idea *was* "right" for them. In fact, it was perfect. There's interest in the West, Montana in particular, and whoever thought readers wouldn't enjoy an insightful piece on one man's reflections on a day in Butte—he wouldn't even restrict it to Main Street—should lose his job.

"Editors," Billy fumed. He decided to send them a bill for his postage. If they were going to treat him in this contemptible manner, the least they could do was reimburse him the sixty-six cents for two stamps. Something for the envelopes and paper, too. Call it a dollar even. He'd find out the name of someone in accounts payable and be sure to be in touch. Perhaps they could trouble themselves to address the check to him. It seemed more than they were capable of when it came to writing letters.

"Dear _____"

It was unbecoming for *The New Yorker* to play fill in the blank. That should be brought to the attention of the stockholders, Billy thought. He hoped he hadn't spilled his beer on that letter. He'd taken them to the bar to read, ready to celebrate an acceptance, ready to drown his outrage. He figured his outrage had gone to the bottom of Lake Baikal shortly before midnight. Down into the depths where caviar sturgeon, those most frightening fish, fin their way around in total darkness. He could picture them clearly, just as they appeared on the Discovery Channel, and he shuddered.

"Billy? Billy?"

Buff was motioning to him.

"Right back here." She waved again, smiling her devious smile, loving the idea of cutting him off.

Billy heaved himself to his feet and moved toward her desk, passing her client as he opened the waist-high saloon-style door that separated them. Automatically, he scanned the woman. Large breasts, tight pants, a practiced roll to her ass as she walked. Was that a phone-sex application in her hand? And what about that delicate necklace nestled between those lovely mounds? A golden *A* hung between the braided chains, drawing Billy's eyes to it, then to either side. Was the precious metal letter too cool to wear under her shirt? Oh, no, Billy thought, certainly not. He hoped it would slip in there, watching impatiently, imagining a cordless phone held between her ear and shoulder. Yes, that was how she'd hold it. Keep her hands free that way.

Hi, I'm A. What do you want to talk about, Billy?

"Hi, Billy." Buff's voice wasn't as sensuous in person as it was over the phone. Certainly not as pleasing as A's would be.

He sat in a plastic chair opposite her desk, hoping it was still warm from the woman. It wasn't, but the coolness that spread up between his legs wasn't altogether unwelcomed.

"How are you?" Buff seemed quite casual.

"Fine," Billy lied. But she wouldn't understand. He should have told her that next to the way the chair was cooling his sweaty balls, the best thing that had happened to him in the past twenty-four hours was the good fortune he'd had of pissing into his toilet rather than all over his living room carpet. He shuddered when he thought how close he'd come to losing another shred of dignity. Who knows, it could have been the *last* shred.

"Well, I finally got ahold of you. Thanks for turning your answering machine on."

Billy curled his toes. He'd be damned if his mother would see so much as a penny of the forty-eight dollars and seventy cents she'd bitched about. That debt was more than nullified. And he'd change his lock, too.

"How's the writing going?"

Don't go there, Billy thought.

"Anything coming out soon?" Buff seemed genuinely interested. Perhaps there was room for fabrication here.

"I've got a piece slated for later this month in the *Times*," he said.

"New York?"

"Yes, their travel section. It's on Butte."

"Really?"

Billy nodded. He hadn't actually had that proposal turned down yet, and he knew that it was next to impossible to get a copy of the *Times* in Butte anyway. No way to verify the story.

"And I'm coming down the home stretch with another novel, too."

"Wow. What's it about? You mind my asking?"

"I'd rather not say. I couldn't do it justice." In truth, Billy figured it wouldn't take long to summarize the six paragraphs he'd written. "All I need is a little more time." Yes, approximately the two weeks I could write if you would be as kind as to push through my final unemployment check.

"That's amazing. I mean, that you do this. I don't think I'm self-disciplined enough. If I didn't have a schedule, I'd be playing all the time, I think."

At least she acknowledged that it took discipline. Maybe she knew more than he gave her credit for.

"Well, let's see . . ." Buff began digging through the papers on her desk. "Looks like you've about run out of unemployment."

No, not quite, Billy thought. Not until the fat lady sings, and I don't hear her crowing yet. Please, please, just two more weeks.

"You're scheduled to get your last check day after tomorrow?"

At 9:25 A.M., as soon as the mail is sorted.

"Yes," Billy said.

"Well . . . I guess that will go through all right."

Billy wanted to kiss her. Take her right there behind her desk. The little receptionist and the people working on their typing tests could watch. Maybe he'd like them to watch.

"This doesn't start until next week," she said.

There it was, Billy thought. A reference to the future as though it was made of concrete.

"I think it's perfect for you."

"Full-time?" Billy asked, trying hard to keep his voice from cracking.

"No, actually it's not. It's part-time."

Things were looking up. Partially cut off was better than fully cut off. But this had the ring of something too good to be true. Billy was always careful. "What is it?" he asked suspiciously.

"Personal attendant," Buff said. "There's a woman relatively new to Butte who needs someone to show her around. Help her out a little. I'm not sure how long it will last, but as soon as I heard about it, I thought of you."

"A woman?" Billy pinched himself to be sure he wasn't dreaming.

"Yes. She was just in, and I had the pleasure of meeting her. She's absolutely fantastic. Her name is Andrea Kauffman. She was a movie star in Germany."

Billy's mouth fell open. A for Andrea? This *was* too good to be true. Booth must have killed him back there on Main Street. He dug his fingers into the soft part of his inner thigh until his eyes watered. Then again, perhaps one feels pain in heaven. Or . . . he hadn't gone *there*, had he?

"She can pay very well."

That's it, I'm dead. Crossed over. Billy shifted in his seat. Paradise looked a lot like Butte.

"She has a lot of time on her hands and wants a friend as much as anything. She doesn't know anyone here."

Thank you, god. A friend it is. And much, much more.

"Does this sound like something you can handle?"

"I think so," Billy said. "Of course I'm very busy, but I think I can fit it in."

"I thought it would work well with your writing."

Bless you . . . why couldn't he remember her name?

"I've got her address right here," Buff said, digging deeper into the papers. "She's expecting you Monday morning. I think she wants to go to breakfast. She likes eating out."

How's she like room service? Billy wondered. He took the Post-It note with her address and stood up.

"Thank you," he said, staring at her longer than he meant to. Something about her, he wasn't sure exactly what, made it hard for him to look away. He was out the door on his way back to his apartment before it occurred to him that she'd blushed. A common enough reaction, he thought. Most women would probably have swooned.

Climbing up the fire escape wasn't as bad as Billy had expected. He hummed the first couple of verses to a song. No, it wasn't a song, it was more the text of a rhyming picture book. A is for Andrea, B is for breasts. Billy couldn't think what C was for, but he knew that in time he would. D is for unDressed. Right now, the prospect of meeting the beautiful Andrea Kauffman clouded his thought process. He thought about her, lying on his sofa, pushed a few inches away from the door by Helmsley, and wondered if he'd been catapulted into the midst of a love story? German actress in the mountains of Montana. He imagined taking her horseback riding through a field full of wildflowers, her white mare galloping in slow motion. Oh, to be that saddle, he thought. It was an inspiring vision, and moments of inspiration being relatively few, he decided to take advantage of it and write.

Billy retrieved a yellow legal pad from his bedroom and carefully printed his return address in the top right-hand corner on the lined sheet. He would query *Playboy*. They paid well and could appreciate the love angle.

"To whom it may concern," he wrote. "Please see that this is delivered directly to your executive editor. It is not intended for the eyes of underlings, and any responses from such shall be returned unopened. My idea is this: a foreign actress in the wilds of Montana. I see about two thousand words, and expect you will have ideas for appropriate pictures. My rate this year has increased to one dollar and fifty cents per word, keeping pace with inflation. I'm sure you understand. And my byline is to go at the beginning of the piece, set in bold type, in something other than the font of the text. A prompt response will prevent me from taking this proposal elsewhere. Very sincerely, William Bristol."

A masterpiece of persuasion. Billy read it over twice, then clipped it to his refrigerator with a magnetized washer he'd found on Main Street one day. When his unemployment check came, he would get it right in the mail.

Writing was tiring. Something else most people didn't understand. And it was also emotionally draining. Billy returned to the living room and thought about moving his sofa, but decided against it. Not while he was fatigued. He slumped onto it, clicked the remote for the television, and listened to the Discovery Channel narrator's English accent.

"It is a fearsome newt, and will consume its own young if given the chance."

Billy held his breath, waiting to see where it lived. It was always so much better when the creatures were not indigenous to Montana. As the rain forest came into focus, he sighed. He would permit the narrator to continue.

· 3 ·

B illy rose early on the morning of his appointment with love, his stomach grumbling to remind him that his unemploy-ment check had not yet arrived and that the free midnight pizza at Chuck's had been his sole nourishment for two days. A man shouldn't have to live like this, he thought. Well, not for much longer. Soon it will be devil's food cake and Flathead Valley cherries. Big, red, plump ones fresh from the crisper drawer of the refrigerator. He could watch Andrea eat them for hours. The thought of her dangling them over her tongue by their stems was almost too much for him.

Billy licked his lips. No devil's food morsels on them this morning. And if Andrea didn't pay him up front or his unemploy-ment check didn't arrive . . . well, he would have to pawn some-thing. He looked at the sparse furnishings in his apartment. There was the couch he couldn't part with because it was where he sat when he wrote, and it doubled as a damn good barricade; a toilet securely bolted to the floor; a monstrous kitchen sink that would make moving the front doors look like child's play; a thirteen-inch color television—out of the question; and a six-slice toaster. The toaster could go, but cinnamon toast over the gas flame on the stove would be tricky without a fire extinguisher in hand.

In a real fix he could pawn the toaster, or he could lower his standards and sell a piece to a magazine or periodical one notch under the best. One notch was as far as he would consider going, and even the prospect of settling for *that* disturbed him. If a writer forfeits his principles it's much easier for him to get cut off, he thought. Forty-hour workweeks might even become tempting. Billy shook like a wet dog. No, he wouldn't do it. It was the toaster or nothing.

"Billy Bristol holds himself to the most exacting standards," he said to his reflection in one of the living room's small win-dows.

What he could see of the day outside looked cloudy. Good. Intense sun highlighted small imperfections in his face—worry lines worn deep from dealing with people who didn't understand his profession. And that included nearly everyone. But other than those occupationally induced creases, he thought he looked quite handsome. His face had good definition: just the right amount of dark whisker shadow, eyebrows thick without being bushy, and a well-proportioned nose.

"You've weathered the storm well thus far, Billy," he said. "Keep the faith and fight the good fight."

Part of fighting the good fight meant making sure he sent a letter to at least one publishing house each week with an update on his novel. With last night's work, he had eight and a half paragraphs, maybe more, depending on how he broke up dialogue. It was coming well, and he wanted to keep the editors chomping at the bit.

"Frothing at the mouth," he said to himself on his way to the nightstand in his bedroom where he kept his leather-bound address book. What to do? Random-opening method, he decided. He closed his eyes and jammed his finger into the middle of the pages. Houghton Mifflin. A fine choice. Good old HM, they wouldn't let him down. Billy looked at the Boston address. Refreshing to deal with one out of New York, he thought. And what's this? An editor's name? It appeared to be. Billy moved quickly to his phone and punched 411 for information. What he'd written last night was good enough to read, and 6:00 A.M.—it was 4:00 in Butte—was when all the best editors were up and about in Boston. He was sure of it.

"We can complete your call for an additional seventy-five cents," the recorded voice on the other line told him. Yes, by all means, put me through. Billy didn't mind spending seventy-five cents. While he waited for the phone to start ringing, he did a quick set of voice exercises.

"La-ohmmmm. La-ohmmmm." He flipped through the two pages of manuscript to last night's additions and cleared his throat, waiting for the editor to pick up, counting the number of rings it took. Eleven.

"Hello," said a tired voice from the East Coast.

"Into the night they rode, all atremble with fear, their horses lame, their ammunition gone, their minds on the things men think of when death is close at hand. And though they were tired, so tired that sleep, even if it meant suicide, was a tantalizing option, they did not stop." Billy drew a great breath and bellowed, "They did not stop, for behind them came . . ." he paused for effect, then screamed, "the Blackfeet." Marvelous. A thoroughly captivating western. So good the editor seemed stunned. Billy clenched his fist and pumped it high in the air. He was coming to the corner, and around the bend . . . the high life.

"What?"

Yes, the editor was in shock. Perhaps he would like to hear it again.

"Into the night they rode . . ." This time Billy was interrupted.

"Who the hell is this? What in the world? Do you know what time it is?"

Overwhelmed, Billy thought. "I dare you to tell me to stop reading," he said. "Double dare you."

"Reading? Is that what you're doing?"

"Only the best western since *Lonesome Dove.* Listen again. Into the night they rode . . ."

"Jesus Christ, you're insane."

Easy enough to confuse with genius.

"Don't ever call me again, you son of a bitch!"

"William Bristol!" Billy shrieked. "The name's William Bristol. You'll hear it again!" The line went dead. Fine, Billy thought. What will HM think when they learn that one of their editors passed on a Pulitzer Prize winner? That man should lose his job. Billy circled the name in his address book and drew an X through it. Cross him right off the list.

Writing was tiring, and so was reading. Reading properly, especially. Billy tumbled onto his bed, wishing now that he'd waited until evening to call. Too bad Andrea's first impression of him might be of someone severely worn down.

In his cardboard blue-and-white bureau, Billy found a clean pair of underwear at the bottom of his shirt drawer and thought it was a good sign. An unexpected pick-me-up. The faded blue jeans and white button-down he chose were not elegant, but they were his favorites and had a handsome western look to them. A modern frontier style that any actress from Germany would immediately find attractive. He outfitted his Hawthorns with laces from his sneakers, passed up his Pegasus Gold hat for a denim cap that matched his jeans, and when he admired himself again in the living room window, he could see no reason for Andrea not to fall instantly in love.

The crumpled address Buff had given him, worn and tattered from countless hours of caressing, said 104 North Excelsior, the neighborhood of the old copper-king mansions. Billy imagined Andrea atop one of the Victorian three-stories, strolling a widow's walk in a negligee as the sun came up, absentmindedly running her hands over her breasts, staring off at East Ridge, silently praying to Mary to bring her lover home safely.

"Here I am," Billy caught himself saying aloud as the fantasy consumed him.

From his apartment on Washoe, it was only a fifteen-minute walk across town to Excelsior, but Billy left half an hour early. Above him, the sky was dropping, shapeless clouds descending toward Butte to cloak the city in iron-gray sheets. Somewhere to the west, probably over the Flint Mountains, thunder rumbled like a train crossing a wooden trestle. Thunderstorms that rolled through in the morning weren't as severe as the ones that hit late in the day after things had warmed up. Those usually brought torrential downpours and hail. The larger and by far less frequent systems that settled over southwest Montana for a full day were more apt to be accompanied by warm, gentle rains. Billy imagined himself in a circular room on the top floor of Andrea's mansion, naked—no, scantily clad, that was more sexy—on her bed listening to the rain patter against the old glass panes of bay windows.

"Here I am," he said again. "Yes, here comes Billy Bristol."

The rain began just as Billy reached Main Street. Where Washoe intersected it, the light was still blinking yellow, and all the way down to Chuck's the street was empty. Deserted, it looked twice as wide. The neon R&R sign glowed a pale red in the sunless dawn and brought back frightening memories of Leslie Booth. Billy spit instinctively, then smiled. He would not mind so much if Andrea liked using her tongue.

To kill time, Billy left Washoe for a narrow alley half a block below him. He toed a broken Rainier bottle toward a green dumpster behind an Italian restaurant and disturbed a tricolor cat snacking inside the metal receptacle. Stricken with some awful affliction, probably terminal, that caused it to hunch its back and limp to the side as it retreated, the cat slunk away toward a chink in the foundation of a beauty salon. Billy averted his eyes as quickly as he could. The cat was only one small notch below him on the ladder of well-being in Butte and could easily be a sign of things to come. The ghost of Christmas future. He couldn't help giving a quick glance at the hole in the beauty shop, the dark oval entrance to a world not far from his, as he turned and retraced his steps to Main Street. True, the cat could have been the worst thing in the alley, but Billy subscribed to the belief that things could and usually did get worse. No point tempting the Fates. They were nothing to fool with.

Granite Street was just one up from Washoe, not much of a hike, even uphill. Where it crossed Main, dipping toward Butte's small college, it was lined with two- and three-story brick houses, most of which had been converted to office buildings or apartments after the heydays of the mines. There was the Montana Legal Aid building, a white-pillared, squat-looking rectangle where young lawyers worked pro bono. Billy remembered a couple of occasions when he'd been obliged to seek their services, once fighting an eviction, once a civil charge of fraud. Neither time had they been of much assistance. If it hadn't been for his counseling *them*, he might have been convicted. Digging the toe of his right boot under a loose section of sidewalk concrete, he kicked a clump of gray rock at the picture window outside the waiting room. It fell short, saying something about his life, perhaps, and he frowned.

A little ways farther, near a drain grate that was already backing up, clogged with sand and other less natural forms of refuse, a woman was taking a red blouse off a clothesline she'd fastened under her second-story balcony roof. Billy waved, and she looked away. Bashful. It had undoubtedly been a long time since someone as handsome as himself had waved to her. He envisioned her abusive husband rushing out into the street to confront him and how he would punish the man. A right, then a left, followed by a crushing uppercut. Yes, then the boots. Finish with the boots. Then a little trip upstairs where the lady could thank him in private. The thought of it—the door to the balcony left open, a cool breeze blowing onto the bed—returned Billy's full attention to Andrea Kauffman. He said her name, seductively rolling the *r*, and hoped she'd not lost her foreign accent.

Billy whirled about face and saluted the Legal Aid building, then skipped half a block closer to Excelsior, whistling a tune of his own composition that he believed sounded German.

Just as Billy reached Excelsior, the rain picked up. He turned his face skyward and let it fall into his open mouth. Do you like the rain, Andrea? And are you wearing something white? Oh, how he hoped that she was. He closed his eyes, thinking of the way she'd smiled at him in the unemployment office, her pouty lips parting to reveal straight, white teeth. Billy sensed something great drawing near. He turned north, uphill, setting his sights on a cluster of enormous houses, one of which he was certain was 104. The highest one. The one with . . . Jesus, was it really a widow's walk? Billy's heart began pumping hot blood through his veins, causing a humming in his groin that he couldn't ignore. He paused his long strides to adjust himself, then resumed his rapid pace, spurred on by love and lust and anticipation of the flesh.

By the time Billy reached the Excelsior Street mansions, large houses where copper barons once held court while their workers chipped away beneath them, the rain had wet his shirt enough to plaster it to his chest, the black hairs plainly visible through the white cloth. He peered down toward his stomach, sucking it in as much as possible, wishing his chest was more muscular. At least it was hairy. He toyed with the idea of undoing the first two or three buttons but decided against it. It would be so much more satisfying to watch Andrea's hands—delicate, white, trembling hands—perform that function.

Billy caught himself stopping to admire the scrollwork under the eaves of the first mansion, even though he knew it could not be Andrea's. It had been converted to an apartment complex, and she would live alone. By herself where she wouldn't be troubled with noisy children, drunken husbands, and loud college students. His eyes moved along the intricate pattern of French curls in the wood, then wandered to the widow's walk on top of another house—a great ways above him, very close to the clouds it seemed, its black, iron railing slick with rain. Billy wondered if it might have a bed on it. If not a bed, perhaps a cot. A fashionably worn foldout sofa. Something to sit upon and watch the sunrises. Something to lie upon . . . Billy forced his eyes back to the scrollwork. Control, control, control.

"What in hell are you looking at?" A pointy-faced man stuck his head out of a small window in line with Billy's stare. When Billy did not respond, the triangular head speared farther into the rain. "If you're thinking about breaking in, my old lady's home all the time and keeps a shotgun loaded with double-ought right by the door. Will blow your fucking head clean off," the man said proudly.

It sounded as if he was happier to have a woman handy with a scattergun than one who worked and could support him. A twisted set of values for a sick individual.

"Do you know where Andrea Kauffman lives?" Billy yelled up at the head.

"Who?"

"Andrea Kauffman."

"Never heard of her. Fuck you!" The man zipped back into the room and slammed his window.

"Thanks," Billy said. He would have to warn Andrea about her neighbors so she didn't call upon Ma Barker.

As Billy plowed farther up the street, his left eye began to twitch, the lid jumping up and down. He swatted at it several times, striking himself hard in the forehead, but it persisted. Fine time for such a thing, he thought. With a quick glance over his shoulder to be sure the living gargoyle was no longer watching from its post, he stared back down the street until the twitching ceased and the redness imparted from the palm of his hand faded. All writers get twitches now and again, he thought, but Andrea shouldn't discover such things until she knew exactly what he did. Then she would better understand.

One more peek at the mist-shrouded widow's walk where he was soon to frolic, and fourteen high-steps took Billy to the front door of what had to be the movie star's house. He raised his hand to knock, proud that it was not trembling, then let it fall to his side where it hung, a separate entity and quite dead. In small gold numbers above the door, the house's location read 102.

What sort of vile prank was this? Billy dug madly at his sodden pants, yanked out the address, and traced Buff's print. One hundred and four, North Excelsior. Did it exist? The previous two houses were 108 and 106. In a stupor of disbelief, Billy slid from the porch back into the rain. Suddenly, he was very tired. His legs ached from climbing the hill, and he began to shiver. Very nice. No Andrea, but a good dose of pneumonia. He hugged himself and stamped his feet. His wet soles splashed water up onto his pant legs, and lightning sizzled down close by, filling the air with the acrid scent of ozone.

"You missed," Billy sneered at the sky. When there was no reply, he began tramping down the street. Perhaps he should climb to the gargoyle's apartment and rattle the door. That would end things quickly. Then again, she might not take his height into consideration and gut shoot him. Gut shoot him or worse. He stopped to stare between his legs. Oh well, no other use for it. With a sad apology to his groin, he looked up, and when he did his eyes fell upon a small house he hadn't seen before, probably servants' quarters for one of the mansions at one time. A neat picket fence ringed its little yard, and a lilac bush grew close to the door. Could it be? Billy's mind shifted to a Hansel and Gretel takeoff. Only there was no witch. Quite the opposite. As he drew closer, he could read the numbers on the side of the house. 104 North Excelsior. Of course. She's modest. Buying a lavish home would call attention to herself. Billy smiled. Not only was Andrea beautiful, she was smart.

Andrea may be beautiful and smart, Billy thought, but she's none too quick opening her door. He hammered the brass knocker into the striker plate again, this time loudly enough to scatter a group of pigeons roosting under the neighbor's widow's walk. In time, when Andrea began making friends, she would venture up there. Oh, the glorious possibilities.

A latch slid on the door. Small hands delicately working the slide, careful not to break any nails. Were her nails painted? Deep red, perhaps. Or mother of pearl. Yes, that would be it. Light shades of silver and pink swirled together. Andrea, Andrea, no pearl as pretty as you. The door began to open, the bottom weather stripping brushing across a smooth pine floor like wind through an aspen grove. Control, control, control.

Andrea's house was dark. Not a light on. Dim shadows blended to form an ocean of rich grays and browns. Was that a bed? Billy stepped inside without being asked, realized his faux pas, and awkwardly back-shuffled onto the porch. As he did, his mind replayed what it had seen. What *was* that standing beside the door?

"Mr. Briztol?"

The voice was not what he had expected. Deeper. Huskier and older. The type of woman who likes to be on top? That would be all right, too.

"Mr. Briztol, is dat you?"

Something wrong. "Andrea?" The surprise and fear were evident in his voice.

"Yez, come in pleaze."

Yes? She had said yes, hadn't she? But . . . stooped, and that hair . . . good god, she was one hundred years old. Billy began to shudder and pinch himself, desperately trying to wake from whatever nightmare had consumed him. Kneading the skin on his left arm into tight arcs with his fingernails, producing enough pain to convince himself he was not sleeping, his brain raced to the only other logical possibility. How had death found him? That flash of lightning? Did power lines come down? Had Ma Barker blasted him in the back? That would be fitting. Gunned down in the streets of Butte.

"Pleaze comes in and sit down, Mr. Briztol." The crone gestured at a small table with a chair at either end, and Billy numbly edged across the room. Behind him, the door closed with a hiss, not at all like rustling aspen leaves this time. No more Chuck's. No more Heineken. No more Discovery Channel. Good-bye, dear world. It's the big cutoff this time for sure.

Billy's eyes adjusted slowly to the gloom, but faster than he wished. After all, he had an eternity for things like that to happen, so why rush?

"Mr. Briztol?" It called to him from beside the door, groping with one age-shrunken hand for the table. "Mr. Briztol?"

"No." Billy mouthed the word to himself. "No, no, no." Andrea Kauffman was blind.

· 4 ·

As he pondered his fate, a low moan escaped Billy. It made him feel somewhat better, so he let out another, longer and more pathetic.

"Iz you not feeling vell?" Andrea called from some crevice even darker than where Billy sat. "Da rain hasn't give yous a chill, has it?"

Billy shivered, trying hard to chatter his teeth loudly enough so she'd hear them bouncing together. Well worth shaving off a layer or two of enamel.

"Iz better den snow, though, yah?"

In July? Yes, Billy thought, "iz better den snow." He looked around the room, eyes scanning for exits. He appeared to be in a kitchen, laid out for the blind or heaven for the obsessive compulsive. The countertops were spic-and-span, everything on them lined in neat rows; nothing was cluttering the floor; and the chairs around the table were all pushed in tight. Two frying pans sat on an old gas stove. Jesus, she used *gas*? Was that part of her cure for his chill? Billy's teeth stopped moving as he stood up and tiptoed to the stove, fearful the hiss he'd heard earlier when Andrea closed the door was the rush of natural gas. He heaved a great sigh of relief when he found the red-handled valve in the off position.

"Vell den, iz ve ready to go outs on da town?"

Billy jumped. How could she move so damn silently without the aid of her eyes? Was it something she had perfected, the way a blind cat might hone its other senses to catch mice? And if so, what was she trying to catch? Billy had a packrat in his apartment once, a fearful creature with a great bushy tail and a forty- or fifty-inch vertical leap. It had frightened him onto the back of his couch, screeching with delight at the big man's attempts to get away. Andrea's house looked like just the sort of place for a packrat. Perhaps she hunted them at night, stalking about with a carving knife like the old farmer's wife. It was an awful thought.

"I don't have a car," he blurted.

"Vhat? I tinks everyone in Montana has a car, yah? Da distances iz so long. Vhat do yous do vithout a car?" Andrea had pinpointed his location, making Billy extremely nervous, and appeared to be looking directly at him. Her eyes were so clear—blue even, in the absence of much light—that he wondered if she could actually see him. Perhaps this blindness was a ruse designed to test him. Something the wicked woman from Job Services planned. See if he would be rude to someone with a handicap so she'd feel better about withholding his final unemployment check.

"I'm sorry," Andrea said. "Pleaze, forgive me. Ve just use my car."

"No!" Billy said it loudly. Careering down the streets at Andrea's mercy wasn't something he wanted any part of. But surely she wasn't thinking of driving herself, was she? "I mean, no, don't think anything of it. Most people in Montana *do* have cars." Most of them have cut themselves off, too, and can afford them, but Billy didn't want to get into that. It was doubtful that Andrea would understand.

"My mother has a truck that I use when I need to go somewhere," Billy said. "Usually I stay in Butte."

Andrea smiled and showed a full set of teeth. Odd. Billy didn't expect that. Not someone her age.

"Okay. I have da car in storage on da flats. Ve call for da taxi, yah?"

"In storage?" Billy was under the impression that she'd just moved to Butte.

"I put it dair ven I could see a bit better," Andrea said.

"You mean this isn't your first time in Butte? I thought that's why you needed . . ." There were a lot of things he thought. He thought Andrea was young and lovely. He thought she lived in a mansion. He thought he might get lucky on a widow's walk. And since he had been disabused of those notions, why not the rest?

"Oh, no. I likes Butte. I been here . . ." Andrea turned away. "Vell, I don't remember exactly. It vas a long time ago. Maybe I tells you about it sometime, yah? Now though, you call da taxi and ve get da car." She said it with an authority Billy didn't think someone of her age could still possess, and it made him uneasy.

Not as uneasy as he felt when the taxi arrived, however, and he saw the driver.

The man hunched behind the wheel of the yellow car, or rather below the wheel, probably hadn't changed his clothes in a month and certainly hadn't seen hot water for at least that long. His beard grew in patches, sprouts of hair shooting from his cheeks like bear grass. His hands were a mosaic of liver spots and grime, and his shirt—a sleeveless Harley Davidson, tattered and torn—exposed his woolly shoulders.

Billy cringed. The sight of hair on a man's back was almost too much for him. And in this cabby's forest of hair, creeping in and out, their six legs hauling them about, were certainly many unpleasant insects. He thought of the Discovery Channel program he'd seen on parasites, the hideous creatures—enlarged thousands of times by powerful, lighted magnifying devices—that all humans play host to. Like the eyebrow mites. Views of them had necessitated a lengthy session in front of his mirror with a pair of tweezers. He'd plucked forty or fifty hairs before the pain grew too intense.

"Here's Old Stan," the driver said as he got out and bowed.

Just like Johnny, Billy thought, looking down Excelsior to be sure the pavement didn't give way to a great black nothingness from which the man had come. Seeing that it did not, that the day was more or less the same as it had been, rainy and warm, he walked Andrea to the Chrysler and started to open her door.

"Yous just show me da handle." Andrea swatted at his hands. "I do it myself."

Very well. Don't bother with your seat belt, either. Come on, Old Stan, full speed ahead.

The driver did not disappoint. He sped away from the curb, forcing Billy to reach for the headrest in front of him to avoid being sucked into his seat. Sucked into a pattern of stains he couldn't help considering the origins of. Drool. That was probably dry and, apart from its offensive appearance, relatively harmless. Dirt. If it wasn't laden with heavy metals from one of Butte's reclaim sites, it wouldn't hurt, either. But was that blood? What had that frightening program on AM radio said about blood-borne pathogens? The wheel. Get to the wheel and stop this madness. Billy reached for the driver's head, but in doing so had to release his grasp on the headrest. As he did, the car whipped around a corner, tossing him onto Andrea who, until then, couldn't have looked more relaxed.

"Vhat are you doing, Mr. Briztol?" She stared at him sprawled out in her lap.

Don't look at me with those sightless eyes, Billy thought. Please, don't look at me. He sat up quickly, sinking into the stains, sinking into contact with virulent diseases unknown to science, confined to the back of Butte taxis. He should have worn a turtleneck. Better yet, a raincoat.

The driver adjusted the rearview mirror so he could watch Billy. "I'm an alcoholic," he said as he floored it down a straight stretch of Excelsior between lights. "Well, recovering alcoholic." He winked at Billy in the mirror. "Recovering from the alcohol I drunk last night," he whispered. "Where did you say you were going?"

"Down on da flats," Andrea said, her hands folded in her lap. "Da Richardson Storage."

"The flats, eh?" Old Stan grinned. "Liked them better before they put in all those stoplights. Christ, some blinking, some not. Some work, some don't. I figure just give her hell and let every man fend for himself. Ain't that what you think?" He jammed on the brakes and slid to a stop at a red light. "Like this one here. Ain't no need of having a light here." He gunned the car through the intersection without looking ahead. Not that it would have done much good. As far as Billy could tell, he was too short to see over the wheel. "And look up here. See, that one's yellow. How long's it gonna stay that way? Might be one of them real long yellows, or it might change fast, just before we make it. Best thing to do is grab a gear and jump on it. No point taking chances."

Billy heard the accelerator greet the floor and the engine roar. He wasn't sure if the light changed before they got there or not because his eyes were closed. Oh, lucky Andrea. Oh, what a blessed disability.

"No carbon buildup in this baby." Stan slapped the dash. "Lots of people, they have cars don't run worth nothing cause of carbon. Know what I mean?"

Billy nodded. Sure.

"See, this here's a V-8, and it weren't meant to be run like no four-banger. On them days when all I get are little trips uptown . . . goddamn narrow alleys . . . on them days, I knock off a bit early and take her up over the pass."

Billy opened one eye to make sure they weren't heading toward the pass. Interstate 90, where it wound over the Continental Divide on the East Ridge, was a terrifying highway. A trip over it would give him writer's block, and that was something he couldn't afford. The block came and went enough without provocation, and the last time it set in had bedeviled Billy for nearly three months. There was no point trying to write with the block. Words simply don't come. But Old Stan wouldn't understand anything about that.

"I'll crank her up to a hundred or so and stand right on it all the way to the top," Stan said. "Clean her all out. But I don't need to worry about that today."

Billy sighed. Thank god.

"No, sir, you are the type of clients I love."

There was that word again. Billy doubted Stan knew what it meant. He'd probably heard it from the woman at Job Services.

"You know that a taxi ain't meant for little hops, skips, and jumps. Use one only when you need it, right?"

Billy nodded. This was serious stuff. Use one only when you need it. Yes, like a pistol or a rubber. Or in the case of this taxi, never again. What in hell would possess Andrea to choose a storage facility so far away?

"By the way, I'm pretty high up. In the business, that is. Look, don't make me wear a name tag no more." Stan turned around, tugging at his muscle shirt to prove there was no tag. "Everybody knows Old Stan."

The car headed for the sidewalk and Billy covered his head.

"Cut that out!" Stan said to the dash, jerking the Chrysler back to the center of his lane. "Yes, sir, she's a trickster sometimes. Gotta keep showing her who's boss."

Billy peeked out from the crook of his arm. Still alive. He thought of the GOD'S RIDING WITH ME bumper stickers he'd seen. God is my pilot, I shall not want. He knew it wasn't quite right but figured the man upstairs would take intent into account and cut him some slack.

"Oh well, not much longer now." Stan rubbed his hands together, holding the wheel with his chin. "Pretty soon I'm gonna hit the big one. The lottery. I can feel it in my bones, just as sure as I can a storm coming. Like last night . . . I knew it was gonna rain today. And it's the same with the lottery. I just *know* it."

Billy shook his head. Old Stan was a perfect candidate to win the lottery. "Cabby Hits It Big," the headlines would read. That type of thing never happened to a writer. He watched the new stores on Harrison Avenue, Butte's downtown thoroughfare, hurtle by. Andrea still appeared calm.

"Say," Stan said. "I wouldn't want you to think I'm cheating you or nothing, but if we swing over onto Continental we can make better time. Here, just check this out. I don't charge by the mile anyway. Ever hear the longest way around is the quickest way there? Watch."

The cab slid easily on the wet pavement and left Harrison in favor of an alley heading east toward Continental, the street at the base of the East Ridge. Billy looked over his shoulder at the broad avenue they'd departed from, then slumped deeper into the stains.

"See, out here I can wind her up to sixty . . . maybe seventy . . . come on, baby . . . miles an hour."

Billy jammed his eyes shut. Stan could stop with the narration anytime.

"Hey, hey, hey," he said. "Here we are."

Amazing. They were at the storage. There were too many people around for Billy to kiss the earth the way he wanted to when he got out, but when he figured no one was looking, he scooped a little gravel from the parking lot up to his lips.

"Thank you," he whispered to Mary, looking down from directly above him. "Oh, thank you."

Andrea got out easily on her own, and Billy would have liked to think she fumbled with her purse when she paid Stan, but she didn't. She seemed to know exactly where everything was, and try as he might, Billy couldn't see how much money she had in her wallet. It appeared she'd divided it into five or six sections, each containing bills of different denominations. She handed Stan a twenty from the middle, then snapped it shut and dropped it back into her pocketbook. If a twenty came from the middle, what was at the upper end?

"Quite da character, yah?" Andrea said as soon as Stan sped off, probably still fondling the twenty.

Billy forced his eyes away from the purse. "I believe that is an understatement." His knees were shaking, just as they had the last time he got the block.

"Iz a good old Butte boy. Good driver, too, yah?"

"Wonderful." Perhaps the blind should be thankful for all they are missing and the rest of us should lament all we must endure through our eyes. Billy sucked on his lower lip. It was an interesting idea. He probably didn't have the block.

"Now, da key." Andrea reached into her purse again. "Yah, here ve go. I tink it's number four. Da big one." She handed Billy the key, and he began a slow walk around the storage facility. He had dried out just enough in the cab to despise the falling rain and the small umbrella Andrea stood beneath, too. Yes, ma'am, I be right back with your key, ma'am. His mind began running through fitting punishments for that terrible woman from Job Services. Mine shafts? Overused. Rivers? Risky . . . could float. Could Leslie Booth be bribed into . . . yes, that was one to keep in mind. Said something for paying his tab at Chuck's, too.

The number-four unit was indeed a big one. It had an overhead door ten feet wide and half again that high. Did Andrea park a bus inside? Probably one of those ridiculous double-decker things they use in England. That would be too much. He would have to draw the line there. Every man has a point beyond which his dignity must not be pushed.

"I am reaching mine," Billy said to himself.

The lock opened with a solid click. It was an expensive lock, solid brass with engravings of a man working at a forge. What would it be worth to a pawnbroker? Billy cursed himself for throwing away the K-Mart savings flyer he'd received with a coupon in it for padlocks. They had been on sale for two dollars, and how would Andrea know if he switched them? He decided he'd have to be more careful in the future. Opportunity came in numerous shapes and sizes.

Billy tucked the lock into his pocket and began hauling on the door. It creaked, moved a few inches, then jammed. Pulling much harder would do irreparable harm to his back. Then again . . . he heaved on the handle, craning his neck to the side, keeping his back straight, bending his legs as little as possible. Slip, disk. Slide on out.

Unfortunately, the door came up.

"Can't even throw my back out today," Billy said.

Light did not penetrate far into the building. Something inside seemed to repel it, and Billy wasn't eager to venture beyond the door. Slowly, one foot at a time, he edged in, keeping a hand extended toward the outside, feeling that if something grabbed him, and he thought that very possible, he might save himself by leaving at least part of his body in the light. Creatures of darkness, are you sleeping? Something whisked across his neck, cold and fast, and he bolted for the door, surprised his legs responded so well.

Out in the rain, he had trouble catching his breath. What was the name of the archaeologist who discovered King Tut's tomb? And hadn't he been bitten by a spider? In a state of terror, Billy began raking his hands through his hair, striking himself about his neck with his hat, shaking as hard as he could. He could picture the spider holding fast to the back of his shirt, lubricating its fangs with some brightly colored poison, its many eyes searching for an artery that would carry the venom quickly through his body. His left hand bumped something hard near the middle of his head, he staggered forward anticipating the bite, then heard whatever it was take flight. He lifted his eyes in time to see black wings—maybe those of a cricket, but probably not—disappear back inside the storage building. Billy crossed himself and turned away from the door. Enough of this foolishness. Better not to work than continue with this.

"Vhat are yous doing?" Andrea had snuck up on him again, and he didn't like that one bit. He would have to get her one of those white canes so he could hear her clacking around. "Have yous got da car yet? Iz da door giving yous trouble?"

Billy's heart beat too fast to answer.

"Von't it start?"

Oh, turn your head, please. What does it matter what you look at? Must it be me? The choice of views for Billy—Andrea's blue eyes or the dark, inner chamber of the storage—was a tough one. And as he started back inside, he would have traded everything he owned, even his novel, for a beekeeper's suit. Things with six, eight, hell, maybe a dozen or more legs were watching him. Multiple quadriceps meant the capacity for getting serious air. They could probably spring on him from twenty or thirty feet away.

Whistling the theme from *Raiders of the Lost Ark* made Billy feel somewhat better. It usually did. He would have liked to have Harrison Ford's bullwhip, but the room seemed lighter now. The car appeared to be in the center, covered with dusty sheets, surrounded by rows upon rows of boxes. What could possibly be in them all? How long had Andrea been in Butte? Well, at least there was no bus.

With two fingers, Billy began peeling off the vehicle's shroud. The sheets were softer than he'd expected and flowed off the metal easily. As they did, the room grew lighter, almost as though the car was glowing. Soft light seeped into the darkness, revealing more than Billy could ever have hoped for.

"Thank you," he gasped. "I'm a rich man." He jerked the cover off fast, revealing the rest of the red-and-white convertible. The '57 Chevy was unveiled.

"It should start right up," Andrea said behind him. "I had a man come in and do da gaz and battery."

Billy put a hand on the driver's door. Smooth. Silky smooth. And cool. Invigorating. How fast do you go, my little darling? And are you all original? My, my, only fourteen hundred miles on you. Hardly broken in. Well, well, we'll take care of that. He lowered himself in, patting the dash lovingly, and let the leather seat wrap around him. Too bad his pants were soaked. Stained seats would decrease the value.

The key turned with the same solid click the lock had made, the long accelerator pedal offered little resistance to Billy's foot when he stepped on it, and the engine turned over. Power, power, power. Raw power. Something almost sexual about it. Caress the steering wheel. Yes, that's it. Oh, the leather. Luxurious. And the backseat! Wide enough to lay two abreast. A starlit night, the top down, overlooking the city, a couple of college girls, innocence giving way. Billy tipped his head back and closed his eyes.

"Yes, of course I'll respect you," he said. "Your friend, too. No, no, that shouldn't make you feel dirty at all. Not at all."

Billy jumped when the passenger door opened.

"Are yous going to back out before ve get fumed?" Andrea snapped.

Jesus, how can she find her way around in the dark so well? Then again, maybe it's always dark for her. At least the idea of getting "fumed" bothers her. Still a little self-preservation in-stinct left. Put one in the plus column.

The gearshift dropped easily into reverse, and the car rolled from the building as if on rails. Rolling toward the high life, Billy thought.

"Better close da storage door, yah? Ve don't vant rain in dair."

Billy got out and pulled the cord attached to the door, then turned to admire the entire car. God, not a scratch on it. Must be worth . . . wouldn't want to pawn this baby. No, get a professional auctioneer. Pull out all the stops. Look at those fins! And the white canopy.

The sound of the horn startled him.

"I can still find da horn," Andrea said when he got in.

Yes, and probably drive a good deal better than Old Stan.

"Now, vhere do ve eat? Iz dat place on Main Street open still? Da R&R?"

The R&R? Someone might remember the encounter with Leslie Booth. "No, that establishment burned," Billy said.

"Burned?"

Maybe she knew better. "No, actually I think the state health inspector shut it down."

"Clozed it down?"

"Maybe just temporarily." Billy didn't dare slam too many doors. The time would come when he could make a triumphant appearance at the R&R with the Chevy and a few young ladies. Show everyone in there who he really was. "How about the Silver Dollar? Do you like hash browns?" He figured they would be easy to chew, even if Andrea's teeth were false.

"Yah, iz good. But I vant da steak, too."

Hmmm, a meat eater. "I'm sure they have steak, too," Billy said.

"Okay, ve go dair. Ve go and yous can tell me all about yourself. Yous are a writer, yah?"

Billy didn't like talking about himself and hoped the question-and-answer period would be brief. On the other hand, there were things he wanted to know about her, too. First and foremost was the car. Did it have a clean title? How often did she plan on using it? Wouldn't she like something a bit more practical? On the way to the Silver Dollar, up the narrow streets of Butte, Billy rehearsed over and over how he would ask these things. Gently. That was best. Ease into it. Don't sound overeager. Go with the flow and establish trust. Slow and steady wins the race.

Billy chose a parking space far from the other cars in the Silver Dollar's lot and didn't feel at all guilty about making Andrea walk the extra fifty yards. She wouldn't want her classic scratched by a door or backed into.

"May I take your hand?" Billy asked as they reached the front door.

"Yah, but gently. Just steer me a little. And ask for a booth. Get us a vide booth vhere ve can relax and talk."

She was determined to talk. Rapid-fire questions? Billy hoped not. And how much might that horrible Buff have told her? Where would he have to draw the bounds? Rein himself in? Lucky for him she was blind and could not ask to see the fruits of his labor. Lucky, too, that in his profession failure was almost fashionable. She might not understand, but he would try to make her see.

As soon as their waiter had taken their order, Andrea started in with the questions.

"So, dat nice young girl . . . vhat is her name . . . da one at da Services . . . she says yous write, yah?"

"That's right." What did Buff know about writing? It was hardly the place of someone who had cut herself off to talk about it. She couldn't possibly know the first thing.

"And she says yous live in Butte your whole life. Vhat is her name?"

"Buff."

"Yah, dat's it. Buff. Iz such a nice girl."

Exactly how the anti-Christ first appears, Billy thought. But here there was hope. If Andrea couldn't recognize Buff for the vicious, conniving creature that she was, her mind must be going. Hmmm . . . vulnerable. Another in the plus column.

"Yous lived right here all your life?"

"Yes." There had been the time in college, but Billy wouldn't, *couldn't*, get into that.

"Do yous write much about da city? Iz very interesting, yah?"

Billy had never considered it terribly interesting. The fact that it hadn't dropped into a mine shaft was of minor note, but other than that, he didn't see anything unusual about living in Butte.

"I write fiction. About places I make up." He thought of his western lying on his bureau, and for a moment wished he was home working on it. See, he thought, this is exactly why it's important not to get too busy working. What if he didn't have the urge to write again for five or six days?

"Vhat type of things do yous write? Da mysteries?" Andrea folded her napkin into her lap without looking. Of course.

Mysteries? Billy was appalled. He was better than those cheap thrillers. Not about to sell out simply to see his name on a best-sellers list. He'd make the list honestly, and then it would mean something.

"No, no," he said. He had always figured he could whip one off in a few weeks if he had to, but it would take a heavy toll on his pride.

"Too bad. I likes dem."

You and the rest of America, Billy thought. All trending toward five-dollar paperbacks. Well, that wasn't his style.

"And Buff said something about da *New York Times*, too, yah?"

"Oh, yes, my travel pieces."

"Dat's amazing." Andrea smiled as if she might not fully believe him. Where was the waiter? "And here in Butte . . . when yous isn't traveling." She was still smiling. "Vhat iz your favorite ting here?"

Billy began to itch all over. His wet clothes made it worse. He dug at his thighs, then the middle of his back, then answered without thinking. "Chuck's. That's what I like best in Butte." Yes, to be at Chuck's with a good credit line this very instant. Forget all this nonsense.

"Chuck's, yah?" Now Andrea seemed amused. "Vhat iz dat?"

The opera house. Haven't you ever been there? Billy picked both feet off the carpet and set them down hard. When they began to itch it drove him mad. He curled and flexed his toes as fast as he could, then remembered the car. The leather, the chrome-trimmed dials on the dash, the power, the college girls. Control, control, control. Deep breath time.

"Chuck's? It's a little lounge on Main Street. Nice, quiet place to unwind after writing."

"A bar yous mean." Andrea's expression hadn't changed.

"Yes, it's a bar." Honesty. Win her trust. Worth a quick go down that road.

The overdue arrival of their meals ended the conversation, but Andrea's smile held on. Well, I suppose Germans like their beer, too, Billy thought. They certainly make some of the best. Half a gallon of Heineken would go down very well.

It took Andrea a mere seven minutes to eat her steak and eggs. Billy didn't see how an old, blind woman could finish so quickly.

Must give her a terrible case of heartburn. He continued picking at his own hash browns, clanking his fork on his plate so she would know to hold off with the questions. This was a good exercise in self-restraint, one that would work its way into his writing. Taking his time forced Billy to experience hunger quite acutely, and experiences were good. The longer he waited between bites, the more his stomach pained him, and the better he would be able to describe starvation someday.

The waiter returned, and much to Billy's dismay, Andrea ordered a cup of tea. When it arrived, the interrogation began once more.

"Do yous have any brothers or sisters?" She took a tiny sip.

Great. Fifteen minutes for her meal and an hour and a half for six ounces of tea.

"No." Keep the answers short. Wasn't that what the fellow from Legal Aid had told him once?

"And your parents? Do theys live in Butte, too?" Another minuscule sip.

"My mother does." This was a topic of conversation Billy had to avoid at all costs. He had just finished the best meal he'd eaten in three days, avoided dying in the back of Old Stan's taxi, and driven a car worth many thousands of dollars that could soon be his. The prospect of pawning the toaster still loomed in the background, but wait . . . what about the brass knocker from the apartment's doors? That was still in one of his bureau drawers and could go first. Memory! It was wonderful. A feeling of pure elation spread over Billy, and he closed his eyes in ecstasy.

"So, vhat does she do? Your mother?"

Billy's eyes flicked open. Can't we drop this?

"She runs an adult activity center." As far as Billy could tell, she did very little. Lots of planning and very little accomplishing. She was always setting up this or that, mostly tours and film presentations. Inevitably they were canceled because of lack of interest. There had been the trip to Seattle to see the Mariners, her one success, but even that wasn't perfect. The charter bus was out of beer before it reached Spokane, and Hector, one of her few loyal participants, a man close to fifty who believed he was Crazy Horse reincarnated, had run off with a whore he met behind the third baseline and hadn't made it back to Butte for a month.

"Adult center, yah? And vhat does she do dair?"

Simple and short. "Sets up events."

"Dat's such a nice ting to do." Andrea took a sip so small it couldn't have done more than wet her lips.

"Sure." The itches were returning, making their way from Billy's head down toward the bottoms of his feet.

"And do yous ever work vith her?"

"No!" Jesus God Almighty, no! The very thought of it made Billy dizzy. Talk about getting cut off. He put his hands on the table to steady himself and stared at his water glass.

"Vhy not?"

"Too busy." That was a good one. Nice, quick thinking. Not far from the truth, too. How could he involve himself with his mother's schemes *and* write? Preposterous.

"I see." Andrea took a larger sip. Good. "Vell, I have been doing alls da talking. I let yous finish your breakfast now and den ve go, okay?"

Billy's curiosity had been aroused since seeing the car, but he was willing to let the questions he wanted to ask slide for now. He stabbed a stray strand of potato that had slid from his plate onto the tablecloth and devoured it. No more taking his time.

When the waiter came with the check, Andrea once more brought out her pocketbook and expertly handed him another twenty. The stack of bills in her wallet did not seem diminished.

On the way past the front desk, Billy dropped Andrea's hand to fish mints from a glass bowl. He stuffed them into the front pocket of his shirt, dried out enough so they wouldn't melt all over. With a bit of milk, they weren't a bad meal.

Outside, the rain had stopped, but it was still cloudy. Billy would have loved to put the Chevy's top down but didn't dare risk it. There was no breeze yet, and that meant showers would return. Definitely not worth it.

"Vould yous be as kind as to drive me around Butte a bit?" Andrea asked as he started the car. "Shows me da city a little? I hear it's spread all out now." She did not seem to get as tired after eating as Billy did. Maybe that was because she ate more regularly. He was ready to go home and go to bed. Get rested up before looking at his novel again. "Pleaze. Just for a bit."

Of course, Madam. Anything you say. How about we go up over the pass? You know how bad that nasty carbon can be.

"Sure. Where would you like to go?"

"Through da uptown. Tell me vhat's new."

Billy looked at the faded brick buildings as he drove the car up an alley toward Granite Street. In the dry, western climate, the hundred-year-old billboard-sized paintings on their sides retained more than a hint of their original colors.

Yes, Andrea, and here's my favorite. He slowed to a crawl and peered up through the windshield at the giant, stout-shouldered blue bottle on the back of what was now an apartment building. HENRY'S BEST RYE WHISKEY the bottle read. Good old Henry. And what's that? A nickel a shot? Jesus, those were the days. Billy hit the brakes hard at the end of the alley. It wouldn't do for Henry to cause an accident.

"Okay, vhere are ve?" Andrea asked.

"Granite Street." Billy made doubly sure no cars were coming from either direction, flipped on the signal light, and swung into the westbound lane.

"Good, yous tell me vhat you see."

Well, there's a drunk sitting on the steps of a boarded-up hardware store. God, I think he's going to relieve himself. Yes, he appears to be going for it.

"Mostly da new stuff. Tell me how Butte has changed."

"Since when?" Andrea looked plenty old enough to view the arrival of electricity, even though it came to Butte before it did to San Francisco, as something new and noteworthy.

"Oh, da last thirty-five years or so."

That was a long time, and a lot had changed. The copper mine had played out, Butte's population had fallen to less than half what it once was, houses were left abandoned for neighborhood boys to play in and sometimes burn down, and the Environmental Protection Agency no longer ignored the toxicity of Silver Bow Creek, the little stream between the uptown and downtown sections of the city. The headwaters of the Columbia River, Billy reminded himself.

"I'll start with the buildings," Billy said, in what he hoped was a slightly sad tone of voice. That would be her point of view, he thought. "Here's the old Anaconda Company Bank," he said slowly. "Now . . . a hotel."

"Yes, I heard they folded up. Too bad. Put a lot of men to work in da mines."

"You know about the Anaconda Company?" Billy took his foot off the gas.

"Oh, yes, big mining group, yah? Who didn't know about dem?"

"Most other German actresses, I would think," Billy said. How did *that* sound? He bit his lip hard. Rude? Had he just lost his car?

"Yah, I suppose dat's true. I have always had an interest in da vest, you see, and as I said, I did spend a bit of time here once. Maybe I should have stayed, yah?" she said quietly.

Billy stopped at the corner of Montana Street and stared at the blond-haired mannequin propped up on the porch of the old Lincoln Brothel. She had her hand placed seductively between Honest Abe's legs.

"Vell, vhere have ve stopped?" The spunk was back in Andrea's voice.

"Montana Street."

"And vhat do you see?"

"Well, there's the Lincoln Brothel." Billy didn't know if he should mention it. The last of Butte's whorehouses, it had held on until the early eighties. He could remember it before it was a museum but regrettably had been too young for any firsthand knowledge of its workings.

"Da Lincoln House? Still going strong?" Andrea sounded upset. She gripped the dash, digging her nails in deep.

"Oh, no, it's a museum now."

"Ve take a look, yah? I like to see a museum."

Not this one, Billy thought. The idea of having to explain to Andrea everything that had gone on inside did not appeal to him.

"Yous give quick tour, okay?"

He parked a couple of places down in front of a great building that had served as a Chinese restaurant, country dance hall, and bingo parlor since deviating from its original function as headquarters for the Butte branch of the Teamsters Union. Wouldn't Andrea be more interested in it?

"I goes good on da sidewalk," she said when Billy took her arm. "I vill ask for help vhen I needs it."

Fine. Just don't blunder into the street before signing over the Chevy. Billy watched her march up the sidewalk, steering her ever so gently up the stairs of the museum.

"Vhat do you see?" she asked.

"A mannequin on the porch with her hand between Abraham Lincoln's legs." He didn't know how to put it any other way.

"Dat's ridiculous," Andrea said. "Iz dat vhat Butte has come to?"

In a way it was. Especially the uptown section. Billy thought about the historic site markers that had been erected over the past decade in an attempt to draw tourists up away from the flats to the dozen or so shops still trying to make a go of it on the hill. He looked down the street, wide and empty, and knew he was witnessing the end of something. He couldn't put his finger on what—perhaps because of an onset of the block—but he sensed that things were changing.

"Ve go in." Andrea opened the door and walked in, stepping around a small counter. Did she have radar? Something like a bat? Billy watched her nervously.

A woman in a long, loose-fitting dress met them and asked if they were interested in a tour.

"No, ve just going to look," Andrea said. She stepped forward, turned to her right, and walked into a large room full of padded chairs.

"The waiting room," Billy said, reading from a plaque on the wall. "Where customers waited for their favorite ladies. It says sometimes there were fifty men in here."

"Yah." Andrea sat down in one of the chairs. "Vhat else does it say?"

"Not much. There are some pictures of the women." Billy stared at them, hard-looking ladies for the most part. The type who could give you more than you bargained for if you got out of line. "Says there was a murder here in 1966. Helena businessman was shot."

"Goodness. Dat's awful." Andrea stood up. "Vell, I don't cares to hear any more. Ve go." This time she reached for Billy's arm and let him lead her to the door.

She was quiet on the way back to her storage building, barely acknowledging Billy's descriptions of the pawnshops, bars, antique stores, and apartments, and until Stan came for them—summoned by a call from a pay phone across the street outside a pizza parlor, a call that Billy made with great trepidation—she didn't say one word. When the cab driver arrived, her spirits picked up.

"Ve going up over da pass?" she asked.

Billy choked. How dare she?

"Not today, ma'am," Stan said. He tore off toward Continental, fishtailing into the street. "She's right up to snuff today."

Right away, Billy noticed the two fresh stains on the seat behind him. A pair of ugly smears of . . . he didn't want to guess. As the car jerked across the road, his body entered a sleeplike state brought on by the powerful sedative fear. He was rather disappointed when they reached Andrea's house unscathed.

"So, do yous vant Old Stan to bring yous home?" Andrea prodded him with her purse.

"No!" Billy snapped out of his trance. By all means, no. The mere thought of it was enough to send him into action, scrambling for the door handle, swinging his feet out onto terra firma as fast as he could.

"I vould pays him a little extra if yous did."

"Oh, no, really. It's stopped raining, and I could use the exercise." Sweat out anything that had gotten into his system from the stains. He made a note to program the Centers for Disease Control's number into his phone when he got home. If he began feeling dizzy, there might not be much time.

"Mr. Briztol?" Andrea called to him over the roar of Stan's engine. He was off with another twenty. "Did you vant me to pay yous today?"

"Yes." He bounced up the walk toward her, his mouth beginning to water the way it might if she'd described in great detail a seasoned New York steak.

"Yah, vell, yous valk me to da door."

At your side, my dear. Here, let me spread my shirt over this puddle for you. Shall I sprinkle rose petals ahead of your feet? Announce your return to the neighborhood? No, wouldn't want to disturb Ma Barker. Might sound-shoot. Billy glanced in her direction, careful not to look so long it could be construed as staring.

"Okay, dat's good." Andrea was breathing hard after Billy's speedy escort to her door. "Now . . ." The purse opened and her steady hand moved toward the wallet and the back of the billfold.

That's it, that's it. Keep going. All the way to the back. Back where you keep the big boys. Come on, what's in there for me? Billy wiped his mouth with the back of his hand and forced himself to blink before his eyes dried out.

"Let's see . . . yes, here ve is. I tank yous, sir, for a lovely morning."

"Oh, you're welcome." You are so *very* welcome. Billy held the fifty to his lips, not quite close enough to touch—money was dirty—and closed his eyes. You are more welcome than you will ever know.

"Yous vill be back next veek, yah? Maybe sometime I tells you a story yous can write."

"Yes." And the week after that, and the week after that. At your service, my lady. And how thoughtful of her to consider his work. Billy patted her lightly on the back, nodded, then skipped away down her walk, legs rising high the way they would in the high life that he felt approaching. Throwing all caution to the wind, he asked himself, What more could a man want?

Standing at the Granite Street post office ten minutes later, Billy found out. There they were, two self-addressed envelopes, much too thin to contain the contracts he had expected. One from *Harper's* and one from *Men's Journal.*

"Don't read them now," he said to himself. "No need to read them now." But he had to. His hands were tearing at them uncontrollably, his eyes reading fast, the presence of the high life no longer felt.

"Dear Mr. Bristol," the *Men's Journal* response began. Hadn't he explicitly told them to call him William? "First, we do not have a prescriptive nonfiction editor. Second, your idea, 'How to Live on Next to Nothing,' is as silly a proposal as I've seen. Do you really think that if you have next to nothing you can afford a magazine? People need to eat, Mr. Bristol."

Billy hurled the letter to the floor. He knew damn well they had a prescriptive nonfiction editor. Whoever responded to his proposal should lose his job.

"What about *Harper's*?" he said. "Will they offend me, too?" He glanced at their response to his idea for a short story involving a rodeo rider and a paralyzing fall from his horse. That's how he had put it to them. Very straightforward, just the way editors want.

"By god, you don't need to know any more!" he bellowed. "What the hell do you mean, 'flesh it out?' Flesh it out?" These people . . . yes, it was from "staff" . . . didn't know anything about suspense. He would have to write and explain it to them. He picked up the letter from *Men's Journal* and tromped out the door, trying to find comfort in the fifty-dollar bill in his pocket.

Somewhere between Granite and Washoe, as Billy came alongside Pendergrast's Pharmacy, an ancient, abandoned building with plywood over its windows, he caught the block. It hit him all at once, taking complete control, slowing his pace to a shuffle.

"Damn all editors," he fumed as he hauled himself up his apartment steps. Maybe he could sue them for lost time. Prove a connection between their rude responses and the block. If he had been able to write, he would have made a note to consider it.

· 5 ·

The block held Billy for five days, and not the way a mother would her baby. No, nothing gentle about the block. It gripped him tight, following him wherever he went, digging at his brain, quick to throw the fact that he couldn't write up in his face. Not so much as a grocery list. The letter he'd written to *Playboy* remained on his refrigerator because he couldn't address an envelope. His unemployment check, when it finally came, went unsigned, and the novel, that wonderful western, collected dust on the bedroom bureau.

Billy had learned long ago that there was no point in fighting the block. Eventually, it would grow bored with him and seek out another writer. He considered calling one or two of Montana's more prominent authors and telling them to be on the lookout for it, but decided against it. No point in alarming them. If they began to worry, it would make them that much more susceptible.

There were things a man could do to encourage the block to move along. Doodling was sometimes effective. Billy remembered once a few years ago when he'd picked up his pen, closed his eyes, and begun scribbling random designs on his paper. And lo and behold, when he looked, there were words. "Hello, blue cat," if he remembered correctly. It didn't seem to make much sense, little more than the babblings of an infant, but it had rid him of the plague. Then there was the time he'd gone to the Peace Corps recruiting office and talked about signing up. The slides of the West African countries where he'd work, countries full of insects a man couldn't get his boot over, even his own size twelves, were enough to send him home ready to fire off two or three first-rate proposals.

Reverse psychology eventually did the trick this time. When Billy woke on the sixth morning, he sang a little tune with the frequent refrain "Who wants to write? Not me, not me." He could tell immediately that it was working. The oppressive weight of the block was letting up, and he danced around the kitchen breaking pencils, putting on a very convincing act.

"Never gonna write no more short stories," he began rapping. "Gonna get me a job and put in my forty." He was onto something here, and wished he could make better puffing noises in between verses.

"It'll make a man crazy, wild, and frantic—to deal with Doubleday, Bantam, and Grove Atlantic. Whatever I write, it won't ever sell—just ask Viking, Random House, and Dell. Hey, who wants to write? Not me, not me. Say who wants to write? Not me, not me!"

Before Billy ran out of breath, the block was gone. He strode into the bedroom, picked up his novel, and cranked out three solid paragraphs between eleven-thirty and noon. On a small, solar-powered calculator, he determined that at his present rate he would be finished in 411 days. And that gave him another idea. He tore off a clean sheet and printed his return address in the top right-hand corner.

"Dear Sir," he began. "Does the name William Bristol mean anything to you? No? I suspected as much. In 411 days, however, it shall. What will it mean? It will be the name of the man who made your career. A man you will be eternally in debt to for writing the book that took you to the top. If knowing this is overwhelming and you wish to sit down, I don't blame you. I suspect it is not every day you receive such wonderful news. For a modest advance now, you will earn the sole rights to my masterpiece, a western the likes of which has not been penned since *Lonesome Dove*. Let me remind you, sir, that book won the Pulitzer Prize. For 411,000 dollars, a thousand for each day between now and completion, you can bring a potential National Book Award winner into your house. Of course, I will retain all paperback, foreign, and film rights. Your prompt response is appreciated and expected. Sincerely, William Bristol."

Well done. Billy didn't see how any young editor could pass on such an opportunity. He would get the names of half a dozen men and women under thirty at the country's best publishing houses. Eager young editors looking to make a name for themselves. If he worked it right, he'd have a bidding war going in no time.

He signed his unemployment check with a great, sprawling signature, folded it into the front pocket of his jeans, took the letter to *Playboy*, and high-stepped out the door on his way to the supermarket. God, it felt good to get rid of the block.

Two packages of real butter, a pair of name-brand cinnamon containers, two loaves of Italian sourdough bread, and a brace of Heineken six-packs. Cold. Billy plopped his groceries down on the Safeway counter and handed the young girl a hundred-dollar bill.

"Can you break this?" he asked, shaking his head as though he had nothing smaller. She could, and he made sure to take his receipt. He would bring it back in the evening and claim he'd been charged double for everything he bought. It was a nifty trick that worked every time.

Back on Front Street, Butte's lowest east–west avenue, far below Washoe where he lived, Billy frowned. There were serious decisions to be made, decisions with lasting consequences, the first and foremost being how to spend the rest of his unemployment check. He owed his mother almost fifty, and while he would argue that when she plugged in his answering machine it nullified his debt, he doubted she would buy it. He owed his landlady for half of June and all of July. And he owed Chuck's, too. At some point Leslie Booth would have to be paid.

Better to think about these things after a few Heinekens, Billy figured. He wrapped the plastic bags around his wrists and leaned into the slope of Main Street, beginning the uphill climb. His progress was so slow that he could not bear to look up from the sidewalk. If he did, it seemed he would never reach his destination. Halfway there, out of breath, beginning to worry about hypoxia, he spied a familiar alley whose potholed tar was sheltered from the hot sun by wide porches extending out from the apartment buildings on both sides.

"Hello, old friend," he said as he started into the alley, already loosening his grip on the bags, swishing an imaginary mouthful of Heineken over his teeth in anticipation. He propped himself up against a garbage dumpster, his back to the flow of traffic in the one-way alley, and chose a bottle from the middle of one of the cartons. Beads of condensation clung to the green glass and cooled his forehead when he pressed the bottle to his face. A much-practiced flip with his pocket opener, the picture of the naked woman on it long ago rubbed out, sent the cap spinning to the ground and released the fragrant odor of fermented hops. He brought the bottle close under his nose, wafting the aromatic fumes toward himself with his cupped left hand, then could stand it no more. He threw back his head, stuffed the neck into his mouth well past the label, and let twelve ounces of golden, imported Heineken rush down his throat. The sensation, similar to opening his mouth under a high-pressure cold shower, caused him to shudder with delight.

"Yah, Andrea, iz good brew," he said, holding the empty in the general direction of Excelsior. "Ve goes and gets more soon."

Looking at the remaining eleven bottles, Billy drew an analogy between them and his money. They were really quite alike, he thought. In both cases, they provided satisfaction in their original forms, yet they could also be used to create new satisfactions. Then it hit him. The more beer he drank, the better he felt, so he should spend his money. All of it. Quickly. Trembling from the genius of this Socratic reasoning, Billy rose nimbly, wondering what new heightened pleasures lay in store for him. What orgasmic thrills would he find when his last penny was gone?

And then he heard his mother's truck coming behind him, the metronomelike slap of the passenger-side mud flap against the tire, the squeak of the tailgate bouncing on its hinges, the raspy horn blaring as proof he'd been spotted.

"All is lost," he sighed.

"Groceries, baby," his mother said through her open window. "That's good. Wasn't enough to feed a mouse in your apartment the other day."

She opened the passenger door and Billy climbed in. It was harder even than climbing Main Street. His mother gently lifted his hands from the bags, and Billy winced as she inventoried the contents.

"Bread and butter." Mrs. Bristol turned out of the alley without looking, something Old Stan would have been proud of.

Billy closed his eyes and clutched at his door, his face twisted into a position he feared it would remain in if people didn't stop trying to kill him in an automobile.

"Got some spirits, too, I see." She smacked her lips, never a good sign.

Billy prayed his mother would not lecture him, mouthing a short plea, pathetic enough to appeal to any deity not more urgently occupied. For the love of god . . . for the love of *any* god, spare the lecture. A man with . . . yes, a man with a job is entitled to a celebratory drink. Good thinking.

"I've got a job," he said between heavy breaths.

"Uh-huh, honey. You need more fiber in your diet. Need to get yourself some raisin bran cereal. Help keep you regular."

Jesus, had she heard what he'd said? Crossing the intersection of Main and Granite, Billy thought of a great many things he needed. Nowhere on that list was raisin bran cereal.

"And some milk," his mother continued. "Calcium. If the lactose upsets your belly, you make sure to get some vitamins. And, honey, you don't need all this booze. Not this much."

Billy bristled. Fine German beer did not fall into the category of common booze. That was like comparing a male peacock in full mating plumage to the disgusting vulture perched atop a bloated wildebeest on the previous night's Discovery Channel program. Billy tried hard to concentrate on the narrator's description instead of on his mother.

"The buzzard will seek an opening in the soft nether regions."

Poor choice. He shifted in his seat, constricting his sphincter in an uncomfortable manner. Soon his whole body would be misshapen. Locked tight by spasms.

"Now, baby, what's this about a job?"

Mrs. Bristol did not turn onto Washoe as Billy had hoped. Prayed, really. Instead, she continued up Main Street. They were going to the center. He concentrated hard, trying to keep his eyes from rolling up too far in their sockets, certain that if he could not do so they would retreat into his head, initiating a severe anxiety-induced seizure. Billy stared out his window at the passing pavement, wondering seriously how badly he'd be injured if he bailed.

"You say you've found some work?" His mother licked her lips loudly, a habit Billy had never been fond of. It made him quite ill. "Why, of course you did. Able boy like you, sure to find respectable work. You bet." More smacking noises.

"Stop," Billy croaked, thrusting his thumbs into his ears so hard he could feel a quivering he assumed was the drums about to rupture. Please, no more. Must I be forced to deafen myself?

The truck slowed in front of a three-story brick building. Already Billy could smell the center. The pungent odor of garlic bread and the sickly sweet aroma of cherry Kool-Aid. It was Spaghetti Day. On the top floor, a great vat of it would be bubbling, two or three old drunks watching as though it was the most interesting thing they'd ever seen. Maybe it was.

"What's your job, baby?" Mrs. Bristol shut the truck off and turned her full attention to her son. To justify her unbounded expression of glee, Billy would have to tell her he'd been hired on as the hospital's new head surgeon. "You go ahead and tell your mommy all about this job."

"Well . . ." How could he explain what it was he'd been hired to do? "Well, I'm employed as a personal attendant." Billy hated to borrow Buff's description, but he had to admit it sounded more formal than anything he could think of.

"Personal attendant." His mother raised her eyebrows, eagerly anticipating a more in-depth response. Billy saw the tip of her tongue work its way out from between her teeth and, wanting at all costs to preempt the smacking that would soon follow, he heaved a great sigh and began speaking in a low tone of voice.

"I work for a German movie star named Andrea Kauffman. She's eighty-eight years old, blind, and still lives by herself. She's hired me to accompany her on necessary business. I'm a consultant of sorts." Billy flattened himself against his door, keeping out of range of the hug he feared his mother wished to deliver.

Mrs. Bristol squealed. "Oh, baby! Didn't I always tell you it was gonna happen? Your mother knew in her heart that it would. She just knew it. I bet you don't have any desire to keep sending your letters, do you?"

She didn't understand. "My novel is actually coming very well," he said.

"Oh. Well, you don't let that stand in the way, sweetheart. This is meaningful work you've got now. Imagine it! Just wait till I tell everyone. Everybody's gonna know about this, Billy. And you say she's blind?"

This was a huge bonus. Mrs. Bristol's need to help people—the need that drove her to show National Geographic specials; institute Spaghetti Day; and spend hundreds of hours setting up museum tours, planning trips to zoos and national parks, and scheming over the best way to bring guest speakers to the center—had been conspicuously and disappointingly absent in her son. She saw this new job as a sign that Billy was coming around. He was making good, and the world would know about it.

"Honey, you'd ought to bring this lady down to the center. She must be so lonely. And a movie star? What a wonderful speaker she'd make! We could cook up some nice bratwurst."

Billy felt himself slipping. Was the block coming for him again?

"Now, you come on in here and tell everyone. Tell them why your mommy's so proud of you."

Her arms came for him rapidly, spreading, groping. Billy believed the only one prouder of him at the moment would be the professional contortionist he'd seen on television. He managed to place his entire body in a two-cubic-foot section of the cab and avoid the hug. He figured at twenty-nine he didn't need to be cuddled.

"Well . . ." his mother didn't seem to care or notice that he'd dodged her. "Hurry up and get out. You come on in and tell 'em all."

Please, anything but that, Billy thought. Hug me, kiss me, smack those lips. Dump the Heineken. Take the money. But don't make me go in there. Don't humiliate your son in this fashion.

Mrs. Bristol opened his door and grabbed his shoulder with the firm grip of a woman on a mission. She was always on a mission. There would be no wrangling out of it.

"And we'll just set this booze in the fridge. You won't need it no more. Not with a respectable job."

Wrong! In fact, the respectable job was one strong argument in favor of the "booze." Billy was sure that if he didn't pour another full bottle down his gullet, and do it soon, too, his tongue would swell and cut off his airway.

"Oh, you're killing me," he wailed softly as he was manhandled from the truck.

Butte's Adult Activities Center consisted of two rooms, equal in size, equally distasteful to Billy. There was the kitchen. One glance in that direction was one too many. Yellow linoleum, wallpaper peeling behind the commercial-sized stove, cheap framed painting of Crazy Horse erected by Hector, immense iron crock of spaghetti, punch bowl of cherry Kool-Aid on the long counter, a humming white refrigerator. If pathetic were a noun, it would be the center's kitchen. Depressing. Horribly depressing.

With an empty look, the eyes of a condemned man resigned to his fate, Billy turned his attention to the dining room. Eddie La-Fontaine, Doug Four-Toes, and Hector Torrerez. Fine, upstanding citizens. Eddie was passed out with his head on his paper plate; Doug was scratching his crotch, going right to town, too; and Hector, Crazy Horse reincarnate, was wearing the chest plate of plastic wolf ribs he'd bought on a trip to Bozeman a few years ago. Big Green, the old film projector, sat in one corner in front of a dozen metal folding chairs, while across the room lay the podium, chalkboard, and wall map of the United States with lines of string held between colored thumbtacks spreading away from Butte to unvisited western cities like a spider's web.

"How." Hector raised his right hand to Billy. Crazy Horse didn't know any Sioux, but he did a fine job imitating the actors who played Indians in the first black-and-white movies. "Many moons since me seeum Billy. How."

Doug hauled his hand from his pants and offered it for a shake. No thanks. Billy sat down next to Eddie, jealous of the drunk and his peaceful sleep. Lucky, unaware Eddie.

"Meal ready soon, yes?" Hector called to Mrs. Bristol, busy stirring the spaghetti. "We wantum eat now, squaw," he said more softly.

Billy couldn't bring himself to laugh.

Eddie woke with a start, snorting as he raised his head, looked to be sure there was no food on his plate, then slumped over again. This was becoming too much. More than a comatose mental patient could bear, to say nothing of a hardworking writer in desperate need to get home to a hot novel. Billy wished his faculties had an on-and-off switch. A breaker he could throw to prevent the permanent damage to his brain he was sure he would suffer. Doug was scratching again, and the sandpaper noises coming from his direction were worse than nails on a chalkboard. Scratch, scratch, scratch, you filthy baboon. Rage began building in Billy's stomach. A lit match against the sensitive lining. Or was it the start of an ulcer?

"So, Billy." Hector tipped his chair back and crossed his arms, assuming the position of the chief. "What you do for long time, Billy? Me not see you and wonder if you dead? Glad you not."

How about that? Crazy Horse was happy that Billy was still in the land of the living.

"You workum now, yes?"

"Yes."

"Not workum for whitie, no?"

"I work for a German movie star," Billy said loudly enough to get Doug's attention, too.

"Ger-man movie star." The chief nodded slowly, then closed his eyes. Without opening them he said, "You think maybe she want play your tom-tom?"

Billy turned away disgusted. A vile picture was forming in his head, taking shape rapidly, like a thundercloud before a storm.

"Me think Billy have good job with movie star. Me wonder if she has sister."

"And what the hell would she want with you?" Doug paused his scratching. "Can't you see Billy's full of shit? German movie star in Butte? My left nut." He dug harder at the object of his expression. "Eddie! Wake up, Eddie, goddamn it!" He punched him with his other hand. "Hey, Billy says he's gone to work for a movie star. You believe this shit?"

"Huh?" Eddie rolled his head sideways to train one eye on Billy. "Fuuuuuck, no." He was out again.

"See, Hector, even drunk Eddie knows better than to believe that."

"Who Hector?" the chief asked.

"You, for Christ's sake. When are you going to lay off the Indian routine? Chief Crazy Horse. Should call you Chief Shit-for-Brains."

Hector shoved his chair away from the table. "Me takum scalp now," he said, looking hard at a butter knife lying on a napkin in front of him.

"Gentlemen!" Mrs. Bristol appeared in the doorway to the kitchen. "I won't have fighting in here. Not on Spaghetti Day. Billy, honey, why don't you tell them about your new job? How you work for a movie star. How you take care of . . ."

Billy cut her off. If he had to tell it, it would be his version. "Yes, that's what I was doing," he said.

Hector pulled up to the table again, a grin of victory spreading across his face. "Me told you," he said to Doug as if he was always right. "Me . . . told . . . you."

"Shut up," Doug snarled, and Hector knew he was serious. He wiped all expression from his face, crossed his arms, and nodded at Billy to begin. The great chief was ready to listen.

"Well . . ." Billy let his eyes roll toward the kitchen to be sure his mother was out of earshot. Finding that she wasn't in sight, he leaned on the table, motioning Doug and Hector closer. "Well, even a blind dog finds his bone sometimes."

"Speakum up!" Crazy Horse ordered. "Me want hear whole story."

Billy stole another glance into the kitchen. All clear. "Yes, well . . . imagine this." Although it was difficult to restrain himself, Billy spoke slowly and calmly, maintaining a hypnotic gentleness for effect. "Imagine a widow's walk. The top of a mansion in the clouds of a warm rain. Mist drifting by . . . the scent of lilacs wafting up from below." Pause and sigh. "Imagine a sofa now. Cushions refreshingly damp. A scene of scattered . . . scattered and torn clothing lying around it. Two bodies on the sofa." This had the makings of something more to send to *Playboy*. In his mind, Billy could see it all. Why, he wondered, did the woman look frighteningly like Buff?

"Get to humpum part," Hector said, obviously excited. "Me want hear humpum part."

"Imagine the most beautiful woman you've ever seen." Billy was pulling out all the stops.

"Havum big titties?" Hector asked eagerly.

"Oh, sensuous breasts." Billy fondled an imaginary pair, as pleased with his word choice as he was with Hector's reaction. "Sensuous breasts, moist lips, bedroom eyes, seductive yet innocent."

"You top, she top?" The chief was panting, and suddenly, as the picture in Billy's head blossomed into a full fantasy, the type of daydream he figured only the very best writers were capable of creating, tapping their deep resources of invention, he could no longer keep his composure.

"She top, me top, six ways to Sunday, Hector." Oh, it was so real. So very real. "Yes, hours and hours of it. Sweaty, hard, beastlike." Billy pounded on the table, thrusting his hips. "Boom, boom, boom!"

A white flash of light somewhere near the center of Billy's brain. Ozone. The electric odor of crossed wires. Falling from the chair, strobes of vision. Mother, rolling pin, floor, floor, floor. Time for one final thought. What shall it be? Bludgeoned to death. Yes, very nice.

"Billy, baby?"

The voice was far away, somewhere back in the realm of the living.

"Honey? Look at me, sweetheart. Open your eyes."

Billy's vision returned painfully, the ceiling light shooting needles into his skull. Is there no limit to the number of times I am to be deprived of death? he wondered.

"That's it, baby. Momma wouldn't have to bash your head if you didn't talk such filth." Mrs. Bristol placed her hand under Billy's neck and lifted his head. It felt as if she was decapitating him, and as his eyes lolled toward the floor he fully expected to see a headless body lying there. "Ain't no need to talk like that. Not on Spaghetti Day."

Evidently, the day was sacred. The gathering of a few drunks in a top-floor activities center had ascended to a level rivaling that of the Sabbath in the eastern European countries where monks still flay themselves for penance. That life wouldn't be so bad, Billy thought. Lots of time to write.

"Eddie, you go get some ice," Mrs. Bristol said.

Yes, or a cat-o'-nine-tails.

"I know it must hurt awful. Hurts your momma, too."

Billy heard the refrigerator door open, a noise that triggered an automatic plea of "beer."

"What's that?" His mother pressed her ear close to her son's lips.

"Him wantum beer, he say." Hector grinned down from his chair. Crazy Horse could scarcely have been happier at Little Big Horn.

Mrs. Bristol jerked her hand out from under Billy's head, allowing it to fall and connect with the floor.

"He doesn't get any beer," she snapped as she stood up. "No booze on Spaghetti Day."

No, certainly not. A hair shirt, solitary meditation, a good, solid go-round with the flogger, yes. But Heineken? On Spaghetti Day? I think not. An act of such unforgivable sacrilege would necessitate the reconvening of the Spanish Inquisition's most dedicated torture masters. Billy winced as the whinny of horses, the squeaking of crude wooden pulleys, and the twang of taut ropes came to him.

"No," he wailed. "Not drawn and quartered."

Doug reached down and pulled him to his feet. Which hand did he use? Better not to think about it. Better not to think at all. Rest the head. Keep the brain, the writer's most precious tool, from swelling. A swollen brain was an easy target for the block, and with the block in there, too, they might need to vent the skull. Billy had watched the procedure on the Discovery Channel, but not without a good deal of squirming. All in all, it had looked like something to avoid.

"Here comes din-din," Mrs. Bristol called gaily from the kitchen, barely clearing the doorway with the huge pot. "Here you are, boys. Eat up. And oh, wait just a minute." The little woman pranced back into the kitchen for the punch bowl. "Look at this." She sounded like she was trying to entice a baby to eat. "It's your favorite . . . cherry Kool-Aid! You just go ahead and help yourselves. Human body needs eight full glasses of water every day. Doesn't need all this sugar, but we'll just cheat a little." She winked.

Cheating? Hardly in keeping with the spirit of Spaghetti Day, Billy thought. He stared at his plate, at the heap of sauce-covered pasta. Nothing like a good blow to the head to take a man's appetite away. He forked a few strands into his mouth, then turned away from the table when his mother began slurping up her portion, the white ends zipping into her mouth like worms into some giant aardvark-like animal. Wasn't there such a creature in Africa? Along the . . . what river was it? The Zambezi? Billy thought so. He rubbed his head and moaned. It didn't seem possible, but the pain was increasing.

"So, baby." Mrs. Bristol paused the slurping. "You're going to bring that nice lady you work for down here, aren't you? Let us make her feel right at home."

Billy gagged. Go back to slurping, he thought.

"Let us cook up some good old-fashioned German bratwurst."

That would certainly sweeten the deal. Perhaps Andrea and Eddie could have a long, intellectual discussion on modern filmmaking. Or maybe the chief could enlist her in his battle against whitie. And Doug? He could scratch his balls to his heart's content without her ever knowing.

"As a matter of fact, Billy, we'd just love it if she'd give a talk. I know there would be a great crowd. Maybe standing room only. We'd all have to get here early."

Hmmm. A good crowd? Surely not as good as the last turnout. Billy and Hector were the only ones who'd come to hear the last speaker. He was someone from the Urban Housing Committee making an obligatory stop in Butte. How his mother had collared him was beyond Billy, but it nearly killed him to sit and listen to someone so thoroughly cut off. The buffoon was running for some office and had talked for an entire hour. It had made Billy quite ill.

"You be sure and ask her," his mother said. "Unless you'd rather I do it."

"No." That could prove disastrous. Kiss the Chevy good-bye. "No, I'll talk to her about it." It hurt so much to speak.

"Don't interrupt nothing on the widow's walk." Doug elbowed Billy. "Boom, boom, boom, you lying sack of . . ."

"Enough!" Mrs. Bristol stood up. "Baby's been punished enough."

Amen to that. Billy exhaled sorrowfully through his nose. A heavy, heavy burden, he thought. He swished a bit of Kool-Aid around in his mouth, growing more and more jealous of Eddie, who'd passed out again. He grimaced when he swallowed. It damn sure wasn't Heineken. Not even close.

"Is baby ready to go home now?" Mrs. Bristol was finished slurping. "Momma will bring you if you're ready. Want some more ice for that knot on your head?"

Ice? Here lay an opportunity. "Yes, I'll get a little more," Billy said strongly enough so no one would volunteer to do it for him. Ten seconds alone with the refrigerator would be enough. Just ten seconds. Ten little ticks of the second hand. He strode into the kitchen and opened the Maytag without hesitation. Better never to hesitate. Ahh, the six-packs. How many will fit in the pants? One, two, three, four. Four comfortably.

Billy nearly forgot the ice. Returning without it would have been a fatal oversight. He fished a handful out of the freezer and limped bowlegged back into the dining room, proud that he did not flinch as the cold bottles rubbed against his bare legs. He waved a quick good-bye to the men at the table and headed for the stairs. They would be tricky and require some fancy stepping.

Down with the right and over with the left. Now down with the left and over with the right. And step one, two, three, step one, two, three. Billy carried the rhythm and the Heineken successfully to the street. He was tempted to crack a bottle in the truck while he waited for his mother, but it wasn't worth it. Soon enough. Soon enough, and more than one bottle, too. He would be home in time for the Discovery Channel's safari. Where were they going today? Back to Africa, he hoped.

The ride down to Washoe was silent, reminding Billy how lovely the absence of noise could be. Jesus, it seemed good to have a bit of peace and quiet. Good for his head, good for his soul. And yet there was still something telling him his trials for the day were not over. Gnawing like a lone rat. Very easy to ignore until it chewed through a power line in the middle of the night and burned your house down.

"Baby?" Mrs. Bristol turned the truck off in front of the apartment building. A bad sign. She didn't think she was coming in, did she? "Baby, I just want to tell you again how proud I am."

Billy doubted that was what she wanted.

"I'm proud as I've ever been." She began to fidget and couldn't make eye contact. Guilty. She felt guilty. For what? The bashing incident? "And, baby, now that you've got this new job, this new very respectable job, I knew you wouldn't mind paying your mother the money you owe her. I knew you wouldn't."

Knew? Billy thrust his hand into his pocket. The unemployment money. Where was it?

"I left you a little. But remember, you owed me from last year, too. There's enough in there so you can buy yourself a pop or a milk. Milk is better for you." Mrs. Bristol reached for him and he drew away, eyes glued to the single dollar bill he'd come up with.

Thievery. Blatant robbery. And does she have any remorse? Perhaps a sliver. In Billy's mind, taking one hundred and sixty-five of his hard-earned dollars should cause her to crumble. Grovel at his feet and beg his forgiveness. He opened his door, feeling as if his chest was in the grasp of a powerful, hydraulic vice. The onset of a heart attack, no doubt.

"Don't be upset, sweetheart," his mother called. "You're on your way now, baby. And don't forget to ask Andrea when she'd like to come and speak, okay?"

Bang. Billy slammed the apartment's front door, regretting pawning the soundproof oak for the first time. He could still hear her voice behind him, chasing him up the stairs through the veneer. One flight up, he drained a Heineken. Not very helpful. He reached into his pants and sucked down a second. Better, but it still failed to produce the Hippocratic effect he sought. Try a third. Ah, that was it. A good buzz.

Billy's buzz carried him to Jesus, but on that step he stopped. There was a note on his door. An envelope taped neatly to the handle addressed to Mr. Bristol. What sort of official posting was this? He trod heavily on Mary and Joseph, then set down his bag of groceries. He looked from it to the envelope, fearing more with each passing second that even a fine slice of cinnamon toast wouldn't offset the horrors in store for him if he opened it. Three minutes passed. Billy knew because he counted. He rubbed at the knot on his head, cautioned himself not to think things couldn't get worse, then reached for the letter.

"Attention Mr. Bristol:" Not dear? Bad sign right from the start. "I shall no longer tolerate your refusal to pay rent."

Refusal? A bit harsh, wasn't it?

"I am giving you fourteen days, the period required by state law, to vacate these premises. If, after that time you have not done so, the town sheriff will remove you and your belongings. I am sorry it has come to this."

There was no signature. Did that fact invalidate the notice? It might. Worth checking at least. Legal Aid would know. Inside his living room, Billy fell onto the couch, immensely dismayed to see that his remote was lying on top of the television across the room. See how every man's hand is set against me, he thought, as he shoved himself up and staggered toward it. He pressed the power button and dialed up the Discovery Channel. Two huge beetles took shape on the screen, and the familiar voice of the English narrator filled the room.

"Locked in passionate congress, the stag beetles remain joined for several hours."

"Stag beetles, huh?" Billy said. "I should have been one of those. Instead . . ." he pulled the last bottle of Heineken from his pants. "Instead, mine are the trials of Job." He tipped his head back and chugged the beer. And later that afternoon as he slept on the couch, he was plagued by strange dreams: women with beetle heads, his mother swinging a battle-ax, Andrea's Chevy driven by a demonic caricature of Old Stan, and Chuck's bartender, Leslie Booth. Booth was coming for him again, and he couldn't run or scream. All he could do was watch and wait.

The dream seemed to be saying something about his life in general, and in it he lay waiting on the sidewalk in front of the R&R. Waiting for her to take him wherever it was such pathetic souls went. Nowhere very good, he suspected.

· 6 ·

4:14 P.M. Billy rubbed his head. It didn't hurt quite so much. Or perhaps he was growing numb. That would be a merciful thing, he thought. He stared at the television, remembering the stag beetles. That program appeared to have given way to one on some sort of exploratory surgery. "If a tumor is present," the narrator said hopefully, "it will lie just under the pancreas." Billy's left hand began stroking his stomach while his right searched frantically for the remote. Where was his pancreas? It could be swollen, swollen and tumor ridden, and he wouldn't even know it. Must make a note to find its location. Key it down in an anatomy book.

Heaving cushions from the couch in a desperate search for the remote, Billy tried to ignore the television.

"Malignant . . . spreading . . . terminal."

Why did those words get through to him? And what awful associations they stirred in his mind. Ah, the remote. None too soon. He pointed it at the TV and jammed his thumb down on the power button.

"Zip," he said as the picture disappeared. As soon as it vanished, he stopped patting his abdomen. There were more pressing things to consider than the location of his pancreas. For now, any long-term pancreatic ailment would have to take a backseat.

4:18 P.M. That meant it was a little after six on the East Coast. And this evening? This evening, an agent. The time had come. The block was gone, the novel was all but writing itself, and with his new job with Andrea he couldn't be bothered by the business end of writing. Takes up too much time, he thought. Can't be negotiating contracts, wining and dining editors, dotting all the *i*'s, *and* writing. That would be too much for any man. He hobbled into his bedroom for the address book.

Agents, agents, agents. He knew there were a few names in there.

"Here we are," he said. He had the names of three of them. Phone numbers for two. And they had better still be in the office, he thought. Working as hard for writers as writers do for them. Well, maybe not quite as hard. That would be awfully difficult. But *almost* as hard. And that didn't mean sashaying home at the stroke of five.

He picked up the phone and began dialing: Two-one-two. Had he ever placed a call to that area with satisfactory results? Billy shook his head. Entrenched in the streets of New York, he didn't see how a person could avoid getting cut off. The agency's voice mail came on after six rings.

Voice mail. The writer's bane. Just another way for editors, publishers, and evidently agents, too, to cut themselves off. To insulate themselves from the real world. So be it. Billy would leave a short message anyway.

"William Bristol calling. It's quarter after six, and I'm glad you're all out having your martinis. We writers are still hard at it. Nose to the grindstone twenty-four/seven. You seem to forget that it is the fruits of our labor that keep you employed. We don't work for you, you work for us. Well, you don't work for William Bristol. And isn't that too bad. I have a very promising novel under way that you shall never see. Not until it is between two hard covers on the best-sellers' rack. Perhaps I shall make it my chief business to find out whom you represent and inform them of your lackadaisical attitude. I hope your martinis are nice and dry."

There, that should get them thinking. They can check their caller ID in the morning and ring him back. Not that it would do any good. They'd blown their chance. Billy looked at the next name. Two-one-two again, goddamn it. He began to shake. If he didn't get to talk to a person, a real live person this time, then to hell with agents.

"Hello." It sounded like a woman, but with a two-one-two number you could never be sure.

"Hello. My name is William Bristol. I'm interested in talking with a literary agent."

"Well, my name is Sarah Conlin, and I've been an agent here for two years."

Two years. Hmmm. Young. Could be good, could be bad. Might be full of ambition, but might lack contacts. Billy knew the importance of contacts. He would feel her out a bit.

"I'm calling because I have a novel in the works that will need the very best representation. The bidding wars it's sure to produce will be a bit beyond my area of expertise. When people start tossing all those seven-digit numbers around, I prefer to let them deal with an agent. Do you know what I mean?"

"I'm sorry, what did you say your name was?"

Inattentive. That would never do. Billy sighed. "Here, let me just read you one short passage. We can go from there."

"Actually . . ."

Billy cut her off. No excuses. "The wolves were howling." Uh-oh. Perhaps this passage was better suited for a morning recitation. Might stick with him the rest of the afternoon and make it hard to sleep. "The wolves were howling, singing to the night sky, that inky blanket of darkness pressing down on the wary riders." He shivered. "The wolves sang to the steady thump of horses' hooves echoing off the steep canyon walls." He tapped the receiver, imagining the shod feet, eyes beginning to dart around his apartment. "Some of the riders plugged their ears, their horses' hooves too close to the dreadful beat of tom-toms they had been dreaming about."

"Mr. Bristol, please . . ."

Yes, I know, very spooky. Not a good bedtime story for a young lady. Lucky for her that's all he had.

"So," he said. "The standard fifteen percent?"

"What?" Why did everyone back east sound tired?

"I said, I suspect you will ask for fifteen percent. I hate to concede that much, but I understand it's the going rate. Oh, yes, and I will expect my own PR person. Someone who can competently handle tours, readings, signings, television appearances. Juggle me into the *Today* show and *Oprah*. That type of thing."

"I see."

Finally.

"Well . . . I'm not able to sign new writers on. You'd have to send your manuscript . . ."

"Why don't I read it to you right now?" Billy shuffled the two pages. "*Crossing Montana*," he said. "That's the title. What do you think about film possibilities? Do you have an agent on the West Coast?"

"Mr. Bristol, please. Please, please. I'm on my way out the door now. It's late."

Billy looked at the alarm clock beside his bed. Late? Hardly.

"Just the first sentence, then. If you don't snatch me up after hearing that, I'll be amazed. Listen to this." He cleared his throat. "Spring, 1866." Billy sighed. "See how it sets the season and the period? Who wouldn't read more? So, do you have the necessary paperwork to bring me on board?" There was an expression someone in New York would like. Billy figured that's where it had been coined.

"Mr. Bristol, this is all a bit much for me."

Yes, he could see that it was.

"I'm going to have to ask you to call . . . no, make that write. You'll have to send a query letter."

"Query letter?" Billy thundered. He hated that term. Hated it with a passion. "I think not," he said.

"Well, suit yourself."

"I will. I'll suit myself right now." He slammed the phone down and began poring over his address book. It was in there. It had to be. Surely he hadn't lost it. Not *that* man's name. Ah, here, right under the *M*'s, where it should be. He dialed as fast as he could, the musical tones coming to his ear like a synthesizer cranked up on speed.

"Larry? Hello, Larry? Yes, William Bristol here."

"Billy." Larry sounded tired, too. Well, that was excusable. He was a writer and knew what it was like.

"You're not going to believe this. Simply not going to." Billy couldn't believe it himself. "I just read a riveting section of my novel to an agent in New York and she told me to send a query letter. Who do these people think they are? Would you like to hear what I read her? I know *you* would appreciate it."

"I'm sure it's very good, Billy."

"See, that's the writer's perspective. That's exactly what I'm looking for in an agent. In fact, why don't you just give me the name of *your* agent? He's done quite well by you and is obviously very well connected." Billy scribbled with his pen to be sure the ink was flowing.

"Well . . ."

"I'm ready." Billy held his pen tightly.

"Well, my agent doesn't allow me to do that. I wish he would sometimes, but he's quite set in his ways."

"Sounds like he could use a dose of Augustus McCrae," Billy said. "He'd straighten his ways out quick, wouldn't he? Wouldn't he?"

"Well . . ."

"Fine, fine, I understand. I'll let you get back to your work. Oh, yes, be careful. I'm just getting over a nasty bout with the block. I think it's gone now, but where to I couldn't say. Take care." Billy hung up, then stared at his address book. Very slowly he drew a question mark beside Larry McMurtry's name. He so hoped Larry wasn't cutting himself off. That would be a terrible blow. Hard to fight the good fight all by himself.

Putting the book away in his bureau, Billy found the brass knocker from the apartment's front door. Well, at least his mother had left him that. With the money it would bring from a pawnshop and the fifty dollars he'd be getting tomorrow from Andrea, maybe he could mollify Old Lady Helmsley. The thought of the sheriff tossing him into the street wasn't pleasant. He would take the knocker to a pawnshop, then stop in at Chuck's. And the receipt from Safeway? He still had it, too. He could get his money back for half the groceries to pay for the beer he'd drink at the bar. And he needed something to drink.

The knocker fit nicely in the large, open-ended pocket of his Mariners sweatshirt. He liked being able to keep both hands on it. Placing his hands on something gave him the illusion that he was in control of more than he really was. He knew it was just an illusion—that all writers are rarely in control of much more than what they write—but it made him feel somewhat better. He stopped before opening the door. Things have deteriorated to a sad state when a man fears leaving his own home, he thought. Well, soon enough it could revert back to Mrs. Helmsley. What would he do then? Strike off Kerouac style? He'd gotten a good book out of it. Spent time in Butte, even. Back when there was more to write about, though. Billy sighed. The good old days. No, now he would face the wild, merciless world penniless and without hope. Avoiding a complete, irreversible breakdown would be accomplishment enough. He shuffled out the door and down the steps, his feet dragging along, his toes burning from the friction of rubber on wood.

"I must persevere," he said to himself. "Persevere and go on."

Rocky Mountain Pawn, a low, one-story building halfway down Main Street between Washoe and Chuck's, stayed open until ten every night except Sunday. Billy looked in its full-length window, past a row of ten-speed bikes, chainsaws, saddles, golf clubs, and entertainment centers, over the shoulder of a life-size buffalo mount, toward the checkout counter. A neon sign was flashing inside, alternating between GET CASH NOW, and PAWN YOUR TITLE, DRIVE YOUR CAR. Billy didn't have a car. He did, however, have a brass door knocker.

Across Main Street, in the Alley of Despair, where his day had taken a tragic turn for the worse, where he'd been nabbed by his mother, it appeared darker than anywhere else. Much darker. Billy figured some god of great misery inhabited its dark borders, using its powers to shut out light. In the dark, it could slither about freely, sliding around in search of unwary travelers.

"Oh, no you don't," he said toward the black alley. "Not twice in the same day."

In contrast to the alley, the inside of the pawnshop was lit too brightly. Six or seven rows of high-watt fluorescent bulbs ran along the ceiling, illuminating every nook and cranny below. And there were many to illuminate. The floor was a maze of household appliances, stereo components, tools of every imaginable species (some dating back fifty or sixty years), lawn mowers, hedge trimmers, pots, pans, camping equipment, compact discs, cassette tapes, computers, cameras, snow shovels, Levi's jeans, leather jackets, and, yes, the buffalo, too. A red-and-white sign hung from his neck proclaiming that all thieves would be prosecuted. What a joke. Billy knew that without thieves many of Butte's pawnshops would go out of business. He looked at a rack of new softball gloves, their original store tags still dangling from their heels. Half the items in there had been lifted.

"Exhibit A," he said to himself as he withdrew the knocker.

Billy knew—was actually convinced beyond a doubt—that the pawnbroker had been handpicked for the job by the devil. Sent up from the bowels of hell as a personification of greed. Leaning over the counter, wiry forearms covered with tattoos, hair pulled away from his face with a rubber band, a ring or two on every finger, an awfully patient look about him, a look that let customers know he would never make more than a pathetically low offer for whatever they brought him, he looked like an evil carnie from some melodrama. Billy prepared himself to be cheated.

The broker folded his arms, glanced down at the knocker on the counter before him, then stared at Billy. It was a look devoid of emotion, save perhaps a touch of displeasure. A god unmoved by the offering.

"It's solid brass," Billy stammered.

The broker didn't blink.

"An antique, too." It could have come straight from the Ming Dynasty without impressing the pawnshop owner. Any more of the man's staring and Billy would suggest they reverse roles and he pay him to take it. Such was the power of Beelzebub.

Something tipped over by the window where a boy and his mother were looking at a bike, taking more time than they needed, hoping the price they'd be quoted would be in inverse proportion to their desire. The broker looked at them and smiled as they hurried out. Billy figured they would find a hundred dollar bill on the way home and come back for the bike. But they shouldn't expect a winged angel to escort them into the next world when their time was up. He shuddered and crossed himself on his thigh where the broker couldn't see it.

"So, what are we thinking?" The broker's voice filled the room, a hiss like January wind.

What are we thinking? Billy wished he would simply read his mind. It would be so much easier than having to talk. Don't force me to humble myself before you. I won't take a knee. No, not here. For the love of Christ . . . why did Billy's head throb when the Son's name came to mind?

"It's worth five dollars." The broker's lips did not move. Did he not care to reveal his forked tongue?

"Yes, yes! Five dollars. Five it is." Oh, give it to me quickly and tell me I haven't sold my soul. Yes, that's it, hand it over. Watch for the fingers now, no contact. There'll be no contact with the dark side tonight. Pure thoughts, think pure thoughts.

Clutching the five, Billy bolted out into Main Street, his heart beating in overdrive, something telling him that if he was fortunate enough to knock on heaven's door someday, he shouldn't expect to do it with that brass knocker.

Over on the East Ridge, the floodlights at Mary's feet shed soft light onto the statue. Hail, Mary, full of grace . . . how'd you like a beer? Lifting a toast to the ridge, he promised himself he would drink one for her, then wondered about the appropriateness of it.

Leslie Booth wasn't working. Amen. Was Billy's luck changing? Was he turning the corner? Probably not. He stopped outside the door and stared at the picture of the underground miner. There were no more gophers in Butte, and hadn't been for a long time. No, now the tunnels beneath Billy were empty. He hoped. He tugged on the iron handle, a new pain shooting through his side. Something more than the strain of walking. His pancreas? It would be fitting for that pesky organ he'd recently learned about to do him in. Was the pawnbroker laughing? Thinking about his five-dollar soul? Billy stepped inside quickly.

Chuck himself was working the bar. A fat, bald man in his sixties with thick eyebrows and a square chin, he poured drinks, broke up fights with his sawed-off pool cue, halfheartedly encouraged any woman who wanted to strip on his bar, and changed stations on the small color television without ever appearing more than half awake. He knew Billy owed a large tab, and he didn't care. Let Booth tend to that. And she would.

"How's she going?" Chuck asked as he sat a glass of Ranier draft down in front of Billy. Chuck wasn't even surprised when Billy paid. Nothing surprised him anymore. Not after thirty years of tending bar in uptown Butte. He'd seen it all. More than it all.

"Not well tonight," Billy said. "I'm being thwarted at every turn."

"The writing?" Chuck liked to talk about writing with Billy. He might have been a good writer himself if he hadn't worked so much.

Billy nodded.

"No sales?"

"No. Well, a couple to the *Times*, but nothing new with the novel. Can you believe it?"

Chuck sighed. "Ever think of doing something else?"

"What?" Well, that settled that. Chuck didn't understand, either. "No. Not in my wildest dreams. See, someone who can write simply has to do it. There's no choice in the matter for them. You'd wake up in the morning—*early* in the morning—and if you couldn't get right at it you'd quickly go mad. That's why it's such a curse." Billy looked up at the ceiling, the entire length of which was covered with rows of baseball hats. Hundreds of them hanging from more than a dozen wires strung like clothesline from one end of the bar to the other.

"Yeah, that's sort of the way I feel about this." Chuck held out his hands. "Used to feel, anyway. Hey, have you heard the news?"

Billy set his glass down. Empty. He was always suspicious of news. There seemed to be more than a fifty-fifty chance that it would be bad.

"I'm cashing in my chips. Throwing in the towel. Hanging it up after thirty-one years. Jesus, doesn't seem like it can be that long. When I say it, I can't believe I've lasted."

Billy felt his throat constrict, not daring to swallow his mouthful of Ranier. There were better ways to kill himself than by pouring beer down his airway. He sat in disbelief, letting the bubbles fizz away until the liquid on his tongue had the smoothness of water. This was the final blow. The straw that would break his back. Send him into a private world of insanity. Oh, dark curtain, fall quickly upon me. Oh, sorrowful, sorrowful existence. Oh, twitching eyelids. Here I go, here I go.

Chuck's firm grip on Billy's wrists prevented him from tumbling backward off his stool. Better to let me fall to the floor, Billy thought. A long, long way to the floor where I might split my skull. Just let go and I'll tip over. Angle my soft temple for a four-by-six joint. Go shake hands with the pawnbroker. At this thought, a vivid image of the man from Rocky Mountain Pawn came to him, so clear that Billy saw the tattoos in detail and smelled his tangy aftershave.

"Very well," he sniveled. "You've beaten me."

"Say what?"

Was that Chuck's voice? Sounded more like Mother.

"Is that you, Mommy? Put down the rolling pin."

"Bristol!" Chuck slapped his face with the wet towel he used to wipe up spilled beer.

Ambrosia? Did I take the up elevator, after all? Billy licked his lips and opened his eyes. Saint Peter looked just like Chuck. Strange. But then again, what better place to arrive?

"Give me another one, Saint Peter," he said solemnly. "I doubt the tap will run dry here."

"For fuck's sake, Billy, what are you talking about?"

Now, now, Peter, no need to be cross. No need to scold the recently departed.

Chuck's door swung suddenly outward, opened violently enough to suck a napkin lying on the end of the bar out into the street.

"Who's coming for me?" Billy asked in a panic. "Don't let them take me away. Please, don't let them take me."

A giant bulk entered from the street, a misguided apparition unable to locate its porthole back to hell.

"No!" Billy begged. "Spare me."

"Billy Bristol," the creature bellowed. "You're coming home with me tonight."

"Angels. I want angels," Billy wailed. "Angels coming for to carry me home, Peter." He grabbed Chuck's shirt. "I know I'm nothing to you. The single soul of a poor, put-upon writer, but I must beg you, please send the angels. Tell this night stalker to leave us. Banish it to the farthest corner of the universe. Please, mine cannot be so dreadful a fate. Angels, angels, angels. Come for me now!"

"Who in the fuck is Angel?" The beast was on him, riled up that its appearance was not as desired as an angel's. "Things I'm gonna do to you would cost an angel its wings, baby." A monstrous set of damp lips planted a kiss in the middle of Billy's forehead.

Lilly? Was it Lilly Four-Toes? Doug's twenty-three-year-old sister? It was, and Billy realized he was not standing at the gates. Only the good die young, he thought, and Lilly had been everything but. A purported bisexual, she could rape man and woman alike.

"Chuckie." Lilly glared at the bartender. "Chuckie, get this man a shot." She brushed Billy's hair away from his ear so she could cover it with her mouth. "I'm getting you drunk," she whispered. "Whole lot of woman's gonna run wild on you tonight."

In that case, get me comatose. Billy threw down the ounce of Jack Daniel's, fully believing the painful burning it caused in the back of his throat would be the most pleasant sensation of the evening. With horror, he thought of the legs. The bristly, sequoian legs that would crush his torso. He tried not to look at her, but like a Himalayan peak, she loomed over him, never out of sight. When he turned his head he could feel her presence, an unbearable pressure on the back of his neck. And when he did face her she consumed his view. True, she was buying the shots, but what price would he pay later? Whatever she had in mind would not be good for his failing pancreas. He stared at her stomach, that gelatinous blob jammed under an extra-large T-shirt, his eyes beginning to glaze, his head numbing.

"So, Billy, you getting primed?" Lilly jumped her stool closer. "Don't think you ought to slow down, do you? Wouldn't want Billy's willy to fall asleep, would we?"

A great, meaty hand fell into Billy's crotch. Roughly. Don't squeeze, Lilly. Please don't squeeze. A childhood memory of squishing purple grapes in the Safeway market came to mind. Pop. Was this punishment for wasting food? Oh, don't squeeze, Lilly.

"Let me see your hand, Billy," Lilly commanded, jerking his arm into her lap.

Jesus, don't make *me* squeeze, either. I don't want to touch it. Lilly, dear Lilly, my dainty spring flower, let's just be friends.

"They say a man's johnson is as long as it is from the tip of his middle finger to his wrist. That true, Chuckie?"

Chuck gave a sleepy shrug.

"Well, for a big man, Billy, you ain't got very long fingers." She separated them and frowned.

Billy couldn't help noticing that if what she was saying were true, and Lilly were a man, she'd be hung like mule. Her hand looked like a heavyweight boxer's.

"You sure don't have very big fingers," she said again. "Your schwanse has gotta be bigger than this."

No, it's not. Really. It's of no interest to you, Lilly. Let's just be friends.

"If this is all you got, buddy, you got fucked." Lilly looked dejected. "I mean, Christ, you must have to tug pretty good to get it out and piss. Or maybe you sit. Hey, you a squatter? I had a squatter once. Wasn't any fun at all."

"It's not the length, it's not the size." Chuck grinned, knowing he wasn't helping matters. "It's how many times you get it to rise."

"Maybe, Chuckie." Lilly still held Billy's hand. "But in case you haven't noticed, I'm no size four. I'm a big woman, and I like a lot of man. You man enough for me, Bristol?"

He looked at her butch-cut bleached hair and shook his head. Where was her humility? Her human decency? Her gender-tied compassion for things that are weak? What sort of gargantuan nymphomaniac was this, and what could be done to escape it? Well on his way to becoming thoroughly intoxicated, Billy found his mind working in slow motion, his thoughts continually returning to Lilly's legs, those oversized tree trunks jutting from her guitar-string-tight shorts. How can I get away? How often does she shave them? Could I beat her out the door? Varicose veins. Fake a seizure? Thick, yellow toenails. Beg Chuck to intervene? Corns and bunions. Sometime between wondering if he could swallow his tongue and thinking that in Lilly even Dr. Scholl would meet his match, the door opened again.

Leslie Booth.

And whom did the softer footsteps behind her belong to? Those light slaps of leather on concrete? Perhaps Lucifer himself was coming to join the party. Billy began to shake, slopping whiskey from his shot glass onto the floor, a terrible waste.

Booth eclipsed what little light shone in from Main Street as she squeezed through the door. It didn't seem possible, but she was even bigger than Lilly. She gave a guttural grunt of acknowledgment to Chuck, then turned her malicious eye on Billy. Behind her, sliding in quietly through the shadows of her broad shoulders, came the pawnbroker. He stopped in the doorway, arms crossed, the last line of defense between Billy and Main Street. The jig was up.

Billy, looking from Lilly to Leslie to the broker, could not figure what grand plan the trio had in store for him, or even where they had descended from. Or ascended. One thing was clear, however, they weren't the butcher, the baker, and the candlestick maker. Nursery rhymes? What brought about that association? Was his mind regressing? Retreating to the blissful ignorance of childhood? Heading back to a time when monsters were confined to closets instead of prowling the streets of Butte and lurking in little out-of-the-way bars?

"Well, well, well." Leslie's voice had a baritone quality that Billy could not help thinking would sound unnaturally deep on an alpha male. His mind floated to the Discovery Channel's program on gorillas—their dark, heavy beards, hairy backs, large frames. Was Booth a simple set of genitals away from them?

"You ain't paid tonight, and it's the boots, my man," Booth said. She scuffed two steps closer, grinding the steel toes of her

Herman Survivors against the floor. "What's the story, Chuck? He make good on his tab?" She didn't look at the bartender. "No? Then get on over to the phone and dial nine-one-one."

The swishing of spandex filled the bar as Booth's legs rubbed against each other.

"Easy, sister." Lilly came off her stool. "Bristol's mine tonight. Already got him drunk."

Sister? Odd salutation. Fleeting thoughts of a Greek myth. What were they called? Hordes? No. Herds? No, not quite it, either. Harps? Closer. Think hard now.

"Harpies!" Billy shrieked, cowering behind his seat.

"Stand down, woman. You don't want none of me tonight." Booth bared her teeth.

"You might have a few pounds on me," Lilly said, "but you ain't no tougher."

Billy peeked from the crook of his arm. It wasn't often two behemoths such as these could be compared side by side. If Leslie was bigger, it was by only a degree. Facing each other in the center of the bar, they reminded Billy of prehistoric elephants. What were they called . . . mammoths? No, the other variety.

"The straight-tusked variety," the narrator had called them.

Mastodons. That was it, mastodons. Billy marveled over how good his memory was. This sensory enhancement had to be due to his close proximity to death. He waited anxiously for his life to flash before his eyes, a phenomenon he'd heard much about and had secretly wished to experience for quite some time. It would make for a wonderful anecdote in a memoir. Was twenty-nine old enough to write a memoir?

Billy slid to the floor, sprawling full length on the dusty boards, and waited. Much to his disappointment, no strobic vision of his life swam through his mind. Here I am, he thought, a pathetic human being. A pathetic creature. Yes, creature was better. Facedown in a bar in Butte, Montana, awaiting the end of my suffering. Awaiting a horrible, undeserved death, and I'm not to be granted so much as a look at my life. Surely that cannot be too much to ask. A look at my life, and then the angels. It is all I will ever ask for.

"What's he worth to you?" Booth's question snapped Billy to attention. "A ten-spot?"

Despite the smallish size of his fingers, Billy figured he was worth at least that.

"Yes," he moaned. "Oh, yes, yes."

"You think I can't take without paying?" Lilly wasn't in the shopping mood. "I can take him, and I can take you, too."

For heaven's sake, Lilly, pay the beast. Billy crawled to his knees. There's no shame. Don't let good old Mr. Hamilton stand between us.

"Besides, I ain't got ten dollars." Lilly said it proudly, as if having the money would have been a black mark on her.

In the tense silence that followed, the calm before the storm, Billy believed he could hear the faint jingle of bells. Angels riding a sleigh drawn by winged horses? he wondered.

"Here I am," he said to no one in particular. "Down here on the floor."

The bells sounded closer. Yes, they were coming for him. He looked to the door, fully expecting the pawnbroker to have departed, frightened by the approach of something from on high, but he was still there, smiling, looking more relaxed than ever. What had he done? Attached bells to the hounds? Pretty trick. Billy now wished he had not announced his location. Was there enough whiskey to mask his scent?

The ringing was very close. Just above him. Directly in line with the cash register. Could it be? He craned his neck up to bar height and squinted through half-open eyes. Chuck was rummaging through the change drawer, sliding coins over each other in his search. The ringing.

"Oh, thank god," Billy gasped, placing a heavy emphasis on the last word. "Thank god, god, god." He said it for the pawnbroker's benefit, hoping for a reaction, getting none. The mere mention of his adversary's name was not enough to phase him.

"Here we go." Chuck sounded slightly more awake that usual. He pulled a crumpled ten-dollar bill from the drawer and offered it to Leslie. "Bristol's bail," he said. Then to Billy, "You owe me."

Billy nodded. What exactly did he owe? His health? His life? His firstborn? All bargains as far as he was concerned. Chuck might be the only truly good man in the world, Billy thought. This act of kindness would be repaid. Chuck could name his price.

One of Leslie's paws shot out for the bill, folded it in half, and tucked it into her bra as naturally as an elephant, or mastodon for that matter, feeds itself.

"He's still mine, ain't he?" Lilly asked suspiciously. "I'd have fought for him."

Chuck's ephemeral burst of energy was gone, and he simply shrugged.

"Good. Come on, Billy boy." A hand wrapped around Billy's wrist, tight as a noose. "Time for the honeymoon."

Billy let his entire body go limp, but Lilly handled two hundred pounds effortlessly. She dragged him to the door and shouldered past the pawnbroker without breaking stride. As Billy bumped along behind her, increasingly concerned that his arm would be wrenched from its socket, he glanced up into the broker's face, into a hideous smile, lips parted to reveal . . . pointed teeth? Yes, it appeared so. He laughed demonically, a terrible noise fading only after Lilly had hauled him a block up the hill.

"I'd rather kick you than pull you, Bristol. Stand up!" she ordered.

Billy complied rather than absorb a boot from one of her horse-sized legs.

"I . . . I have a bad pancreas," he said as he pushed himself to his feet.

"A bad what?"

"Pancreas." Billy held his side where he imagined it to be.

"Don't have nothing to do with your crank, does it?"

"It's killing me, I fear." Billy sighed and looked plaintively into the night sky, searching the heavens for the mercy that had thus far been denied him.

"Humph." Lilly grunted. "Better get you home and in bed where you can die a happy man in that case. You still live on Washoe?"

In two weeks, if Helmsley had her way, Billy would not be able to answer in the affirmative, and that thought brought a sudden wave of sorrow, a hard lump forming in the back of his throat. Could it be another tumor? A lymph gland run amok? He shuffled toward Washoe in a daze, thinking the whole time that this forced march up the long street beside Lilly, the sex-crazed juggernaut, was somehow symbolic of his existence. A lot of hard work for nothing. Worse than nothing. Toiling toward the top where great misery awaited.

It took Billy three tries to fit his key into the lock on his apartment door. Jesus, Mary, and Joseph hadn't appreciated Lilly's weight, and he wondered if they'd pay him back by collapsing the next time he stepped on them. Send him crashing to his death a few floors down.

Inside, Lilly made straight for the couch.

Not the couch, Lilly. Not my favorite couch. Don't sit. Please, don't sit.

Lilly didn't sit, she sprawled. Planked herself down, leaned, back, spread her legs, and grinned.

"You just gonna stand there, or are you gonna start?" she asked. "Get on over here and give me one on the lips. I want to feel some tongue, too."

Billy clamped his eyes shut, and even behind their lids it was not dark enough.

"You get all this woman tonight, baby." Lilly reached for him. Roughly.

Sometime later, Billy wasn't sure how much later, after he'd given in, after his unspeakable torture, he found himself thinking about memory again and how long it would take for the day's mental scars to heal. This time he did not find memory such a wonderful thing.

Vell, Mr. Briztol, you iz late."
True, but how did Andrea know? Did she have one of those horrid clocks that spewed out the time in a monotone voice when you pressed a button? Or perhaps the sun's ultraviolet rays still registered in her retinas. Maybe she had a Braille sun dial. Stonehenge in miniature. That idea interested Billy. He imagined her in druid garb huddled over a circle of rocks behind her house.

"Ver yous delayed en route, or did yous get off to a late start?" she asked.

Billy was ten minutes late. *Only* ten minutes. Why did it matter? In truth, Lilly Four-Toes had done her best to kill him the night before, and he'd been slow getting out of bed, taking great precautions not to wake her and risk another go-round. As it was, he doubted he would ever be whole again. Certainly never so pure.

"Ve must be punctual, Mr. Briztol." Andrea was not going to let it drop.

Ve must be scolded, too, I see. Shall I fetch the flogger?

"I've a big day, and now I doubt ve be able to take breakfast."

"I'm sorry," Billy said sincerely.

You would deprive me of nourishment? In my weakened state, I will faint. He stroked his head, focusing his eyes on Andrea's little kitchen table, hoping he wouldn't faint at the wheel. Ah, the wheel. The Chevy. The college girls. Summon strength and soldier on.

"Yah, vell . . . I suppose iz okay dis time. You call for da taxi, yah?"

A softie. Andrea was a softie. What a stroke of luck. Billy really could entertain hopes of owning the car. In fact, he *would* own the Chevy. He knew it, and being convinced for the first time in more than twenty-four hours that something very good was going to happen to him gave him energy. Not as much energy as the Western omelet he craved, but enough to pick his feet up from the linoleum in Andrea's kitchen on his way to the phone. If he didn't stop shuffling soon, the soles of his Hawthorns would wear through. When his novel was published and he was invited to the *Today* show, the shoes would be worth showing, a fine symbol of what writers must endure, but in the meantime they would cause him a great deal of grief.

"Make sure yous get dat Stan driver," Andrea said. "Request for him by name."

But of course. Billy shuffled the last two steps. Wouldn't want to have too many things in the plus column, he thought.

Stan dropped his taxi into neutral and tacked out the rpms when he pulled up in front of Andrea's. The engine responded with an ear-splitting roar that caused Billy to recall obscure decibel levels above which permanent hearing damage is caused. He remembered a jackhammer operator interviewed on *60 Minutes*. That man had to buy increasingly powerful amplifiers to hear his television.

"I do miss the birds," Billy said, imagining what he would tell the camera crews after he went deaf. "Yes, all the little birds." Heavy sigh. "I can see their beaks moving . . . chirp, chirp, chirp . . . but they don't sing for Billy anymore." Pause for the next question. "What's that, sir? Could you speak up a bit, please?"

"Vhat are yous talking about?" Andrea had snuck up on him again. Her uncanny ability to do that was wearing thin.

"Just talking to myself," Billy said.

"Yah, vell, if ve vant breakfast, then ve goes now."

Billy weighed the ride with Stan against missing another meal and hurried to the car. Starvation was so much slower.

"Ah, my most favorite clients," Stan said as soon as they were seated. He cocked his head to the dash, revved the engine twice, eyes closed in concentration.

Billy hoped he would open them before driving away.

"Carbon!" Stan sat up and slapped the empty seat beside him. "Goddamn carbon. She's gone and gotten plugged up on me. Needs a high-test enema and a couple runs over the pass." He caught Billy's eye in the rearview mirror and said, "We know all about how to cure what ails her, don't we?"

Before Billy could answer, he found himself plastered to his seat, his seat with three more immediately noticeable stains on it, as the cab accelerated down Excelsior. Out of the corner of his eye he saw that Andrea was smiling, no doubt lost in memories of youthful escapades on the autobahn.

Stan skidded to a stop at the intersection of Granite Street. "Binders still work good," he said, though it was clear he thought it small consolation in view of the carbon. He couldn't look into the backseat without bracing himself up, and he used the gas pedal to gain the required leverage. "Old Stan's gonna win the lottery," he said.

The light changed, and Stan popped his foot off the brake.

"Yup, I'm taking home the jackpot. You bet," he said confidently.

Billy began to fidget. Stan had made this prediction before.

"Want to know why I'm going to win?"

Billy did. That piece of knowledge would save him a lifetime of these meaningless jobs that cut him off. He could overlook Stan's driving for a clue to the lottery.

"Yah, ve do." Andrea was interested, too. But why? She didn't need the money. Being old and blind made her a good bet to win, but she should let well enough alone. Spread the wealth around.

"I know because Jesus told me." Stan pointed to a rosary of blue and white beads hanging from his mirror and shrugged. "Don't know why he chose me, but he did. Told me in person, too," he said proudly. "Didn't send one of those little kiddy angels or give me no sign. Did it all by himself."

"Yah, did he really?" Andrea nudged Billy's leg and he pulled away in disgust. Why indulge so ludicrous a fantasy? It bordered on blasphemy to encourage such talk. If Andrea had seen the pawnbroker—if she had been able to witness the dark side—well, she would not take Stan's foolishness so lightly. Billy considered plugging his ears.

"Well, Jesus did it in a dream. Told me I was going to win, that is." Stan ripped around a corner, the tires squealing.

Billy looked up at Our Lady of the Rockies and silently apologized. Guilty by association, he was.

"See, I'd been drinking at Chuck's," Stan said.

Andrea reached for Billy again, and it wasn't easy to dodge her prodding fingers. What did she have, some rare ability to locate flesh by small amounts of escaping heat?

"Been belly up to the bar . . . I know, I know, it ain't right, especially with me being an alcoholic, but I got to tell it like it was. I was swiggin' like a bum." Stan passed a Volkswagen van full of modern hippies dressed in gaudy tie-dye. "Free love, baby!" he screamed to the girl driving. "Now, damn, those were the days! I went to Woodstock, you know. I'm telling you, that was the time. *The* time. But anyway, where was I? Oh yeah, I was drunk."

"I don't mean to interrupt, but maybe yous tell about it over breakfast?"

Had Andrea lost her mind? This cretin wasn't fit for the public world. Any more of his offensive language and Billy would have to write to the Better Business Bureau. Or, what about a lawsuit? File one against the cab company for . . . Billy wished he had a subscription to the court TV channel. He would learn all the little ins and outs that way. Still, he was convinced Stan was laying the foundation for a big civil suit. A big, lucrative civil suit in which, having been injured—and no, injuries need not be physical—Billy could collect an enormous settlement.

"Breakfast?" Stan slowed down to just above double the twenty-five-mile-an-hour speed limit. "Ain't nobody asked me to breakfast since . . . well, I guess it was Lilly Four-Toes after Chuck's closed one night. And she just did it cause she wanted some."

Billy spat on the floor mat between his feet. Oh, horrible twist of fate.

"Yes, ma'am, it would be an honor," Stan said, bunching his T-shirt up and drawing it across his eyes.

Don't get teary eyed. Billy felt his shrunken stomach contract. If he weeps, I will vomit. Retch until I rip something.

"Where would you like to go? Name your destination, and Old Stan will take you there directly."

Stan never went anywhere unless he went directly.

"Vair did ve go last time, Mr. Briztol? Da Silver Dollar?"

Billy kept his mouth shut. He would have no part in this. If he did, he would pay for it with the block.

"The Silver Dollar it is," Stan said, as he yanked the car into an alley and gunned it back up to cruising speed. "Whatever my most favorite clients wish for."

If that was the case, Stan would turn into a toad, Billy thought, and Andrea would be young and lovely and have her hand on his thigh. No, Stan would not at all like what one of his most favorite clients would wish for. He should choose his words more carefully.

"Mr. Briztol, vould yous escort me into da restaurant?" Andrea turned her blue eyes on him as soon as they reached the parking lot. "Guide me a bit, please?"

I would steer you into an oncoming car if I could get away with it. Billy stopped, ashamed of the thought. Andrea had been good to him, and to think such a thing was wrong.

"Yes," he said quietly as he opened her door and offered her his hand.

Inside, the aroma of bacon returned Billy's every thought to his appetite. When no one was looking, he tugged his T-shirt away from his body and peered down the opening at his stomach. Soft and flat, it reminded him of a dead fish left out of water too long on a hot day. This starving business will be the end of me, he thought, as the hostess seated them in a booth.

Coffee arrived, steaming and black, wafting its beckoning odor into the air. Billy stared at his cup, wishing through some derivative of alchemy he could change it to a solid. So fine-smelling a substance would be worth eating two or three times a day. Giving it serious consideration, tapping his brain for any hocus-pocus that might have the slightest grounding in science, he took too big a sip and burned his tongue rather severely. As he fished an ice cube from his water glass, setting it gingerly in his mouth, he decided alchemy and black magic were nothing to fool with. Leave such nonsense to Stan and other blasphemers who were already doomed.

"Yeah, so like I said, there was this dream." Stan drained half his mug without flinching, an action that caused Billy a great deal of discomfort. The roof of his mouth burned, and his throat began to swell.

Why must I bear suffering meant for others? he wondered. On the off chance that some bizarre Corsican phenomena had settled in over the booth, he plunged his fork into the meaty portion of his thigh, stifling a cry when the pain rushed to him instead of Stan. Not even in the most twisted set of game rules was this fair.

"Quite a dream it was, too." Stan reached onto the waitress's tray, forking hash browns toward his mouth before she had time to set down his plate, mopping up the extra strands that clung to his beard with a thick tongue.

Not having been subjected to the view, Andrea smiled.

"The dream starts out in Paris, right?" Stan nodded at Billy, half asking, half telling, and when no one disagreed he dove headlong into the story, talking loudly and freely. "Begun in one them places with shelves all full of pretty bottles. Even had one shaped like a corkscrew. Must have been a perfume store or something. Anyway, I was looking at that twisty fella wondering what it'd go for when the owner . . ." Stan whistled and raised his eyebrows. "Oh, my, the owner . . . appears. She's wearing this pink-flowered dress and carrying an umbrella. Had it opened right up in the store. She's fifty-five or so but don't look a day over forty. Quite a sight. Had one of those things that suck in your belly and make your boobs look real perky. One of them . . . what the hell are they called?"

"Corset," Andrea said calmly. "Iz dat vat it vas?"

"Damn straight it was a corset. All's I could think to call it was a *closet,* and I knew that weren't quite right."

Billy's left leg began to twitch and his hairline felt as if it had come to life, crawling across his forehead like a centipede. How much discomfort must he endure humoring this fool? Customers in the nearby booths had stopped eating to stare and listen.

"Well, you know where my eyes were glued. Right smack on them titties. Ooo, la-la." The thick tongue appeared again, rolling slowly over Stan's lips, drawing a moan from Billy. "But at the same time I was looking, I was also thinking."

He could actually do them both at the same time? Billy was skeptical. He salted his eggs.

"I was thinking that since women don't wear them things no more, I must be back in history someplace. Didn't make no difference to me though, 'cause I figure a man's a man no matter where he is, right?"

Not if he lives where his phone number begins with two-one-two, Billy thought. But Stan wouldn't understand that.

"Course I'm right," Stan said. "And there I am. One man in history staring at them . . ."

"Yah, da breasts. Ve got dat part." Andrea sipped from her water glass.

"Well, I'm staring at those jugs, knowing I've gone back in history, thinking about how much that curvy little bottle's gonna run me, when pow!" Stan brought both hands down on the table hard enough to slosh water from his glass.

Andrea jumped and Billy grinned. Didn't see that one coming, did you?

"Just as sure as sheep shit, I'm in the desert." Out came Stan's tongue, slow as a bear from hibernation. It moved back and forth, evidently not finding anything to its liking, and retreated. "Yes, sir, the burning sands. Camels, mirages, sun, sweat, the whole nine yards. And damn it, seeing's how this is a dream, I don't even bat an eyelash. Seemed all square with me. Yup, right on the level."

Stan paused to soak up a pool of gravy with a piece of toast, wiping the bread vigorously across his plate. Billy turned away before he ate it, beginning to think he should drop Mrs. Helmsley a thank-you card for her eviction notice. If it was going to be the best thing that happened to him this week, he owed her some gratitude.

Stan smacked the tablecloth again. "It's like I said, in the desert it was hot. I did say that, didn't I? Sure. The bottoms of my feet in particular are real heated up. Burns each time I take a step. I'm walking along—step-ouch, step-ouch, step-ouch—when I hear this voice. Big, deep voice, too, and it's saying, 'Moses.' Only real slow. 'Mo-ses.'"

Stan's eyes grew small and he puffed out his chest, booming his words into the restaurant for interested and uninterested ears alike.

"'Mo-ses, Mo-ses,' says the voice. Close, too. Well, I always make a point to mind my own business, so what's it to me if someone's calling for Moses? Hell, ain't none of my concern. I figure whoever it is gotta be a grade-A idiot, too, cause it's plenty clear that I'm the only poor bastard staggering around in the desert. Excuse me a minute."

Stan opened his mouth and inserted half of his right hand. Billy averted his eyes, but the cacophony of gagging noises that ensued hit him hard. Coughing violently, Stan punctuated each expulsion of air by a low growl from his stomach.

Let the true beast be revealed, Billy thought, as he quailed away. These other customers—these swine lacking the decency to have fled this establishment at the beginning of the tale—will wish they had when the metamorphosis taking place across the table is complete. Will it have two heads? A forked tail? Certainly cloven hooves. Very well, get on with it. Shuck off your human shell and reveal your true hideous self to the world.

A drawn-out moan concluded Stan's retching. Billy assumed the transformation was complete and was not about to open his eyes. Strange how he found himself contemplating the many times he'd been forced to use his eyelids lately.

"It is an evil world," Billy whispered. "And more's the pity for us unlucky few who are burdened with the majority of its trials." A poem? Yes, or perhaps part of a modern sonnet. Not a very good market for either, but he would not discard the thought right away.

"God almighty, it's a foot long," Stan exclaimed.

Billy, startled to hear a human voice instead of the demonic braying he'd expected, opened his eyes. Stan sat straight in his chair, eyeing a piece of phlegm-covered string with awe.

"Wondered what had been tickling my throat for the past few days," he said. "Hey, how do you figure she got in there? What do you bet I could build a candle around it? Probably burn like gangbusters, too. Which reminds me . . . I was burning in that desert. Burning right up. Didn't make matters easier to have to listen to that voice, neither. Time come when I couldn't take it no more, so I holler, 'Goddamn it, shut up!'" Stan lowered his voice for the first time. "Well, Jesus Christ. I mean *Jesus*. I mean it's *him*. He's floating along over the dunes, coming right at me, moving at a good clip, too. Don't look any too pleased, either. He gets right up to me, close as from me to you, and it ain't till then that he realizes he's made a mistake. He looks all puzzled, like he don't know whether to shit or go blind, and then he gets this big grin on his face and sticks out his hand. How about that? Jesus Christ wants to shake hands with Old Stan. Just like we was pals. Course I take his hand—ain't got much of a grip, but anyway—he says, 'Why, it ain't Moses at all. And here I was set to give that fool merry hell. Always wandering around in the desert. Can't get it through his skull that there ain't no pharaoh no more.'"

Billy tore his napkin in half and rolled a pair of earplugs, both of which fell from his trembling hands long before reaching their intended orifices. In his mind, a vivid image of an Inquisition-era torture chamber was pulsing hard. A stocky, bald-headed fellow was fishing through a barrel of rusty knives while something closer to an ape than a man cranked the rack. In the shadows, another person, probably a monk—yes, it appeared to be a monk—was busy stoking a fire beneath a vat of boiling oil. And the grins. These were men who delighted in their work. What was this vision? Had Stan's heresy summoned these evil souls up from the depths? What retribution would they exact upon an innocent bystander? A good man forced to be privy to the rantings of a lunatic? If only the unemployment checks had not run out.

There, the root of blame. Billy ground his teeth. This was Bush's doing entirely. The unemployment queen. Hecuba. She'd dealt him this hand. How could he return the favor? Fleeting memories of a Discovery Channel program on the Salem witches cruised through Billy's mind, but he couldn't put them together. Ah, disjointed thoughts. The onset of premature and aggressive Alzheimer's? Stray, stray, little neurons. Short out, burn up, send me reeling to the floor. Take me away.

"So Jesus . . ." Stan glanced down at his plate, where he had placed the horrid string. "Well, Christ, he says to me, 'Old Stan, you've been a pretty fair man, ain't you?' He was looking me right in the eye, and I knew lying weren't the thing to do so I fessed up. Told him I drink. Yes, drink and then sometimes drive, too. And I told him I like to cuss. Even told him about the deal with my cousin when she was fifteen. That seemed to rile him up a bit, but when I made plain that she was willing, he took it better. Yes, sir, went out of my way to let him know she was okay with it."

"Oh, enough, enough!" Billy mouthed the words only to find that he had been stripped of the power of speech. "Deprive me of my hearing as well," he begged. If there is a god . . . if there is *any* god . . . oh, Christ, I didn't think that. I'm sorry, I'm sorry, I'm sorry. But you see, it's wearing off on me. How could it not? This test is too much. Reduce me to a pauper, force me into slavery, turn my own dear mother against me, evict me, too, if you must, but spare me the sermon on incest. It is truly more than I can stand.

"What's the matter with you, bub?" Stan worked his jaw as if he were still chewing. "Look like you're gonna keel over."

Haven't you ever seen a man teetering on the edge? Not all of us take that next step as blithely as you. For some, madness is an undesirable realm.

"If I must enter, let me do so of my own free will," Billy uttered.

"Speak up!" Stan hollered with the authority of an inquisitor extracting a confession. Hmmm . . . there it was again. Sixteenth-century Spain.

"Something you eat make a mess of your insides? Happens to me when I eat cabbage. You need to be excused?"

Billy managed to shake his head. A remarkable accomplishment.

"Okay, then, listen up. I'm just getting to the good part."

Can't we forgo that? Just let everyone use their imagination? Billy recalled an assignment from grade school in which his teacher had begun a story and each student had to write an ending. What would his be to Stan's dream? He thought hard, soldiering his beaten brain into working order, and then it came to him.

"Suddenly I woke up," he whispered.

Andrea turned in her chair to face him, cocking her head as if she'd heard but did not understand. Billy shifted out of the path of her stare, but he felt more eyes on him. The eyes of other customers; the eyes of the unseen, all watching closely as if bets had been taken on his breaking point. Be still, lip. No more trembling. Give them no satisfaction. Endure it all manfully. Yes, manfully.

"So Mr. Christ, he says that all in all I've been a good man. Kind of touching, ain't it?" Stan worked his napkin between his fingers.

If he brings it to his eyes, I will vomit, Billy thought.

"Yes, sir, he says, 'It ain't easy keeping the faith, Old Stan, and I know you've always done your best, so I want to reward you. Want you to reap the benefits of living the good life.'" Stan raised his hands, turned them palms up, and closed his eyes. "Christ said, 'You've turned back evil on every front. Hardened yourself to the devil's seduction. Fought tooth and nail against injustice. Fought it like a motherfu . . .'" The evangelist routine came to a close. Stan dropped his hands, looked sheepishly around the restaurant, and sighed. "Jesus said he'd reward me by letting me win the lottery. Said his pa might frown on it, but that if I promised not to say nothing about it, he wouldn't, either."

"Well, what are the numbers?" Billy blurted. If he was damned, he might as well take a chance on being rich.

"Ah, brother, not so fast." Stan licked his lips. "I was all ready to scritch them down in the sand so I wouldn't forget, but Jesus told me they'd come as signs. I'd just have to wait and find out what they were. Guess he wanted to make a game out of it."

"Dat's quite da dream," Andrea said. She had assumed the all-knowing smile that in Billy's mind had come to characterize her.

She was well aware of everything that would happen and could never get over being slightly amused when she saw that she was right. The I-told-you-so look of a child. "Iz too bad yous have to vait, though, yah?"

Billy cleared his throat. What would it take to dispense with all talk of the dream? Whatever the price, he would gladly pay it. Perhaps the customers would like to hear some of *his* dreams. How about if he tried to describe the sheer panic of waking under the impression that the ambulatory disorder that prevented him from opening his Heineken in his sleep had followed him into the real world? That would be entertaining.

"Okay, Mr. Briztol, yous seem anxious to be going, yah? I leaves da money on da table." Andrea opened her purse and laid a crisp twenty beside her plate. Before closing her wallet, she handed another twenty to Stan. "For da fare and da entertainment," she said.

Billy scowled. He'd never considered driving a cab a lucrative profession. In fact, he was convinced that in the grand scheme of things, the divine design, it wasn't intended to be. Reserve that line of work for cretins and simpletons who don't mind being cut off.

In the parking lot, Stan opened Andrea's door. "You know, I think I'd trade winning the lottery for that woman in the perfume shop," he said.

"Yah, vell, I tink yous make good choice if yous do." Andrea smiled. Again. "Now ve goes to da Richardson Storage."

Billy's mood brightened. The storage meant the car, and on so fine a summer's day—there hadn't been a cloud in the sky for a week—college women would be out sunning themselves and he could put the top down. And he would find reasons to blow the horn. Would he wave, or play it cool the whole way? Decisions spread out before him like the open road.

Stan hit the gas hard leaving the lot, sending Billy back into the stains of reality. Back to a dismal present in which vulgar cabbies were rewarded and he was forced to walk, not drive, a long, hard road. Back to a place where fantasies gave way to whatever had been coughed up on the seat's fabric near his cheek.

· 8 ·

"Yea, though I walk through the valley of the shadow of death, I shall fear no evil." Billy entered the storage, racking his brain for the rest of the prayer. "There are no scorpions in here," he sang in a high voice. "No vampire bats . . ." That sounded less convincing. "Black widows . . ." Almost a question.

He knew that the car lay immediately in front of him, but he couldn't see it. What had the Discovery Channel said about caves? A complete absence of light, a constant forty-two degrees, stalactites and stalagmites. Which were which?

"Entering the inner chamber," he said into an imaginary microphone on his chest. "I, Billy . . . I, William Bristol, sole survivor of the expedition"—appropriate pause to mourn lost comrades—"will soon take possession of the greatest treasure known to mankind. Here, under the desert . . ." That would make a fine title for a National Geographic documentary. Billy whistled a bar of the theme music. "If I do not return, tell . . ." Tell whom what? Tell Mrs. Helmsley she needn't evict me? Inform the boys at Columbia that I'm not in the running for their little prize?

Billy stubbed his toe on the driver's side front tire. Very well, spelunking was dangerous. Realizing where he was, he wasted no time climbing in and turning the key. The shifter dropped easily into reverse, and, convinced that the engine had triggered a series of booby traps culminating in a massive cave-in, he gunned the Chevy into the sunlight. William Bristol, explorer extraordinaire.

"I thought maybe yous got lost in dair," Andrea said. She climbed in, holding tight to her purse. "Now, brings me to Helena, yah?"

Helena? That wasn't so bad. There were some nice advantages in that, not the least of which was the capital-city women. Professional women. Billy licked his lips. There were women in Helena who would appreciate his fine automobile even more than college girls. They would be out for lunch by the time he got there, and some would be wearing suits. Yes, this was going to work very well.

Billy cruised slowly down Harrison toward the interstate, his left arm resting out the open window, his head tipped back, not so far that he resembled a chauffeur—they weren't much better than cabbies—but enough so that in his mind he could pass for Robert De Niro or Andy Garcia in a gangster movie. He watched oncoming drivers out of the corner of his eye, pulling to the far left of his lane at the stoplights. Force the hit man to swing into the wrong lane if he wants to whack me. He imagined the trunkful of cash from a numbers racket and could feel the cold steel of a tommy gun in his right hand.

"*Rat-a-tat-tat,*" he said in the direction of a suspicious-looking gentleman on the sidewalk. "Gotcha."

"Yous must learn to speak up," Andrea said sharply.

Billy thought this was a fantasy she need not be privy to. What role could she play in it, anyway? A rival's mother? Well, yes, that might not be too bad. He would be taking her out for lemonade to see if he could get her to reason with her unruly son. Just before he took her home he would say something like, "I've had a lovely time, Mrs. Kauffman. Always a pleasure. You talk to Mickey now. He's a good kid and should listen to his ma. But if he don't listen, if ya can't talk no sense into him, well . . . we're gonna bury him. Here, here, now, don't cry."

Talent. Billy sat through a green light, convinced that if he applied himself for a week or two he could write the whole thing.

"No," he said. "I can't think about it." That was the lure of thrillers. Big money, movie sales, Book of the Month Club orders. And all for something he could do with his left hand. No, William Bristol writes literature. His pen would stay true no matter what it meant.

The car behind him honked its horn. If he was going to play the part, this is where he'd get out and pistol-whip someone. The obligatory scene where a beefy woman-beater gets his just desserts. What about a screenplay? Was that selling out? Not if he didn't set his novel aside to work on it, he didn't think. Not if he kept his priorities straight.

"Literature first," he whispered as he drove through the intersection and turned into the eastbound lane of Interstate 90. "No matter what, literature first."

Billy stepped on it, getting the convertible up to seventy in the quarter mile before swinging north onto 15 at the base of the East Ridge. He couldn't see Mary up there, but he felt that she was watching, agreeing that his literature must come first.

"So, Mr. Briztol." Andrea slipped her shoulder belt off to face him. Why did it matter where she looked? "I understand yous had some schooling."

Billy yanked both hands from the wheel and began to beat his chest. What had she said?

"Vhere did yous attend?"

Attend? It was like giving his throat a direct order to close. His nostrils, too. Billy fought for air as he continued pounding his breast, trying for all he was worth to keep his heart pumping. The car veered toward the shoulder and began sliding sideways. Through two slits in his lids, Billy saw Andrea grip the seat. There, he thought, are you happy you brought this up? A split second before contact with the guardrails, he nailed the brakes, spinning the Chevy around in a tight circle, bringing it to rest in a blue cloud of smoke. He opened his door and coughed his breakfast up onto the pavement. Cruelly deprived of another meal.

"Vat in da world vas dat?" Andrea sounded more angry than scared.

That, my good woman, was what you deserve for mentioning my brief enrollment. Billy leaned out his door again as a series of dry heaves assaulted him.

"A deer, a deer," he stammered. Let it go at that. Please, let's count our blessings and agree never to speak of this incident. But it was too late. Andrea had triggered repressed memories that would not easily be buried. They came swarming to the front of Billy's thoughts, consuming his mind, transporting him as neatly as any time machine back a decade to a land of buildings forever tainted with the smell of Lestoil, chairs affixed to wooden desks far too small for him, schedules, libraries, the unbalanced weight of a full backpack slung over his left shoulder, glass trophy cases full of dusty black-and-white photographs, tiled dormitory showers, three-subject notebooks, the squeal of chalk on the blackboard, and the acrid odor of fear in the air as a bespectacled man passed out final exams. Borrowing from a dead author he'd been forced to read, forced by a—no, he'd vowed that word would never again cross his lips. It was the worst of times.

"Vell," Andrea said, returning her shoulder strap to its intended position, "since ve isn't dead, maybe yous tell about da schooling now, yah? Help pass da time on da vay dair."

Billy wondered why Andrea thought he'd open up to her. A psychiatrist had tried for several sessions to get him to talk about his collegiate experience without reaching first base.

"Begin!" Andrea commanded.

Well, that was an approach the shrink hadn't tried. One that Billy dared not disobey. With both hands on the wheel, chest pulled close to them in case of emergencies, seat belt painfully tight around his waist, he allowed himself back into the world of academia, a world he had forgotten so completely that in his mind the univer . . . the university . . . no boils popped up on his hands . . . had become synonymous with being cut off and nothing more.

"I have always wanted to be a writer," Billy began. The bottoms of his feet did not itch. Perhaps enough time had passed. "It is all I have ever wanted," he said, glancing out across Elk Park, the high sage plateau on top of the Continental Divide, known to its handful of residents as Little Siberia. "And when I was young, I believed a college education was a good first step toward my goal." A hawk's shadow passed over the highway in front of the car, sending ground squirrels scurrying for their holes in the median. "I enrolled at a well-respected university on the eastern shore of a large New England lake."

Billy shivered. He remembered how the wind would come whipping across the ice in the winter, blasting him on his way to class with a damper cold than he had ever imagined possible.

"New England, yous say? Vas it very beautiful? Da leaves in da fall?"

"Yes," Billy answered, cringing in anticipation of her next question. "Yes, the leaves were lovely."

That wasn't a lie. They were one of the few things he'd enjoyed. The leaves and—what was her name? Had he ever known? It seemed to him that he had, that he must have. He could see himself falling down with her into the heap of leathery oak leaves along the sidewalk, could feel her hands on his back, her tongue on his face—why had *this* memory been pushed aside? Billy adjusted himself into a more comfortable position. There had been a full moon. A full moon and a warm breeze. A gorgeous night all the way around. Around. Yes, he'd moved his hands around her. All around her. He could feel his trousers sliding off again. My, this was good. The soft glow of a street light . . . oh, Christ, no wonder he hadn't visited this episode for so long. There it was, the policeman's light in his face, the difficulty he had dressing himself, the stern words of the judge, "lewd" standing out in particular, back muscles convulsing from the raking he had to do for the elderly. Raking, raking, raking. There was no end to the leaves then. No end to the leaves, and no end to the hundred hours he'd been sentenced to rake, pile, bag, and cart them off. It was safe to say that experience had soured him on leaves.

"Beautiful pines," he said, looking into the canyon where the interstate left the north end of Elk Park. "Beautiful, beautiful pines."

"Vhat vas your declared major?" Andrea was looking at him again as if she knew.

In a flash, Billy could see his adviser, a fleshy woman in her early forties, wide ass, stubble field of chin hairs, exactly the type to file a sexual harassment suit in an attempt to convince herself that there really were men willing to violate her. She sat in front of him, drooping off either side of her chair, lips pursed, the perpetual look of disgust she wore growing more evident as she discussed majors.

"Undecided" had seemed the right route for Billy. Better for a writer to learn a little about a lot than vice versa. He would take a semester to sample writing and literature courses. He'd read lots of books. After all, he wanted to write them himself someday.

"B . . . b . . . books," he stammered, recalling the voluminous amounts of required reading, the small print, the acute despair that swallowed him when he began the first sentence of a book whose pages totaled several pounds, and the confusion created during classroom discussions. There were hidden meanings—deep metaphors ingeniously woven into the stories that usually involved some cynical commentary on society or latent homosexual feelings of the author. Odd how it seemed only the—only the man at the head of the room, the detached-looking man whose disjointed interjections of wisdom were forever showing up on tests where they were expected to be regurgitated verbatim—odd how only he could decipher the readings. According to him, the stories were no more than thin veils for what the author really intended to say, and most of the time it seemed that the author's intent was to chastise society through the use of phallic symbols. Billy imagined a Rosetta stone cut in half, one side full of words like *gun, pen, upright,* and *strong,* all pointing to a crudely carved penis, and opposite it words such as *flower, born, safety,* and a few assorted feminine colors all leaping from a great vagina.

"Ah," Andrea said. "Da arts. Of course. Vithout da printed word, vhat do yous have? Who vas your favorite author?"

Details. Andrea wanted details. Just like the exams. The age of generalness, if there had ever been such a time—and with as many ages as Billy's history teacher seemed to think occurred, there must have been—was over. So, who was his favorite author?

"Vell, do yous remember?"

Demanding and impatient. Andrea should have been a . . . Perhaps she'd like to wreck again, Billy thought. He let the Chevy drift toward the side of the road. Your side, my dear. Here come the trees on your side.

"Vhat did he write about?"

The West. Just as Billy was doing. "McMurtry," he said. "My all-time favorite."

"Ah, iz good choice. Da *Lonesome Dove* gentleman, yah? Vhat was it dat appealed to yous about him?"

Now Billy understood where the test questions had come from, once again feeling cold sweat on his neck, a secretion he attributed to not knowing an answer.

Andrea tapped the dash, rekindling a terror Billy had not known for many years. The time had come to answer.

"I liked the exposition and breadth of his story," Billy said. That should be worth partial credit.

"Yah, yah, I can see dat." Andrea nodded, satisfied at least for the moment. "And other modern authors? Any of note?"

Billy shuddered, recalling the course in women's literature he'd struggled through. That had been yeoman's work. Taught by a man-hater—odd that she'd gone to great lengths to look like the object of her hatred—whose curriculum centered on obscure writers of her own ilk. Writers who loved man-bashing. Writers with agendas. Writers who, in Billy's estimation, should have spent more time fooling with sharp paper cutters as children so the world might have been spared their hideous rhetoric. He recalled one of the instructor's own pieces about a woman and a dog. God, there were no bounds to that creature's indecency.

"Vell, are yous still thinking?"

Tick-tock, tick-tock, time's running. Please stop writing and pass your test booklets to the front of the classroom. Billy's skin began to crawl, and he wondered seriously if it was block, searching hard for an entrance. He pushed the Chevy up to eighty. He'd find out just how much endurance the block had. See how well it could keep up.

"No, none of the other authors we read were worth a damn," he said.

"Yah, seems to be da case," Andrea said. "Yous iz an exception, though, yah?"

Billy didn't like the way she looked at him when she said it. She didn't get the *Times* in Braille, did she?

"Vell, Mr. Briztol, if you vill permit me da final question, I vould appreciate it."

Final? For the first time in Billy's life, that sounded heavenly.

"I must ask if yous got your degree?"

Cold sweat again. And hiccups. Nosebleed? Soon.

"Da nice lady at da Job Services said you told her once dat yous left before da required number of credits."

Billy had. In fact, he'd left three and a half years early. What a regrettable oversight telling Buff had been, too. He'd done it to prevent being considered for a full-timer a year or so ago. A job that would have cut him off for good, but one he wouldn't be considered for without a degree.

"If it's none of my business, yous don't have to say if yous don't want."

Oh, I don't, I don't. Isn't that obvious? Irreparable harm has already been done this morning. My tender mind has been dealt a terrible blow, and to delve further into this subject could—no, certainly would—finish me.

"Did yous have trouble vith grades?"

Billy stared at the speedometer. Eighty-seven. Where in the hell was Helena? Had the road been rolled up in front of him? That would figure.

"Or da administration?"

Billy wheezed. In through the nose, out through the mouth. I can breathe, I can breathe, he told himself. No shortage of air.

"If yous iz a successful writer, yous have prospered vithout da degree, so vhat does it matter? I am curious."

Billy felt a wave of anxiety coming for him, as eager to wash over his head and drown him as the sea monster responsible for annihilating all those aboard the *Marie Celeste* had been. More bad memories. What had the history teacher said? "Implausible theory?" Yes, something like that. Better not to pick at those old wounds. What to tell Andrea? The truth? No, not the truth. But what if she already knew? What if this was a test, the stakes being the Chevy?

"Let's just say there were irreconcilable differences between me and a department head," Billy said.

"Ah." Andrea sat quietly for a few moments—long, torturous moments for Billy during which he squirmed in his seat, wishing wholeheartedly for a few dozen extra sets of hands to scratch all the little places on his body that itched. "Differences vith da department head, yah? Yous have a name for dem. Vhat is it?"

"Stop!" Billy croaked. She was getting too close. Too close to the single word that he could not hear without shutting down. Too close to his Rumpelstiltskin. He wondered what it would be like, fading away to nothing before her eyes. Well, scratch that thought. She wouldn't even know. "Just one body found in the wreckage," he whispered.

Billy applied more pressure to the accelerator. This baby really moved. He watched the speedometer climb over the century mark. Beside him, legs crossed and arms folded calmly in her lap, Andrea waited patiently. Mother Superior holding out for the heretic's confession so the boiling oil could be lowered. Jesus, that idea was turning into something uncontrollable. An obsession. Something that must be looked into before it began showing up in the novel.

"Vhat vas it dis chancellor . . . dis . . . vhat is da word?"

"No," Billy begged. "Please, not that. I couldn't bear it. Please, please, please." He let up on the gas and put his hands to his head. It was throbbing so badly.

"Yous have da special term for dem. Vhat is it?"

A word that shall never pass these lips, Billy thought. The foulest four-letter word in the English language. A word whose utterance will prompt a breakdown of catastrophic proportions. Andrea, dear Andrea, if you have the slightest shred of pity in your body, you'll drop this.

"I tink it begins vit *D*."

One of Billy's hands slid down to his throat. Breathe, breathe, breathe. See, no noose there. No tight coils of rope.

"Ah," Andrea said confidently. She had it. "*Dean.* Yah, vas it da dean?"

Twitches. Yes, they would come first. Billy felt his cheeks jump and watched closely in the rearview mirror as the fingers on his Adam's apple began to shake. Squeeze hard, little fingers. The car slowed and started weaving. A hoarse cough welled up in the base of Billy's throat, and even before it reached his mouth he knew it would be the last noise he would ever make. A fitting good-bye to the world that had treated him so cruelly. A guttural, unintelligible farewell known only to a few dedicated entomologists as the purest expression of defeat. With this thought in mind, he drew it out into a long, raspy bark, keeping hard at it for the better part of fifteen seconds.

"My goodness," Andrea gasped.

Goodness? Here was some irony. A sightless beast capable of using the D word without suffering any ill effects had no business talking about goodness. No, that wasn't her department. With superhuman effort, Billy extended a trembling finger in her direction and mouthed, "Evil," then let his hand drop to the seat, where it flopped violently, though not entirely of its own accord.

"Vhat about dis dean? Vhat sort of man vas he?"

Terrible. Worse than that, really. Thinking about him was like Chinese water torture. *Drip, drip, drip.* Surely Billy's skull could not take much more. Split, you thick, stubborn bone. Come apart. Burst asunder.

"Yous must have a story here, yah?"

Don't make me tell it, Andrea. Oh, where's Helena?

"You tell now."

The Big Belt Mountains southeast of Helena were coming into view. Billy looked at them on the horizon and moaned. So far away.

"I vant to hear," Andrea said.

"The writing. It was over my writing," Billy said slowly. Oh, god, oh, god, it hurt. "I wanted to use my writing in place of the required literature assignments. The . . ." No, he couldn't say it. "*He* wouldn't let me. He failed me. He recommended I be . . ." Billy choked. "Expelled." There, it was done.

"Dat vasn't terribly nice, yah? And yous a successful writer?"

"I was," Billy said, trying to convince himself as much as anything. "I was, I was. And dedicated." That wasn't entirely untrue. The entire semester had been block-free, and Billy had written a great deal. Dozens and dozens of first-rate proposals.

Billy could see the dean clearly again, enthroned behind his polished hardwood desk, fingers tapping its glossy surface. *Ta-ta-ta-tap, ta-ta-ta-tap.* The British are coming, the British are coming, *ta-ta-ta-ta-ta-ta-tap.* And he could hear him, too. Hear him passing judgment.

"Mr. Bristol, there are certain things this institution cannot tolerate. Dishonesty, disregard for the law, and, in your case, sloth. A writer? You call yourself a writer? You bombard magazines with these idiotic ideas." He'd held some Billy had taken to the meeting in his defense, raised them over his head, and let them slide down to the desk. "This isn't writing. It's a waste. And so is your time here. You understand if we tailor our classes to you, we must lower our standards of excellence to the degree that we cease to be the pillar of higher education that we are recognized as. The doctorates and double doctorates"—he'd pointed to his framed diplomas behind him—"the undergraduate degrees . . . everything people have taken from here would become cheap and meaningless. They might as well tear their diplomas to shreds, rescind their degrees, and shudder at the very mention of our name. You understand that your lack of effort contradicts everything we strive for in these halls and that their sanctity must be preserved. If we let you stay on, the price we would pay is too great. Your grades are abominable, your attitude abhorrent. I'd like to say that it gives me no great pleasure in telling you what I'm about to, but that wouldn't be entirely true. I admit I take a certain amount of satisfaction in cleansing so fine a place of a blight like you. So I'm not sorry to see you go. And go you will. You will immediately remove all personal belongings from these premises, forfeit any privileges you hold at this university, and I sincerely hope you will never again attempt to enroll. You are hereby expelled. Good-bye."

And so the ax had fallen. Billy remembered walking out of the building into the cold winter air, staring at the man's car, a black BMW, unable to tear his eyes from the green license plate, DUBL PHD. It was the worst moment in his life, the beginning of years of block and suffering. It was something no one should force him to relive.

"Vell, perhaps maybe someday yous show him, yah? Publish da big book." How could Andrea smile? How could she not know what she was doing? "Maybe yous tink of da great story some-time."

Crossing Montana. Yes, it was a great story, but any further thoughts of the university experience would delay its completion by several years. Billy would have to write those young editors again with an update. Tell them not to wear themselves out antic-ipating his book. He stared straight ahead, the white lines in the middle of the interstate zipping by, appearing to run together. And when Helena finally appeared, a pillar of smoke from its lead smelter rising in salutation, it was—save the stripper in Elko, Nevada, who'd done that nifty trick with the shot glass—the most beautiful sight Billy had ever seen. Sleeping Troy had not looked as good to Odysseus from inside the wooden horse.

"Here we are," he announced. Yes, praise all heaven, here we are.

Andrea had business at the bank. The big First National on Main Street. Transferring foreign accounts, Billy figured. Swiss? It wouldn't surprise him. What did surprise him was the fact that he was able to negotiate downtown Helena's moderate traffic with-out wrecking, though it occurred to him his competence at the wheel might be a product of shock. What would happen when it wore off and he entered the next phase? PTSD, if he had the let-ters in their correct order, manifested itself in odd ways at odd times. Better to have a fender bender in Helena than leave the highway coming down into Butte from Woodville Hill, the notch at the south end of Elk Park where the interstate fell away toward Berkeley Pit.

Whatever business Andrea had at the bank didn't require Billy's assistance.

"Yous help me to da door, and den maybe I see yous back in half of an hour, yah?" she said as he escorted her along the sidewalk.

Maybe you will, and then again . . . Billy stared north, pictur-ing the wide plains eighty miles farther toward Great Falls. He could burn up a lot of road in the '57 going that way. There was the canyon along the Missouri River between Helena and Craig where he'd have to watch himself, but after that it was smooth sailing clear to Saskatchewan. A little jaunt over the border to see a farmer's daughter would do his spirits immeasurable good. He could picture the Saskatchewan sunset, different somehow from one in Montana, soft light filtering into the loft, the delicious aroma of fresh-cut hay all around him. And, yes, she *was* getting out of her overalls. Billy stopped. The farmer's daughter looked suspiciously like Buff. Enough of that.

The First National was not an appealing structure. Planked down between two older buildings, a feed store converted to a hair salon and some type of law office, Billy found the new four-story offensive. He imagined creeping up Main Street on a great, tracked crane, a bulbous wrecking ball swinging a long arc toward the copper-trimmed awning over the bank's front door.

"Okay," Andrea said. "I give yous some change, and see yous later." She handed Billy ten bucks and he steered her into the bank, wondering as he looked at the huge, multilayered vault behind the tellers if there should be a safecracker in his novel. Someone good with toluene might spruce the story up.

Back on the sidewalk, Billy shifted his thoughts from the novel to Mr. Hamilton. He spread the bill open between his hands, then flipped it to admire the green ink, his favorite color. There was a coffee shop less than two blocks down the street, just the type of place professional women would gather for lunch. And between the bank and the coffee house was a Hallmark store, where he could buy a notebook and pen. He would chew it pensively at his window-side booth, making sure everyone knew he was a writer. A *novelist,* he told himself as he shelled out almost four dollars in the Hallmark store. Not just a writer, a *novelist.*

In the air-conditioned coffee shop, Billy went with an iced cappuccino, asking for it calmly so anyone listening would believe he drank them regularly. He studied the young man behind the counter carefully before paying, sipping his drink as though it didn't entirely suit him. There was an open booth next to the window, and Billy took it even though the bench hadn't been cleaned. It wasn't easy to brush the pastry crumbs away, but he used a napkin and told himself they'd fallen before reaching anyone's mouth. Settled in, he flipped open the notebook and began nibbling his pen. As if on cue, three women came in. Billy chewed harder on the pen.

The women, tall fast-walkers no doubt down from the capitol building, opted for a table directly across from Billy. Another piece of good luck. There were two brunettes and a blonde, all well dressed and expertly groomed, any one of whom would find it fashionable to have an artist in tow. Billy wished his hair were just a little longer. He rested his chin in his hands and sighed.

"All the money and love," he said. "And still not enough for Isabelle."

The women stopped talking and looked at him.

"Poor Isabelle. What more could I have done? The Pulitzer? Would that have been enough?" Billy shook his head. "But that was out of my hands," he said to the ceiling. "I had all the good reviews, the high sales, the best authors pulling for me. Oh, Isabelle, Isabelle, why did you leave me?"

The blonde cleared her throat. Billy figured she'd replace Isabelle just fine.

"I'm sorry," he said, "Am I disturbing you?"

The woman smiled.

"I don't mean to. I'm so sorry." He turned to the window and moaned. "Oh, Isabelle, don't you know that I would *give* you the house in Spain? No need to contest it. And the royalties? I would never deny you them. Don't you see, I *want* you to be comfortable forever. And your son, too. No matter whose he his. He is half yours, and all wonderful."

The blonde cleared her throat again.

"Oh, dear. I really am sorry," Billy said, wringing his hands. "It's just . . . well, this writer,"—he wanted to be sure they understood—"has fallen on hard times."

"Writer?" the blonde said.

"Ah, but no more." Billy clapped the notebook shut. "My soul is broken, and my words are empty. The feeling is all gone. I must cancel the three-book contract and go overseas. Perhaps some time alone in the North Atlantic . . . just me and the sloop."

"You have a boat?" one of the brunettes asked.

Billy nodded. He would have a yacht if she wanted. The QE2, if it made any difference.

"What do you write?" The blonde seemed genuinely interested. And why not? What was there not to fall for?

"Novels," Billy whispered. "Epic stories of love and loss. And now . . ." he faced the window again. "And now, I must live like Samuel. I have become the man I deprived of so much in my fifth book."

"How many books have you written?" It was the brunette again.

Billy counted on his fingers. On both his hands. "Eight," he said.

"And what did you say your name was?"

"William Bristol," he whispered.

"William Bristol. Hmmm . . . Doesn't ring a bell."

"Oh, thank god," Billy said standing up. "It's so refreshing to find someone who doesn't know. Someone who isn't trying to get me to hurry my next book. Hurry, hurry, hurry. No one understands about the time it takes. So nice to find a woman"—he looked at each of them in turn—"to find some *women* who aren't clamoring for me to sign copies. Copies or body parts. That's the worst. Can you imagine it? So hard on Isabelle. And her not being able to stand. Oh, my, oh, my. Wait, was that it? Was the lady in Paris, the one who thrust her legs at me to sign with that glitter pen, the last straw? Oh, Isabelle, I should have wheeled you away from that crowd much sooner. I'm sorry, I'm sorry." Billy stumbled toward the table, hoping that the blonde and at least one of her friends would rise to catch him. "So faint," he said. "Not the cancer. Not again."

The blonde stood up and stopped him in his tracks. A real firm-gripper. Must have one of those exercise machines at home, Billy thought. Bow Flex, maybe. He lowered his head to her shoulder.

"Hold me, please," he begged. "May I cry?"

May I cry? Yes, that was a dandy. Let her see that he was thoroughly in touch with his feminine side. And from the way she was holding him, hands all but bursting his shoulders, Billy figured she could stand to get in touch with her feminine side, too. He sniffled on her shirt, then straightened up. "Forgive me," he said, lowering his eyes. "I was overcome. How may I make it up to you? Can I buy you lunch? Dinner?"

The blonde smiled. "Hey, don't worry about it."

"Really . . . I would feel so much better. Is there somewhere nice I can take you?"

The woman looked at her friends. They could come, too. "Well, I'm not sure what you mean," she said.

Smooth. Billy was making all the right moves.

"Are you asking me out?"

Billy shrugged. Let her interpret for herself.

"I mean, not that I'm not flattered, but . . ."

But. Goddamn buts! This is a good story, *but*. This reads well, *but*. I'd love to go out with you, *but*. *But* was the only three-letter word in the English language that meant no. Unequivocally.

"But I think we're standing on opposite sides of the plate. Not that I wouldn't enjoy a dinner . . . I just wouldn't want you to think it was going to go any further."

Would any such thing ever cross his mind?

"Oh, goodness, no," he said, realizing even as the words came out how insincere it sounded.

"I guess what I'm trying to say is that I like men, I just don't like them in the way you probably think I do." Her friends stood up and headed for the door. "It was nice meeting you, though."

Billy watched in horror as they headed up the sidewalk. Were they holding hands? Well, he thought, at every turn. And now he had wasted money on the notebook and pen. Let his iced cappuccino get warm, too. When would such things cease to surprise him? Why did he still want to caress the blonde's chair? Why did he wish he *was* the blonde's chair?

Billy stepped out of the coffee shop and shuffled up toward the bank. The women were already three blocks ahead of him, and, yes, they were holding hands.

"Well, everyone needs someone," he said to a fire hydrant.

Andrea had finished her business and was waiting for him in a plush dark-blue recliner near the bank's door. She knew immediately when he came in.

"Ah, yous is back," she said. "Did yous find any big fun?"

Three of them, Billy thought. Wouldn't even invite me to watch, however.

"Vell, I iz ready to go back to Butte now. And tired, too. I vill probably sleep."

That was a blessing. No more talk of . . . well, no more of the talk they'd had on the trip up. Billy helped her down the sidewalk to the Chevy, and it appeared that she was out before they reached the interstate. He looked at her leaning against the door and wondered if she slumped enough so passing cars couldn't see her. He hoped that she did, and if she wasn't old and blind would have tugged her out of the way a little more. Wouldn't do to have her spoiling anything if a young lady lawyer pulled alongside in a sports car.

"No," Billy said. "I won't hope it." Hopes had a way of being dashed to pieces and, when possible, were best avoided. Driving south on Interstate 15, he wondered if there was a particular spirit charged with hope-busting. A foul-tempered troll that carried an oversized, wooden Louisville Slugger everywhere he went and was always on the lookout for some hopes to take a swing at. If so, he seemed to pay particular attention to Billy.

"Keep your eye right on the hope," he whispered, imagining the bat connecting with a resounding crack. "Going, going, gone."

· 9 ·

S ee how the summer wears on and I wear down," Billy said
to his reflection in the little mirror above his bathroom
sink. He studied the lines in his face, the grooves cut deep
in his once-fair skin: twisty signatures of the block, indecipher-
able names of editors, and jagged, branched lines that seemed to
appear after a hope had been dashed to pieces. True, his face had
character, but much more character would leave it looking like
a prune. Billy needed something good to happen, and he needed
it soon.

Things with Andrea were going about as well as any work
could, he'd staved off his eviction with fifty dollars—though only
for another two weeks, he reminded himself—and he'd done well
dodging his mother. But that wasn't enough. Not enough to com-
bat the increasing number of furrows in his face. So what to do?
Billy shuffled into the living room and plopped down on the
couch, flicking the power button for the television.

"And I'll be giving a reading at two this afternoon," a man's
voice said.

Billy held the volume button down to hear more. The picture
came in just in time to show a well-dressed gentleman cradling a
slim paperback. A how-to book, unless Billy was mistaken. Eighty
or ninety pages of self-help material that had probably sold millions of copies. Certainly a Book of the Month Club selection, it
had probably been picked up by the airline companies for distribu-
tion on flights, too. But a reading? Now *there* was an idea. He
switched to the Discovery Channel as its narrator went on about
Louisiana's walking catfish and their "adaptations for finned
propulsion over dry ground." Billy pored over his novel, already
well into a session of voice exercises. It was high time the bookstore in the downtown mall had him give a reading. Give him a
chance to take some satisfaction in what he worked so hard at.
Give others a chance to listen to this wonderful story. Why hadn't
he thought of this earlier?

Billy clicked off the TV. Walking catfish made him nervous. He imagined one of about sixty pounds finning its way over Jesus, Mary, and Joseph, whiskers trailing along behind. Surely one couldn't come this far, he hoped. Not all the way to Montana. But then, there *was* the Missouri. What if one crept out around the dams in the dead of night? Plodded over the divide during a day of heavy rain, thrashing from one puddle to the next? Billy listened carefully, thankful that he didn't hear anything with scales on the stairwell.

"Hello," he said aloud to the sprawling crowd he knew would gather in front of the bookstore to hear him read. "Hello, ladies and gentlemen." Should he call them fans? They would be by the time he finished. And what a great way to build an audience for his work. Friends and fans. That's what he'd say. This was a stroke of genius. Exactly the pick-me-up he needed. Inspiring. Moments of inspiration, being relatively few, were nothing to let slip past. Billy tore a clean sheet from his tablet, page eleven, he thought, and, after marveling over the fact that he had ten pages of *Crossing Montana*, printed his name and address in the top right-hand corner. "Dear Panel," he wrote. The National Book Award winner was determined by a panel, wasn't it? "William Bristol writes to take issue with you." New paragraph.

"By considering only published works for your award, you discriminate against a great many authors. How, in all fairness, can you say that the best book each year is one that has been published? I believe you would be thoroughly enlightened if, in the spirit of democracy, you opened this competition to all manuscripts, published and otherwise. As an example of what I'm talking about, please read the following, a short excerpt from *Crossing Montana*, my own novel, which, although it is still a work in progress, I can't believe you wouldn't consider.

"'Meteors streamed from the sky, streaks of blue and green, brighter than the stars. Riding under them, their horses silhouetted against a stark background of sage and rock, the little party pushed on, each man afraid to say what he was thinking, afraid his thoughts were shared by every other man. Afraid that their time was ending. Afraid time *itself* was ending. Afraid that the entire sky was falling.'"

Billy was shaking. When had he written that section? And how could he have forgotten how captivating it was? The panel would consider very carefully what he had to say. He signed his name, then added a postscript.

"P.S.: In the event that you have already chosen this year's recipient, I will allow my book to be considered for next year's award. Please inform me where I may send it. Thanking you in advance."

First, Billy would find out where to send the letter. McMurtry might know, but if not, there were other ways. He tacked it to his refrigerator with the magnetized washer, then headed for the bedroom and a clean set of clothes. The bedraggled look was fashionable for second and third readings, but better to play it safe for the first one. A white Wrangler button-down, clean jeans, and the Hawthorns. Classy without being pretentious. Just like my writing, Billy thought. Simple yet elegant.

The Butte Plaza Mall, a low, narrow strip of connected stores, including a bookstore, lay the better part of a mile below Washoe down on Harrison. Billy stared out the kitchen window, over the fire escape, past the great brick McQueen Hotel toward the downtown. He would need to do everything in his power to be sure the reading went well. The hike back up to his apartment after a less than satisfactory appearance at the mall would be pure hell. The type of journey that could break him physically and mentally.

He gathered his novel, checked to be sure each page was there and in place, combed his hair twice, and started slowly down the stairs. It was important to pace himself. Not sweat. Outside, Billy slid into an alley between his apartment building and an old law firm that had operated more recently as a Chinese restaurant. It was abandoned now, the partners' names still visible on the brick below the brighter yin-yang symbol, so that it appeared they might be the restaurant's managers or kung fu instructors. Either way, Billy figured it would be a step up for them.

The alley was shaded, out of the late July sun's blistering heat, but even so, Billy reminded himself to pick up a bottle of sunscreen. Something with a good, high SPF. Ultraviolet protection, too. He stared at his reflection, mirrored in the side window of a frame shop, looking carefully for any signs of melanoma, grateful his profession didn't involve much time outdoors. It weathered him enough as it was.

It took a long time for the traffic lights on Harrison to grow larger than the miniature yellow boxes they resembled from uptown. Billy measured his progress toward them by seeing how much of his thumb he needed to hold before his eye to cover them. He'd take twenty or thirty steps, close his left eye, raise his thumb, and sight on an intersection at the foot of the hill. He crossed four streets before it took more than his nail to eclipse the lights, and he wondered if just for fun the powers that be kept moving them away from him. Maybe he would reach Harrison and turn to find all of the uptown miles away on the northern horizon.

Harrison Avenue, when he finally reached it, was busy. The main artery of modern Butte, it funneled cars east to west in front of insurance agencies, fast-food restaurants, touristy shops with neon signs in their windows, Butte's major supermarkets, hardware stores, and the mall. As Billy tromped toward his destination, he wondered what passing motorists thought of him, walking alone on the sidewalk. He stopped once under an old railroad trestle to examine a clump of grass that had pushed itself through a seam in the concrete, drawing an analogy between it and himself. Something about the difficulty of writing but how, with perseverance, even the greatest obstacles would yield to him. He wanted to bend and stroke the grass, telling it what a good job it had done and how it was important to keep trying.

"Someday you'll be a field," he said as he started walking again. Yes, the grass would grow and spread, and so would his fame. "I am the little shoot that becomes the redwood," he said, then wished he'd chosen a tree that grew faster. According to the Discovery Channel, it takes a redwood several hundred years to mature, and that was a long time for Billy to wait.

"The little shoot that becomes the apple tree." That was better. They could bear in half a dozen years, he thought. "The seed that becomes the rose," he said to a park bench painted with an ad for a bead shop. No, no good. Too many thorns. He'd stick to the apple tree.

The mall lay beyond a huge car dealership, its lot full of expensive, shiny vehicles. Billy looked them over carefully, trying to decide which one he would buy when *Crossing Montana* made the list. He'd need something to go with Andrea's Chevy. Four-wheel drive with lots of clearance. Something that sat up high enough so he could look down into passing cars. Down the loose-fitting shirts of college girls. Centered in a cluster of used rigs, a behemoth Dodge loomed, STUMP JUMPER painted in bright red letters on its side. Something like that would do nicely. And when people asked him how many miles to a gallon it got, Billy would tell them if he had to figure it out then he couldn't have afforded it. One of the many axioms he'd use when he made the high life. Perhaps he could hire a butler. A handyman. An eager-to-please simpleton who could hose off the truck, vacuum his house, and take care of his laundry.

Billy was trying to decide between employing a man of limited intellect—that would look good when he went on the talk shows—and having a half dozen good-looking young women to wait on him when he walked into the Butte Plaza Mall, its air conditioning so heavenly that instantly all his thoughts turned to it and how good it felt to be out of the heat.

The bookstore was right in the middle of the mall, between a movie theater and a hair salon, its two windows full of books from the list, hardcovers and paperbacks alike. Billy imagined his own novel in the foreground, a giant poster-picture of himself behind it. He would wear a suit for his author photo, he decided. Custom-tailored in England, too.

"Can I help you find something?" a middle-aged man asked.

Billy straightened himself, extended his hand, and looked down at the proprietor.

"William Bristol," he said. "I'm here for a reading."

"A reading? I don't think we've got one scheduled for today. Where did you hear about it?"

"No, no." Billy chuckled. "I'm *giving* the reading. William Bristol."

The bookstore manager studied him, eyes narrowing, fingers searching for each other, head beginning to shake.

"Who set this up?" he asked.

"My agent, of course," Billy said calmly.

"And you're from . . . ?"

"Right here in Butte. The book is *Crossing Montana*. An adventure story and so much more," he said.

"I see. Is it a recent title?" The manager looked nervous now. Downright worried. His eyes darted over the books in his windows and, not finding *Crossing Montana,* he sighed heavily. "I'm afraid there's been some sort of mix-up. No one told me . . . and it's Bristol, right?"

"Yes. William Bristol."

"Well . . . I hate to say it, but we don't have the book. I don't know how this can be. When did your agent set this up?"

"A long time ago, I suspect," Billy said. "I've been on tour for the past three months. This isn't exactly the homecoming I had in mind, either."

"No, no, I'm sure it isn't. Let me just check the computer." The man headed for the counter, but Billy cut him off.

"I can tell you right now you'll get an out-of-print notice. Ingram and . . ." What were the other distributors? Billy mumbled something unintelligible. "List it out of print. Sold out the first thirty thousand already. You'll have to order from the second go-round. Look, it's not your fault." He put his hand on the man's shoulder, frail and small, and steered him away from the computer. "I'll read from my copy. Do you think you could make that announcement to your customers?"

There were seven or eight other people in the store. Mostly women, mostly older. Very well, Billy thought, *Crossing Montana* is a book for everyone. He watched the manager hurry to each of them, then point to a chair in the back of the store, an apologetic look on his face. Billy waited before he pulled the yellow paper from his pocket. Five women sat before him, a tough audience, without a doubt.

"Friends and fans," he said cordially. "Today, it's *Crossing Montana.*" Billy held the manuscript high in his left hand. "A first look at a great book."

"Where can we buy it?" one woman asked.

"Right here, ma'am, as soon as it's out."

"Out?"

"Well . . . back in print. I'm sorry to say the publisher is between printings. Won't be too long, though." Billy nodded and winked. "So, let's see." He shuffled the pages quickly. Over the racks of books before him he could see the manager fiddling with the computer. Better hurry. "Ah, yes," he said. "A touching section from early on, in which the main character faces the death of his lifelong friend." Billy raised his eyebrows, hoping for a reaction. Some *ooos* and *ahhs* would have been welcome.

The women said nothing.

"I see. Well, here we go," he said. "'The man's face was pale, his eyes dull and glassy, his thoughts in another place where there was no pain.'"

"Excuse me," one of the women said. She was a burly lady in her forties with an armload of self-help books. "Is this going to gross me out?"

Billy smiled. "No, ma'am, and remember, please, it's fiction. All made up." He looked back at the paper. "'The arrow had paunched him, spilling his innards onto the dusty earth before him, its wicked flint tip undulating slowly as he breathed.'"

The woman took her self-help books toward the counter as fast as her squat legs would carry her. Billy shrugged and smiled at his dwindling audience.

"'The captain leaned forward so his friend could whisper to him, a tear forming in his eye. A tear that surprised the captain so much he didn't wipe it away. There was no shame in crying. After all, the dying man had been his best friend.'"

"When does this take place?" a lady with a big JCPenney bag asked.

"The mid-1860s," Billy said.

"Like *Lonesome Dove*?"

Yes! The first of many comparisons, Billy thought as he nodded.

"I hated that book. The movie, too. I can't believe it won that prize."

What? How dare she? This was blasphemy.

"I can see this isn't for me, either," she said, stomping off.

Down to three, now. Billy cleared his throat. Readings were supposed to help build an audience, not drive fans away. Perhaps a different section? He flipped through the pages.

"Indians," he said. "Here's a good description of the Plains Indians."

"Excuse me!" A lady whose hairdo made her look part poodle put her hands on her hips. "*Indians?*" she said. "That word is archaic, derogatory, and most offensive."

Strange, Billy thought, especially coming from someone with blond hair and blue eyes. But then, there was that tribe in Newfoundland. What were they called? The descendants of Vikings and Inuits, right? He'd seen the Discovery Channel program on them.

"This is exactly why it's so hard for me to buy books anymore," the lady said. "Racism, racism, racism. It's everywhere. All the big publishing houses are off my list. Most of the smaller ones, too." She held up a slim copy of some plant-identification guide. "I'll take my mushroom book and go. And just so you don't forget, it's Native American, not Indian. They were here long before we were and deserve our respect."

Well, that leaves two. Billy waited to see if they were going to stick around.

"Horses?" he said. "Is it okay to read about horses?"

Billy hoped that it was. The store manager was on the phone now, a look in his eyes that could mean only one thing. Mall security was on its way.

"'He spurred his steed onward,'" Billy read.

"*Spurred?*" the remaining women said at the same time.

Billy covered his face with his hands.

"They should be outlawed," the older of the two ladies said. She was a well-dressed woman in her mid-fifties, a thick hardcover, *Love After Middle Age,* tucked under her arm. "How would you like it if someone stuck a metal spike in your side?"

"Yes," the other woman said. "And whipped you, too."

Right now Billy figured that would be par for the course.

"Do you know who the largest buyer of horses in Montana is?" Love After Middle Age said.

"Canners," the whipping lady answered before Billy could speak. But he didn't mind, that wouldn't have been his first guess. "I once rescued a pregnant mare at an auction. Can you believe they were willing to spend eight hundred dollars to turn that beautiful animal into dog food?" She looked as if she would cry. "Her little unborn foal, too."

"You think that's something?" the older woman said. "I used to work for a veterinarian, and we had a horse come in with a broken leg once. Owner wanted it put down." She shuddered when she said it. "I told the vet he'd have to stick the needle in me first. Got him to set its leg and let me take him home."

Billy felt sorry for her horse and figured it wished the vet had "put it down."

A uniformed man appeared at the front of the bookstore. Not here for the reading, Billy suspected. The manager nodded toward the back as the ladies cleared out, talking loudly, each assuring the other she was a better champion of horses.

"Do you protest the stunts in the movies?" Billy heard one of them say as they left.

"What do you mean, protest?" the other said. "Of course. Who do you think chained herself to the set when Redford made that movie out here a couple of years ago? They had to torch me out of that Kryptonite lock."

As Billy waited for the security guard, he looked at the hundreds of books around him. Hundreds of books, hundreds of authors.

"We are a put-upon lot," he said to a row of mystery books.

"Okay, buddy, time's up," the security guard said. "You're out of here. Reading's over."

Obviously. Billy shuffled toward the front of the store, the guard a half step behind, pausing for a moment to stare at one of the books on the list. A celebrity biography, Billy thought. Figures.

"Hey, man, no hard feelings, huh?" The security guard held the door. "Shit, I know what it's like. I'm a writer, too."

Stop. Say no more. Billy felt himself falling apart.

"Keep a journal every day. You know, I think I should write a book sometime. How long you figure it'd take? A month or so?"

Billy covered his head as he stepped into the parking lot, as hot now as a blast furnace.

"You have a good one," the guard said as the door closed.

Have a good one? After a reading like this? Billy shuffled across the tar, the thought of how far away he lived as depressing as anything he'd contemplated in a long, long time. All uphill, too, damn it.

"And what are you looking at?" he snarled at Mary. "Weren't there writers around back then, too?"

As if by way of an answer, Billy suddenly saw what she was staring at. Saw it plain as day, though his eyes and mind fought each other, his brain telling him it simply couldn't be. He shook his head hard, crammed his eyes shut, but when he opened them it was still there. It cruised silently through the lot, tinted windows rolled up, and, yes, it appeared to have a green license plate. A black BMW, a green plate.

Billy clutched his stomach. This was too much. Not here in Butte. Not after all these years. Coincidence, right? Fate, even in its foulest of moods, wouldn't do *that* to him.

Billy wondered about it all the way back to Washoe, a walk that seemed to take forever, each step harder than the last. And he wondered about it all through the afternoon programs on the Discovery Channel, too. He hadn't seen the numbers on the plate, or worse yet letters, but he feared the car was the same one. Feared that he would again see the man who had cost him so much.

Billy locked his door, thought about pushing the sofa in front of it, but didn't have the strength. If his suspicions were correct, he'd need all the strength he had just to get by. And a day such as the one he'd had did not leave him feeling strong.

Almost too weak to answer the phone when it rang. Its loud jingling announced something awful, Billy feared. Better not to answer it. But it wouldn't stop. Twenty-two rings later, he lifted the receiver.

"Yah, yous is home."

Andrea. Well, could be worse.

"I vas wondering . . . are yous attached?"

"What?"

"Does you have someone you are seeing? Da wife or girlfriend?"

Not propositioning. Surely this cannot be. "No," Billy said slowly.

"Yah, then is good. I have da nice young lady who wants to meet you. Very pretty, too."

How would Andrea know? Was this some sort of cruel trick?

"Do yous feel up to it?"

Billy put a hand down his pants. He wasn't sure he'd *ever* be up to it again. The miracles of modern medicine notwithstanding, if *he* was in Butte . . . no, Billy didn't think up was a possibility. Even so, the prospect of a date was unexpected and not altogether bad.

"You think she'd like me?"

"Yah, I tinks so. You vill see her, den?"

Billy sighed. "I suppose."

"Yah, good. I have her over tomorrow night. Yous can come see. Have big fun maybe."

Andrea hung up, leaving Billy wondering if he'd blundered into something terrible. It would have to go a ways to be worse than he was accustomed to, but that was just it—maybe he was becoming *too* accustomed to misfortune. Were the Fates hoping for a better reaction from the BMW sighting? Disappointed that Billy had not keeled over right there in the parking lot, perhaps they were arranging something even more diabolical. He would find out soon enough. In all probability, too soon.

· 10 ·

What of dreams? Billy rolled onto his back and stared at the ceiling, grateful to be alive, then pinched his cheek hard to make sure. No, not crossed over yet. All night he'd been awash in dreams of unspeakable terror, and now he was growing suspicious that their origin was due to an evil entity that had taken up residence in his apartment. A horned devil, perhaps, whose hooves had trod upon his forehead during the night. Almost certainly that was the case. Where was the ugly little fellow hiding now? Might he be conspiring with the block?

Billy scanned the room, then swung his legs as far out onto the floor as he could, fearful that something would reach for them from beneath his bed. Cold floor. A sure sign of a creature from the dark side. No doubt it had slithered along over the very boards he stood on. He lifted one foot, then the other. Better not to let the chill seep in. In the doorway to the living room, he stopped.

He looked at the door leading into the stairwell where Mrs. Helmsley had tacked another eviction notice. And how will you throw out my new friend? he thought. If he likes it here, and Billy fervently hoped that he did, enough to stay long after he had gone, it could be tricky persuading him to leave. A good exorcist would be needed, and off the top of his head Billy couldn't think of one.

"Come into the light," he croaked as he headed for the bathroom, peeling back the shower curtain an inch at a time, hoping the demon was not in the mood for a bath. "Cleanliness is next to godliness," he sang. No, no demon in here. He turned the water on and climbed in, sitting at the back of the tub as it slowly filled, letting the hot water envelop him. When it reached his stomach, which he had sucked in and was thinking looked quite firm, he extended his legs and closed his eyes. So, what of dreams? His psychology professor—damn that Andrea for making him think of such things—could attach meaning to every one of them. A subscriber to Freud, the pinch-faced weasel was always relating them to underlying feelings of sexual inadequacy or incestuous desires. Billy turned his eyes to his groin.

How are we today? Disappointed that there was no response, he remembered something frightening from the Discovery Channel on Darwinism. Things that serve no purpose will, through evolution, be lost. If matters didn't improve soon, it would be impossible to go to bed without fearing that some morning his penis would have dropped off. In fact, wasn't that one of his dreams? Good god, it was. Maybe there was more to that professor than he'd thought.

Billy wasn't going to towel off, but he didn't want to leave wet footprints on the living room rug. They were just the sort of thing he would forget about making, then wonder where they came from. With that in mind, he ran the towel over every inch of his body, paying particular attention to his privates, making sure nothing felt loose enough to cause immediate concern.

Intact. That's the best he could think of, and that wasn't very comforting. No ego-boosting adjectives for size. No powerful-sounding nicknames. Nothing to inspire equestrian comparisons. Very well, take comfort in the fact that it's still there. Besides, aren't the Swedes always advertising enhancing tools in the back of *Hustler*? And maybe, like the professor, they're onto something, too.

Back in his bedroom, careful not to stand in one spot too long, Billy detected a breeze. Cool air was drifting into the room, slithering up under his towel, further shrinking his extremities. Like cutting a nickel in half, Billy thought, as he strode into the kitchen intent on finding the source of this obnoxious wind. Ah, an open window over the sink. Billy shuddered, imagining the little devil that had entered his apartment clawing its way over the dishpan, and was surprised he had the strength to close the window. Immediately, the breeze stopped, the first relief Billy had felt in some days, but a chill reminiscent of fall remained, a chill he hoped did not prophesy another autumn of picking sugar beets in cold, eastern Montana. Could the demon arrange such events? Just how badly could it misbehave? Above all, Billy didn't want to be working in the sugar-beet fields come fall. He backpedaled away from the sink, slumping down into his couch in the living room, his mind returning him to the fields along the Yellowstone River he'd labored in three years before.

"Picking sugar beets is worse than *anything*," he said with conviction, shivering as he remembered how his mother had tricked him into accompanying her to those little towns near the North Dakota border, towns with odd names like Forsythe and Terry, where it was no accident that hotel rooms cost exactly as much as a day's wage in the sugar-beet trenches. How she'd enticed him with the promise of finding dinosaur bones among the beets and wonderful small-town anecdotes he could use in his writing. Oh, it had been an awful time in his life, full of wind, cold, sore fingers, and hopelessness. Never had he been so seriously cut off. He remembered how starting in on a new, freshly turned-over field had given him at first great sympathy for Sisyphus, then made him jealous of a task as simple as rolling a little stone. Far better work than picking those heavy, elongated, fleshy tubers, he thought. Picking mountains of them. And how angry it had made him when the bucket loaders filled the eighteen-wheelers that hauled them away to be processed. How they could, in a matter of seconds, lift without effort everything Billy had broken his back piling all morning. And to what good end? So his mother could lounge around the hotel until ten or eleven every morning, then sally out to pick up agates along the river?

Billy thought of the loot she'd returned with. The scaley, white rocks that, when cracked open, contained wonderful designs of blue and red. Intricate fern patterns frozen for all time inside the stones' glassy centers. He thought of the friendships she'd forged with local museum curators and craftsmen, the prices she was paid for her agates, and what had become of the agate he'd found—the one thing he'd taken from the beet fields that hadn't ended up on its way to the processing plant. The great, spheroid as big as a volleyball he'd lugged all day, certain a bright financial future was in store for him as soon as the monstrosity hit Christie's auction block. Where had that geological wonder disappeared to? It hadn't left the hotel room on its own. And what connection was there between its untimely departure and his mother's acquisition of a new winter coat? Surely she hadn't bartered away a stone worth millions for that mackinaw. Or maybe she had—done it as much out of jealous spite as ignorance.

Jesus, Mary, and Joseph announced someone's presence on the stairs. Billy sat bolt upright on the couch, jerked away from the sugar-beet fields, breathing silently through his mouth, waiting for the knock on his door. Even though he expected it, he twitched with fear when it came, four solid raps followed by four more. Well, they were too hearty to be feeble old Helmsley. Who, then? Billy wondered if the legislature had slipped a bill by him reinstating debtors' prison. Was there a uniformed officer of the law at his door? He glanced to his ankles and imagined the leg irons. Clink clank, clink clank. Bread and water for you, Bristol.

"Billy, honey, open up." It was no sheriff's voice.

Mother. Billy coughed.

"That you, Billy? You open up for your mother. Don't make me dig out my key."

Billy heard his mother's purse open, the snap of the oversized buckle like the initial crack of an old percussion cap rifle. Like the ones from the reenactment of the Battle of Gettysburg he'd seen on the Discovery Channel.

"I got it in here someplace, Billy, you'd better open up." Aspirin rolled in its bottle, change—quarters, it sounded like—shifted, more metal noises, papers wrinkled. Jesus, he was running out of time.

Billy glided into the bedroom, and even as he moved, that's how he envisioned it. Floating. Soaring. He *was* smooth. He shucked off his towel—invigorated by the thought of his nakedness—and pulled on a pair of pants, hesitating only a moment at the thought of how things might get twisted up without underwear. Very well, let them bounce around. Maybe it will stir some life into them. His T-shirt went on easily. Was he losing weight? Yes, most likely. The sneakers didn't feel too bad without socks, either. Cool, synthetic leather. Onward to the kitchen window, whistling a bar from the James Bond theme.

Bend the legs when you lift, Billy remembered, cursing himself for so recently closing off his escape route. Now was one of the very few times he wouldn't welcome a back injury. The window slid up, and Billy slid out. A wasp, its iridescent blue body glinting in the sunlight, flushed off the iron fire escape and made straight for him with deadly accuracy (the shape-shifting demon, no doubt), lit on his forehead, and drove its wicked cargo deep into his left eyebrow.

Billy reeled forward, catching himself just before he plunged over the metal railing. Already his face was swelling, the onset of a severe allergic reaction, he feared, and the pain was terrible.

"You . . . you little winged asp," he moaned. "Why me?"

To that question, a logical answer rapidly appeared: Why not? It all made sense. Billy was exactly the type of person a wasp would seek out to sting. It would sit contented as hundreds, perhaps thousands of people walked past, waiting for just the right one. Well, wait no longer, my fine friend, here I am. Billy staggered down the steps, his left eye closing. Half blind is better than full blind, he thought, then quickly wished he had not. Long ago he had learned to be very careful about seeing any good in the bad. Better not to tempt Fate.

The alley at the foot of the fire escape rose up to meet Billy, stealing his balance, sending him spinning forward, clawing at the air. His fingers found the side of the apartment building, great gobs of masonry slopped on between the bricks tearing at his hands, cutting deep furrows into his palms. Just what I deserve for believing being half blind was a good thing, he thought, a certain satisfaction coming over him. At the brink of falling, he steadied himself, took one step around the corner of the building, and *pow!* No, not pow, more of a thwack. The sound of a heavy rug on a clothesline being struck with a flat shovel.

His mother swung her pocketbook again, the giant hold-all whistling toward him, eclipsing the sun. Boom! Above the left eye this time, driving the wasp's stinger toward his brain. Billy sank to his knees, unable to beg for mercy. His mother took a full step back, twirled her pocketbook with all the elaborate motion of a 1920s major-league pitcher, bringing her hands together high above her head, stepping into the blow with fierce determination, now at the plate, Barry Bonds hitting big number seventy-one. The purse connected broadside with Billy's cheek in an explosion of pain. On his way to unconsciousness, the helpless state he hoped would signal submission, he couldn't help thinking that he'd definitely heard quarters jingle.

"You know Mommy hates a sneak, Billy, honey." She squatted over him, her hands still double-looped through the straps of her pocketbook. "You know better than to go sneaking around on your mother."

"Ohhhh."

"No? No?" His mother clicked her tongue and stood up slowly. "Hurts me awful to have to crack you again, baby, but you can't tell Mom no." Down came the pocketbook with all the force of an Oregon lumberjack's splitting maul.

Billy was out longer this time. When he came to, his mother was sitting beside him, rubbing his chest in a maternal manner, stroking his shirt lovingly. Dr. Jeckle was back, and Billy was damn glad to see him.

"Mmmmm," he sighed, careful to avoid the long o sound. That had gotten him into serious trouble, and he didn't need another pocketbook lesson. His whole head hurt.

"What terrible thing bit you, honey?" His mother traced the welt above his eye.

"Mmmmm."

"What's that? Well, never mind. Mommy will take your mind off it."

Hadn't she already done a remarkable job of that? Billy's cheek throbbed and his nose felt broken.

"Get you a good mud poultice."

How about a body cast? He watched his mother scrape a little mortar dust from along the base of the building, dry flecks of brick and dirty spiderwebs. She spit on the mixture, rubbing it into a paste.

"Mmmmm."

"Yes, gonna feel all better soon. Mommy knows." She smeared the grime around the stinger, none too gently, either. "Let's get you back upstairs now. You can let your mother in this time."

By the time they climbed to his apartment, Billy *couldn't* let his mother in. He tried the key she handed him a couple of times, then gave up. One of many simple tasks he could not perform half blind.

"Here." His mother snatched the key and rammed it into the lock. "Like this. What's the matter with you, Billy?"

Was she looking for a long, drawn-out answer, or would the usual and sincere "I don't know" suffice? He shook his head and mumbled.

"More mumbling. I raised you better than to mumble, honey, remember?"

He did indeed. Mumbling had been punished by lessons with the metal spatula. Thinking back on it, his mother had used her kitchen utensils at least as much in discipline as in cooking. The spatula for mumbling, the salad spoon for back-talking. Yes, back-talking and sloth. Lying around on the couch was an offense punishable by the salad spoon. Then there was the wooden cutting board with its slender handle and wide paddle. That instrument of torture was reserved for swearing and forgetfulness. Forget to put the toilet seat down, and *bam!* Forget to empty the coffee grounds, and *smack!* Worst of all, however, was the waffle iron. That hinged device he was forced to put his hand in—cold, thank god—for stealing his mother's change.

"Billy," she would say in a solemn tone, "Billy, I'm missing eleven cents today. You come along with me to the kitchen." And come along he would, usually hauled by an earlobe. The waffle iron would be down on the table, low enough so she could exert a great deal of pressure when it closed. "In Turkey, they'd cut your little hand clean off," she'd say, and there was something in her voice that always made Billy wonder if she wished she were a Turk. In would go his hand, into the gaping maw of steel bumps. He'd close his eyes as his mother lowered the top, both hands wrapped around its handle, her feet coming up on their toes, all her weight descending on his hand. After a waffle-iron session, his hand would sport more than a dozen red indentations, sometimes for a couple of hours. It had been a hard way to earn eleven cents.

"Billy, you got to get back on track." His mother glowered at him from across the living room. "Back on the straight and narrow."

That didn't sound like much fun, even compared with being stung by a wasp.

"Find you a good job. A *real* job. Make you a nine-to-five man."

Billy shuddered. How could his own mother be a proponent of cutting him off?

"How do you expect to meet your wife without a job?"

Well, there was Chuck's.

"Your mother would be so pleased if her baby had a nice woman. Someone instead of me to take care of you."

That would be a blessing. Maybe this finding-a-wife idea was worth looking into.

"You get yourself cleaned up and on track, and there ain't no shortage of nice ladies who'd love to take your hand."

How about my crank? Figure they'd take it, too?

"How long's it been, baby?"

Billy looked at her with suspicion, hoping she had more couth than to ask what he feared she was about to.

"How long's it been since you've . . . *been with* a lady?"

Well, would being raped by Lilly Four-Toes count? If so, it hadn't been that long. But a lady? Probably not since the leaf escapade during college. *She* was a lady. My, was she ever. A tiny glimmer of hope stirred in Billy's pants. Be still for now, he told himself. I'm grateful to see you're alive, but you've got to lie quiet now.

"Are you afraid, honey? Is that it? If you are, there's videos you could watch."

Okay, too much.

"Actually, I have a date tonight." Billy prayed his misfortunes thus far were payment in advance for the good time he was going to have later. If his time with Andrea's surprise date was proportionately as good as his day had been bad, there was a real chance that the evening would end on the widow's walk.

"A date, Billy?" His mother began to smile. No, to beam, her mouth opening in an ear-to-ear grin. "That's my boy." Then, as quickly as she'd started, she stopped smiling and took a fast step across the room toward him. "Is she respectable? That's important to me, honey. We want a nice, respectable lady for you."

We is right. One with a good job to boot. A real knockout who brings down six figures a year. That's what *we* want.

"A woman with stature, Billy. You'd never want to settle for anything less."

At last we agree on something. How about a senator's daughter? A lawyer? Perhaps a good businesswoman. The lady who runs the espresso shop on Granite Street is easy to look at. And she could make me a few of those flavored coffees every day. Or the doctor from the clinic. *What* would I do if it was her? Billy began to tremble at the thought of a stethoscope dangling between bare breasts. Lab coats, blood-pressure cuffs, examination tables. Oh, Andrea, let it be her.

"You should have told me about this before . . . before . . . well, wouldn't have had to get your face all swole up." Mrs. Bristol sighed. "Billy, you bring a lot on yourself."

Maybe. Or perhaps none of it is my doing. Cruel fate . . . every man's hand.

"You come into the bathroom now, and we'll see about that stinger. Can't have a stinger in your eye if you're going out on a date. What time are you meeting her?"

"Five," Billy lied. He feared his mother had plans for him and he didn't want to be tied up until seven. Especially not at the center.

"Well . . ." More tongue clicking. "Well, that's not very romantic, baby. Don't you know evening is better? How do you expect to get her in the mood with the sun still up? Never mind, though, you'll figure these things out. Let's see . . . five . . . well, you've still got plenty of time to help me out at the center."

What if I leave the stinger in my eyebrow? Could I do that instead of going to the center? I'd even press on it from time to time. Stifle cries of pain.

A moment later, under the glare of the bathroom light, his mother was poking and prodding at his forehead with all the grace of a Brahma bull. What on earth was she doing to him?

"Mommy sees it. Yes, it's a big one, isn't it?"

Billy shifted.

"Hold still," she barked.

Her fingernails dug into his scalp, converged on the stinger, a firebrand lodged in his head, and then she had it. Instantly, he felt better.

"Thank you," Billy whispered, and he meant it wholeheartedly. After all, his mother wasn't given to unsolicited acts of kindness. "Thank you."

"Of course. Now you go get dressed . . . got some filth on that shirt . . . and we'll head up to the center. I'm planning something wonderful, Billy," his mother said.

Doubtful. Planning something, yes. Wonderful, no. Not at all likely. Billy hated feelings of suspicion. He had a good imagination, and he usually suspected the worst. And he was never disappointed.

Don't let her size fool you, he thought as he stared at his mother behind the wheel of her pickup, her head barely poking over the dash. Chugging their way toward the center, he wondered what it would be like tooling around in Andrea's Chevy. Minus mother, of course. He would look forward to red lights then, maybe even wait a few moments after they'd turned green before passing through the intersection. Give people time to recognize him. *There goes Billy Bristol. Look, kids, that's Billy Bristol. Honey, I saw Billy Bristol today.* It would be a grand life.

"Why, here we are," his mother exclaimed when she pulled up in front of the center. It was as if it surprised her. An appropriate reaction if they'd stopped at Chuck's. Billy wished he had a cold beer. He could taste it. Feel it burn the insides of his split lips. "Come on in and see what Mommy's got cooking."

Cooking? Was it Spaghetti Day already? Billy's stomach growled. He wasn't sure if he could wait until seven to eat. One meal a day was going to kill him.

Billy looked up the narrow staircase. He didn't like walking ahead of his mother. Someone behind him on the stairs was too much like being chased.

"Let's go," his mother snapped. "Up!"

At least there was a railing. Something to haul on. Billy pulled his feet over the stairs one at a time, his toes scraping on the vertical boards.

"Pick up your feet when you walk. Wouldn't want your date to see you shuffling. Too young to be shuffling, honey."

She had no idea what he had been through. Most men who suffer a lifetime's worth of monumentally bad luck need to be spoonfed by husky nurses in an insane asylum. If I can still shuffle along, that's pretty damn good. Put yourself in my shoes for one day and see what it's like to walk, or shuffle if you will, along the edge. Billy reached the top of the stairs. It was his greatest accomplishment in some time.

"What bite-um you?" Hector pointed to Billy's face. "Lookum like shit."

Did this fool *live* at the center?

"Hector, we'll have no profanity in here. I've spoken to you about that before. We're better than all of that," Mrs. Bristol said.

Billy wished his mother would hit Hector with something. Why was she so quick to beat her own son and so slow to lift a finger against a man who could benefit from corporal discipline? It wasn't fair. He looked around and frowned.

"I was hoping more of you would be here," his mother said.

More of us? Why? You've got Hector the buffoon and your shanghaied son. Isn't that audience enough? It was so ludicrous, he smiled.

"That's right, honey, you've got reason to be happy. Mommy's going to buy Chuck's."

"Drinkum, drinkum, drinkum." Hector began to chant and stomp his feet. "Drinkum hi-yai, drinkum ho-yo."

Bash him, Mother. Please! Billy looked around the room for a club.

"No drinking. Not booze. None of the devil's brew."

What? Buy a bar and allow no drinking? What sort of down-the-tubes venture was this? And how in god's name did she have the money to buy a bar in the first place? Had she . . . had she been holding out on him? Allowing him to drift through life in abject poverty while she squirreled away enough money to buy a bar? For Christ's sake, she'd made him pick sugar beets! Or was this some sort of inheritance Billy was being cut out of? If that was the case, a lawyer would straighten it out in short order. Billy knew a good one in Great Falls. A real go-getter who'd never allow someone to usurp his inheritance. Mother had some explaining to do.

"How . . . how much?" Billy stammered.

"How much what, baby?"

Money, goddamn it. How much have you denied your only son?

"How much money?" His mother tightened her grip on the pocketbook. He was coming dangerously close to mumbling.

"Well, Billy . . . enough. Enough to make a very respectable bid."

"But . . ." He was thinking about his eviction notice and impending removal from his home.

"Waste not, want not, honey. Like I've always said."

It was true. That had been one of her favorite sayings. Billy never thought it made much sense. He wasn't particularly wasteful, and yet there was a good deal he wanted.

"I've been saving all my life to make a difference, and now's the time." She gestured around the room. "This little place is getting cramped."

Billy coughed. Cramped? There were three people there. What did she want, a gymnasium?

"Getting too small for our big plans."

She was crazy. Yes, maybe that was it. What about power of attorney? Get her clapped in a home, a big one if that's what she wanted, then put the money to good use. Billy made a mental note to search the yellow pages for psychiatrists who were willing to give free evaluations. They were supposed to be smart fellows, and he didn't figure it would take much to see that his mother had lost her mind. Just have her explain she wants a bar but won't serve booze. Ought to be enough to get her carted off.

"Can you imagine Spaghetti Day in a bar, Billy?"

He could. The Knights of Columbus served it every once in a while, and draft beer was only fifty cents a glass.

"I could set up behind a real counter, and you could serve it, honey! Can't you just picture it?"

Billy tried not to, but in fact he could. An ugly picture.

"Servum, servum, servum." Hector began to laugh. Evidently he could picture it, too. "Me wantum more, waiter." He thrust an imaginary plate toward Billy.

By god, this man knows no bounds. Swing that quarter-laden purse, Mother. Crack his skull if you can. Billy rubbed his face and believed she could. How could she ignore such foolishness and still fly off the handle over a bit of mumbling? More evidence that she was crazy. Exhibit B.

"But surely you don't think I brought you here just to tell you this, do you?" she said.

"Tell them what?" It was Doug Four-Toes. He loped into the room and put his arm around Billy. "Hey, brother." There was something in the way he said it that made Billy sure he'd found out about Lilly.

"I just was telling about how I'm going to buy Chuck's."

"No drinkum," Hector said sternly.

"Well, if you end up with it, the first thing I'd recommend is firing that awful Leslie Booth. She's bad for business," Doug said.

Amen to that. Billy wiped his swollen forehead. Send her packing.

"No talk of firing in here, Doug. We're in the helping business."

Exhibit C.

"Helpum, helpum."

"How about scalpum, scalpum?" Doug began fiddling with the Leatherman on his belt.

"Boys, no more!" Mrs. Bristol let her pocketbook swing to the full extent of its straps. Hector and Doug shut up. They probably heard the quarters. "We'd better get down to business now. Have to be done before five so Billy can go on his big date."

That was unnecessary.

"A date, huh?" Doug grinned and Hector started his pelvic thrusts. "Heard you had one of those with sis. Looks of you, you did, too." He touched Billy's cheek. "Try to fight her, did you?"

"Doug, Billy was set upon by bees. And he *still* looks very handsome. We've got to stop this teasing. Feelings will get hurt. And I've got just the thing to take our minds off it. Super-clean!"

Instant silence fell, and instinctive steps were made toward the door. Super-clean was the semiannual cleansing that the center received whether it needed it or not. It involved mops, brooms, dusters, all manner of horrible-smelling detergents, buckets of warm water, buckets of hot water, buckets of soapy water, rags, chamois cloths, sponges, heavy duty scrubbers, and lots and lots of supervision.

"Now, who would like . . ." Mrs. Bristol rummaged through a cupboard, "the feather duster?" She hauled it out, the great pink wad of dyed feathers dancing on its long plastic handle. "Who wants to be the duster boy?"

Hector flinched first and the job was his.

"Dustum, dustum," Doug said.

"And look here." She flew to a corner in the kitchen where the bristle brooms were stored, lined single file against the wall. "Who's up for a little sweeping? Doug?" He grimaced, and like an auction in which any movement of the body constitutes a bid, he won the prize.

Billy didn't like dusting or sweeping, but they were infinitely better than mopping or, worse yet, scrubbing. That was a perpetual task. It always seemed that the more he scrubbed, the less he'd done.

"Looks like you're the only one left, Billy."

Billy looked around, hoping she was wrong. After all, didn't she say the center was getting cramped? Where were the fifty or sixty other people who made it seem so small?

"We'll start you out with this bucket."

Not the black scrubber's bucket. Please, anything but that. His mother took her time retrieving it from under the sink, working it slowly into view like a torture-chamber master showing his victim a new tool of the trade. More Inquisition thoughts? Best not to let any hired psychiatrist in on those.

"Here you are, baby. Mommy will watch and make sure you do okay." She handed the bucket to Billy, his eyes clamped shut in fearful anticipation. One of his fingers brushed a matted clump of steel wool, setting his teeth on edge. "Go ahead and start with the stains and scuff marks on the kitchen linoleum. Sponge the stains, scrub the scuff marks. No brushes, wire, or plastic. And only soft soap." She dropped something into the bucket that felt like a bottle of liquid soap. Damn it, it felt full. "No cleanser this time, either. Too abrasive. Elbow grease does just fine."

"What *you* do?" Hector asked Mrs. Bristol.

Careful, Billy thought. That was a good way to get to dust *and* mop.

"I'm going to sit and figure."

Interesting synonym for "make sure you all do your jobs."

"Figure exactly how much I can bid on the bar."

Billy felt his face grow hot. Why couldn't she figure what it would take to get his landlady off his back? Help him finish his novel uninterrupted and not cut off?

"I'll just take a few wet sponges over here to the table with me in case I get in the mood to help." She soaked three sponges in cold water, set them on a plate, and enthroned herself at the table, lips working as she "figured."

Billy peered inside the bucket: sponges, steel wool, Brillo pads, brushes (circular, straight, and tooth), bits of old T-shirts, squares cut from jeans, the bottle of soft soap, four or five dead flies, and a spider. A live spider that came dashing up the side and over the lip, causing Billy to spill his treasure trove of cleaning utensils. One of his mother's wet sponges hummed through the air and socked him in the back of the head.

"Can't figure around clumsiness, baby. You pick that up, now," she said.

Did she mean the sponge or the bucket? Billy saw the spider tear away toward the stove. It would lie in wait for him under there. It looked like a dreaded brown recluse. Didn't the man on the Discovery Channel say they were six and a half times more venomous than black widows? It seemed he had. Maybe that would get him out of scrubbing. Worth a try.

"Mother, I believe that spider was a brown recluse. Very poisonous."

"A what?" She picked up another sponge, turning it over in her hand, finding her grip. "I doubt there's any such thing, honey. If I were you, I'd get to work. Five o'clock's coming."

"Not nearly fast enough," Billy mumbled. Good god, was he stupid? He heard the sponge coming, pinwheeling water away in every direction. He tried to duck but wasn't quick enough. Splat! Right in the center of his chest. Very well, he was guilty. He felt the cold water trickle down inside his shirt toward his belly button and didn't bother wiping at it when it headed for his groin.

There's nothing more humbling than scouring a floor, Billy thought an hour later, as his back began to cramp and his hands felt as if they'd absorbed a pound of water apiece, his fingers thick and his palms swollen. Too bad I didn't have a cat-o'-nine-tails to flay myself with while I worked.

"Ohoom, ohoom," he chanted to himself, keeping a watchful eye on his mother. He didn't plan on getting sponged again. Out in the dining room, he could hear the slow swish of Doug's broom and the occasional whisper of the feather duster. Every once in a while his mother would click her tongue as she figured. It certainly was taking her long enough. Those five-digit numbers must be rough on her. Five-digit numbers! Billy attacked a scuff mark. Even now Mrs. Helmsley was undoubtedly talking with the sheriff. Preparing for the eviction. Why was that word so easily confused in his mind with execution? And why was Billy incapable of thinking about an execution without remembering what the Discovery Channel had said about ancient Indian capital punishment? How they had used elephants as executioners, crushing the condemned man's head underfoot.

"In with his head," he could hear the narrator saying. Billy's own head began to throb.

"Me finished now," Hector announced.

Somehow Billy doubted it. His mother rose, walked slowly around the dining room, then shook her head. "Not quite," she said. "You've still got the insides of the cupboards, and isn't that dust on the ceiling?"

"Back to work!" Doug bellowed.

Billy wished she'd sponge them both. If she wasn't going to, maybe he should. He looked at the pile of sponges, stacked like yellow bricks, and could feel their soggy weight in his hands, wanting to hurl one the way fondling a gummy bear made him want to bite it. He eased into the kitchen and picked one up. Who first? Hector, he thought. He's most deserving. Billy began his windup, a compact motion like Pedro Martinez out of the stretch. He'd show Hector servum. Right down the middle, too, by god. Billy reached back and let loose with everything he had, and at the same moment his mother stepped in front of Hector.

Whump. Like a water balloon dropped onto pavement from a great height. The impact, a direct hit to her left ear, bowled her into Hector, too shocked to catch her, and together they tumbled to the floor.

Billy headed for the door, his instinct for self-preservation telling him to get out as fast as he could. This was surely going to hurt his bid to wrest his mother's money—his money—away from her. Had he thrown away forty or fifty thousand dollars with one errant pitch? Behind him, as he went down the stairs two at a time, he could hear Hector raise the war cry.

"Killum, killum, killum," he whooped.

Billy doubted his mother needed Hector's encouragement. He imagined her rummaging through the kitchen drawers, searching for the long-tined roasting fork. She'd skewer him with it for sure.

Billy's Washoe Street apartment was south of the center, and two reasons came to mind why this was both good and bad. On the plus side, south meant going downhill. Down some of the steepest streets east of San Francisco, where, in his already weakened state, hypoxia could easily reduce his mental capacity to that of a six-year-old, like the Discovery Channel climbers on Everest. But it also meant that he would have to stick to the streets, because virtually all of uptown Butte's alleys run east to west. On the streets, he felt vulnerable—a young wildebeest separated from the herd. He remembered how the one he'd seen on television was—what had the narrator said?—"cut down" by lions. Better to be pursued by lions, Billy thought, as he began crashing downhill. He'd gone less than a block when he heard his mother's truck start up, the engine roaring, tires squealing on pavement, spurring him onward. Now the sensation of being chased was very real, an acute sense of desperateness he normally found only in dreams or when dealing with editors.

"Pace myself. Must pace myself," he whispered. That's how the man in *The Naked Prey*, that frightening movie that was on a couple of times a year late at night, had survived. Billy imagined running through the African bush. The buildings he passed became giant baobab trees, the sidewalk a game trail, the electrical lines jungle vines. Behind him, he heard his mother's truck, the cacophony of loose springs, squeaky brakes, dragging tailpipes, and dry belts blending together into one awful clatter like the cries of a thousand Zulu warriors. He glanced over his shoulder and saw that all three of them were in the cab, pressed in tight as sardines: his mother behind the wheel, Hector in the middle, Doug hanging out the passenger window holding his broom like a spear. Billy ducked as they bore down on him and heard the broom strike brick inches above his head. A near miss. The truck rocketed by, whipped down a side street, and appeared moments later behind him again. What would Doug try this time? Jesus, was that the long-handled ice chopper? Where did they find that horrible instrument? Billy distinctly remembered burying it under some boxes of old *Reader's Digest* magazines in the center's storage closet last January. This was a bad time for it to resurface.

On came Doug, the ice chopper held lance-style, King Arthur in a jousting match. Billy flattened himself against a building, the old Anaconda Company Bank, he thought, and heard the broad, four-inch blade swish close to his chin. This was becoming intolerable. He watched the truck disappear down the side street. Then, blessedly, he heard something come apart—in the engine, it sounded like. Billy lowered his head and pushed on toward Washoe for all he was worth. He hoped his near-death experience hadn't left all of him as limp as his legs felt. In a few hours, he was going on a date and, if the opportunity arose, to the widow's walk as well. True, things had gone badly for him all day, and while he cautioned himself not to believe he'd seen the worst of it, he figured it was acceptable to acknowledge that the future is unpredictable. What harm could there be in that?

Billy stood in front of his bathroom sink, eyes fixed on the drain, not daring to look up into the mirror. He'd bathed again, twice in one day for the first time since . . . he couldn't remember. It was pushing six o'clock, the time fast approaching when he needed to leave his apartment and take his chances on the streets of Butte. If his mother's truck was back in running order, he didn't figure his chances were too good.

"Mirror, mirror, on the wall," he said softly as he raised his eyes.

Please, he thought. Please don't look dreadful. Not so bad that she'll leave before there's any talk of the widow's walk. Let her stay and at least hear me out. Billy opened one eye. His good eye. The swelling had gone down around his cheeks, but it was quite evident that something was wrong with his other eye. The brow was a dull purple color and the lid, especially when closed, looked puffy. What could he blame it on? What selfless act had he been performing when he was injured? Women, Billy thought. What do women like to hear? Not those awful things Lilly Four-Toes had insisted he say to her. She was an exception. What do *ladies* like to hear?

Children. It should have something to do with children. Or, better yet, babies. All ladies love babies. What had happened to his eye? Poked with an umbrella? The wound would go nicely with such a tale. Yes, he'd sheltered a mother and her child with his umbrella, standing off to the side, out in the rain, the downpour, with no regard for his personal comfort. The child reached for the umbrella, Billy passed it off, and poke! And then he'd told the woman what a lovely baby she had and wouldn't dream of letting her pay for his doctor bills. Fantastic!

Cologne. Billy opened his medicine cabinet and began pawing through boxes of Band-Aids, bottles of aspirin, large square patches of gauze, a compression bandage, hydrogen peroxide, isopropyl alcohol, iodine, eyedrops—better snag those—nasal spray, cold and flu tablets, burn ointment, calamine lotion, and a few red pills to chew after brushing his teeth to show the spots he'd missed. Billy felt so much better just knowing what was in there. He really was a pillar of preparation. Doesn't do to be caught off guard in an emergency, he thought, as he let his eyes wander to the burn ointment.

"Made with real aloe," he read aloud. Good. That could be the start of a fine conversation if his date turned out to be the doctor. Good thing he'd watched the program on holistic health the other night, too. But now, where was the cologne? Essence of Tiger, it was called. Billy hoped it didn't smell like cat piss. Ah, here we are. He found the thermometer-sized vial with its tiny stopper and skinny tiger picture. Billy cracked the stopper and held it to his nose. Very pleasant. Not at all like cat piss. He dumped the entire bottle into the palm of his hand and rubbed it all over his neck, more toward his ears, where he hoped it would cause her to nibble. Not bite, he told himself, nibble. Billy had heard about biters, and he didn't figure they were his cup of tea. Especially the ones who filed their teeth.

Check the time, check the time. Five after six. Billy didn't need to leave for half an hour. Funny how he could walk so much faster on his way to a date than to work. He opened the top drawer of his dresser and began rummaging through his socks and underwear. Where was a good pair of crotchless boxers when he needed one? He pulled out his silk shorts, held them open, then let them fall to the floor. Chewed. Jesus, there were at least a dozen pairs of new tighty-whities. Why did the mouse seek out the only sensual item of clothing he owned? Why?

"Why not?" Billy said sadly. He pulled on a pair of Fruit of the Loom and wondered if Fruit of the Loin would be a better name for them. Maybe it was something he could market himself.

No slacks, but be sure the jeans are clean. A nice, faded blue, too. That light, well-worn look that epitomizes casualness. Casual was best on a first date. Jeans didn't come off as easily as slacks, but that was okay. Let her work at them a bit.

Billy made a conscious effort not to shuffle down Washoe on his way to Andrea's. Soon, perhaps any day now, I'll be high-stepping, he thought. A wad of mother's money to stretch my wallet, Andrea's Chevy under me, all around me the open road ahead. He stopped in front Pendergrast's Pharmacy, the mortar-and-pestle painting fading to a dull silver against the bricks. The building was abandoned now, but not empty. Certainly not empty. Billy turned his stare to the other side of the street as he passed. The drugstore was a hangout for feral cats, and he didn't care for the way they moved. That slinking motion and wicked stare gave them away as creatures in league with forces he would just as soon not have any dealings with. The windows had been boarded over, but Billy could imagine the inside of the store, a great apothecary counter . . . he stopped and scratched his head. Was it possible? And what it would it be worth to the right pawnbroker? Plenty, no doubt. But there were probably candles or, worse yet, their waxy remains on it, ghostly smoke rings on the ceiling, a perfect oval worn smooth from countless paws of dancing cats on the floor. The apothecary counter could stay. Billy thought he heard a claw scrape against the inside of one of the windows, the rasping sound of splintering wood. He wasn't shuffling now.

Billy kicked a Ranier bottlecap ahead of him, a kind of side-walk soccer, skipping it along over bits of broken glass, cracks in the cement, and the leafy dandelions that had managed to find toeholds in the concrete. He kept it going almost all the way to Main Street, close to a record, he guessed, and would have tried to play all the way to Excelsior if it hadn't taken a bad bounce and slid down a storm grate. He stood and stared down between the iron slats into the darkness under the road. Poor little bottlecap. What if it drifted into thousands of miles of mine shafts under the city? More than once Billy had dreamed he was lost in that labyrinth. Injun Joe in the great cave.

"I say."

Billy didn't move his eyes from the storm grate. He knew that voice.

"I say, could you tell me where I might find Chuck's Corner Bar and Lounge?"

And Lounge. Was that its full name?

"Can you hear me, sir?"

Face your fear, Billy told himself. Look it in the eye and let it know you're not afraid. But it had been so long. So many years had passed. Recovery was nearly complete, and now, after healing time had done her best to make him whole again, were old wounds to be opened? It didn't seem fair.

"I say, sir."

Billy raised his head. The black BMW from the mall parking lot, yes, it was the same one, was pulled tight to the curb on Main Street, close enough to the junction with Washoe so that if someone—Old Stan, perhaps—whipped around the corner, there would be a collision.

"Yes, you there. I'm wondering how to get to Chuck's Bar and Lounge."

A pretty woman sat with her hands folded on her lap in the passenger seat, her silhouette through the tinted glass slightly arousing—a naked fan dancer behind her ostrich feathers. The driver was peering over the roof at Billy, and slowly, very slowly, their eyes met. Until that moment, Billy had thought the trademark line of black-and-white horror movies was rather foolish.

"Oh, no," he whispered. "Oh, no! It can't be, but it is."

It was, all right, and it was still wearing the same hat. That same goddamned gray-and-red fedora. That professor's hat. That . . . Billy choked on the very thought of it. That dea . . .

"Dean's hat," he said in the high-pitched voice of pure terror.

"What's that? I'm afraid you'll have to speak up."

"Deeeeeeean," Billy stammered. "Deeeeean."

The man was becoming exasperated. His face, especially around his little glasses, was growing red. Did his beard still twitch? Yes, it did. He drummed his fingers on the roof of the car, a rhythm he'd perfected on the glossy surface of his hardwood university desk. *Ta-ta-ta-tap, ta-ta-ta-tap.*

Words came to Billy. Single words whose definitions were tied up in a time of his life, and, to a certain extent, *were* a time in his life. Halls. Standards. Code. Expulsion. *Ta-ta-ta-ta-ta-ta-tap.*

"Yes, well, fine." The dean dropped back into his car, and Billy watched his lips move as he spoke to his wife. "There's something wrong with that man."

Yes, well, fine. The car pulled away from the curb, its green license plate, DUBL PHD, growing smaller and smaller as it accelerated up Main Street. If ever there was an appropriate time for shuffling, it was now. Billy's feet never left the tar on his way across the street. He focused on the scratch of rubber on blacktop, forcing his mind to concentrate on each step. On the west side of Main, he stopped and looked up at the sky.

"When does it end?" he asked. "Even Job . . ." He couldn't finish. He shook his head and shuffled on, his brain too jumbled for coherent thoughts. How dare he have believed the future would be bright?

Scuffing toward Montana Street, Billy felt as if he were outside his body, a nice new way to feel sorry for himself. There goes poor Billy. Look at him, a beaten man. Never has such a put-upon individual laid leather to the streets of Butte. He knew the real tune people would sing about him now.

Honey, I saw Billy Bristol today. I don't know how that man goes on. This thought process was interesting. Like attending his own funeral. From high among the rooftops, Billy watched himself shuffling. Your cross is a heavy one, Bristol. He saw himself turn and start up Excelsior. Onward to Golgotha!

The widow's walk on top of the house next to Andrea's didn't look so inviting. Its railing was probably rusting through, and there were almost certainly wasps living under the eaves. He rubbed his eyebrow, delicately massaging his forehead, and reminded himself to remember the umbrella story, though after his run-in with the dean he wasn't sure if he was up—interesting way of putting it—for anything more than a kiss on the cheek. He worked his right hand into the pocket of his jeans, groped around, feeling through the soft, lint-covered lining. Nothing. Not so much as a shiver. He had that fedora-wearing, BMW-driving dean to thank for that.

"Dean," he hissed through clenched teeth. Billy felt a little better. "Dean, goddamn it! Dean, dean, dean!" Saying it seemed to have a therapeutic effect. Like the woman he'd seen on television who felt so much better after admitting to her psychiatrist— remember to find one for Mother—that she had been molested as a girl. Billy thought it was her father who had done the deed.

There was a car parked in Andrea's driveway. A red Pontiac Grand Prix. The sporty model, Billy noticed. Good, a professional woman who hadn't lost her sense of adventure. Too bad he wasn't up to a Tarzan/Jane role-playing game. Ah well, perhaps in time. He peered through the tinted windows, cupping his hands to the glass to see into the driver's seat, the tiniest bit of excitement coming over him. The seed that will bloom someday on the widow's walk? Perhaps. A Tazmanian Devil air freshener hung from the rearview mirror, and the factory radio had been replaced by an Alpine CD player. Oooh, she *was* a wild one. A small pair of sunglasses lay folded on the dash. Were they Oakleys? Nice. And had she put them on the dash instead of the passenger seat for any particular reason? Say, so he wouldn't sit on them? Very thoughtful. Billy gave a quick glance at Andrea's—nothing doing in there—then eased around to look in the backseat. The first beats of the *Pink Panther* theme music came to him, and he adjusted his movement to the rhythm. This was almost as good as going through someone's medicine cabinet.

The windows in the back were darker. What activities did she plan for back there? Discreet is good, he thought. Billy had been interrupted once before by a policeman, and it wasn't an experience he cared to repeat. A leather briefcase lay on the floor behind the driver's seat, an ornate *B* tooled into the front. Beatrice? Billy liked the way it rolled off his tongue. What did she keep inside? Files? The doctor from the clinic would have files. Or maybe it was a portable love kit. He'd seen such things advertised in the back of certain magazines. It looked about the right size to contain handcuffs, a flexible crop, fishnet panties, a couple of leather masks, a little chocolate spread, and a Polaroid camera. Maybe one with a built-in zoom. Billy leaned closer to the glass, careful to avoid contact. She probably had a car alarm. Why didn't that appeal to him more? Proximity sensors, motion detectors, rocker switches, and laser grids. Rarely did the thought of such devices fail to turn him on. Damn that dean to hell!

The woman had backed into the driveway, and the license plate on the front of her car sported an oversized pair of neon-red lips. What was on the back? This wasn't the type of girl who'd settle for the generic. No, she'd need something like MD 1 or LAWYER. CATCH ME would be good, too. Billy walked around to the trunk and looked down. JOBS 4U.

"Jobs for you," he said. "Jobs for you." What type of jobs? Was there a connection between the lips on the front of her car? Jesus, God would never drop something like that in his lap. Or was his period of trial over? Maybe this was how he was to be rewarded.

"No, don't even think it," he said loudly. But he *was* thinking it. He was thinking it would be his just desserts. A wealthy nymphomaniac would be fitting compensation for all he had endured. Anything less would not be enough. He'd earned Miss JOBS 4U, and not many men could say the same.

"Jobs for me," he said as he moved his hand around inside his pocket. Still nothing. That would all change once he realized it wasn't too good to be true. Once it sank in that his life was getting back on track. Once he began high-stepping. On his way to Andrea's front door, he lifted his feet well above the cement walk. Billy Bristol begins the rest of life right now, he thought.

How to knock? What can a woman gauge by a man's knock? Billy lifted his hand, then stopped. This bore consideration. Soft, hard, slow, fast, or firm? How many raps? Seven firm ones, he decided. Good luck plus middle-of-the-road strength.

"Who iz it?" Andrea sounded as though she was in the kitchen, near the door. Billy hoped she hadn't cooked anything. Lord knows what might wind up in her meals. Sweater fuzz, shirt strings, or a hundred other foreign objects worse yet. He shuddered at the thought of the spider he'd seen at the center earlier in the day becoming entombed in a meat pie or drowned in some stew.

"Billy," he said. "Billy Bristol." Good enunciation, especially the last "l." No mumbling there.

"Yah, comes in."

The moment of truth. Like a sultan lifting the veil on his never-before-seen bride. Billy opened the door and stepped in. "Here we go," he whispered under his breath. "Let's do it."

Andrea was indeed standing at the stove, but it appeared that she was simply boiling water for tea. Tea was good. Not chai tea, of course, but one of those sweet brews made with fruit or exotic flowers. A cup of that would go down nicely.

"May I give you a hand with that?" Billy asked, loud enough so his date, wherever she was, would hear. A firm knock and polite. He hadn't been there fifteen seconds and already he was making a good impression.

"No, dat's okay. Iz just tea. You can vait in da living room. I be right in."

Into the living room. Where was she? Ah, a purse on the couch. Small, shiny, and black. Sensible. A leather recliner sat opposite the couch, and Billy opted for it. Let the ladies sit together, he thought. Be a gentleman about this. Be a gentleman until it's time to *not* be a gentleman. Until it's time to play with the crop. Giddyap, little horsie. Oh, he could see it all so clearly, and yet, as he reached for his pocket, still nothing.

"I tink . . ." Just as Andrea announced the name of Billy's date, the tea kettle began whistling. He didn't catch it, but he didn't think it sounded long enough to be Beatrice. "I tink she's just in da bathroom."

Not Beatrice. Too short. One syllable, it sounded like. Belle? Belle was a nice name. Rather like an Old West harlot, but Billy didn't figure that would make her a bad girl. It would fit with the lips on her license plate, too. But Belle would want him to sit on the couch. Be more forward. No, he wouldn't do it. He was the type of man who did not mind being dominated.

The bathroom door was open a crack, and from the recliner Billy strained to see inside. He hoped she wasn't on the can. That thought made him uneasy, causing his feet to itch. The bottoms of his feet, right smack in the middle where no amount of wiggling or toe curling helped. He looked back toward the kitchen, where Andrea was just coming in with a tray. Spooky how she got around without her sight. What were those on the plate next to the teapot? Scones? Billy's mouth began to water, and there, did he finally feel something in his pants?

It was darker in the living room than it was in the bathroom, so when Belle opened the door, Billy blinked.

"Hello," she said as she glided toward the couch. He liked the way she walked, and her voice sounded familiar. Probably from a dream. "How are you?"

Billy blinked again. Her voice *really* sounded familiar. Was it the clinic doctor's? If he could get her to say "amoxicillin," he'd know. He touched his eye, knowing that if she were a doctor she'd comment.

"I'm glad you could make it," she said.

Well, fine, but not exactly the diagnostic response Billy had hoped for. He closed his eyes, lowered his head, then opened them very slowly, letting them adjust to the light before he looked up. Good god, he *did* know this woman.

"Hi." She smiled and waved.

And that voice. It was from a dream, all right. A nightmare.

"Would you like a cup of tea?"

Laced with hemlock, please. Or arsenic. Or cyanide. Billy ran through a list of half a dozen potent poisons he wished she'd serve him. Go back to Pendergrast's Pharmacy and rummage around in the cupboards for something in an amber bottle covered with spiderwebs. Chugalug, old boy. Bottoms up!

"I'm feeling a bit tired." Andrea exaggerated a yawn. "Maybe I just goes in and lie down for a bit. Leave yous two alone. Yous can talk."

"No." Billy stood up without really meaning to.

"It vill be okay. I feel better soon. Go on, drinks some tea. I be back soon." Andrea made her way to a door next to the bathroom, felt for the handle, and slipped out of sight.

Alone. The word pounded in Billy's head. Alone with . . . goddamn it, what *was* her name? Was it Bush? Yes, he thought it was. B for Bush. And then everything began to make sense. It was crystal clear. JOBS 4U. Ah, that was a good one.

"I thought this would be a good opportunity to get to know each other away from my office," Bush said.

Billy was shaking. What more did she want to know about him? In this day of compounded misfortunes, could there be anything good? Once before, he'd been tricked into believing there could be, and now it seemed that he was paying for it. He wouldn't make that mistake again.

"Rain on me," he said silently. "Floodgates open wide." Too bad he couldn't bare his chest to heaven and beg for hail.

"Does this make you uncomfortable?" Bush was sipping her tea as if she knew damn well that it did. She had the smugness of a sister teasing a younger brother. "You don't look very relaxed."

Really? Have the hives set in? Twitches? Billy took a deep breath.

"I was poked with an umbrella." Brilliant. What would come next? Should he tell her he corked his mother with a sponge, too?

"Your eye?"

Wait a minute, Bush sounded concerned. Careful of this twist, Billy told himself.

"Yes."

"Oh, no! How did it happen?"

Hmmmm. How did it happen? "I was holding it for a woman and her baby. The little . . ." Girl. Yes, a girl. "The little girl wanted to see it, and when I let her hold it she poked me with the metal tip."

Metal was a good touch. Steel would have been better, but metal wasn't bad.

"Recently? It looks like it hurts."

"Yes, just today." This conversation has to stop, Billy thought. For god's sake, this is *Bush!* Archenemy slave driver. Job Services Puss. Twat, the Wicked.

"I didn't even realize it had rained."

Rained? What did that have to do with anything? Oh, the umbrella.

"Shade," Billy said. "She was using it for shade."

Don't play along. Jesus, let her think you're an idiot. Tell her it poured cats and dogs. Say something rude. Tell her she looks like an African bush pig and be on your way.

"You look nice." Billy clapped his hand to his mouth. Had the demon from his apartment possessed him? Was there a sponge-hurling, compliment-spouting demon in him? That type of fellow could get a man in hot water.

"Really? Thank you." She appeared to be blushing. Yes, she was blushing. "So do you."

Tell me she didn't bat her eyelashes. No fluttering eyelids. Billy looked away. Why, he thought? Why does the first woman to acknowledge my good looks since my little lady of the leaves have to be Snatch? Oh, it is a strange world. Full of complexities and always unpredictable. He scratched his head. That sounded like a fine way for a character in a play he could write to begin a soliloquy. A heartfelt lecture to the stars. Was there any money in writing plays? Only for the author's descendants, Billy decided. It was one of those noble professions, even more so than fiction writing, that didn't pay until you were dead. Like painting and poetry.

"So, how long have you worked for Job Services?" Idle chat?

"A little more than a year."

Yes, that was true. Billy couldn't remember seeing her in there before that. And what a black day it was when he discovered his octogenarian friend—the little old man who filled out his papers without asking questions and told jokes about the fat women he worked with—had been replaced by the girl with the name that always reminded him of what was between her legs. God, what was her name? Her *real* name.

"And before that?" Why didn't he just shut up and drink his tea? "What did you do before that?"

"I lived in New England. Back east. I worked at a lot of different things. That's how I became interested in Job Services. I figured I'd always been able to find something to do, so maybe I could help other people do the same. Besides, my parents were starting to . . . worry. They didn't want their daughter . . . what was it they used to say? 'Bouncing around.' Yeah, that was it. They didn't think I should be bouncing around so much." She blushed again and said something that sounded like, "God, if they only knew." "They're out here now, in fact. Dad's got some crazy idea about moving here. Nice to know you're missed, but distance isn't always a bad thing to put between yourself and your parents. You'd understand if you met them."

Billy understood perfectly. He'd like to put some distance between himself and his mother. How close was the moon? He'd seen the Discovery Channel program about it.

"Just listen to me rambling on. What about yourself? Have you always lived in Butte? Butte . . . odd name. Everyone back east thinks it's pronounced *butt*. Butt, Montana."

Fitting. "Yes, all my life," Billy said. Blown opportunity for lie number one. Was he host to a truthful spirit?

"And you're a real writer?" Buff sounded keenly interested.

Billy nodded.

"I'm impressed," she said. "Novels, right? Didn't you say you write books?"

"Fiction." Get her on his turf. "Well, of course I also do the travel pieces for the *Times*."

"Don't you have one coming out soon?"

Billy chewed his lip. "Yes, fairly soon. The one on Butte." That's what he'd told her, wasn't it?

"Well, I'm impressed again."

She seemed to spend a good deal of her time in that state.

"Can I ask what your books are about?" Buff wiped a stray drop of tea from the side of her cup with her tongue.

"Oh, I couldn't do them justice describing them," he said. Too bad she hadn't come to his reading. At least the first part of it.

"No, I'm sure that's true. God, listen to me. I'm getting nosy, aren't I? You'll have to think of a way to shut me up."

"Oh, it's okay." Billy figured if she kept talking there was a better chance another drop of tea would get loose, necessitating more tongue-lapping. And he could think of half a dozen ways, all vulgar beyond description, to shut her up.

"You know, I'd love to see some of your work sometime," Buff said.

There's a curve ball. Billy pretended to choke on his tea.

"Are you all right?"

"Yes, thanks. Just . . . went down . . . the wrong way."

"You probably don't ever let anyone read your work until it's finished, do you? I've looked for your name in the stores, but I haven't seen it. Do you go by Billy or William? I'd use William, I think."

Billy was thinking about those nasty ways he'd like to shut her up.

"I'm sorry. Listen to me. I'm hardly one to talk about names. I've always thought mine was stupid. Buff. Who ever heard of a girl named Buff? Sounds like . . . god, I don't even want to think about it."

I do. Billy grinned. There were already many synonyms for that special part of a woman. Why not go ahead and add Buff to the list? He ran it through a quick set of tests, substituting it in silent conversations for one of the more common names. "Love to see her buff. Jesus, look at the buff on that one! Didn't get any, but I felt her buff." Yes, it worked splendidly.

"Is it short for anything?"

"No, afraid not. Plain old Buff."

Billy was beginning to believe there was nothing plain about it. In fact, he began to picture it. Actually see it. No, this buff wasn't one of the ordinary variety. He stared pointedly at her crotch. Ah, yes, there you are.

"Are you hungry?" Buff picked up one of the scones.

Mmmm, scones. She handed it to him, his fingers brushing the back of her hand. Wonderfully soft. He suspected her of using Calgon Moisturizing Lotion. He'd seen a television ad for it recently, and Buff's hand felt just the way they described it. Billy wondered if she had any lotion in her leather valise. He imagined her Calgon-saturated hands massaging his back, and suddenly he realized that he was not possessed by an evil spirit. That he was quite in control of himself. That the element of danger—the risk of getting close to someone as powerful as a Job Services employee, someone who could deny him unemployment, force him to seek work, and cut him off—had a primitive, erotic appeal.

Like sex in a public place or an affair with a rich married woman. How could he advance to the next level? What did she want him to do? Talk. Next to alcohol, conversation was the best way to break down inhibitions.

"Are your parents retired?" Billy crossed one leg over the other and leaned back into the recliner. Nice and easy, he told himself.

"Yes. Well, Mom never worked much anyway, and Dad retired this year."

"What did he do?"

"He was a teacher."

Billy reminded himself not to take too big a bite out of his scone, but this was really getting good. What better therapy to heal his academic-induced trauma than to be with a teacher's daughter? There was none. It was like a minister's child falling for a heathen. A convict doing the judge's princess.

"Revenge," Billy blurted.

"What?"

"How are yous kidz getting along?" Andrea floated into the living room just in time. "Having some lovely talk? Yous know, I vas telling Buff how much I enjoys your company." It still made Billy uneasy when she looked at him. "It iz so nice to have someone to help me out a bit. Really very good of yous."

It appeared Andrea was on his side. Careful, my good woman, do you really want to aid in the desecration of this temple? Billy looked at Buff and smiled.

"But yous vould probably rather go somewhere fun tonight, yah? A picture show, maybe? Vhat time is it, about eight?"

How in hell did she know that?

"Almost." Buff was smiling back at Billy.

"Vell, I tell you vhat. I treat yous to a picture show, yah? Do yous have time for dinner, too?"

"Oh, yes." Billy couldn't help sounding eager. "I think we do."

"Good. I treat yous to dinner, too." Andrea pulled a bill from her shirt pocket and handed it to Buff. Billy thought he caught Benjamin Franklin's profile. Good old Benjy. He was one of Billy's favorites. "And, Mr. Briztol, be okay to go for another ride in two days? On da Saturday?"

"Of course," Billy said.

"Okay, tanks you. I let yous go now. Go, go. Have big fun, yah?"

"Thanks, Andrea." Buff hugged her.

"Yes, thanks a lot." Billy would have hugged her, too, but with her being blind and all he didn't quite dare. "I'll see you Saturday."

Out to the Pontiac. Quick glance up at the widow's walk on the way. Now, test the waters. "Look at that." Billy pointed to the rooftop. "Isn't that something?"

Buff squinted slightly when she looked up, a real turn-on for some reason. "Nice place to watch the sun set from, I bet."

"Yes, I bet it would be." There was hope. "Be nice to sit up there at night, too. Above all the lights of the city."

"I bet they get a great view of the fireworks on the Fourth." The house was only a few hundred yards from where they set them off every year.

And the rockets' red glare, the bombs bursting in air. It was all Billy could do not to puff himself up and begin singing.

"Are you coming?" Buff stood with her door open, leaning on the roof of the car like a model in a mechanic's calendar. Lose the shirt and she'd have it to a T.

Hmmm, lose the shirt. Billy didn't mind thinking about that. Not one bit.

"Yes, I'm sorry," he said. "I was still thinking about the fireworks." And the fireworks that might yet be in store for him.

Through the streets of Butte in style. Billy tipped his seat back slightly and extended his legs. This was something he could get used to. As he watched the passing buildings—the ornate mansions of the late-nineteenth-century copper kings, whose lawns were green even in the middle of Butte's dry summer; row upon row of similar-looking white, wooden, two-story houses where the miners had lived; larger brick buildings that had once served as banks, accounting firms, or fine clothing stores; low, long-windowed pawnshops, and lower, windowless bars—he decided he'd allow Buff to drive the Chevy sometimes, too. He held his breath as they passed Chuck's, fearing the BMW with green plates would be parked out in front, but it was not. With any luck, Leslie Booth had run that man, that man and his pretty little wife, all the way back to New England. Billy looked sadly out his window at the bar's thick wooden door. The sidewalk was cracked, bits of amber glass lay strewn about for several yards, a crushed plastic to-go cup was wedged between the slats of a nearby storm grate, and tattered pieces of masking tape—their signs announcing bands, uptown sales, or softball tournaments long gone—clung to the side of the building like tinsel hanging from a dead Christmas tree. The uptown is dying, Billy thought.

"Where would you like to eat?" Buff's question startled him. "Ever been to Rosalero's?"

On a writer's salary? Buff had a lot to learn. The swanky Mexican restaurant where the waiters wore huge, gaudy sombreros was out of Billy's league. Not above his tastes, but out of his league. He looked at his blue jeans and wondered if they were appropriate. He'd hate to be turned away. There might not be time to find another place, and he was beginning to feel faint.

"That sounds good," he said.

Rosalero's was in the heart of New Butte, the flat downtown section of the city where the mall, half a dozen electronics stores, twice that many body shops and car dealers, a pair of office-supply outlets, and a strip of modern hotels spread away to the Southeast, running, it seemed, as far and as quickly from the uptown as it could. Here, Butte was just another western city, laid out in neat grids on level ground. There was no danger of stumbling down a mine shaft, stepping over someone sleeping off a hangover on the sidewalk, or skating through a steep intersection during the winter. It was as characterless as any other town, uglier than most, Billy thought.

On the way into the restaurant, he remembered playing dodgeball with bits of rock in the uptown streets when he was a boy. He remembered the rough men with dirty faces filing into bars on every corner when a shift at the mine ended, the fights that spilled out onto the sidewalks every night, the broken bottles, smashed noses, and the interesting shapes of blood stains on the concrete. He remembered the center when it was a vibrant place and Spaghetti Day drew more than one hundred people, and the Lincoln Brothel with its mysterious, scantily dressed women who ran young boys off with a broom when they dared one another to go up and ring the doorbell.

Enough reminiscing. Billy held the door for Buff, following close behind her, ready to throw himself into the good life without looking back.

"How'd you like to wear one of those things?" Buff asked, pointing to their waiter's hat as soon as he turned his back.

Billy eased his bottle of Corona onto the table, no small effort considering how wonderful its contents tasted. Was she thinking of getting him a job? "I wouldn't," he said quickly. "Not at all."

"I think you'd look kind of cute."

Was she hinting at some bedroom game they might play later on? Billy Bristol, conquistador? In that context, wearing the hat wouldn't be too bad. Did the first Spaniards in the New World crop their horses? It seemed that the Discovery Channel had portrayed Cortés flaying his steed onward into battle with the . . . were they Incas or Mayans? Whichever, he had used his crop quite liberally. Billy looked at Buff, and it was only with the greatest effort that he restrained from licking his lips. Giddyap!

Nothing feels as good as a full stomach, Billy thought, as he and Buff stared at the sign outside Butte's mall forty-five minutes later, trying to decide which movie to watch. He patted his belly, running both hands slowly over his abdomen, closing his eyes, lifting his eyebrows, smiling without opening his mouth. So, this was happiness. Not half bad.

"Do you want scary or funny?" Buff was reading down the list of films.

"What . . . I mean, which do you prefer?" Billy liked that she asked what he *wanted*. Here was a woman who wasn't afraid to please her man.

"Both, but since I'd never go to a horror movie alone, why don't we see it? That is, of course, if you won't get embarrassed when I scream and crawl up onto your lap."

Embarrassed? Have you lost your mind? I'll welcome you with open arms. Billy turned away from the sign toward the parking lot and casually worked his hand into his pocket. Let's go now, boys. Rally the troops.

"Sometimes I just can't help myself."

Billy fervently hoped that tonight was one of those times.

The theater seats had been reupholstered recently and smelled of some strong industrial cleaner. Billy was afraid to sit too far back in his chair because he worried that the fumes might be carbon tetrachloride, the agent used in dry cleaning, and he'd seen a Discovery Channel program on the carcinogenic effects of that substance. He couldn't remember if only those who had endured "prolonged exposure" had suffered or if the substance produced much quicker results. He'd limit himself to a few gulps of air every minute.

Throughout the previews, Billy conducted experiments in peripheral vision, greatly pleased with their results. He found that he could face the screen and get a good enough view of Buff's chest to form a vivid mental picture. A picture he transposed to the screen. And look at that! There he was, in a starring role beside her. My, my, this didn't look like something to take the children to.

The real movie began in an Egyptian tomb, first-century thieves peering into an antechamber as a sandstorm raged above them. This made Billy uncomfortable. He wasn't keen on mummies, and he felt certain that at any moment the thieves would share his sentiments wholeheartedly. They crawled through a small opening in a hieroglyph-covered wall. Tight spaces, tight spaces. Billy's chest contracted. Don't care for them, either. He moved closer to Buff. For someone who was frightened by horror movies, she seemed to be taking this quite well. Billy looked away when they showed the sarcophagus, just catching the ornately carved god . . . which one was it . . . Ra? Damn those peripheral vision exercises! And when the mummy came boiling out, scattering scarabs everywhere, Billy nearly crawled over the armrest between his seat and Buff. Before he realized what was happening, his arm was around her and his face was buried in her hair.

Mmmmmm. Oh, the aroma of a lady. Soft soaps, fruity lotions applied with a loofah, shampoo and conditioner massaged in during a shower, a mist of hair spray, and a hint of perfume. Would she have dabbed it on the back of her neck if she didn't want him to discover it there? Oh, Buff, protect me!

The movie moved to the present with the throbbing of a helicopter blade and the hero—a young, good-looking archaeologist—running across a rooftop toward the airship above the words "Cairo, two days after the millennium." Billy peeked at the screen and reluctantly withdrew to his seat, leaving his arm around Buff, wishing it was long enough to reach down onto the front of her shirt.

While an enormous ocean liner carried the mummy toward unsuspecting New York City, Billy marveled at how it was impossible to predict fate. How one minute he could be smashed to the ground and the next find himself walking on air. Maybe life was like a yo-yo, he thought. If so, he figured he was due for a dozen or more years on the upswing. Pull me up, up, and away. He looked at Buff, turning his whole head this time, and found she was looking at him. Was this a moment? She leaned over and whispered in his ear.

"This mummy is ridiculous, don't you think?"

Billy watched it rocking to the waves in its crate, and he did not think so at all. He should caution her against such strictures. Mummies were nothing to fool with.

"I can't imagine such a thing," she said.

Billy could. Perfectly well, too. He could imagine the embalmed fellow creeping over Jesus, Mary, and Joseph on its way to his apartment, and he shuddered. To the bassy strumming of stringed instruments and low incantations, he pictured the mummy seeking out his boot closet, and he tightened his grip on Buff's shoulder.

"Besides, what do I have to be afraid of with you here?" she said.

Brave? Is that what she thought of him? Billy turned back to the screen. Very well, mummy, you've met your match. Very quietly, so no one else heard it, he began to whistle the *Raiders of the Lost Ark* theme. That always made him feel so much better.

An hour later, the mummy had been dispatched, the world had been saved, and sometime along the way Billy's hand had found Buff's. When the theater lights came on he blinked but didn't let go. He held it all the way to her car, sure now that she used Calgon.

"Where to?" Buff asked before turning the key.

What type of question was this? A your-place-or-mine question, or was she simply asking directions to where he lived? My place, Billy decided. That should be a safe bet either way.

"I'm up on Washoe."

"Whereabouts?"

Billy squirmed in his seat. He really wished he knew what her intentions were. If they were more than platonic, and that would be splendid, he would have to tell her that he lived in a small upper-floor apartment. If, however, this was going to be a kiss-on-the-cheek date, well . . . in that case there was room for improvision. Yes, in that case she could drop him off in front of the large house with the lovely gazebo in the backyard.

"What time is it?" he asked.

"Eleven-thirty. Why?"

"Do you have to work tomorrow?"

"Yes."

Put one check in the big-house column.

"Don't you?"

"Me?"

"Your novel, I mean?"

"Oh, of course." Billy felt sweat beading on his forehead. "Excuse me if I act surprised, I just never think of it as work. Not something I love that much. No, writing itself is never any work."

"But what about the rest of it?" Buff said. "The marketing. Do you have an agent?"

Billy felt the hairs on the back of his neck stand up. He would just as soon never hear that word again. At least she hadn't said *New York* agent. That would have been too much.

"Not right now. I haven't found one who matches up well enough with me."

"Really? I'm surprised. I figured everyone had an agent these days."

Well, figure it again. Not Billy Bristol. He wouldn't be forking over fifteen percent of his earnings to someone unless they were worthy. And measuring up wasn't easy.

"Is it as difficult a market to break into as you hear?"

Billy wondered what she'd heard? Unless someone sat her down and traumatized her with tales of authors' suicides, great works that went unpublished for decades, and life below the poverty line, it was a much harder market to break into than she could begin to imagine.

"It's very difficult," he said. "At least until you become established."

"And what's that involve?"

Good question. Billy wasn't sure he knew. Luck had something to do with it. And persistence too, probably, but there seemed to be more. Something intangible. Some divine assistance, perhaps. Some force that randomly selected authors and springboarded their work onto the best-sellers' list. If that was the case, Billy figured he could stand being selected any time.

"Well . . . good work. And time. Not . . ." He almost said something about cutting oneself off, but she wouldn't understand that. "Not giving up."

"Amazing." Buff turned onto Washoe. "It must take a great deal of faith."

And then some.

"Well, I'd still love to read something of yours. Anything at all. Especially romance. If, of course, you ever write any."

"Maybe I'll do a short story just for you sometime." Billy wouldn't want to sign away any rights to it, but it wouldn't hurt for Buff to get a copy.

"Oh, I'd love you to death," she said.

Jesus, what a way to go! Better than being bludgeoned by Mother or starving. Billy pictured how she'd do it. Would she get her tits involved in the execution? Ride roughshod over him in a fit of passion, knocking him about, pulling hair and pinching? That would certainly be more than his heart could take. Just thinking about it made his chest tighten. Stay back, angels, she's not quite finished with me.

"Are we getting close?" Buff asked.

"Oh, yes. Yes."

"To your place, I mean."

Billy blinked hard. Back to the real world, Bristol. Where do you live?

"Just up here." He pointed to the apartment complex.

Buff pulled up to the curb and Billy looked out his window to the corner of the building. It seemed like years ago that his mother ambushed him there.

"I had a nice time tonight," he said as he opened the door.

"Yeah, me, too." Was there a hint of disappointment in Buff's voice? Did she want to come in? "What are you doing this weekend? You're with Andrea Saturday, right?"

Billy nodded.

"Would you like to do something Saturday night?"

"Very much."

"I'll call you, then?"

"Yes. I guess you have my number," he said.

It would be a much more pleasant call than her last, when she'd informed him of the job with Andrea. Billy wanted to walk around the car and kiss her through the window, but he'd been a gentleman all night—if not in his thoughts, then certainly in his actions—and he decided that was the impression he'd leave her with. He started up the steps without looking back, thinking to himself as he heard her pull away that Billy Bristol was definitely on the upswing. The high life was just ahead, one or two steps away, so close he could taste it. Truffles. That's what the high life tasted like. Dark, sweet truffles.

· 12 ·

Peter Pendergrast III, M.D., Board Certified Psychiatrist. Free initial consultations, professional evaluations, flexible hours, prompt responses to all inquiries. Specializing in helping you heal what hurts the most. On-site extended-care facility. Anaconda, MT."

Billy loved the yellow pages. Here at his fingertips was just the sort of man he needed. He punched the number into his phone, hands trembling with excitement. Mother was going down the road.

"Good-bye, Mother, it's been nice, it's so hard to see you go." He sang the verse a couple of times in different pitches. There was a country song there, he was sure of it. "And how we cried when the men in white suits came . . . Things around here ain't the same . . . Not since Momma went down the road." Splendid.

"Hello."

Billy knew that the man who answered was the doctor himself. He had one of those flat, sad voices that helped his patients open up. He sounded part monk. *Hellohmm.*

"Hello. My name is Billy Bristol, and I was wondering about getting a consultation?"

"Yes, Mr. Bristol."

Jesus, cheer up! Billy wondered if his melancholy tone was part of a job-security ploy. He could have the Powerball lottery winner feeling bad about something in no time. "Well . . . it's about my mother."

"No, no, Mr. Bristol, not over the phone. Call me old-fashioned, but I still believe face-to-face is the way things should be done. Where are you?"

"Butte."

"Ah, what a wonderful city. My father's natal home."

That sounded like genuine enthusiasm. Perhaps the pharmacy had been his father's.

"And when can you come in?"

Billy paused. He wasn't sure how long it would take him to hitch a ride. Mother's truck was out of the question, if not out of commission.

"It's all right, Mr. Bristol, I always have the time to see someone new. You tell me what works for you, and we'll plan on it."

"How's three this afternoon?" That should be plenty of time for some writing before he'd need to catch a ride. Anaconda was only twenty miles away.

"Very, very good."

Very, *very?*

"Let me get that in my book. Billy Bristol, three o'clock. I've got you in for a half hour. Most of the sessions are an hour, but today let's just get to know each other a little and see where things go."

"Well, this is just about my mother."

"It often is, Billy. May I call you Billy?"

Billy looked at his hands. Perhaps his fingers should have done a bit more walking through the yellow pages. "Sure."

"Well, good. That's good. That's very, very good. And you may call me Peter if you'd like. In fact, I'd like you to if you can. Do you think you can do that?"

Peter, Peter, pumpkin-eater. Peter Pecker Prick. Peter Piper picked . . . Yes, calling him Peter would be easy enough. He could call him Pete, too, if he liked. Or Doctor, or Mister. What did it matter? This was about his mother and nothing more.

"That's fine," Billy said.

"Good, I'm so glad! It's like I tell everyone, we'll never get anywhere if those silly little letters in front of my name stand in the way. Doctor, schmockter! Sometimes we *all* need a helping hand. A little push to get us over the next rise. Billy, we'll work on getting over any ridges together. I'm looking forward to seeing you at three. This is very, very good."

Billy set the receiver down slowly. He was beginning to think that a man would do well not to own a telephone. It had never been any use to him. Well, there had been a time when late-night nine-hundred numbers had helped, but that was before the documentary he'd seen on the women who talk on the other end. Big, ugly women with deceptive voices who play out their own fantasies over the phone. They weren't the young, lovely teenagers they pretended to be at all.

So, what to write today? There was the novel, but projects like that couldn't be hurried. And working on it every day, even every other day, would mean pushing it along faster than it should go. He would wait to work on it until it absolutely drove him crazy not to. Today, he could still resist. He tore a clean sheet of yellow lined paper from a tablet and printed his address in the top right-hand corner. He would lay the foundation for a short story in the *Atlantic Monthly*. They were a reputable magazine, worthy of his talent, and would compensate him adequately. Especially if he made it clear that they must.

"Dear Sir," he began. He knew the editor's name there—the man had been there forever—but decided to keep things as formal as he could. There would be time for first-name casualness after he received the go-ahead for his story. The go-ahead and a sizable advance. After all, it wasn't William Bristol's style to propose something that could be whipped off in a couple of weeks, and he would need to make certain that they were seriously interested. The best way to guarantee a publisher's interest was to get them to pay enough money, Billy thought. He skipped a line, indented sufficiently, and kept going.

"I am not discouraged." Well, if the poor quality of his handwriting didn't betray the lie, the *Atlantic Monthly* might be impressed. They'd told him recently not to be discouraged, and he was offering proof that he wasn't. What had they said? Something about the large number of submissions they receive and the fact that a rejection is not necessarily a comment on the writing. Billy wasn't sure exactly what it was, but he wanted them to believe he'd taken their advice to heart. He dropped down to the third line, reminding himself that query letters should be short.

Now, what should he propose? Billy looked around his apartment for inspiration. He didn't find any. Was the block setting in? He scrawled his name in small letters on the back of his left hand. No, it wasn't the block. Billy closed his eyes and tried to think what he would *like* to write about. Wasn't that why he'd chosen the writing profession? To create something from nothing? To be the master of an entire universe? He tapped the pen on the coffee table, stopping suddenly when he remembered the tapping fingers of the . . . of the man Andrea had forced him to think about. The dea . . . no, he couldn't bear it.

Ah, but there it was! Inspiration in the face of the unthinkable. He wrote fast, trying to keep all his letters the same size, evidence of a perfectionist who wouldn't settle for anything short of the best.

"Up on the Highline, in a Montana high school near the Saskatchewan border, in country marked by rolling fields of winter wheat, crisscrossed with deep coulees (some of which might or might not have fossils in them), where the sky looks so big you believe it covers the whole world, in a little town that to so many *is* the whole world, a teacher falls in love with one of his students."

Billy was trembling. He'd really hit on it this time. Place-based and with real current interest. How far could he ride this wave?

"The teacher's love is reciprocated by the student, who, in order to avoid going to college (where her overbearing parents insist on sending her), purposely fails her senior year. But over the summer, the teacher, away in Boston, becomes engaged to another woman. He brings her back to Montana, and after a heartfelt apology to his student is gunned down on the first day of classes by the girl he promised to marry as soon as she turned eighteen. He is shot with a handgun, too."

Billy had to get up and walk around the living room. This was the best short story idea he'd ever had. Too thrillerlike for a novel, but a stroke of genius nonetheless, as good as it gets for a shorter project.

Mainstream and fast paced. A stunning mirror of contemporary society. Forces the reader to come to terms with American life in the twenty-first century. That's what people would be saying. That and much, much more.

"By god, I've done it," Billy said out loud. He looked at the proposal, marveling over the idea, struck by the power of his pen.

"P.S.," he wrote. "I will need five thousand dollars up front, and another five when the piece is completed. Also, I must have my name at the head of the story, in bold letters, in a different font from the text. I thank you in advance."

"They should thank me," he said as he folded the letter into an envelope. "I may just write for them again sometime." He flipped through his address book, paused when he saw the large, red X he'd drawn through *Atlantic Monthly*'s address, then chalked it up to a moment of despair. They couldn't possibly turn *this* idea down.

Carrying the envelope with both hands (above all, he didn't want to lose it—works of genius were hard to replicate), Billy walked softly down the stairs to the front door of the building. It was nearly noon, a fine time of day for someone progressing toward the high life to be up and about, and it was hot outside. Close to ninety. A cold beer—one of the Coronas from Rosalero's—would taste good. Billy thought back on his night with Buff. By god, he'd remembered her name this time. He imagined her sitting in the air-conditioned office at Job Services. It was probably cool enough in there to firm things up nicely. Oh, yes, he could see her clearly.

"What have we under here?" he said out loud, pretending to lift a shirt, letting go of the envelope with one hand. Melons. Billy's mouth began to water.

"Mel-ons." He loved that word and said it again, rolling his tongue around as he did.

Billy strolled to Main Street, then onto Montana without meeting anyone on the sidewalk. He wondered why Butte bothered with sidewalks. Apart from the Saint Patrick's Day celebration, when the city's population doubled and revelers packed the uptown streets, the sidewalks were as empty as the mine shafts beneath them. Creepy, he thought. Like a ghost town.

At Montana, he turned south and headed downhill toward a blue post-office box three and a half blocks away. Far below him, on Interstate 90, he could see tractor trailers cruising the highway, inching along toward Spokane, Seattle, and all points west. Maybe a truck driver would pick him up. He thrust his hand into his pocket and turned the wad of loose bills Buff had given him to return to Andrea over a few times. He had thirty or forty dollars in there. Would it be safe to ride with a trucker? He'd heard stories of people murdered for a lot less money. What if the trucker's partner was lying in wait for him in the sleeper? Billy imagined the coarse wire pulling taut around his neck from behind. Okay, no rides in eighteen-wheelers.

Halfway down Montana Street, the letter safely on its way to Boston, Billy stopped to look up at the statue of the Virgin Mary. Yes, she was still up there, basking in the sun. He hoped she had taken note of what a gentleman he'd been the night before with Buff. Perhaps she'd put in a good word for him someday.

"Excuse me!"

Billy had assumed that no one else was on the sidewalk and hadn't seen the woman until he bumped into her.

"I'm sorry," he said, replaying the soft feel of her chest in his mind. Too bad he hadn't put his hands up. "Are you okay?"

"Yes, thanks," she said.

Billy liked her voice. It was like . . . he wasn't exactly sure, but it was pleasant. Kind and inviting. "I hope so. I guess I wasn't watching where I was going. I was staring over at . . ." He stopped. She probably didn't care. What would such an attractive woman—late forties, short blond hair, slender legs, pretty white shirt—care what he'd been staring at?

"The statue?"

"Yes, that's it. Mary."

"I've heard there's a tour ride up to it every day," the woman said. "Do you know anything about that?"

Billy had heard a similar rumor, but the thought of riding in a bus up the steep East Ridge didn't sit well with him, and he hoped it wasn't true.

"I'm really not sure," he said.

"Well, I hope so. I hope I can get my husband to take me up there, too."

Husband? Too bad. "Are you going to be in town long?" Billy wasn't sure why he asked, or even what made him so sure she was a tourist, but as the woman didn't appear to be in any hurry, he figured he'd keep the conversation going.

"Well, that's a good question. We're visiting our daughter."

Billy bit his lip. Could this be? Look sharp, now, he told himself.

"My husband's got this crazy notion in his head that we should move out here. We live back east. Back in New England."

"Really? That's lovely country. Nothing like the leaves in the fall." Good, good. Let her know you're a well-traveled man. "I remember going to school back there." Nice job—now she knows she's talking with an *educated* man, too.

"I think our daughter would just as soon have us stay there."

"Oh, she loves you very much." Billy blurted. But Jesus, that was stupid, he thought. Why screw things up when they were going so well? "I mean, I'm sure she'd love to have you closer." And that was dangerously close to mumbling. Billy decided he'd quit before he dug himself a hole he couldn't get out of. He was probably only a slip or two away from telling her he'd like to have her daughter on the widow's walk. Or worse yet, telling her he'd like to have her daughter *and* her on the widow's walk. "Well, I've got to get going. It was nice meeting you."

"Yes, nice meeting you, too."

Billy could feel her eyes on him long after he'd turned his back. Why was she still looking? He hoped he hadn't made an entire ass of himself. He didn't need to get on the bad side of Buff's parents. Not while he was being a gentleman. Once he'd played with the crop a few times, he didn't particularly care what they thought of him, but right now, in the courting stages, he didn't want to spoil his chances by offending Mom or Dad. He stopped at a streetlight and turned around, surprised the woman was gone. He could still feel eyes on him, and decided they must be Mary's. Billy didn't like it when she watched him so closely.

Waiting for the light to change to cross the street, Billy took off his hat and wiped his forehead. He was sweating, more from his chance encounter than from the sun. He didn't want to come into his appointment with Peter—he reminded himself to call him by his first name—looking bedraggled. This was a professional meeting, and he had to conduct himself accordingly. He closed his eyes, ran the back of his right hand across them, then looked into the street, into the dark windows of the black BMW.

The son of a bitch was in there, crouched over the wheel, enjoying his air conditioning, no doubt tapping on the dash waiting for the green light. *Ta-ta-ta-tap, ta-ta-ta-tap.* It was the rhythm of discipline. The beat of authority. The cadence of all things bad. Billy cringed. He could smell the lacquer of the oak desk, see the high glass bookcase, and hear those awful fingers drumming as his sentence was handed down.

Billy stared into the car, his whole body shaking. And what was this? The dean's wife pointing at him? Through the dark window, it appeared that her hand was raised in his direction. Were they talking about him? What if he'd been recognized? Unlikely, he thought, but so were the workings of Fate. One never knows what to expect from that force. Billy watched the car accelerate smoothly away, its green license plate growing smaller and smaller. He turned around once more, half hoping Buff's mother had reappeared, but she was gone, and he was left with only the far-reaching stare of Mary.

"What do you think of deans?" he asked the statue as he crossed the street.

There was a minimart crammed in next to the on-ramp of Interstate 90 at the foot of Montana Street, a tiny one-room building with a set of gas pumps and a high rotating sign that Billy believed could easily come crashing down on him as he passed beneath it. The only thing that would calm his frayed nerves was a drink—a nice cold beer—and even the prospect of being crushed by a sign wasn't enough to deter him from going into the store. Andrea's money was damp in his pocket, the bills sticky with sweat, and it took him two tries to peel away a five and pay for his bottle of Coors. It wasn't Heineken, he told himself as he gulped from the can on his way up the on-ramp, but it was cold, and beer always helped.

Heat waves rose from the tar as far as Billy could see, running up the sides of the Flint Mountains in the west, climbing skyward like the spirits of snakes. Maybe this was where serpents came when their time was up. That wasn't a very comforting thought. The idea of a fer-de-lance or gaboon viper ghost rising up underfoot was enough to give Billy pause. Perhaps a cooler day would be better to meet with Peter. Much less apt to step on a mamba. The man on the Discovery Channel had taken almost as much pleasure in talking about them as he had the spitting cobras.

"Capable of outracing a horse, with a propensity for biting in the neck." Billy pulled his T-shirt up to his chin. The bridge up ahead was alive with snakes, gushing into the air by the hundreds. If someone was going to give him a ride, it would have to be before the bridge. Among those legless ghouls, there was sure to be a mamba and, dead or alive, they were best left in peace.

Billy's thumb went up automatically as the vehicles passed, and though he told himself he shouldn't, he began counting to see how many would go by before one stopped. This was an exercise that could only be discouraging, yet it held a certain amount of appeal. A type of satisfaction for the pessimist. See, Billy thought, I knew more than one hundred cars would go by without anyone stopping. I was right. And being right, no matter what about, couldn't be all bad.

The hundred and ninth vehicle to pass stopped. So much for reaching two hundred. It was a pea-green National Forest Service truck, and the driver had hit the brakes hard enough to screech the tires, then roared backward so fast Billy stepped over the guardrail. The truck's passenger door swung open and a tall Indian grinned from the driver's seat.

"Climb aboard, brother," he said.

Billy eased back onto the highway and pulled himself up into the cab. There was a blue-and-white car seat between him and the driver, overflowing with men's clothes, a wedding picture resting in a glassless frame on top.

"What's your name, friend?" The driver reached over the car seat and shook Billy's hand in the four-step manner common among patrons of Butte's uptown bars.

"Billy."

"Harold Badmarriage, Billy. And ain't it the truth, brother, ain't it the truth." He patted the contents of the car seat. "That's all I'm getting this time, friend. She's took me for everything else." He squawked the tires out into the highway without checking to be sure the lane was clear. Old Stan would like that move, Billy thought. "Where you headed?"

"Anaconda."

"Sorry to hear it. That's where she was from, Billy, and she was easy on the eyes and hard on everything else. Hard on my wallet, hard on my heart, hard on my equipment . . . should have seen the way she'd bust things up around the house when she got pissed. We're talking stereos, TVs, microwaves. She wouldn't touch nothing that didn't cost a hundred bills or more. Yes, sir, go raging around with a hammer and smash the living shit out of everything. Car windows . . . she liked those the best. Especially in the winter. Check her out, man." Harold tossed the picture into Billy's lap. "Check her out, bro, and take a good look. She's one to stay away from."

She *was* easy on the eyes. Tall and thin and with flowing dark hair and puffy lips, she looked like she spent a good deal of time making herself up. It wasn't time wasted, either.

"Got bitch written all over her, don't she?"

Billy studied the picture.

"Don't she?"

"If you say so," Billy said.

"I do say so. See, look here. This is all she left me with. Came back from the fire in New Mexico—that's what I do, fight forest fires—and she'd hauled everything else away. Well, she ain't getting this, too. Maybe she's got the big screen and the blender and all the CDs and every one of those goddamn kitchen tools she made me buy her—never could figure that, because she sure didn't cook—yeah, bro, maybe she's got all that, but she ain't getting this. And I got"—Harold rummaged through the pile of clothes— "I got two pairs of jeans." He twirled them about the cab. "Three pairs of underwear, washed. Some socks, a couple of Ts, my sneakers, and a sweatshirt. What else does a man need?"

"Beer," Billy whispered. He could use another himself. Flaunting his wardrobe around the truck didn't seem like the best way for Harold to get them safely to Anaconda.

"Beer?" The government truck skidded sideways as Harold jumped on the brake and slid toward the Rocker exit. "Goddamn right, beer!" He got the Dodge back under control and headed down the ramp, his foot on the gas again. "Scare you?"

Billy couldn't speak.

"Well, we ain't dead. Not this time, Billy. Hey, you think you could buy us a round? I'm good for it, man, really. You can trust me. Trust!" he thundered. "I shouldn't have trusted you, should I have?" he said, picking up the wedding picture. "Not as far as I can . . ." He sailed it out his window. "There. To hell with her. This watering hole open?"

One exit west of Butte, Rocker wasn't much more than two tremendous truck stops on opposite sides of the interstate, but its small bar, neon signs in every window, was open. The bar was open, and Harold was thirsty. He chugged his beer in less than ten seconds and motioned to the bartender for another. He was good for it, he said. His second went down as fast as his first, and so did his third. In half an hour, Billy had managed to put away two beers to Harold's eight.

Harold stared at the empty cans in front him, then swept them off the bar.

"That . . . that old whore," he said. "Sure thought she gart everything, didn't she? Mmm-hmm, that's whart she thought. Old whore, anyway."

The little clock above the hard-liquor rack read one-thirty, and judging by Harold's slurred speech Billy didn't think his chances of riding into Anaconda with him were too good. It would be hard to avoid a trucker now, but Billy was down to twenty bucks, hardly worth the effort of strangling someone for. He stood up from his stool, but Harold caught his arm.

"Come arn," he said. "Have another one. I'm good fer it."

Billy shook his head. He couldn't miss his appointment. Not with thousands of his mother's dollars at stake. Thousands of *his* dollars.

"Okay, then." Harold pulled himself up Billy's arm. "Let's go, bro. Here, you drive." He handed Billy the keys and stumbled out the door.

The big Dodge wasn't as comfortable as Andrea's Chevy, but it sat nice and high and had plenty of power. Billy saw why Harold drove it fast. There was something exciting about driving a government vehicle, too. Agent Bristol, he thought as he gunned it up onto the interstate. That had a good ring to it. Agent Bristol, 007. He glanced in the mirror to be sure he wasn't being followed. No, no suits back there.

"Turrrn the fuckin' tunes on." Harold reached for the radio, cranked up the speakers, and began to accompany Garth Brooks. "Ahr showed up in boots . . . yer tie affair. Wheeee!" He was dancing with a pair of his jeans, twirling them in front of him. "Bye, bye." With a flick of his wrist, Harold tossed them out the window.

"Therrrre. Bitch won't get those, will she? Caurse I got friends in looow places." A handful of underwear spun out toward the sagebrush along the ditch. "Whiskey, whiskey, whiskey drowns!" Harold's sneakers bounced down the highway in back of the truck. "Drown the bitch!" The socks flew out, too. "Think I'll slip on down . . . come here, you bastard." He wrestled the car seat up onto his lap. "What you gonna trot your kid around in now?" It exploded in a cloud of plastic splinters and bits of fabric, pieces skipping across both lanes.

Billy pushed the accelerator down and focused on Anaconda's green exit sign. Two more miles, he told himself. Make it to the border, and I'm home free. He imagined a battalion of enraged . . . bedouins . . . yes, that's what they were, in hot pursuit. Riding camels. Big double-humpers. The kind the narrator on the Discovery Channel said could go a month without water. Well, they'd need some after this chase.

The big Dodge cornered well for its size, gripping the pavement nicely around the bend of the exit ramp. Billy set his sights on Anaconda's immense smokestack, the multistory brick structure left as a monument to the town's copper-smelting days. He'd heard it was large enough to drop a Volkswagen down with room to spare. He looked past the stack to the Pintlars and Flints, their peaks almost entirely free of snow, and imagined a mad scientist preparing to hose them down with radiation. Never fear, Special Agent Bristol is on his way. He held the truck at an even 75 mph, wishing there was a pair of dark sunglasses to put on, but by the time he reached Anaconda, the huge smokestack now behind him, the fantasy had played out and Harold was asleep.

Peter Pendergrast's office was on the west end of town, across from an Arby's restaurant with a large parking lot. Billy left the Forest Service truck there and gave the keys to one of the cashiers. Harold would come looking for them when he sobered up. It was too early to meet with Peter, so Billy ordered a chocolate malt—much better than a plain shake—and took it outside to a picnic table where he could see the doctor's office. It was a small, old building with a newer, low row of connected apartments behind it. The extended-care facility. Which cubicle would Mother get? He studied them, trying to decide if she should be boxed in by other crazies or allowed to have a room on the end. She could take one in the middle, he thought. Maybe she'd want to turn it into a center and institute Spaghetti Day. An all-you-can-eat-with-your-hands affair.

Beyond the apartments, on the northern horizon, a buzzard soared lazily on a thermal. Billy didn't like those birds. They never strayed far from something dead. What if it began circling above him? That would be worse than seeing a black cat or hearing an owl. A circling buzzard would fly in the face of his high-life theory. A theory that he realized could be flawed anyway. After all, he'd seen the *dean*, and he'd gladly take a flock of buzzards over a single one of those. Is there anything worse than a dean? he wondered. War is hell, heartbreak and sorrow are bad, pain is terrible, labor is awful, but a dean? A dean tops everything.

"Devil's right-hand man," Billy said to himself, thinking back on his college days. His infant stage as a writer. Days full of hope, endless ideas, and unbounded optimism. And then booted out by a man whose entire life experience wouldn't fill a thimble. Who was hopelessly cut off. Whose concept of the world was limited to the padded university campus. The "halls," as he liked to call them. Billy wondered how he was enjoying the halls of Butte and what he wanted with Chuck's. Had destiny intertwined their paths to give him a chance for revenge, or was his appearance mere coincidence—one of those anomalies Fate is so famous for? Time would tell. At least now Billy could think about it without breaking out in hives, a remarkable accomplishment if he did say so.

Dr. Pendergrast's secretary was a middle-aged woman with baleful eyes and a soft voice. The type who could advertise the business by announcing that not only was she an employee, she was also a patient. If that was the case, she looked like she could use a bit more doctoring. She wrote Billy's name in a large, hardcover book with a bright rainbow on the cover beneath the words "Happy Happy," and it appeared that she mouthed them to herself a couple of times. The evocation didn't seem to improve her spirits.

The waiting room was circular, a pair of soft chairs in the middle, a magazine rack full of Dr. Seuss books and photocopied Peanuts comic strips next to them. Four closed doors left the room at different angles, neatly stenciled words above each one. There was the PROBLEM IDENTIFICATION ROOM, the CRYING ROOM, the STRATEGY ROOM, and the I FEEL ALL BETTER ROOM. That one had a yellow smiley face on the door. A narrow hallway leading toward the apartments was situated between the Crying Room and the Strategy Room, perhaps for patients who were unable to get ahold of themselves after therapeutic bawling. STAY AWHILE was stenciled above it. Billy imagined wheeling his mother down that hall in a straitjacket. Stay a good *long* while, he thought.

Suddenly, the Strategy Room door opened, and a woman came out carrying a bundle of colored construction paper bound through holes with heavy red yarn. Billy noticed that the first sheet said "Today I will wake up." Behind her, clipboard in hand, came Pendergrast, tall and thin, receding hairline, small glasses, worn sweater, slacks, and sneakers.

"Plan, plan, plan, Dorothy," he said. The woman nodded and glanced at the I Feel All Better Room with nothing short of longing. "You're so close it's scary," Pendergrast said. With this encouragement, the woman hugged her construction paper to her chest and hurried out the door. Pendergrast sighed deeply. "Ah," he said. "Leaps and bounds."

"Hello," Billy said. "Peter?"

"Yes." He lifted his left hand and waved, moving only his fingers, bringing them down against his palm as he raised his eyebrows.

"I'm Billy."

"Shhh, shhh, shhh." The doctor's eyes darted around the room. "This way," he whispered.

Billy followed him back past the reception desk to a room designated the HALF HOUR ROOM. Inside was a table and two chairs, one of them on wheels. The walls were covered with movie posters from *Awakenings, Instinct,* and *One Flew Over the Cuckoo's Nest.* Pendergrast took the chair on wheels and shoved himself backward with his feet, humming through the gears like a race car. He screeched like a hawk when he stopped and slapped the clipboard down on the table hard enough to make Billy jump.

"Yeah?" he said as he scribbled something on the paper. From where Billy stood, it looked like "nervous."

Pendergrast pointed to the other chair. "Sit, sit, sit."

Billy eased himself down, keeping a close eye on the clipboard and the doctor's fountain pen.

"So, here we are." Pendergrast leaned back and put the end of his pen into his mouth. "Just us. Just Peter and Billy. And what would you like to talk about today, Billy? What would you like to tell Pete? Or maybe you'd rather tell Petie . . . ?" Pendergrast's hand moved quick as a snake to a box on the floor beside him and emerged wearing a puppet whose features closely resembled his own.

"Petie says hello." He opened the puppet's mouth, exposing a bright blue set of gums and oversized teeth.

Billy didn't have much money, but he would gladly have given it all to Petie to return to the box and never speak another word. "I'd rather talk to Peter," he said.

Pendergrast rapped Petie's head on the table, flipped him over on his back, tiny hands flailing in the air, and moaned a long, drawn-out wail. The now-lifeless puppet slid from his hand back into the box.

"Peter it is then, Billy." The doctor propped his elbows up on the table and dropped his chin into his hands. "Tick tock goes the clock, time's running so we'd better talk. Talk, talk, talk, Billy."

Billy looked at an *Awakenings* poster. Why wasn't he fortunate enough to get a doctor like Robin Williams? "Well, it's my mother. She needs . . . she needs help. Long-term, I think."

Pendergrast scratched a note on the clipboard. "Third-person speech? Identity crisis?"

"She doesn't know what she's doing." Billy scratched at his leg, an action that prompted Pendergrast to scrawl "fidgeting" on the pad.

"This—this mother, Billy. What do you mean she doesn't know what she's doing?"

"She's about to throw her life savings away."

"Life savings? How do you mean throw them away? Is this mother going to take them to the dump?"

"No. Well, sort of. She plans to buy a bar and not serve alcohol."

"The A word!" Pendergrast leaped to his feet and Billy shoved his chair back away from the table. Let him write "nervous" again if he wants. "I suspected this from the start. Yes, yes, now we're getting somewhere. Are you sure you wouldn't rather talk to Petie about the A word?" He retrieved the puppet once more and began giving it chest compressions. "And one, and two, and three, and four." Petie gasped, then sat up and stretched.

Billy thought that if he could get his hands on Petie there would be no future resuscitating. He'd tear his little head clean off.

"No?" Pendergrast removed the puppet and wrung its neck. This was a slower death than the first, one that involved coughing and gagging for quite some time. Billy had to look away. "Yes, I know, it's awful, but we can't have him spying on us. You don't want to talk to Petie, that's fine." Pendergrast plopped him back into the box. "Just take your time."

"Well . . . there are other things, too. It's not just the bar."

"Enablers?" Pendergrast readied the fountain pen.

"There's the center, too."

"Center. Hmmm. Yes, the center. The heart. The root. Center, center, center. Go slow now, Billy. Baby steps."

"She runs the Adult Activities Center and thinks it's crowded when two or three people show up." Pendergrast's pen was flying. "She wants the bar for more space, but she doesn't need it. I just don't want to see her do something she'll regret. She isn't in the proper state of mind to make decisions involving so much money. I'm sure you'd agree."

The doctor moved closer. "Billy, for just a minute, do you think we could forget about Mother," he winked, "and talk about you? I don't want to rush you, but I think we're getting somewhere now, and perhaps it's best if we leave Mother," he winked again, "if we leave mother out of this. Let her and Petie go do something together. No Petie, no mother. Okay?"

Billy began to fidget in earnest. He looked over his shoulder at the door.

"Another room? Is that what you'd like? We can do that. Up, up, Billy." Pendergrast strode to the door. "Hold my other appointments, please," he said to his secretary on his way by.

"Sir, you don't have any other appointments," the woman said.

"Hold them anyway. And don't argue. Remember what we decided about arguing?" He shook his head and whispered to Billy, "We talked about arguing once in the Crying Room."

Billy was relieved when they walked past that room. He figured that while it might be a fitting place for Mother, it wasn't anywhere he'd enjoy visiting. He followed Pendergrast into the Problem Identification Room.

"Billy, Billy." Pendergrast sighed. "Here we are at the beginning. Beginnings are good places to start, don't you think?"

Logical enough.

"Would you like to tell Peter a little story? A little once-upon-a-time, maybe?"

Billy stared at the floor between his feet. The gray carpet had tiny pink swirls in it. What would it be like to be a piece of carpet? he wondered. A simple, and not altogether bad existence, he figured.

"No? That's okay. That's just fine, Billy." Pendergrast pointed to a wall with large Roman numerals on it. "Do you know what those are, Billy?"

He looked up. "Yes."

"And would you like to tell Peter?"

"They're the numbers one, two, and three."

"Very, very good. Do you know why I have them there?"

"No."

"They are to help us take a break. To help . . . slow things down. What I'd like you to do is tell me something about yourself.

You tell me one thing, and then you get to take a break. You get to count one, two, three before you say anything else. You can count fast, or you can count slow. See, watch. My name is Peter." The doctor counted to three on his hand. "I like to help people." One, two, three. "Billy is my friend." One, two, three. "Nothing to it. And every time you tell me something, you get a break. Okay, now you try."

"My mother is crazy." One, two, three. Billy counted fast. "She wants to throw her life away on a bar." One, two, three. This wasn't so bad. Sort of like waltzing. Pendergrast must have thought so, too, because he appeared to be conducting an orchestra, his hand moving in the triangular, three-beat pattern. "She needs lots of help."

Pendergrast didn't stop his hand when he spoke. "No Pe-tie, no moth-er. Re-mem-ber?"

Billy said nothing.

"You're count-ing too slow-ly," Pendergrast said in a singsong voice that made Billy think of his second-grade music teacher.

"I don't want to count anymore."

Pendergrast stopped conducting. "No breaks?"

"No."

"Well, that was quick. Quick, quick, Billy."

"Would you be willing to meet my mother? Evaluate her? I really couldn't bear it if she went ahead with this foolishness."

"I don't know, Billy. I just don't know," Peter said. "Tell me, have you and your mother always been close?"

"What do you mean?"

"Whatever you want me to mean. Answer any way you want. You tell Peter anything that comes to mind."

"Yes, we've always been close. Except for the time I was in college."

"College?" Pendergrast scribbled on his pad. "Is there anything from that time you'd like to talk about?"

Billy hesitated.

"Not all a bed of roses, was it?"

"No." Billy spoke without realizing it.

Pendergrast's eyes narrowed and his mouth twitched. He clenched his fists, rolling his hands over each other in front of him and began to wiggle his hips and moon-walk backward. "Ba-da-bing, ba-da-boom!" The doctor rushed forward and poked Billy in the chest with both fingers, then brought his arms into the Egyptian position—one palm up, the other down—and strutted a tight circle.

Billy looked at the door. He remembered the mummy movie he and Buff had seen, and the whole Egyptian thing didn't sit well with him.

"Can you feel it, Billy?" Pendergrast had come back from the banks of the Nile and was holding Billy's hand, gripping it tightly, massaging his fingers. "It's progress, Billy, and it's all around us." The doctor's eyes darted around the room. "It's *everywhere.*"

All Billy saw were the Roman numerals. Progress must be something not everyone can see, he thought.

"Tell, tell," Pendergrast said. "What about college? What happened when you were away from your mother?"

"I met someone."

"Was this someone a man, Billy?" The doctor winked and nodded. "Did you meet another man?"

"Yes."

"Slowly, now, Billy. One step at a time. Come out slowly."

"Out?"

"Yes, out. You know, *out.*"

"Out of where?"

"You tell me, Billy. Where do you hang your clothes?"

"The closet?"

"Yes, Billy, well done. How do you feel now? Better? I bet you do. Hasn't a great weight been lifted from your chest? Don't you feel so very free? You may dance if you want." Pendergrast stepped back to give him room.

Good lord, he thinks I'm gay. Billy frowned.

"No, no. Happy face, Billy." Pendergrast pulled his lips into a wide smile.

"No, it was nothing like that. Not at all," Billy said.

"Oh." The doctor looked disappointed. More than disappointed, really. He shook his head, then his eyes brightened. "An experiment? Just one time? Tried something new? You can let go of the guilt now, Billy. Let it all go. Bye, bye, guilt." He waved. "Can you say bye-bye?"

Billy was about to. "It wasn't like that, either. This man was the . . . the dean."

"Dean?" Pendergrast bit the end of his pen. "Dean. Hmmm
. . . the head. The director. The leader. Antiauthority? No, I don't
think so. Power? Tell me, Billy, what about this dean?"

"He had me expelled."

"The bastard!" Pendergrast pounded his fists into his thighs.

"And now he's back. In Butte."

"Is he really?"

"Yes."

"Billy, I would like to meet this dean. I would like to meet
him, but he would not like to meet me. This dean sounds like a
meddler. The type who likes to play with people instead of dolls.
Billy, I would like him to see firsthand what he has done. Ruined a
fine man like yourself. And I know he has, Billy. You can't hide it
from Peter. You put on a good face, but I know what it must be
like deep inside. Well, no more. You put on your battle face now.
You and I, we'll fix things. Make you whole again. Whole, whole,
whole. And then you'll dance. I just know it. And to think all
along I thought it was you I was supposed to help. I see now who
needs the help, Billy, and it isn't you. No, it's this dean. And help
him I will. That's what I'm here for. You see these?" He extended
his hands. "These are helping hands. They can even help people-
hurters like him. You wait and see." He pulled a business card
from his shirt pocket. "My home number is on here, Billy, and
you can call anytime you want. You let me know if this dean
turns up again. I promise you'll never regret it. Petie and I are in
your corner, okay?"

Billy took the card and broke for the door. He was absolutely
certain he'd dream about Petie that night, and he wasn't looking
forward to it. Not one bit. Outside, he headed fast for the road, the
whole time imagining Peter coming after him with an oversized
butterfly net.

"Physician, heal thyself," he said as he hit the pavement.

Ten minutes later, in the parking lot of a large grocery store, a
cold bottle of Heineken wrapped tight in his hand in a paper bag,
Billy looked east toward Butte. He could just see the East Ridge,
but he couldn't make out Mary.

"What do you think, old girl?" he asked in the general direction of the statue. "Do *you* know how all of this is going to
work out?"

· 13 ·

Old Stan won the lottery. Billy sat in the back of the taxi with Andrea and listened in stunned disbelief to how he'd picked his numbers.

"Yes, sir," Stan said. "Just like Jesus told me in my dream. Signs was plain as day. Just check this out. Been married twice and never had no luck at that, so I figured two weren't my lucky number and went with three. This taxi here is number eleven, and even if she gets carboned up every once in a while she's still a pretty good rig. Then, of course, I picked seventeen because that's how old I was when I . . . well," he winked in the rearview mirror, "you know. Ooo, baby."

Stan shoved the accelerator to the floor and slewed around a sharp corner at the foot of Excelsior Street on the way to Andrea's storage shed.

"I took twenty-two cause it's triple good luck. Seven times three, right?"

Billy groaned. Stan's ignorance had made him one hundred thousand dollars richer. It wasn't fair.

"The last number . . . oh, you're gonna like this. My neighbor's cat threw kittens the other night and one of them had thirty-four toes. You ever hear of such a thing? Thirty-four friggin' toes! Well, if that ain't a sign, I don't know what is."

Billy stared at the arsenic-laden sediment ponds along Silver Bow Creek and thought them a more likely cause of the cat's toes than some divinity looking out for Stan's financial future. A great backhoe was doing some trench work around one of them, an EPA agency worker seated comfortably in its air-conditioned cab. Billy wished he'd swing his bucket out over the road and clip the taxi. Wipe number eleven right off it.

"Dat's vonderful." Andrea was beaming. She obviously didn't understand what it was like to be poor. German movie actress, she'd *never* been poor. Billy could have used that hundred thousand, and she didn't seem to care one bit. "Vhat are yous going to do vith it?"

"Here's the best part." Stan swiveled his head around like the great gray owls Billy had seen on the Discovery Channel. It was an unnerving habit to say the least. Bad enough when the owls did it. "I'm going to buy Chuck's. And then I'm going to put a big sign over the door that says OLD STAN'S. Or maybe it should say OLE STAN'S. Which do you like better?"

"Dey are both good. I likes dem both." Andrea was very pleased. "Vill you tend da bar yourself?"

"You think I could?" Stan was still looking over his shoulder. How the hell did he stay on the road? Uncanny. "You really think I'd be right for that? I ain't too good with memory, and some of the customers are mighty particular about their orders. I confuse things easy sometimes. Bourbon and rum, for instance. See, to me there ain't no difference, but to some . . . well, I don't know. A good bartender is the key, so I might just hire out. Jesus, I didn't never figure I'd have an employ working for me. Guess I never thought I was cut out to be a boss. Boss. A man could get used to hearing that, though, couldn't he?"

Billy felt ill. How was it that everyone around him was so well off and he couldn't even pay his rent? Thinking of it reminded him of yet another note from Mrs. Helmsley's he'd found when he'd returned from Pendergrast's the other day.

"Attention, Mr. Bristol." Attention. That wasn't terribly cordial now, was it? "This is your last and final notice."

Last *and* final. Billy began to fume thinking about it. Rude *and* redundant. Someone ought to take that old hag down a peg or two.

"Your rent is now a full two months in arrears, and if it is not paid in full by one week from today I shall instruct the town sheriff to remove you and your belongings."

That was it. Direct *and* to the point. What did she have going with the town sheriff? Billy wondered. What made her so sure he didn't have better things to do?

"You know something?" Stan finally turned around and faced the road. "I might just keep driving on the weekends. Maybe try to get on with a limo service. I've always wanted to get behind the wheel of one of those big stretched-out fellas. Not much for the corners, I'm sure, but I'll bet they're fun on the straightaways. Shuttle back and forth between here and Bozeman. I'd give 'em a ride."

"Limousine, yah?" Andrea had that smirk that always made Billy uncomfortable. What was she thinking?

"You bet."

"You'd like to drive dem?" she said.

"More than anything. I'm not talking those glorified caddies, either. I mean something thirty feet long. Big bar in the back. Real dark windows and lots of leather. Lots of leather. Maybe even a Jacuzzi in her. Now that would be something!"

"Yah, dat's da truth."

Even Billy had to agree that a limousine ride immersed in hot, bubbly water would be worth taking. Certainly that would be part of the high life. Maybe Buff would join him.

"So how much vill you bid on da bar?"

"Well, good question. Government seems to think about half that money belongs to them. Taxing bastards." Stan sped up down Harrison Avenue, swerving into the passing lane. "If that's the case, I figure somewhere around fifty or sixty thousand. Fifty or sixty thousand. Jesus, I never figured Old Stan would have money like that. Not free and clear, anyway."

"Vill dat be enough, do you tink?"

"Hope so. But if it ain't I may just *buy* a limo. There's money in that, too, I'm sure. Gotta be. And I don't look half bad in a tux, either. Wore one at my cousin's wedding a few years back. Well, his second wedding, that is. Had women on me like flies on . . . well, you know. They were all big, hefty ladies, but they need loving, too." He winked at Billy. "It's all good, brother, ain't it?"

Billy wondered how much money his mother was prepared to sink into Chuck's. Surely not as much as Stan. That was the one good thing he could think about this. At least if Stan bought the bar, he could go in and have a drink. That sounded a great deal better than serving Doug and Hector on Spaghetti Day. As they pulled up to the storage facility, Billy thought about his mother. Odd that he hadn't heard from her since the sponging. What was she planning? What retribution would she try to exact? She bore watching at all times, and it made him nervous that she was lying so low. The calm before the storm, he thought.

Andrea handed Stan a twenty when he stopped at her storage, much too generous in Billy's opinion. Why not go ahead and give him another hundred thou? She fished the storage key out of her purse and handed it to Billy. He eyed the building fearfully, half afraid that Peter Pendergrast would be waiting in there perfecting his Egyptian dance.

As the giant door creaked upward, Billy closed his eyes. Let the light enter first, he thought, as he imagined the scrape of claws on concrete, small creatures retreating.

The door stopped a moment later, and Andrea jingled her keys. That was the sign.

Billy turned sideways to give himself plenty of room between the rows of boxes on his way to the Chevy. He pictured enormous sets of antennae protruding from the cardboard, insects with sharp fangs and sticky feet eager to spring on him. This building was a good place to let off one of those foggers that spewed lethal gas into the air.

"Fire in the hole," Billy whispered as he lobbed an imaginary grenade into the corner. On cue with its landing, a stack of boxes toppled in front of him, instantly sapping his strength, sending him to his knees. He covered his head with his hands. Play dead, he told himself. Dead, dead, dead. But what if the fiend is a scavenger? Billy flipped his hand around on the cement, quivering like a fish out of water. Better to play *almost* dead.

"Vhat is going on in dair?" Andrea's voice filled the room.

A fine question, Billy thought.

"It's okay," he said, though his voice was hardly convincing.

"Ve have long vay to go. You hurry, yah."

Billy pushed himself to his feet, peeking toward the boxes through his hands. Two of them had broken open, their contents lying scattered across the floor.

"What in the world?" he asked out loud. "Wigs?"

One of the boxes appeared to be full of wigs. Blond, red, black, long, and short, more than a dozen wigs lay on the concrete. Billy stared at the synthetic hair, fine wisps swaying in an undetectable breeze. Must be from her acting days, he decided, trying to imagine a much younger Andrea wearing them. They were all very elegant-looking, nicely styled and undoubtedly expensive. Maybe they were *real* hair. Billy wondered when they started making artificial wigs. The thought of having to touch someone else's hair, especially someone who might well be dead now, gave him goose bumps. And so did what he found in the other box: satin bedspreads. Lots of them. Blue and pink silky sheets, lacy pillowcases with fancy ruffles, and nine—he counted them twice—lingerie-style nightgowns. Billy held one up by its narrow straps. Jesus, the thing was see-through. What type of movie star had Andrea been? Don't even think it, he told himself. But he was thinking it. And now, after god knows how many years had passed since Andrea had worn one of the—he wasn't sure what he'd call them—it wasn't a pretty sight. He imagined the blind woman fumbling with her garter belts, wrinkled fingers working over wrinkled legs.

Quick, stuff everything back in the box and drive these thoughts away. Billy wadded an armload of fabric into a ball and shoved it into the box, unable to help wondering what he'd find if he explored the other containers. There must be more than one hundred, he thought. In places, they were stacked to the ceiling.

"Vhat are you doing?" Andrea snapped.

"Be right there. Just a second." Billy slid the boxes out of the way and climbed into the car. It fired as soon as he turned the key, and the shifter dropped smoothly down into reverse. This was a truly wonderful automobile, and no matter how Andrea had earned the money to pay for it, Billy loved driving it. He coasted backward into the sunlight, noticing how the chrome around the gauges on the dash shone, and thought how much Buff would enjoy going for a ride.

"Ve go to Missoula, yah?" Andrea swung her head to the west.

As you wish, ma'am. Billy let the car coast onto the entrance ramp, then pushed the long gas pedal to the floor. He loved the way it first resisted his foot and then, as he pushed harder, seemed to drop on its own. He was going almost eighty when he merged with the westbound lanes, wishing his hair was just a bit longer so that it could stream out behind him. Hair trailing in the breeze, a pair of small, dark sunglasses, a ragged denim coat, and the open road. What appealed to him so much about that? And why was it that lately his mind never strayed too far from an endless highway? Ancient migration instincts stirring, he thought. Billy remembered the National Geographic special he'd seen on the first humans to come to North America: Indians who'd crossed a great land bridge between the Soviet Union and Alaska. He wondered what the two countries were called back then and if he had any Indian blood in him. He pictured himself weighted down in a woolly mammoth coat, a walking stick tipped with the jaw of some extinct species of wolf gripped tightly in his hand. Billy Bristol leading the way to a new world. And then he remembered that there were giant cave bears with a particular lust for human flesh and was just as glad he was going to Missoula instead of across the Bering Strait. And that reminded him, why *was* he going to Missoula?

"I have business." Andrea's answer was simple, and from the way she said it, Billy didn't think it was a good idea to prod her further.

Anaconda's great smokestack came into view, and Billy thought about Peter Pendergrast sitting in one of his rooms. Maybe he was working a patient with Petie. He remembered what the doctor said about the dean and wondered if the two would ever meet. There would be a sight, he thought. He was still thinking about it, playing out various scenarios, all of which involved him watching, sometimes from behind a two-way mirror, sometimes from an elevated seat in an arena, always with a six-pack of cold beer, when the ponds along the Clark Fork River east of Warm Springs appeared, flat expanses of water where big brown trout finned their way through dense patches of aquatic vegetation. Billy had gone there with his mother one evening to watch the birds. Back when she wanted to take the center patrons there on a field trip. He remembered the ducks, the yellow-headed blackbirds, a pair of bald eagles, and long-legged herons that filled the marsh around the ponds. It had been as teeming with life as the Galapagos Islands must have been when Darwin visited them.

It had gotten dark quickly that night, before he and his mother made it back to the parking lot, and Billy remembered the splashes of feeding trout he'd heard. Great gulping slurps as browns longer than his arm pulled things off the surface. He could still see the silvery rings on the water in the moonlight, and for an instant—no longer than it took to hurtle past the exit, where fishermen parked to try their luck in the spillway downstream from the largest pond—he thought it had been a pleasant evening with his mother. Then he recalled the shore rat he'd seen strike out across a narrow bay, its little legs propelling it toward the other side, and the swirl of fish it vanished in halfway across. He figured it was a sign for all land dwellers to stay away from the depths, and he'd taken it seriously. Fish eats rat; what eats man? He looked at the ponds in the rearview mirror and wondered what would pull him under if he tried swimming in one. It certainly wasn't worth thinking about for too long. Not if he wanted to avoid nightmares.

Below Warm Springs, the Clark Fork ran through fifteen miles of farmland before reaching Deerlodge, the home of Montana's state prison of the same name. Billy looked across the river toward irrigated fields of alfalfa, green against the blue sky above them. It had been days since he'd seen a cloud, and he wondered when the annual forest fires would start up. He'd thought of fighting fires the summer after his stint in college, when the block held him fast, but decided it was too dangerous. He'd gone to work as a campground attendant in Glacier National Park instead, cleaning tent sites, walking around with an air of authority, finding it tolerable work until someone told him they'd seen a grizzly bear nearby. After that, he couldn't sleep, certain each noise was the bear, eager to maul someone (very likely the attendant).

A week of sleep deprivation was enough, and from Glacier Billy took a single paycheck and headed to the Pacific Northwest. Over into Washington and upper Oregon in his beat-up station wagon. He'd liked the big trees along the coast. Giant frond-leaved cedar, tall larch, and ponderosa pine, whose bark flaked off in endlessly interesting patterns of red and orange. He'd seen where the Columbia River dumps into the Pacific, and now, driving past Drummond, the halfway point between Butte and Missoula, he remembered thinking at the time that if he'd waded in its waters, molecules from the streets of Butte, molecular chunks of sidewalk washed into the great river's source, Silver Bow Creek, might wash over him, and how bizarre it was to think that they had arrived at the same place as he had without the aid of six hundred and eighty-two dollars. He'd wondered about it all afternoon, sitting in the dense fog in Portland, until in the end it had made him homesick. He'd felt Butte was washing away an atom at a time, draining out into the ocean he heard and smelled in front of him.

Andrea was asleep by the time Drummond dropped out of view, resting her head against the door. Why did she need to close her eyes when she slept? Billy wondered. He looked at her for a second, but visions of the lingerie he'd seen in the storage shed quickly sent his eyes back to the road. The Rock Creek exit came and passed, the cliffs along the interstate there, where bighorn sheep sometimes gather, giving way to the clear-cut sides of the Sapphire Mountains.

There were half a dozen cars parked near the natural hot springs twenty miles east of Missoula. Billy had heard tropical fish swam in their waters, introduced from a pet store in Idaho years ago, and that had fully cured him of any inkling he'd ever had to soak there. What if a deadly poisonous stonefish was among the implants? Innocent-looking enough as a fry, it could conceivably have been mixed in with the guppies. Now, a decade later, it was lying just off a sulfur-spewing vent on the bottom, its hundred spines blending perfectly with the gray rock around it. Little did the frolicking bathers above know that below them lay one of the world's most venomous creatures. The Discovery Channel narrator had put the stonefish in the same class as the gaboon viper and the red South American frog whose name but not appearance slipped Billy's mind.

Stonefish, coelacanth, monkfish, pallid sturgeon, walking catfish, shore-rat-eating brown trout. Billy ran through a small portion of the list of fish that he reminded himself of each time the thought of wetting a line entered his head. The whole problem with fishing was that you never really knew what you'd catch. For some, this was the thrill. For Billy, it was the horror, and he couldn't get the thought of lobed fins out of his head until he reached Missoula.

"Andrea." He said her name loudly and hoped she would wake up. He dreaded having to reach over and touch her. He wasn't sure why that thought repulsed him, but it did. "Andrea!"

"Don't yell. I hear good." She stretched her arms toward the dash and brushed at her hair. "Ve are in Missoula?"

"Yes."

"Then ve go to da Stardust Saloon," she said.

The *Stardust*? Were there two of them? The only Stardust Billy knew was the big strip club out on the western edge of the city. In the current wave of political correctness that had swept over Missoula, it was in the news two or three times a year, most recently less than a week ago, when one of the strippers had been bitten by a trucker.

"Are you sure you mean . . ." Billy wasn't sure himself how to explain to Andrea that she'd asked to go to what he, Doug, and Hector referred to as the titty bar.

"Yah, I mean da Stardust. Yous don't go in if yous don't vant."

Little chance of that. Billy grinned. This job was panning out pretty well. Paid to go to the Stardust. Not a bad way to be cut off.

"In case yous iz wondering, I vant to help da girls."

"Help?" Had she been a dance instructor?

"Yah. Dey iz treated very poorly, I tink. I heard about da one who got bit, and I tink I can maybe assist some. It iz a good ting to do vith my money."

Billy wasn't sure about the Save the Strippers Foundation. He had always assumed most of the girls enjoyed their line of work, but Andrea was old and blind, and if this meant something to her, he figured there were worse ways to spend a little money. Like his mother buying Chuck's, for instance. Well, she'd get hers when Old Stan stepped up to the auction block. She'd get hers, and then maybe he'd get his. His money. His thousands. His rent, his car, his high life. It was all coming, and damn soon, too. And in the meantime, what could he see for six dollars? While Saint Andrea went about her business, Billy would find out.

Inside the Stardust, it took Billy's eyes almost a minute to adjust to the dim lighting. He looked at Andrea beside him and thought to himself that whatever else being blind was, it wasn't adjusting to the dark. A narrow corridor lined with psychedelic velvet paintings beneath rows of black lights led to a large room with a cathedral ceiling covered with stars. Billy looked for Orion, the belted hunter, but couldn't find him. A stage ran twenty feet from a curtained doorway out into the room between a couple of dozen sets of tables, some occupied by men, several of whom had large stacks of one-dollar bills beside them.

"I go do my business now. Yous check out da entertainment if yous vant." Andrea drifted off, accompanied by one of the three bouncers, a pudgy-looking man who was probably a black belt or very good with a club.

Billy took a stage-side seat just as the DJ announced the next dancer.

"Put your hands together for Storie," he said. Billy clapped hard as Storie burst through the curtain at the end of the stage, her white plastic outfit glowing violet in the black lights.

Billy laid a dollar bill on the edge of the stage. Down to five now, he thought, while Storie twirled around a shiny pole a few times, then threw herself down in a split next to the dollar. Oh, oh. That was a nifty trick. She bent forward and picked up the bill with the tip of her tongue, winked, then blew Mr. Washington over her shoulder. Nice, but someone should tell her how filthy money is. Billy brushed a hand across his mouth. Once upon a time, Storie, there was a girl who couldn't keep money out of her mouth. He'd like to tell her that tale while she sat on his knee.

By the end of Storie's three songs, Billy figured it was the wisest six-dollar investment he'd ever made. He wondered how many of the things that Storie did might Buff be able to do? A good many, he hoped. Especially that work with the ice cube.

Out of money, Billy was forced to sit farther from the stage, and though he tried, he couldn't get a satisfactory view of the dancers. They knew exactly who had the money and just how to give those men a private peek. Judging by the way they smiled, he couldn't believe Andrea would convert any of them. He looked for the girl who'd been bitten, but she didn't make an appearance, and it wasn't until the bouncer told him Andrea was waiting outside that he saw her. The two women were talking near the Chevy, the dancer bandaged on her cheek. He politely kept his distance, but the ladies were finished. He smiled and said hello to the dancer as she walked past him, and she returned the greeting, though it was evident that the bandages made her self-conscious.

"It iz settled," Andrea said firmly as soon as Billy started the car. "All of dem is leaving."

All of them? They must have humored her to no end.

"Where are they going to go?" Billy wondered what Andrea had offered.

"To a much better arrangement. Safe place."

"What were you talking about with the girl who was bitten?"

"I tells her if it vas me I would have killed the man who did it."

Oh. Billy didn't like how matter-of-factly Andrea said that. It didn't sound like an empty threat. He decided he'd better make it a real point never to be late for work. Never late, and never, never bite. Not even his own lip.

"Ve go get good food now, yah?"

Billy swung the car toward the center of town. There was a steakhouse on the Clark Fork decorated with all manner of antique weapons, implements of war from every culture, endlessly fascinating and at the same time quite frightening. Billy remembered the great opening of the blunderbuss from England and the crossbow that could shoot an iron bolt through a barrel of sand. There were samurai swords from Japan and knobkerries from central Africa, and the last time Billy had been there, on his way back from the mouth of the Columbia, the restaurant had made plans to purchase a French catapult. One of the great trebuchet models. One like the Turks used to hurl bodies infected with the black plague over the walls of European cities. The Discovery Channel had taught him all about it.

But now, to Billy's immense disappointment, the restaurant had changed hands, and its new owners had dispensed with the weapons. They'd even taken the glass case of derringers down. No more multibarreled pepperboxes to look at while you ate your steak. Too bad.

"Tells me, Mr. Briztol." Andrea expertly worked a spoonful of soup into her mouth without taking her blue eyes off him. "Did yous and Buff have fun on da date?"

Billy realized he hadn't thanked her. "We did. Thanks for setting it up."

"Yah, you iz quite welcome. And yous go out again tonight?"

"Yes, I think so." She'd called the day before to set it up, drawing out the hours for Billy into interminable periods of light and dark when all he could think about was how good Buff would smell. He loved Calgon so much.

"I tink her parents maybe come tonight, yah?"

Billy coughed hard. Soup was meant to be swallowed, not inhaled. Parents? Buff hadn't mentioned that.

"Maybe yous all go for a ride or something nice. Yah?"

It would be nice if they did no such thing. Billy coughed again.

"I'm sure it vill be big fun. And den the two of yous can maybe take a stroll at night." Andrea closed her eyes and slowly shook her head. "Does you know how long it has been since I tooks a stroll at night vith a man?"

It wasn't a question she wanted answered, and staring at her rocking back and forth in her chair, Billy suddenly felt sorry for her. It must be lonely being old and blind, he thought. If the waitress hadn't come with his T-bone just then, he might have told her he'd take her for a nighttime stroll some evening. As it was, the immediate prospect of holding off starvation for a few more days took precedence.

Billy dove into his beef with a passion, slicing huge, juicy chunks off his steak, forking them into his mouth with gluttonous speed. He cleaned his plate in five minutes and spent another fifteen wondering if he could snake Andrea's baked potato away without her knowing it. If she hadn't made the comment about strolling with a man, he might have tried.

Billy thought about what she'd said again that day, as he walked back from her house to his apartment in the late afternoon sun. Passing Pendergrast's Pharmacy, looking at the boarded-up windows, he drew a parallel between Andrea and the shop and again felt sad. If he were a painter, he'd paint a picture of a woman standing in a garden of every imaginable flower. And the woman would have a blind person's cane. It was an image he had trouble shaking, one that did not go away until he'd showered and dressed for his date, and then all thoughts turned to Buff and her parents, and while he knew it wasn't a good idea to ask the spirits for assistance in these matters, he couldn't help saying a quick prayer to Mary. He didn't ask for a wonderful time, only that he not regret it. He doubted that would offend her.

The duck-billed platypus is one of Australia's more venomous land animals. Its spurs contain a neurotoxin that proves most unpleasant to the unwary handler."

Billy listened to the Discovery Channel narrator while he waited for Buff, trying to figure out exactly what the platypus was. Whatever genus it fit into, he'd never lose any sleep that it hadn't evolved in Montana. Australia, home of the deadly bushmaster snake, was a good place for the platypus. Billy didn't figure he'd be heading to the land down under anytime soon. Yes, there were opal mines and the chance of stumbling across a gem of untold value, but compared with the odds of being bitten by something that would require the victim to "immediately receive antivenom or face dire consequences," they were infinitely small. And as one of the locals gleefully told the narrator of the program Billy now watched, "Australia's got a lot of ways to kill you, but she don't always like to do it very fast." The camera panned over a flock of sheep, one of them writhing about on its side, "felled to the vicious kick of a platypus."

Enough. Billy changed the channel just as the phone rang. Why did that noise always send his heart into his mouth?

Was it Buff? Damn the oversight of not having caller ID. Billy let it ring five times before picking up. Like fishing, the problem with answering the phone is that you never know what you're going to find on the other end of the line, he thought.

"Hell-o, Bill-y," a voice said.

Pendergrast. Jesus, what could he want at . . . it was almost six-thirty.

"How are youuuu?"

Was that *Petie*? Billy imagined the bespectacled puppet waving at him.

"We want-ed to check in on you. See how Bill-y is do-ing."

Billy shook his head.

"Si-lence is not a good sign." Pendergrast's voice went neatly up the scale as he spoke. "Want an-other vis-it?"

"I'm doing very well, thank you." He imagined Petie's little head nodding vigorously at the prospect of another visit. "Getting ready to go out on a date."

"Hear that, Petie? Billy has a date," the doctor said.

Billy hoped Petie wasn't the jealous kind. He didn't need a malicious puppet stalking him.

"This is good news, Billy. Very, very good. And what about the dean? How are your dean thoughts?"

Billy said nothing. Let him take the silence any way he wished.

"Not so good there." It sounded as though Pendergrast was writing. He probably had that clipboard with him. Or maybe Petie was writing. "I've . . . well, we've been thinking a lot about our nice talk the other day, Billy, and we just wanted you to know that we're in your corner. You can turn to us any time you want. You go ahead and call in the middle of the night if you'd like. Do you think you'd like that? Or maybe you'd prefer us to call you. Would that be better? What time would be good? One? Two?"

If Pendergrast ever rang his phone in the wee hours of the morning, Billy would do whatever it took to make sure he found a . . . a duck-billed platypus in his mailbox a day or two later. Spurs pointed outward and in a foul mood.

"Not that late," he said.

"Well, you just let us know. And keep your eyes peeled for that meddler, too. We're onto his tricks, Billy."

A woman said something in the background, but her voice was too weak to make out what. "The Crying Room," Pendergrast bellowed at her. "I'll be in after a minute. That one may not make it, Billy," he said sadly. "Petie doesn't think so, either." The doctor sighed. "Well, we're off to do our best now. You remember to call."

"Bye, bye, Bill-y."

Petie signed off and Billy hung up. And then the phone rang again. What did he have this time? Another stonefish? He lifted the receiver without saying anything.

"Billy, honey, you there?"

Monkfish. Or maybe a burbot. Unpleasant either way. Billy set the phone down. Better to cut the line. The next time it rang, he let it. Mother would assume she had the wrong number the first time.

"Hey-ho, nobody home," he sang on his way down the stairs, the phone ringing in the background. He'd wait outside for Buff. She should be there within fifteen minutes, and then he could put mothers, psychiatrists, telephones, and platypuses out of his head. And he was eager to do that, too.

Buff had techno-dance music cranked up on her Alpine. Billy heard the steady throb of bass before he saw her car, and as the Pontiac cruised up Washoe, he grinned. A nice, sporty red car was going to stop and pick him up. He loved the way Buff looked behind the tinted glass, mirrored sunglasses against blond hair. Mmmmm. He noticed she had her leather bag in the back again. Was she going bronc busting tonight? Billy hoped so.

Inside the car, Billy was surrounded by speakers. He could feel the music coursing through him, his loose-fitting shirt pulsing from the beat.

"You and me, baby, ain't nothing but mammals, so let's do it like they do on the Discovery Channel." The metallic voice boomed out from all around him, and Billy bit his lip hard so he wouldn't laugh. All he could picture was one of the platypuses hopping up on the other in a mating frenzy. He looked over at Buff, then looked away. Was platypus style in any of the books?

Buff snapped the stereo off when the song ended, but kept tapping on the wheel. Billy noticed that she had a fine sense of rhythm.

"I thought maybe we would meet my folks and go for a ride. Is that all right with you?" she said.

It was a good thing Andrea had prepared him for this. It took a little of the sting out of it. "That's fine."

"Are you sure?"

Billy squirmed in his seat but hid it well by adjusting his seatbelt. "Yes."

"Okay. We won't go too far. Then you and I can do something if you want."

Oh, yes.

"They're staying over at the McQueen," Buff said.

The McQueen. The eight-story, recently renovated hotel named for a section of Butte swallowed by Berkeley Pit. Billy had heard that they'd even brought in Italian stonecutters to redo the granite pillars. It probably cost a pretty penny to stay there, and because having rich in-laws never hurt, Billy settled back into his seat and concentrated on breathing deeply. Think about later on and the little leather bag, he told himself. He wondered if Buff had the *Lone Ranger* theme on CD for her stereo. That would be quite a thing.

"We'll make them ride with us," Buff said as she pulled into the carriage port at the McQueen. A moment later her mother, the same woman Billy had spoken with on his way to Pendergrast's, walked through the revolving door. Billy got out and opened the back door for her, an action that seemed to both please and embarrass the lady, though he doubted she was used to anything other than first-rate treatment.

"Your father's got a touch of the flu," she said to Buff. "He's been lying around all day complaining. Personally, I think it may be an excuse to get out of taking me up to the statue. He said he didn't feel like going this evening. Sounded like I was supposed to stay with him, but I didn't come all the way out here to mope about in a hotel room." She reached her hand over the seat, and said to Billy, "I'm Susan, Buff's mom."

Billy took the lady's hand and shook it gently.

"Billy," he said. "I actually think we met the other day on the sidewalk."

"Oh, of course. I didn't recognize you all dressed up."

Billy had a nice Wrangler button-down on. Sharp, but hardly dressy.

"Buff tells me you're a writer."

Billy nodded.

"And what wonderful country to write about. Or, maybe you aren't regional. I guess I'm jumping the gun. It is wonderful country, though."

Billy stared out his window into the setting sun. It was dropping behind the Pintlars, falling far to the north of where it would be during the winter. He wondered what he would be doing when winter came. Huddled in his alley with his belongings? Not if he could help it. But that, he thought, was the whole point—he couldn't help it. Men were in charge of their own destiny only to a certain point. From there, the Fates took over, and it seemed to Billy that they took a great deal of pleasure in watching some suffer. He imagined them sitting around a table in the sky discussing the day's schedule.

"Whom shall we make shuffle today? How about Billy Bristol? He's always fun."

Billy wondered if they resided in the west or the east. For all he knew they could be watching him right now.

"Well, what would you like to see, Mom?" Buff waited for an answer before pulling into the street.

"Could we take a look at the pit?"

Billy's mouth grew dry. The Berkeley Pit should be the eighth wonder of the world, he thought. It was the only place he'd ever seen, and he'd only seen it once, where the more you looked the deeper it appeared. A few years ago he'd made the mistake of peering down into the great hole from the observation deck on Continental Drive, and he'd damn near lost his balance to vertigo. Good thing there was a railing there or he would still be falling. In his opinion, the Berkeley Pit was a testament to man's ability to carve. Michelangelo might look at a block of marble and see an angel waiting inside for his chisel, but to look at a mountain and see a hole to hell, now that took vision.

"Oh, why do you want to see a big hole in the ground?" Buff didn't move the car. "It's filling with water so fast it doesn't look like much anymore."

Billy begged to differ, but he certainly wasn't going to argue in favor of viewing the pit. Once had been enough. He had heard something about the rate at which water was seeping in, and there had been a few nights when he'd lain awake wondering what would happen when it filled up, but because his apartment was uphill from the pit, he hadn't given it too much thought.

"Well, your father and I came into town on a lovely road—lots of corners on it—right over the Continental Divide. That was nice."

This woman certainly had a sense of adventure. Harding Way, the old road over Pipestone Pass through the Highlands east of Butte, was a close second to the Going to the Sun Highway. There were places on it where a slight miscalculation meant tumbling a thousand feet or more off a mountain. And Billy would be on the side closest to the cliffs.

"That works. We can drive over to Whitehall. There's an ice cream shop there that stays open until nine or ten."

Billy cringed. Harding Way was a route he avoided at all costs, and even the prospect of a big dollop of maple-walnut ice cream wouldn't ordinarily entice him over the pass. He looked at the slit in the mountains where the road wound through. It was dotted with white crosses its entire length, memorials to luckless travelers who had plummeted to their deaths. Before the interstate went through, there were five or six fatalities each month. More in the winter. Billy had always wondered if that's what had happened to his father.

Now, heading out of Butte on Continental Drive, past the turnout for the pit, past the old brick hospital, under the East Ridge and Mary—her stone robe glowing in the evening sun— Billy closed his eyes and thought of his father, a man he would forever connect with the smell of a pipe, coarse chin whiskers, and Carhart coveralls. He'd left when Billy was three. Gotten into his Malibu, revved the souped-up engine, and roared off toward Harding Way. Billy remembered watching as the car became a light-blue speck against the dark-blue Highlands.

"Billy, honey, you come inside now," he could hear his mother saying, and he'd never seen his father again. Not that night at supper, or the following morning at breakfast, or even at Christmas. In time, Billy decided he must have gone off the road and so never would accompany his friends on salvage runs to the bottom of the canyons along the highway, where they picked through the twisted remains of cars each spring, bringing home eyeglasses from glove boxes, maps and atlases from under the seats, and occasionally a suitcase or other personal effects from a trunk they managed to jimmy open. Billy never went with them, because he always wondered if somewhere at the foot of one of those cliffs was a light-blue Chevy Malibu. He kept his eyes closed the whole way up the pass, head turned toward the window so Buff and her mother thought he was looking out. And despite closing his eyes, he could see rusted cars, broken every way imaginable, their windshields shattered and roofs caved in, tires flat and wheels missing. The Malibu was mangled worse than any of them, twisted almost beyond recognition.

Billy didn't open his eyes until he felt the car crest the top of the mountain. He was sweating and felt as though he'd been holding his breath. He reached over and touched Buff's leg, wrapping his hand tight around hers when she lowered it to him. Before them, the sky over the Tobacco Root Range was turning deep purple, the bare rock peaks jutting into it, their individual features standing out sharply. One star shone bright above them, and as Billy stared at it, he wondered how long it took for its light to reach them. The Discovery Channel narrator said some stars were so far away that they had burned out millions of years ago, and yet their light was still visible because it took so long to travel the distance. He wondered if he could see earth from the star, and if it shone, too. If so, it would shine long after the world was gone. Billy reminded himself to keep track of that thought. Maybe there was an essay in it somewhere.

The green, irrigated fields along the Jefferson River were filling up with whitetail deer, does and spotted fawns venturing into the alfalfa from the cover of cottonwoods along the river. Susan remarked on them, and Buff pulled over to watch one group of seven or eight that was feeding close to the road. Billy kept his eyes peeled across the field in the lengthening shadows of greasewood and rosebushes. He was certain a great buck lurked back there, waiting for it to grow dark before making himself visible, and Billy had always been a little uneasy around antlered game. He'd found a winter-killed bull elk one spring when he was a boy, its body ravaged by coyotes and ravens, its antlers cocked back over its head at an odd angle, their dark tines beginning to weather, one tip chewed off by a porcupine.

Then there had been the nontypical mule deer that made an appearance when he was picking sugar beets near Terry. That freak of nature had twenty or twenty-five points to a side, its antlers grown together like wild vines. It had trotted the length of the field, head held high as if proud of its genetic mutation. No, Billy didn't mind the does and fawns, but he was relieved when Buff headed down the road again toward Whitehall before anything else appeared.

The ice cream shop was only ten miles away, but by the time they got there it was dark. Billy remembered how when he was in college it had taken him several weeks to cease being amazed at the phenomenon of twilight. In the West, day changed to night as swiftly as summer to winter.

"It gets dark fast here, doesn't it?" he asked Susan.

"Yes." She was looking back toward the Highlands. "And it sure is dark. I never knew a person could look at so much country without seeing a light. Those mountains must be thirty miles long, and there's . . . well . . . there's nothing."

Billy stared at the Highlands, a dark smear against a darker sky. She was right. Well, almost right. There was more than nothing up there, he thought, but sometimes he wished it wasn't true.

"Easy to see how Sasquatch legends persist out here," Susan said.

Jesus, could she read his mind? Billy hoped not. He would have to be extra careful not to think about the widow's walk in her presence. He strained into the night, then shuddered. He wasn't at all sure that the Sasquatch was a legend. People thought the coelacanth had been extinct for 300 million years until one turned up off the coast of . . . Madagascar? Yes, that's where it was. Billy remembered because he'd made a note never to set foot on those shores. Leave that great luminescent-eyed fish to the scientists and evolution experts.

"I wonder if Sasquatch stories existed before whites moved west?" Susan said.

Billy nodded gravely and said they did, though in truth he had no idea.

"My grandmother used to tell stories about a similar creature that hunted at night and ate horses." Another lie. Billy had never known either of his grandmothers. "My great-great grandfather's trapping partner, a Flathead Indian, supposedly found a dead one when he was young. Frozen into a glacier in the Bitterroot Mountains near Idaho." He was getting out of control now, but Buff's mother seemed to like a story. She stared wide-eyed, letting her ice cream slowly melt. "Said it was covered from head to toe with long, silky hair. And bigger than any man."

"That's amazing," she said.

Yes, indeed. Billy stole a glance at Buff, not as easily fooled as her mother, he figured, but she didn't seem to be paying any attention. She was watching two little girls engaged in a race to see who would finish their ice cream first.

"Too bad Carl wasn't here for this. He loves history." Susan licked at her cone, and Billy saw where Buff got her lovely tongue.

"That is an understatement." Buff sounded just as happy her father was missing out. "My dad's the only man in Montana who can tell you when every war there ever was began and ended, how old each of our presidents was when he took office, and how many square miles there are in Mongolia. And all of it, with seventy cents, might get him a cup of coffee at the R&R."

"Buff." Her mother elbowed her in the side.

"It's true, Mom, and you know it."

"Your father has spent a great deal of time studying. It's been his passion."

"Lucky you."

"Hey!" She elbowed her again, and Billy began to feel uncomfortable. He would have walked away if he hadn't been trying to figure out why the name *Carl* had unsettled him.

"And so what's the deal now? He's suddenly going from books to bars? Not that I think it's a bad choice, but isn't it rather sudden?" Buff said.

Books to bars? Billy thought it a fine choice. Books to bars, books to brews. This Carl couldn't be all bad. Not at all.

"Yes, well . . . I admit it's different." Susan turned to Billy. "My husband has it in his head that he's going to buy a bar. Wants to turn it into an authentic Irish pub. I think he's read about one in a book somewhere. I told him New York City would be a better place for such a thing—he's talking bagpipers and the whole bit— but he misses his daughter. It really is too bad he didn't come tonight. His worst fear is that Buff will end up with a lousy man. I've told him a million times she's too smart for that, but he seems convinced."

Unfounded fear? Billy wondered. Let's see . . . what could he offer this book man's daughter? A romp on the widow's walk. Well, that's one thing. And what about his mother's thousands? That would be a fine little nest egg. But, more important, what could the book man offer him? Any man who entertains the notion of having bagpipers at his beck and call must be well off. Susan didn't look as if she was used to anything but the high life. Her fancy perm wasn't something new, and her clothes were of the best brands not because she cared if others noticed but because that's who she was. Billy looked at her and saw Buff in twenty-five years. Still easy on the eyes, he thought. He imagined them out for a Sunday drive in the Chevy. Not over Harding Way, either.

On the ride back to Butte, mercifully on the interstate this time, Billy again thought of Buff in the Chevy. He could see her so clearly in the seat beside him. No, better yet, in the driver's seat.

Let him ride in style. Were cigars worth taking up? Perhaps those fat Cubans that were kept in fine hardwood humidors. Billy's nostrils flared, and for an instant he believed he smelled tobacco. Or maybe he would smoke a pipe. Not a yellow corncob like his father's, but something ornate and very expensive from a country like Denmark. Did they make pipes in Denmark? Ebony bowls with German silver tips? Inlaid strips of teak? Such a creation would be worthy of his lips. He puckered his mouth and inhaled deeply. Yes, he could smell tobacco.

Topping the Continental Divide for the second time in less than two hours, Billy could see the lights of Butte before them, a great circle of yellow and white points against a greater darkness that was the rest of Montana.

"It looks so big from up here," Susan said. "My god, like Chicago."

It was true. At night, Butte appeared ten times as large as it was, an odd illusion as the city had no suburbs. Billy liked this nighttime view, especially since he couldn't see Berkeley Pit, the most dominating daytime landmark. He could almost forget about the underground tunnels and shafts he lived above.

"The runway's pretty." Buff pointed to the mile-long strip of blue lights that led away from Butte toward Harding Way. A small plane was taking off, the rotating red beacon on its tail blinking as it taxied.

Billy had heard that some couples parked at the end of the runway and let Delta's big 727s come in over their cars. That sort of sport wasn't for him. He'd heard too much on the Discovery Channel about wake turbulence to risk being blown end over end for a cheap thrill. One of those babies comes in too low, and it's all over, he thought.

So where would he take Buff when they dropped her mother off? It wasn't a question he'd given any thought to, because until very recently it wasn't in the realm of possibility. Better not to think about something that won't . . . that can't happen. A good way to have high hopes dashed to pieces and make a man shuffle. Billy scuffed his feet on the floor mat. Yes, they still remembered how.

The McQueen was lit up with orange lights, its yellow bricks glowing in a way that made Billy wonder if the old building harbored something evil. He wished they'd parked farther away.

"Buff, we brought a bag of stuff for you," Susan said before she hauled open the hotel's enormous front door. "We're parked behind the hotel. You want my key so that you can stop by and get it?"

Buff took the key from her mother's ring. From where Billy sat watching in the car, it looked to be a delicate tool. He hoped it fit a Jaguar or Mercedes. Buff kissed her mother quickly on the cheek, then let the hotel swallow her, the big door closing with a *whoosh.*

"So, where to?" Buff said eagerly, shutting the door hard enough to make Billy believe she was glad to be rid of her mother.

Yes, where to? What about the M? The giant lighted letter erected by Montana Tech on the hill above the city? That was a popular spot, but doubtlessly well patrolled by the police. These days, they seemed big on indecent acts, too, and would probably be as happy to bust a writer as a pro football or baseball player. Billy shrugged.

"No suggestions?"

"No, I guess not," he said.

"Would you like to get a drink somewhere?"

Billy hoped that this lady would marry him. "That sounds good." And oh, did it!

"Chuck's?" Buff said.

I'm in love. Billy imagined little winged hearts flitting about his head the way they did on Saturday-morning cartoons when a pretty cat walked by Sylvester. That was his name, wasn't it? He thought so.

"Chuck's it is," he said with authority, already feeling the first beer on his tongue.

Buff wheeled away from the McQueen and toward Main Street.

Billy stared up the street toward the traffic light and between the yellow flashes said to himself, "It all starts here." Mary was shining behind him, still watching, no doubt, but even she couldn't begrudge him a drink or two at Chuck's.

"I'll be good," he whispered.

Every parking spot on both sides of Main Street for one hundred yards up and down from Chuck's was full. Buff cruised past the bar and turned onto Iron Street, one of Butte's narrow, east–west streets named for a metal. Platinum, Iron, Silver. Billy knew which he would live on, and it wasn't sold by the ounce. They pulled in next to a long, two-tone van with a bumper sticker that read IF THIS VAN'S A ROCKIN', DON'T COME A KNOCKIN'. Billy watched Buff read it to herself and smile. How odd it is, he thought. A few weeks earlier he never would have guessed.

Someone had pulled the poster advertising the upcoming auction down from Chuck's door, possibly in response to Buff's father suggesting that he would bring in bagpipers. He pulled the door toward himself and held it for Buff, a blue haze of cigarette smoke curling out into Main Street. There was a sign behind the bar proclaiming WE SMOKE, SO FU, and it was the truth. The ceiling in Chuck's was low, and the air was as thick with smoke as it had been all over southwest Montana in 1988, when Yellowstone Park burned. Billy remembered how it had blotted out the sun for days, ash settling on the streets of Butte like snow each time the wind blew from the east.

"Bristol!" Leslie Booth roared and the bar fell silent. Even the song on the jukebox ended. Billy had forgotten about this foul-tempered beast, and now, edging back toward the door, keeping a close eye on Booth, who brandished a bottle of rum in her man-like hand, he figured he'd be lucky to get out alive.

"Thump-um thump-um," Hector shouted from somewhere in the smoke. Billy groped for the door handle, his hand finding nothing. The motion was detected instantly by the Amazonian bartender.

"I don't think so." Booth was over the bar in a flash, quick as a Discovery Channel tiger pouncing on an Indian water buffalo. And she still had the rum bottle.

"Bust-um skull!" Hector sounded closer. "Killie, killie, killie!"

Where was Buff? Billy searched the smoke, his eyes darting from one end of the bar to the other. Oh, Buff, let my last sight be of you. Wasn't there a Marty Robbins ballad . . . ? And what would it hurt to give me a little peek under your shirt? A dying man's last request. Booth raised the bottle high over her head, her other hand finding Billy's neck, thick, calloused fingers tightening around his windpipe.

"You gonna pay your tab tonight?"

Booth's eyes twitched, and the hairs on her chin—thick, black stubble that undoubtedly resisted every manner of clipper short of a hedge trimmer—bristled like the guard hairs on a

Russian wild boar. That's what she reminded Billy of. A giant forest hog like the one that had put its Siberian pursuers "to flight" on the National Geographic special he'd seen on the Soviet Union's wildlife.

"Yes or no, Bristol?" The pig arched backward, its bottle raised to the full extent of its elephantine arms.

Billy squeaked something that sounded like "yes."

"Speak up, you little pissant." Booth's breath was hot and sour in his face. What the hell did she eat? Or what the hell *didn't* she eat? "I'll crack your head like an eggshell."

"Brains," Hector said solemnly. "Spill-um." He emerged from the smoke and nodded approvingly, a grave expression on his face, his hands folded across his chest in his best Crazy Horse imitation.

And then there was Buff, sliding into view from the ladies' room, firm legs bringing her closer, one hand outstretched, an angel ready to whisk Billy up, up, and away. He reached for her, but instead of taking his hand she snatched the rum bottle, twisting it free, a feat of strength the world had not witnessed since King Arthur pulled Excalibur from the stone. Booth snarled, let go of Billy, and turned her head just in time to catch the bottle against her temple, where it exploded in a mist of glass and liquid. Her beady eyes dimmed, her knees buckled, and she sank slowly to the floor, one great paw finding a barstool to keep her from toppling onto her back. As stunned as Billy, she lifted her eyes to Buff, shook her head, and licked her lips, a thick tongue lapping the rum that dripped from her forehead.

"Nice shot," she whispered, as she pulled herself to her feet and stumbled back behind the bar, striking a young man full in the face for snickering, sending him off his stool into the puddle of alcohol.

Hector unfolded his arms to give the umpire's safe signal as a sign that it was finished, and the jukebox broke the silence with a Guns N' Roses song. As Buff led Billy toward the back of the bar, everyone gave her plenty of room, and Booth was both quick and pleasant when she took their order.

It took Billy three gulps and three quarters of his beer before he could speak, and the "thank-you" he stammered seemed to go unnoticed by Buff, who sat across from him at their little table, peeling the label from her Coors, not so much as a hair out of place. She drank slowly and easily, and as Billy watched he began to worry that he had bitten off more than he could chew. What could he look forward to if he failed to satisfy her? Being dominated was one thing, having the shit kicked out of him was another. And she'd smashed Booth with so little effort. What could she do if she really exerted herself? Billy ran a hand down his ribs, trying to remember the best position to hold if attacked by a bear. Knees drawn in, hands clasped behind the neck, he thought, hoping very much that it wouldn't come to that. He stole a glance at his crotch. Buck up, boys, we've got a live one here.

"I probably didn't need to do that," Buff finally said. "Learned it from a great big southern gal working in a dance club in Orlando one summer. Cleo. That was her name."

What else had Cleo taught her?

"I'm glad Daddy didn't have to see it." She looked around the bar and frowned. "I can't believe he's seriously considering getting into this business."

"So's my mother." Billy said it without thinking. He would just as soon leave his mother out of any conversations with Buff.

"Really?"

Too late. The door had been opened. "Wants to expand the Adult Activities Center she runs."

"That's not a bad idea."

Yes, yes it is. How to tell her? "Well, she doesn't really need to."

"No?" Buff said.

"No. And she said she wouldn't serve alcohol here. Just spaghetti."

"I know a great recipe."

This wasn't going anywhere Billy wanted it to. What did?

"I'm kidding." Buff reached for his hand, and it was only with the greatest effort that he didn't draw away. "Do you think she's got a chance at buying it?"

"I hope not. I expect Andrea's cab driver will end up with it. Old Stan. He won the lottery and plans on sinking it all into this. But I guess that wouldn't be too bad."

"So he's the one who hit the Montana Cash. I read something in the paper about a Butte man's numbers coming up. Lucky guy."

Not really. Billy figured it was preordained for people like Stan to win lotteries. Luck didn't have much to do with it.

"Your father is serious about bagpipers?"

Buff took the longest sip of the evening from her beer. "God only knows. I certainly hope not. Can you imagine it? I mean, look around. Is this the type of crowd that's going to belly up to Guinness? I don't see it happening."

Billy did look around. He knew almost everyone in the bar. They were the same people who'd been coming in for fifteen years. Occasionally a new face would appear, and every once in a while someone would disappear, but for the most part Chuck's, and all the uptown bars, had a regular set of customers who, like union workers on strike, wouldn't dream of crossing the line to another establishment. Billy wondered what would happen when Chuck's patrons grew too old to drink every night. There was no young blood for the uptown bars anymore, and suddenly he felt sad. Ten or twenty more years and a whole way of life would come to a close. Everything would be down on the flats and the uptown would be nothing more than a historic curiosity to tourists. He thought of Pendergrast's Pharmacy and how lonely a place it was.

"That's what it's all coming to," he whispered. "One big ghost town."

"Ready?" Buff set her bottle down and stood up.

Billy rose slowly, and walked even slower to the door. The row of square pillars in the center of the bar, names carved into them, some from fifty years ago, stood like tombstones in the smoke, the rows of hats hanging eerily over them like the souls of the long dead. Billy shook his head and didn't look back. He did hope Stan could buy it. However he ran it, it would remain essentially the same, and in that thought there was comfort. He understood that change was inevitable, but it didn't need to come tomorrow.

Buff drove west out of town without asking Billy where he wanted to go. That was just as well. Let her make the decision. A mile past Rocker she swung south on Interstate 15, the radio on, her fingers tapping the wheel, an old rhythm from Billy's past that he couldn't place. Melrose? Was that where she was taking him? That was a nice little town—on the Big Hole River at the foot of the Pioneer Mountains. And there were a couple of small bars there, too. Billy eased back in his seat, picturing a quiet game of pool in a Melrose bar. And perhaps the owner would let them stay after closing. Close-cropped green felt, the leather bag . . . it was almost as good as the widow's walk. Two ball, center pocket. The fantasy faded as Buff flipped her blinker on and braked to make the Feeley exit. Billy sat up straight now.

"Ever been on this road?" Buff asked as she wheeled onto the dirt lane leading up the back side of the Highlands. A small brown Forest Service sign read BUTTE 27.

Nearly thirty miles of narrow road through inhospitable country. No place to break down, no place for a sporty automobile, no place to travel at night . . . just the sort of place for a Sasquatch. Billy began to shiver.

"Cold?" Buff turned the heater on. "I love roads like this at night. You never know what you're going to see."

No, indeed you don't. Better to keep your eyes closed and see only darkness. Billy turned his head and shut his eyes. He could feel the wheels bouncing over loose stones, probably getting ready to come off and strand them miles from anywhere. Mountain men. He opened his eyes and began to panic. If James Dickey had ever visited the Highlands, then *Deliverance* would have been a western novel. Who knew how many freaks there might be clinging to a subsistence living in the mountains' old mining cabins? And who knew how long it had been since they'd seen a woman?

"Do you really think this is a good road to take at night?" Billy asked.

"One of the best. There are always elk on it. See, look." A band of animals streamed across the road in the headlights.

No bull, no bull, no bull. Billy held his breath and wished hard, but to no avail. Last in line he came, velvet-covered antlers held low against his back, his shadow galloping alongside, eyes red in the lights.

"Ahhhh!" Billy cringed.

"God, he was a big fella, wasn't he?"

"Ahhhh!"

"I should get a hunting license some year and come up here," Buff said.

A hunting license? This woman never ceased to amaze.

"That would really set Daddy off. He's . . . well, he's excitable to begin with. Ought to see him when he gets worked up."

Billy was getting worked up himself, fighting not to hyperventilate. Slow and deep, he told himself. One breath at a time.

"There's a spot up here I really like. The old Cow Camp."

Too much. That dilapidated set of buildings undoubtedly housed great numbers of unspeakables. Things that wandered the hills in search of cow skulls to use during nighttime rituals. To the steady beat of tom-toms, Billy imagined hideous beasts linked arm in arm whirling around a charcoal six-pointed star. Not the Cow Camp, Buff. Anything but that.

"Isn't it pretty in the moonlight?" She pointed to the cluster of buildings, pale against paler sagebrush. "Come on." She brought the car to a halt and turned the key. "Walk with me."

Leaving the car was hard for Billy, though staying in it alone would have been much more difficult. He got out and wondered why he began whistling the slow, end-of-war version of "When Johnny Comes Marching Home?" It wasn't the sort of tune that inspired bravery. He hurried its pace as well as his own, walking fast to catch up with Buff, and side by side they made their way to the Cow Camp and the creek beyond.

Billy heard a frog vault off the bank and splash into the water. Better hope there aren't any big browns up here, little man. At the stream's edge, Buff turned quickly, so fast that Billy was afraid she'd seen something on the far bank, and put her hands around his waist. She kissed him then, quickly on his neck at first, standing on her toes to reach his cheek, her tongue hot on his lips.

"Relax," she whispered.

Impossible. Not with the forest so close. Not under the hungry eye of a mountain lion. Billy knew there was one nearby. And what was that? The soft thud of padded feet?

"Notice the involuntary twitch of the tail just before the charge. It is an action common to all felines." The narrator's voice came to him as he watched the sagebrush for a tail tip. Black, aren't they? The tip of a lion's tail is black, right?

"Oh, Billy. Look." Buff spun him toward the Cow Camp, and there, perched on the peak of the highest roof, was an owl. And not just any owl. A great gray owl with eyes the size of saucers. It spread its tremendous wings and stared at them, then pitched forward and sailed away into the night, toward the cries of a pack of coyotes whose haunting chorus sent chills down the length of Billy's back.

"Demons," he whispered as he started toward the car, and though it was an uphill grade he found he did not run out of breath before reaching the road. He climbed in quickly and belted himself into his seat, locking the door as fast as he could.

"Did I do something wrong?" Buff's hand started toward the ignition, then stopped.

Turn the key. Just turn the key. Billy stared at it as hard as he could. "No, it's not you," he said, without taking his eyes off the steering column.

"No? What is it, then?" She was sliding toward him, pressing him against the door, that thin barrier of metal between him and . . . god only knew what. Or perhaps god did not know. Perhaps the fellow who knew lived down below. Billy imagined fork-tailed Lucifer stalking about beneath them.

Please start the car, Buff.

"What's that?" Buff straightened up and looked through the windshield. A gray shape moved into the road, stopped, then drifted out of sight.

Billy began to tremble, his frayed nerves reaching the breaking point. What would happen then? he wondered. Would he come unraveled like a cut violin string? Quite possibly.

"Almost looked like a wolf. Do you think it could have been?" Buff was excited.

Of course, Little Red Riding Hood. Shall we take another stroll down to the Cow Camp? Buff needed to work on her addition of signs. A bull elk plus a great gray owl plus a wolf. The sum of pure evil. Susan wouldn't think these mountains were so empty now, would she?

"Okay, I suppose it's getting late," Buff said.

The witching hour. The time when all creatures offended by daylight take to the wilderness for their nighttime sport. Were there woods nymphs? Billy perked up a little, then shut his eyes and did not open them until he heard the hum of tar under the tires half an hour later. Buff had driven the width of the Highlands without incident, something he never would have supposed possible, especially in the dead of night, proving beyond a doubt that she *was* a remarkable woman. Stopping at the Cow Camp could be forgiven, chalked up to her not knowing any better.

"If you don't mind, I'll grab my stuff from my folks' car," she said as the lights of Butte came into view. From this angle, more to the south, it didn't look so big.

"Sure." Billy could handle a stop at the McQueen, nothing compared with where he'd been earlier. A walk in the park. He'd relaxed enough to let his hand wander toward Buff's leg, and now he wondered if he'd felt a shiver when he touched her. All aquiver with lust, aren't you? Well, well, we're back on my turf now. He moved his hand to the inside of her thigh. Hello.

He was thinking hard about the leather bag when they pulled into the hotel's rear parking lot, and as soon as Buff got out he looked over his shoulder to be sure it was still there. It was, and he liked the view of Buff walking away from him. A very fine wiggle. Billy watched her pull the key her mother had given her from her pocket . . . ummm, tight-fitting pants. And then he saw which car she stopped beside and in an instant, less time than it took him to blink, his life returned to shuffle mode. There, in the orange light of the McQueen, sat a black BMW, its green license plate glowing yellow, DUBL PHD plainly visible.

· 15 ·

At four minutes past midnight, Pendergrast picked up on the first ring, wide awake and attentive. Perhaps he'd just finished a late-night session in the Crying Room.

Billy held the phone with both hands, his entire body trembling, the receiver jumping in front of his mouth like some sleek black creature he was trying to strangle. "Deeean," he stammered. "Da-da-da-deeean."

"Slowly, Billy. Tell Peter very slowly. I'm right here with you." The doctor's voice was calm and encouraging, a demolition expert talking a member of the bomb squad through a complicated defusing.

"Dean has . . ." Billy's breath came in short puffs, restricting his speech to one or two words between gulps of air. "Dean has . . ."

"It's all right, Billy. Take your time. Very, very, slowly."

Billy moved one hand to his chest and began massaging the area directly over his heart. Yellow wire, now. Cut the *yellow* wire. He pictured the tangled mess of wires that was the detonator. Solid state circuits, a mercury switch, needle-nosed pliers all atremble.

"The dean has a daughter," he said.

"How dare he?" Pendergrast thundered. "Who has copulated with this people-hurter? By god, I'll seek her out."

Billy had a vivid sudden vision of a Scandinavian truffle pig, its nose blackened with forest muck, and while truffle pigs in general made him quite nervous, he welcomed this sight because it gave his mind momentary freedom from—as Pendergrast had called them—dean thoughts.

"Of all the great justifications for involuntary castration, this takes the cake. Heads and shoulders better than even the great Philbert's definitive writings on the subject. Billy, do you realize you've offered the world irrefutable proof in favor of a procedure that until now was believed appropriate only for pedophiles, incest mongers, rapists, and sexual sadists?"

Billy shuddered, his hand slipping down to his groin. Whatever the great Philbert had written should be confiscated and set on fire in an Eastern European city square, the blaze ringed by soldiers with automatic weapons . . . Kalashnikovs like the African game wardens carry.

"It is a terrible pity this man was not deprived of his seed, Billy. I fear now his . . . his offspring"—Pendergrast's voice cracked when he said it—"may be in need of more than even I can offer."

"It's worse," Billy whispered.

"Yes, Billy, that is the way with deans. It's *always* worse. What more is there? No, who do I think I am? What more is there? . . . I should be flogged for pressuring. Petie?"

There were several loud thumps on the other end of the line, each one followed by a stifled moan.

"No more," Pendergrast finally pleaded. "Please, no more." But Petie was a vicious bastard, not easily dissuaded, and Billy listened to another round of thumping, every blow resonating more than the last.

"Stop," croaked Pendergrast. "You'll kill me."

While Petie disciplined the doctor, Billy began to wonder if perhaps this bespectacled storm trooper was better suited to helping him than Pendergrast.

"Petie?" Billy's voice was stronger, more commanding.

"Yes, Bill-y." The doctor moaned in the background.

"Peter pressured me just now in a way that made me feel extremely uncomfortable. He was pushy and assuming."

The puppet flew into its master with unbounded zeal. Billy thought it sounded as if Pendergrast was getting it in the face.

"*Very* assuming," Billy said, pushing the phone to his ear and listening carefully.

"I beg . . . I beg of you in the name of god to stop this." Pendergrast gagged. Had Petie applied a choke hold?

"Enough!" Silence followed Billy's demand. "Petie?"

"Yes, Bill-y." Eerie how damn calm Petie sounded even as Pendergrast continued to moan.

"Petie, I'm dating the dean's daughter."

"Bill-y, must I come and see you?"

Lock the goddamned doors tonight. Billy wondered what he could barricade the kitchen widow with? "No, Petie, I don't think so." How would that be to awaken with Petie present? Manacled to the bed, a strap of leather run through his mouth . . . no, Petie's presence would not be required. "The dean's daughter . . ."

"Name, Bill-y." Petie probably had the clipboard. Was he drawing a bull's-eye?

"Buff."

"Bad, bad, bad," sang the puppet.

"Yes, I know."

"Knowing is good, Bill-y. Not e-nough, though."

"I usually can't remember her name. I always want to call her Bush."

"More sen-si-ble. Go on."

"She is, despite her father, a very good person."

"Doubt-ful."

"I never would have believed it possible, but it's true. But here's the problem."

"Very, very good." Pendergrast said weakly.

"Bill-y is talk-ing now," warned Petie. The doctor fell silent.

"Prob-lem i-den-ti-fi-ca-tion, Bill-y. Pro-ceed."

"When the dean finds out who I am . . ." Billy breathed deeply. This was almost inconceivably bad luck. Almost. "Well, I'm afraid . . ."

"No fear!" Petie wasn't fooling.

"Well, I wonder . . ."

"Won-der is o-kay."

Thank god. "Well, I *wonder* what will happen? The dean seemed to hate me in college."

"I'm sure he didn't hate . . ." Pendergrast should have kept his mouth shut, and it sounded as if Petie reminded him of that fact in no uncertain terms. The doctor cried out in pain.

"Hate-ful creature, Bill-y," Petie said. "Does he need a less-on?"

Here was a defining moment, and Billy recognized it as such. Here could be the kiss that turns the frog into the prince.

"Yes," Billy said slowly. "I think he needs a lesson."

"Want re-venge?"

Oh, yes, Petie, I do. I want it more than anything. High-stepping over the dean would be worth any price.

"Yes," Billy whispered, feeling like the president of the United States signing off on some black operation in a little country the world would never expect U.S. forces to be in. There was a story idea. Billy blinked hard. Laos or Cambodia?

"Plan-ning time, Bill-y." Petie had the clipboard now for sure. Billy could hear the swish of the pen on paper, rapid strokes that outlined a cunning, devious, get-exactly-what-he-deserves operation that for the first time in many years empowered Billy with a sense of control over his future. A sense that perhaps the rules of Fate were not carbon steel and could be bent to accommodate improvisation.

"Take charge," he mouthed silently to himself. "Take charge."

More than ten hours later, rested after a deep, demon-free sleep, Billy hammered down the stairs to the apartment's front door, slinging the monstrous porthole open, peering out at another hot summer day, the sun already high over the East Ridge, Mary basking in its light like a great white reptile. Was it okay to think of her as such? Billy wished he hadn't. He remembered the Discovery Channel program on reptiles, in particular monitor lizards and Komodo dragons. What would he do if he saw one of the great beasts skitter across Washoe? He imagined the furious flailing of legs, thick tail whipping back and forth, still retaining instinctive movement from its fishy ancestors. He scanned the street up and down. Far to the west, close to its junction with Main, something waited on the sidewalk. Better to wait, too, Billy thought. Lizards were good out of the gate, but they weren't much for endurance. He could probably get back inside before it got to him. Even so, how would it hurt to move back onto the steps? He sat down on the steps of his building, the cracked concrete warm through his jeans. It was flaking off in thin wafers, rusted rebar poking through where the steps had seen the most wear.

"Buff," Billy whispered to himself, letting her name trail away like winter wind seeping through a windowsill. Thoughts of her flooded him, warming from the inside all the little places that the sun could not reach. Though he could never let on to Petie, he was beginning to like the name. Like a feather pillow, he thought. The sound his bed made when he flopped down on it after a long, hard day. Buff.

The sun ducked in behind the old Anaconda Company Bank, leaving Washoe bathed in shadows, a perfect example of the progression of time, Billy thought. He stood up and stretched, checked to be sure the money Andrea had given him after their trip to Missoula was still in his pocket, his hand finding the comforting bulge of tightly wadded bills, took a few strides toward Main Street, then stopped and returned to the steps. If he was going to make it to the high life, he'd better work some on his walk.

"Up with the left foot, raise, raise, raise," he sang to the tune of an old Christmas song . . . something about Santa filling Little Will's stocking. He marched in place, arms pumping at his side, back as straight as a Marine's. Good posture, Bristol. Sir, yes, sir! Now, up the street at a good clip.

"Mr. Bristol." The woman's voice came from behind him, sharp, steady, and almost unemotional—a judge reading a death sentence he secretly very much approves of. "Mr. Bristol."

Billy turned around slowly, his erect stance now lost, the slump of bad luck, the more comfortable position of despair, back in place.

"Mr. Bristol."

"Your rent, Mr. Bristol." It was Helmsley. "You are in arrears two months."

No surprises there. Brace yourself now, here comes the town sheriff. Helmsley was awful, but she was also predictable.

"I have taken measures, Mr. Bristol. The ball is rolling. And if, as I strongly suspect, you are not prepared to rectify this situation right here, right now, and I do mean with cold, hard cash . . . no bartering services . . ."

What was she referring to? He'd told her right up front he wasn't a *real* plumber and wasn't *sure* he could fix the leaks. And he *had* pounded the loose nail back into the steps.

"If I don't have some money . . . if I don't have a considerable amount of money, more than a token few dollars. That nifty fifty isn't going to cut it this time."

So that wasn't going to work again, either.

"In the next five seconds, I'm going inside to call the town sheriff and will instruct him to move your belongings into the street."

Five seconds? But she was at least fifty feet away, and there was no way such a distance could be covered shuffling. High-stepping, maybe. Shuffling, even scuffing along so fast the friction melted the soles of his sneakers, which he wasn't about to sacrifice, wouldn't bring him to Helmsley in five seconds.

"I started counting two seconds ago, too," she said bitterly.

Well, down to three seconds. Not even the high-step would work. Billy stared at her beady, close-set eyes dark against her white hair. Ugly, ugly, ugly, he thought as his feet began inching toward her. He glanced at the East Ridge and grimaced. Mary, may I? Why, yes, you may, Billy. Forty-one baby steps. And haul out that hard-earned cash, too.

"Are you prepared?" Helmsley left it at that.

Prepared for what? A low-swinging chariot drawn by the winged brothers of Pegasus? That would be all right. Not too high, boys. Gee over here, haw. Billy imagined careering down Harrison at the reins.

"Well?" For a small woman, Helmsley carried herself well. She didn't come up much past Billy's chest, but then neither did his mother, and she could be lethal.

"I've got . . ." He worked his hand into his pocket and touched the bills. This is when it hurt the most. Knowing he was going to give them up. He shouldn't have twisted them together.

"I don't have all day." Helmsley thrust an open hand at his belly. "Make it snappy."

Billy withdrew the money, and no king ever relinquished his sword to a conqueror with more sorrow. Vanquished once more, he thought.

"What's this?" The landlady peeled the bills apart and frowned, her eyes growing more beady. Again Billy thought of the giant lizards.

You're a skink, Billy said to himself, wondering how often she shed her skin? I'll bet she doesn't close her eyes when she sleeps, either.

"Mr. Bristol, do you mean to tell me this is the best you can do?"

He wasn't thinking of telling her anything. The surrender was unconditional, right?

"What am I supposed to do with this?" Helmsley said.

Buy a case of Heineken, four cans of Spaghettios, two dinners down in the flats, a night at a fancy hotel on Georgetown Lake with your lover, and a bottle of generic-brand Pepto-Bismol to coat your stomach from the knives of existence. That's what Billy had earmarked it for. Maybe a little something for Petie, too, but he guessed that fellow derived enough enjoyment from his work to do it cheap.

"This doesn't count for much." Helmsley tucked the one hundred fifty dollars away in her purse, where Billy had as much hope of seeing it again as a Turkish prisoner does the outside world.

Letters from a Cell in Turkey! A title to definitely keep in mind. Billy watched Helmsley turn and tromp off, and it was easy to imagine a dirt floor, damp ceiling, heavy bars, and cold, cold chains around his ankles. He saw her whip around once, his heart beating fast at the thought that she was coming back, but instead she headed down an alley in the general direction of the Mc-Queen, its high brick front just visible over his apartment building. Somewhere inside, sheltered from the light of day, lay the dean. Billy pictured him fanning himself with a colored ostrich feather while he flipped through a great book written in some long-dead language. A book of incantations, perhaps.

"*Mumblo jabba mi koo,*" Billy said in baritone pitch, instantly running a hand down between his legs to be sure he hadn't instructed some spirit to deprive him of his manhood. That was the problem with random spells. You just couldn't ever be sure what might be summoned. "I can call demons . . ." He puffed out his chest, an actor on an Elizabethan stage, then took a quick step back, changed posture slightly, and replied, "Yes, and so can I, and so can any man. But will they come when you do call?"

A window flew open across the street and a man thrust enough of his body out so that by all rights he should have fallen to the pavement. "Shut up, you crazy son of a bitch!"

Billy stared at him, not altogether surprised. Hecklers weren't uncommon. Too ignorant to appreciate the Bard. He bit his thumb at the man and headed up the street, feet breaking contact with the sidewalk just enough so he wasn't shuffling. But where was he going? Helmsley had neatly altered his plans for Heineken and Spaghettios, to say nothing of the way she'd thwarted the reservations he wanted to make at the inn on Georgetown.

"Damn all slumlords," he muttered. "And that place had a varnished hardwood deck!"

Passing Pendergrast's Pharmacy on his way to the post office, Billy heard something bumping about behind the boarded-up windows. Had Petie come to set up shop? He tiptoed by, especially careful not to step on any loose cement. A car slowed down on the street beside him, the driver undoubtedly prepared to say something unfavorable, but instead the vehicle coasted to a stop against the curb, its engine still running. Billy looked at the driver, slumped against his window. He was an old man, small and gray, with stringy hair and a face as wrinkled as a jack-o'-lantern left outside until Christmas. The bumping inside the pharmacy stopped, and Billy felt something cold pass through him. Could it be? Oh, god, what a thought. What an awful thought. He rubbed his hands vigorously against his chest, concentrating very hard on the functions of his heart. Keep beating, old friend. Don't get any ideas about . . . he nodded at the man in the car . . . stay to your own course and keep thumping. He placed a finger under his jawbone and felt for a pulse. Weak, but it was there. Billy took two forced steps up the street, lead feet almost impossible to lift. Behind him in the pharmacy, he knew the cats were twirling and the dead were dancing, clumsy, robotic moves, rigid limbs animated by some force from the other side. How was their new recruit faring?

But wait. How could he be *sure* the man was gone? What if he was still clinging to life, fighting to remain part of the world? What if a little resuscitation was all he needed? That might be worth a handsome reward. How often did old men have large sums of cash on hand? Billy wondered. Often enough so that he couldn't risk passing up an opportunity.

Billy backed up even with the car and peered through the driver's-side window. He rapped gently on the glass, his hands working toward the door handle, still hoping for a sign of life from the man inside. He heard the latch disengage, thinking a well-oiled door said something promising about the man's wealth. Then the driver moved. His wrinkled face twitched, and a bony hand came up from between the seats with a can of Drop 'Em pepper spray, its distinctive red nozzle pointed at Billy's eyes. In super-slow motion, he watched an arthritic finger tighten on the curved trigger, silver hairs undulating on the back of an ancient hand. Billy tried to draw away and was enveloped in a cloud of gas that seeped into every pore, burning his lungs, stinging his skin, setting fire to his eyes, sucking the air from his chest. He gasped, unable to breathe, the terrible fumes filling his throat.

Spin into the street, he told himself. Into oncoming traffic, where this will all end quickly and I will be free of a world of deans, mothers, misfortune, and cayenne-pepper spray. Billy whirled toward the center of Washoe, outstretched arms eager to embrace the grill of some fast-moving vehicle. And when he reached the other side of the street alive, he fell to the sidewalk, rubbing his eyes in agony.

"Every man's hand is set against me," he moaned, a suspicion soon borne out when a passerby, one of Butte's rare pedestrians, asked curtly, "What the hell's the matter with you?" before continuing up the street.

It was half an hour before Billy could see, and when his vision returned, the world blurry, the sun a great silver disk, dull as a well-worn coin, he began thinking that Andrea's blindness was a blessing in disguise. Oh, spare my eyes the offenses of this awful place. He shut them tight and groped along the side of an old hardware building, his fingers tracing the mortar lines between bricks. With the exception of certain delicate curves on an attractive woman, earth held little he cared to see, and even the women had their drawbacks. Physical reminders of the unobtainable high life—that's all they were. And if a man did succeed . . . *if* he did . . . Billy opened his eyes and lengthened his stride . . . if he did procure one, the chances were that her father would be a dean.

At Main Street, Billy turned downhill to the post office. He waded in through the door, head held low, avoiding eye contact with anyone who might recognize the signature of mace. Fumbling with his box, he tried the key three or four times before getting it open. Looking at its contents, he quickly realized that his journey there had been an awful mistake.

"Dear Mr. Bristol." Billy's eyes hurt as much from the words before them as from the mace. "We can offer you no encouragement at this time."

Encouragement? Is that what he'd asked for?

"We rarely accept freelance work and don't have time to read anything unsolicited."

They hadn't even read his proposal? What was he to do, lie around waiting for the magazine to call him up with an assignment?

"We're sorry we can't be of more help. Sincerely, Staff."

Billy wadded the letter from *Outdoor Life* into a tight ball and pitched it toward the wastepaper basket. He didn't want to do a piece on Montana trout streams, anyway. Especially not if he had to fish himself. It would be all right until he hooked something . . . *something* being the operative word.

He opened another envelope, growing hopeful when he saw it wasn't a form letter.

"Dear William Bristol."

Well, they'd used his name properly. And he liked the way it looked right there at the top of the page. It should be in a different font, but . . .

"Rarely have I had to write the type of letter I'm sending you."

I'll bet, Billy thought. It wasn't every day *Story* received ideas so clearly cut out for publication in the Pushcart Prize collection.

"There are two things one needs in order to write."

What? How much money I'll accept and when I'm available to be flown back for awards? Billy thought he'd mentioned both of them.

"First, you need ideas. You've certainly got that covered. But second, and more important, you need to be good. Mr. Bristol, I understand that writing or, more precisely, the *appreciation* of writing, is in large part subjective. But I believe that I speak for all readers when I say that this profession isn't right for you. Please, please, please, consider a different line of work."

Billy threw the letter as hard as he could, bouncing it off the wall above the trash basket.

"No good news today, Billy?" the postmaster asked.

Billy wanted to hit him. What did he know? He'd been cut off his entire life. He booted the door open and shuffled onto Main Street, turning downhill toward Chuck's. It was instinctive for him to do so, as natural as the course of water, and he wondered in what other ways he was governed by the basic laws of the universe.

"Oh, baby."

Billy bristled at the voice. There were times when those words would have brought him joy, but because they were not coming from the little speakers in one of the adult bookstore's peep booths, had not been uttered uncontrollably from atop a widow's walk, and were not the entire extent of Cheryl or Marilyn's vocabulary (the women he imagined sometimes visited him late at night), this was not one of them.

"Billy, honey, you've been avoiding me," his mother said.

See, he thought. A plebeian might as well aspire to be a nobleman as I to stroll on the road to the high life. He listened to his mother's footsteps, thick-soled shoes coming toward him. There was a pair of feet that had never shuffled.

"You turn around and look at your mommy."

Billy drew a deep breath and swiveled slowly. Was she getting into her batter's stance?

"Billy." He braced himself, gritting his teeth in fearful anticipation. "Billy, why did someone mace you?" The little woman displayed no signs of sympathy. Or surprise.

Was it that obvious? What was he, a walking advertisement to the effectiveness of Drop 'Em?

"You speak up quick and tell your mommy the truth." She began to swing her purse, no doubt laden with rolled quarters. The prospect of ten or twenty dollars' worth of change coming in contact with his face wasn't an appealing one.

"I was trying to help someone." He couldn't muster much conviction, but he made a conscious effort not to mumble.

"Help? I'm not getting good vibes, baby." The pocketbook lengthened its arc, swinging like Poe's pendulum. "Mommy's only going to ask for the truth once more. You remember what I taught you about honesty?"

How could he have forgotten? Honesty had been drummed into him with the soup ladle. She'd figured out just how to hook her index finger into the looped handle and twirl the scoop with a force that would make the most practiced knobkerrie-wielding Masai warrior green with envy. Those were hard lessons, not easy to forget.

Billy stared past her to the top of Main Street, where the road met the sky beneath the massive iron gallows frame of a mine shaft, steel girders marking the entrance to a subterranean labyrinth of tunnels. Even now a close kin to the Minotaur could be scraping along under him, its horns cutting through the darkness in search of something to gore. Send Mother down with her purse, he thought. A very worthy adversary.

"Makes Mommy sad to think she didn't teach you the truth, Billy."

Good god, now was the time to answer. Offer her some satisfactory explanation for the macing. As his mind raced, a car heaved into sight at the head of the street, its glossy black exterior materializing from the gallows frame. It came toward him fast and quiet, its big foreign engine silently bringing it closer, its green license plate visible from two hundred yards.

A wildebeest, Billy thought. A *hamstrung* wildebeest facing hyenas. That's what I am. As the BMW slowed down, Billy wished with all his heart that the crack in the sidewalk at his feet would widen sufficiently to drop him down into the path of the Minotaur.

"Hooves and horns," he said. "There are worse things."

"Hello." Susan Austin had her window partway down and was smiling. Billy stole a glance into the passenger seat, careful to look with just one eye. If the dean was in there, perhaps only half his body would turn to stone. He wondered if the pawnshop had a cheap pocket mirror he could use. A little flip-open vanity case from Avon or Mary Kay that still smelled like the woman whose daughter had stolen and hocked it. He stared at the palm of his hand, trying to figure the correct angle at which he'd need to hold it to see into the car. Humble, modern-day Perseus. There's something to that one. A musical? Billy imagined cavorting about onstage, little puffy wings attached to sheepskin slippers, a big plywood sword stenciled with the words ONE FOR THE LITTLE MAN held high over his head. Dodge, parry, counter, thrust! He pictured the lights going down as the dean gasped his final breath.

"Run through." That's what he'd say, and it would be wonderful. The power to conceive such masterpieces in the face of so much misery was the mark of a man destined for greatness.

Billy's mother eyed the woman in the car suspiciously. Surely this was someone asking directions. "Is there something you need?" she asked.

"Oh, I'm sorry if I'm interrupting. I just wanted to thank you, Billy, for our ride last night."

There. How do you like that, Mother? This fine, upstanding, BMW-driving lady has stopped to thank me. And to think you were prepared to bludgeon me.

Mrs. Bristol displayed none of the shock Billy had hoped for. Instead, she trained her eye back on her son, more suspicious than ever. "What do you say to this nice lady, honey?"

Billy coughed a "you're welcome" at the sidewalk. He didn't think Buff's mother would understand being maced or care to see the results. His face still burned, and he feared that his eyes were swelling shut.

"Did you and Buff find something to do afterward? I see she took her things."

Under different circumstances, Billy would have liked to have a little sit-down with Susan and see if he couldn't get her to have a mother-daughter talk about the dangers of cruising through the Highlands late at night. He'd stress the importance of staying away from places like the Cow Camp. As it was, he simply nodded.

"Baby, you got yourself a girlfriend?" Mrs. Bristol let her pocketbook stop swinging. "Got someone you'd like your mommy to meet?"

Billy didn't know what to say. His skin was crawling, and he wished he was somewhere else. Anywhere. At home, at Chuck's, even on Borneo beneath a tree that had just been fogged with insecticide. Let all the canopy dwellers drop down upon me. Bring the eight-inch centipedes by the bushel and let it snow metallic-green horned beetles. Billy envisioned his outstretched arms breaking the fall of half a dozen new species. Look at this one, he imagined saying with the heavy British accent of the narrator on the Discovery Channel. It has pincers fore and aft.

"I'm Gloria Bristol, Billy's mother." One high-step carried her to the curb, where she studied the automobile and the woman inside, still not entirely ready to accept what she saw.

"Susan Austin." The pretty woman extended her hand, and it was shaken with a force she was unaccustomed to. "I've met your son a couple of times now."

"Really?" For the briefest of moments, Mrs. Bristol's eyes sought Billy's. It would go hard on him later for keeping her out of the loop.

"Yes. My husband and I are here visiting our daughter, Buff."

"Really?"

Damn her! This incredulous tone wasn't called for.

"Beautiful country out here."

"Ummm." Mrs. Bristol took a curl of pocketbook strap up in her hand. Not a good sign. "Billy, baby?" She kept looking at Susan. "What have you told this woman?"

"Quite a bit," Susan answered, perhaps sensing that this was an uncomfortable conversation for her daughter's boyfriend.

"Really?" Mrs. Bristol was getting worked up. Billy could see the veins in her hands, and they didn't show unless she was seriously agitated. Lessons about truth weren't far away.

"I think it's wonderful what he does. Writing. I'm going to have to start getting the *New York Times.*"

Billy cringed. Still looking at his feet, he felt the great weight of his mother's eyes on him. They were eyes that, over the years, had worn him down. Along with painful lessons about truth, she more than anyone else—save perhaps the dean and the block—had taught him shuffling, and he knew that he was only moments away from an advanced course on that subject. After this, he'd have it mastered for sure.

"Yes, sir." Mrs. Bristol nodded. She knew every bend down this road.

"You said your work most frequently appears in the travel section, didn't you? About one Sunday a month?"

Billy felt things closing in around him. Hang on, he told himself. But it was hard. So hard when he knew worse was yet to come. When would he hit bottom? Was there a bottom? God, what a frightening thought. What if there was no low point from which he could begin to claw upward? Or what if it was so far down that when he got there he'd spent all his strength slowing his descent and could look forward only to a slow and painful death in the basement of misfortune?

"Too bad you did your piece on Butte before my husband bought his lounge. An authentic Irish pub would have been a colorful addition, don't you think?" Susan said.

"What?" Mrs. Bristol whipped her head around to face the car.

"Yes, I know, it sounds strange, but my husband has it in his head that he's going to buy a bar out here and turn it into something. I don't know where he got the idea for it, but he seems quite determined. At first I wasn't sure, but now I think maybe it's just what he needs."

"Which bar does he intend to buy?" Billy watched his mother suck up more strap.

"The one down on the corner. Chuck's."

Play them against each other, Billy thought. That may be my only hope. Drag myself away while the predators fight. He inched a step back.

"Stand where you are," commanded his mother, and he dared not disobey.

The salad spoon had taught him obedience long ago. Mrs. Bristol stared hard at the BMW, numbers no doubt whirring through her head. Billy could almost see her counting. She looked as displeased as Helmsley had. Matters of finance seemed to bring no joy to anyone today.

"I assume you told Billy about this?"

Susan shifted in her seat. Direct examination wasn't something she encountered very often.

"Well . . . I mentioned something about it last night, didn't I?" She was begging assistance now, but Billy couldn't interfere. He had his own neck to think of.

A face full of mace, a head full of worry . . . he needed one more thing to go with it. A face full of mace, a head full of worry, a heart just barely hanging on. There it was. A good, solid refrain in a country song.

"Oh, look at this." Susan lifted the sleeve on her left wrist, so distraught she didn't realize her watch was on the other hand. "I'd better head out," she said as she rolled up her window. "Nice meeting you."

The car pulled away instantly, all eight cylinders shoving it down the street. Billy continued looking down. Better not to see it coming.

"Baby, you shouldn't conspire against Mommy."

What was the penalty for treason?

"Hurt her feelings terrible."

Well, at least that was an acknowledgment that she had them. Sometimes Billy wondered.

"Hurts me right here." She tapped her chest with the purse, its strap now wrapped entirely around her hand. "And to tell that respectable lady you write for the *New York Times!* I know sometimes you try, baby. You've got your ideas and all, but to put on airs . . . makes my ears ring to think of what you must have said.

"An apology letter will be written now. You'll write it and let your mommy sign it before it goes in the mail. You tell about the macing in it, too. The *truth* about the macing. If this girl loves you, she still will. Takes a big man to admit he's done wrong, Billy. You tell me right now what you'll write."

Billy ran his hands together, fingers pulling hard against each other.

"Go ahead. Mommy knows it's not easy. The right thing never is. I'll help. Dear Buff . . ."

Billy didn't respond.

"Dear Buff . . ." His mother sounded as if her patience was waning.

Dear Buff, how would you like to elope with me? And what do you think of widow's walks?

"Baby, Mommy doesn't want to give a lesson on Main Street. You tell me you'll put *I'm sorry* in the first line. We both know that's where it's got to go."

"Dear Buff, I'm sorry," Billy whispered, and it wasn't altogether untrue.

"Thatta boy," his mother encouraged. "Now we have to tell her what you're sorry for. What are we sorry about, honey?"

Not being a millionaire. The fact that there's never a cold Heineken within reach when a man needs one most. Mistakenly believing a neighbor would enjoy a little Shakespeare this morning. The list was endless.

"We're sorry about ly—" Mrs. Bristol waited for Billy to finish, and when it became clear he wasn't going to, stood on her tiptoes and whispered hoarsely toward his ear, "We're sorry about *lying*, aren't we, baby?"

Oh, yes, that, too.

"You let me hear you say it now, okay?"

"I'm sorry."

"The whole thing, Billy. I need to hear the whole thing and know that it will go in the first line."

"I'm sorry about lying." It was like having to admit to heresy during the Inquisition. What came next? A session on the rack?

"Lying about what?"

Oh, too much! Billy felt as if his head would burst. How would she like to see that? Stand back, Mother, wouldn't want to get brain on you.

"I feel the truth coming, sweetie. It's going to be so much better then. You just tell your mommy what you lied about. It can go in the second line if you want. But not the third. Definitely not the third, so I need to hear it now. Want me to give you a hint?"

Why not? Billy moved his head up and down once.

"Has something to do with that big newspaper in New York. Does that help?"

This was painful. Worse than a drubbing, although Billy wasn't sure that he would escape without one of those, too. Dear Buff, whatever I lied to you about I have paid for. I have been publicly humiliated and soundly thrashed. Love, Billy.

"Has to do with the *New York Ti—*"

"*Times,*" Billy stammered.

"Oh, yes it does. That's what it has to do with. Now, what did you say you did for the *New York Times?*"

"Wrote."

"Yes, wrote. And was that true?"

Well, in a sense it was. It was only their poor judgment when it came to publishing the pieces that kept him out of print. For a week or two, he had written exclusively for the *Times.* And by god, his idea about Butte supermarkets at two in the morning . . . no one had written about who buys vegetables—in particular, tubers—late at night. There was a segment of the population that was fascinated by such stories, he was sure of it.

"Billy Bristol, was it true?"

"No," he mouthed.

"Ah, finally. Mommy will let you decide on your own what to put in lines three through ten, baby. Needs to be heartfelt and honest, though. Then I'll sign it—just to be sure you do it—and we can put it in the mail. Wait and see if Buff doesn't fall head over heels."

Fall to pieces is more likely.

"Now I'm going down to Chuck's and find out all about this man's idea for an Irish pub, baby. And I haven't forgotten about the sponge incident, either. We will talk about that when you bring me the letter. It had better be in your best handwriting, too. This is something you should be proud of." She high-stepped by and crossed the street, leaving Billy alone. He looked over at Mary, high on the East Ridge.

"At least *you* can't sneak up behind me," he said to himself, though he wasn't convinced that she could not.

· 16 ·

T his little piggy met a dean's daughter." Billy sang to himself in the tub, pulling at his toes, the water less than an inch from spilling over the sides. "This little piggy told a lie."

He began to rap now, bouncing up and down, marveling at his weightlessness.

"This little piggy got a face full of mace . . . when my little piggies gonna die?"

He imagined running a needle across a fast-moving record in time to the puffing noises he'd make into the microphone.

"Hey, little piggie. Say hey, little piggie. Gotta watch out for the big hog!" He shoved himself up onto his knees, pointing Elvis style at his groin, then shook his head. Little piggy didn't have much to worry about. The act was a bust, and he'd sloshed water all over the bathroom.

Billy stayed in the tub until all the water had drained, not because it gave him any great satisfaction but because he could not bear the thought of getting out and toweling up his mess. It had been a long time since he'd scrubbed the bathroom. In fact, he wasn't sure that he ever had, though it would have been unlike him to move into an apartment without giving it a thorough cleansing first. Surely the possibility of tub fungus had occurred to him, necessitating a complete sterilization. Even so, that was more than a year ago. Plenty of time had passed for a good crop of dust bunnies to move in, frightening clumps of lint and hair—hair from god only knows what—that float eerily across the floor late at night, propelled by undetectable wind currents, and come to rest in places like in back of the lion-claw legs of the tub or under the refrigerator. He'd ferreted a great family of them out from under there with his bristle broom not long ago, half a dozen varying in size from a quarter to just slightly smaller than a tennis ball. Billy shuddered thinking about them, in particular the massive old grandfather, hairs from tenants past sticking out like porcupine quills.

How long would it take for the water on the bathroom floor to evaporate? That was probably the best idea. Let it vanish on its own. Billy closed his eyes and eased back into the porcelain, thankful it retained the water's heat.

"Buff." He whispered her name. It was always there in his mind now, never far from the front, and unlike dean thoughts, financial worries, problems with his mother, problems with Petie, problems with his career—the other thoughts she vied with for position—all contemplations of her were pleasant. He thought of her often, sometimes consciously, sometimes quite unexpectedly. Those were the thoughts he enjoyed most. The times when he was doing something that even by the wildest stretch of imagination could not be connected to her, yet he inexplicably found himself thinking of her. It was as if she were there with him, searching for change in the pay phones, opening a can of Spaghettios at lunch, wondering how long it would take the water to evaporate.

Stranger still, and equally wonderful, was the fact that when he thought of her he could never quite imagine how she looked. His thoughts were of her as a whole. Her smile, laugh, figure, and mannerisms blended together to form something altogether different from the physical person he knew, and the closest he could come to describing how he felt was happy. It was as if a special part of her resided in him, there to help him through the day, never more than a thought away. Lying in the tub, Billy wondered if she felt the same way and hoped she did.

Hearing the phone ring, the shrill jingle that could only mean someone expected him to dance attendance on them, did not feel right. Not at all. Neither did splashing naked through the puddles on the floor on the way to answer it. Neither, for that matter, did tromping about naked. Must have something to do with the lack of fear "big hog" inspired earlier. Billy reached for a couch cushion to cover himself with before answering the phone. Why did the back of his neck always prickle when it rang? That wasn't supposed to happen unless someone he knew had died or an evil spirit passed close by.

"Hello." He held the receiver with two fingers, careful not to let it touch his wet ear. Electrocution wasn't on the menu for today.

"Yah, iz Andrea. Ello."

Deep sigh of relief. Very deep.

"I knowz ve didn't plan, but maybe yous come and ve go for a ride, yah? Buff go, too."

Buff? Hmmm . . . In the Chevy? This sounded workable. More precisely, it sounded like work that wasn't work. And that sounded pretty damn good. He hadn't seen Buff since their High-lands date four days ago, and while thoughts of her were good, they weren't going to get him onto the widow's walk.

"You come over right away, den, yah?"

"Fine."

Andrea said good-bye and left Billy holding a dead line. He re-placed the receiver gently, still mindful that a damp surface makes a hell of a conductor. The cop show he'd watched a week ago had focused on a southern coastal city devastated by a hurri-cane. There were looters, flood victims, property damage, and, worst of all, lots of downed power lines. He remembered the way electricity arced from the transformers to saturated cypress trees, long blue and orange streaks lighting up the night, elimi-nating any possibility of his ever living in the Southeast. Butte was a much safer bet. No tornadoes, hurricanes, catastrophic hundred-year floods, earthquakes, or volcanoes. If the city didn't sink into the tunnels beneath it and Berkeley Pit didn't over-flow, he was a lot better off than he would have been in most places.

Billy sorted through his bureau. The time was fast approach-ing when he'd need to do laundry, and the mere thought of it made him tremble. There was something about having to go to a public laundromat that nauseated him. Perhaps it had to do with their clientele. On average, there would be two or three all-but-helpless old ladies picking through a basket of stained underwear, one or two unkempt kids playing some spying game beneath the clothes-folding table, and a stern-faced man whose sole job was to watch the change machine and who never took his eyes off Billy. Laundromats were such depressing places.

Maybe he could wash things in his sink and let them hang dry in the alley. No, that was even worse. The only apartments with clotheslines in their alleys housed tenants whose toilets never worked, who were perpetually in competition with rodents for food, and who fought viciously with each other over who con-trolled the prime city dumpsters. Better to use the laundromat. Just go late at night when he would not be recognized.

Today, Billy was down to his last pair of jeans and three short-sleeved shirts. He chose a faded tan one, loose enough to ripple in the breeze of the convertible. It was the type of shirt he could also slip a little deodorant through in a supermarket without detection. That was always a good thing to keep in mind. He never knew when Fate would decide it was time for him to sweat. The last time he used that trick, however, someone had beaten him to the punch, and the brown hairs that clung to the bar of Old Spice made him violently ill. On his way down the apartment steps, he wondered where his serious aversion to others' hair came from. And why in the world was he thinking about it? This could be the beginning of an unhealthy obsession. Something to nip in the bud before it blossomed, for sure.

As always, Butte's sidewalks were deserted. As devoid of people as the streets of London during World War II when the German V2 rockets rained out of the sky. Billy had seen a program about it on public television once, and as he looked up Washoe toward Main Street, it was easy to again picture the shattered glass and rubble. He hoped no fire alarms would go off before he reached Andrea's. In his current state of mind, it would be all he could do not to cry "incoming" and dive for cover. Such actions would certainly not go unnoticed by someone driving by, and he would be rebuked. And he would just as soon at least one day go by without bearing the brunt of another's chastising. Not too much to ask for, he thought.

The auction of Chuck's was only a few days away, and between Main Street and Excelsior, the steep north–south avenue he never looked forward to climbing, Billy wondered who its new owner would be. He also wondered how things were coming with Petie. And that got him thinking about Buff. She knew nothing of the trouble between him and her father. Nothing of the years of agony he'd been through, years when the very mention of the man's title set Billy on his knees and brought clusters of hives to his hands. Years when he could not pass a school, not even an elementary school, without shuddering. Years of the block when the only employment he could find was menial labor: picking sugar beets, cleaning a campground, filing, stapling, and folding. While his peers went on to MFA programs all across the country, Billy floundered through the school of hard knocks in Butte. While his classmates were signing copies of their first novels, he was signing unemployment checks . . . when he was lucky. And while others appeared on *Oprah*, the *Today* show, and *20/20*, Billy stood before his mother on Spaghetti Day. No, Buff knew nothing of the suffering that had begun in her father's office many years before. She knew nothing of the degree in shuffling Billy had received or how often he was forced to put it to use. Even now his feet slowed into the familiar tempo. *Swish-slap, swish-slap, swish-slap.* There was something comforting in it. Something Billy had come to rely on.

"My bosom friend, despair," he said, placing both hands over his heart. "Right here with me all the time, never going to let me down."

A dozen pigeons flushed from the eaves of a Victorian mansion on the corner of Washoe and Excelsior. Billy watched them wheel together into the sky, banking sharply over the rooftops toward a church steeple. Wonder was they didn't pass over him and let fly a stream of indescribably foul liquid. Well, one thing to be thankful for. Worth two or three high-steps? No, not quite. He continued shuffling along, knowing the time was approaching when he would have to apprise Buff of his dealings with her father. And Petie's plans for him, too. Once that puppet was set in motion, Billy knew he would not deviate from his course. Nor did he want him to. The little man had said it best himself.

"Peo-ple-hurt-ers must pay."

Buff's car was in Andrea's driveway, just as it had been on the night of their first date. He leaned against it, catching his breath from the haul up Excelsior, and looked over at the widow's walk. There it was, jutting into the huge, blue sky. Beckoning. He stared at it until his breathing slowed, his chest no longer billowing under his shirt, his pulse, weak as it might now be, falling back into a steady rhythm, allowing him to hear more than its pounding. And there was something more to hear. Billy raised the brass knocker on Andrea's door, let it slip from his hand, then jammed two fingers between it and the striker plate. Inside, they were laughing. Giggling. And dented fingers was a small price to pay to learn what caused them this merriment. Laughing women weren't to be trusted.

"Read it again," Andrea said. "More, more. Da part about finding your name. Oh, dat kills me."

Billy pressed his ear to the door. He'd never heard Andrea laugh before. Whatever lay behind her mirth was worth hearing.

"'Dear . . . dear . . . dear.'" Buff couldn't control herself. Billy heard her gasping for air. "'Dear Buff, I'm Billy's mommy.' *Mommy!*" Buff shrieked, breaking into raucous laughter.

One door away, Billy wasn't laughing. He hadn't expected this. He began working his shoulders in tight circles, his eyebrows twitching, his mouth growing dry as sand. How was this possible? He asked himself again, his mind drawing blanks.

"'It is late at night, and my eyes hurt from looking through my phone book. Even though Austin was near the front, I had to be sure there were no other Buffs. Baby, you are the only one.'" Buff slapped something, the coffee table, perhaps, and Billy felt his chest tighten. "She went through the phone book," Buff said.

Of course she did, Billy thought. Page by page, name by name, motivated by hatred and spite.

"'It is with much sadness that I write to you, but I know you are respectable and want to know the truth. You may wish to sit down.'"

Billy did. He wished he could crawl under a rock. Even one above a colony of sow beetles. He sank to the ground, pulling his head into his lap, slowly rocking back and forth.

"'My son has told you lies. I am ashamed of him.'" Buff wrinkled the paper. "Look, look, she's made them separate paragraphs."

"Yah, iz vonderful," Andrea said.

Buff cleared her throat. "'I have tried to be a good mother and have bashed him many, many times for lies. Truth lessons are so hard for my boy. You must know up front that there may not be any hope for him. Oh, it hurts me so much.'" Buff and Andrea began laughing together.

"Vhere's da part about writing? Read da part about writing." Andrea's voice was high and loud.

"It's coming," Buff said. "Listen. 'Billy has never written for the *New York Times*. He just hasn't done it, so don't let him fool you. I know he will try, but you must not believe him. Do not believe. Being respectable, you may not understand how lazy Billy is. Too lazy for writing. Not even once-upon-a-time stories. Lazy, lazy. But Mommy tried. Please don't blame me.'"

Billy pulled his head harder, bending his back into a tight curve, wondering if he had the strength to break his own neck. *Snap*, goes the vertebrae. *Snap, snap, snap.* He jerked with all his force, his face coming close to the ground between his legs.

Misfortune has made me too supple, he thought.

"Okay, we're coming to the end," Buff said. "'Buff, my baby has told you awful, terrible lies, but if you can find it in your heart to forgive him, it would make me so happy. Please show him this letter. I have left a space for him to sign it, if you would like him to. I think sometimes that helps him see what he's done wrong. Mommy does love him. P.S. . . .' Oh, god, listen to this . . . 'P.S. I know your father wants to buy Chuck's. I am going to try, too. Please understand that business and friendship are separate. You and your family are welcome there anytime. We have Spaghetti Day every Thursday. Love, Gloria Bristol.'"

"Dat iz priceless!" Andrea said.

Billy disagreed. He very quickly assigned it a monetary value equal to everything he was about to lose with Buff. Andrea, too. Good-bye, Chevy. So long, big dowry. Oh, this little note was anything but priceless. It had stripped him of all hope for the high life. Smashed that dream to pieces with the force of his mother's coin-heavy purse swung with all her might. Well, Mother, you've beaten my body and broken my spirit. Congratulations.

"Vhat are yous going to do about it? You're not going to showzhim, are you?"

"I haven't made up my mind."

Oh, good. Leave me on pins and needles. Billy slumped into the door, disappointed there was no jagged sliver of wood to impale himself on. Damn all smooth doors. He scuffed his back side to side, waiting . . . *hoping* to find a pine shard.

"Did yous hear dat? Is dat someone at my door?" Andrea said.

"Maybe it's mommy." Buff began to laugh again. "Come to bash her boy."

Billy knew he was the only one at the door, but hearing Buff's explanation he couldn't help looking up. Eyes wide with fear, he tipped his head back, hands over his face to block the blow. He could see the sky through his fingers and the corner of the widow's walk. And then he felt himself falling backward, his balance gone. Finally, he thought. The carpet of hope has at last been jerked out from under me. Oh, rapid be my descent, and far may I fall.

"Billy? Are you all right?" Buff stood over him holding the open door he'd tumbled through.

Here's a grown man sprawled out on a kitchen floor, hands over his head, but yes, Buff, I'm fine. Let me hop right up and high-step it into the living room. Give me a moment to gather myself and we'll be off on the open road in the Chevy.

"You're not hurt, are you?" She knelt next to him.

Hurt? What would give you that idea? My furrowed brow? Trembling hands? The expression of insurmountable pain on my face? You really haven't known many writers, have you?

"How long have you been . . ." Buff reached for Billy's hands and tried to pry them from his eyes.

Good luck, he thought. The light of day will not pass these fingers. But, Jesus, she was strong. She peeled his hands from his face, set them at his side and touched his cheek.

Soft, warm . . . mmmm . . . fragrant finger, leave me alone.

Buff leaned over him, her lips inches from his mouth.

"Vell, are ve ready?"

Andrea came into the kitchen smiling. Billy got up as quietly as he could, leaning against the door frame for support. His legs were still wobbly, and it didn't seem right for a man who'd gone through as much as he had to have to stand.

"And yet I persevere," he whispered to himself, words from a late-night television evangelist coming to him as he stepped outside. "Yea, though I trudge up Excelsior, the devil behind me stride for stride, I shall fear no evil. And deep in the valley of night . . . and despair . . . and misfortune . . . and shuffling . . ."

Far below him, down near the corner of Washoe, he heard Stan's taxi peel away from the light. Not much carbon in her today, he thought, as he watched the yellow Chrysler barrel up the street. It screeched to a halt in front of the house, and Stan exited with a flourish. He was wearing a suit.

"Armani," he mouthed to Billy as he led Andrea to the car.

Good. Old Stan has an Armani suit, and I've got . . . Billy tugged at his T-shirt. I've got this shit-brindle thing. All very fitting.

Andrea rode in front, and Buff sat in back with Billy. He looked at her twice on the way to the storage shed, but both times she was staring at him with the smug look of a woman who knows more than she's telling, and it made him so uncomfortable he began to squirm in his seat. And that made it hard to keep from tipping over when Stan roared around the corners.

"Yous still vant to drive a limo, yah?" Andrea asked as the stoplights on Harrison whipped past.

"You bet. Damn near more than anything. I don't get that bar, and that's what I'm doing. Buy myself a big, double-stretch rig. Long as you would believe. Jacuzzi and the whole works. Nice Bose stereo system. And I wouldn't be playing any Mozart. No, sir, Old Stan's limo would be one rocking mother . . ."

Buff pinched Billy's thigh, but all he could think about was whether they made waterproof interiors for limousines? The way Stan drove, the Jacuzzi would be dry in a hurry.

"And leather!" Stan pounded his fist into the dash. "This SOB would have more leather in her than a herd of beef." He stroked his chin, no doubt marveling at the recently razored skin. "You know, part of me hopes I don't get Chuck's."

"I don't think he needs to worry," Buff whispered.

Billy's heart sank. Lower. Stan was his only hope for ever enjoying another beer—American beer, at least—in Chuck's. Soon, it would be Guinness stout or Prego meat sauce. He wasn't sure which was worse.

"My most favorite clients pay nothing today," Stan announced when he whipped into the storage lot.

"Vell . . ."

"I won't hear of it. Not today."

"Vell, yous iz a good man, Stan. Maybe I comes and cheer yous on at da auction."

"By all means, ma'am." He bowed to her, a gesture he didn't realize she could not take notice of. "By all means." And then he whispered to Billy, "Hey, that one you've got there is a hottie. You just let me know if you'd like to borrow the suit." He tugged at his lapels, winked three or four times, and climbed back into the cab, foot on the accelerator before the door was fully closed.

"Yah, he iz a good one," Andrea said. "Iz a good old Butte boy." She fished out her key and handed it to Billy. "Ve just open it up, yah. Don't need da car just yet."

Here was a twist. Not necessarily for the better, either. Billy remembered the rows of boxes, and the wigs he'd seen spilling out from one of them. He would rather do almost anything than deal with those boxes.

"Ve going to sort through a few of my old tings."

Well, that figures. I'd done no more than think of how unpleasant that would be before she suggested it, Billy thought. How can it be that my every fear is soon realized while all that I wish for remains unobtainable? Perhaps a readjustment of desires was in order. Maybe if I were terrified of receiving the National Book Award . . . it was worth giving some thought. Right now, however, there were more pressing things to think about. Like getting the storage shed's overhead door open without something toting a bulbous egg sack dropping from the rafters onto his head. He turned the lock and pulled on the handle, arms far from his body, back bent as little as possible. Good form to throw out a disk, he thought. Maybe Andrea would pay long-term.

"Remind you of any movies?" Buff asked as the door came open and fresh air whooshed inside. "Can't you just picture the mummy hiding out in a place like this?"

Perfectly well without your assistance. Billy could, and had, pictured the mummy in there. Many times. He imagined him bursting out in a whirlwind of loose bandages, his oval, toothless mouth gaping wide.

He rubbed his eyes, trying to adjust them to the darkness inside, then tilted his head and said with satisfaction, "Tutankhamen, I presume."

Buff squeezed his shoulder.

"I needs to take some inventory. Find outs where my tings are, yah?" Andrea drifted to his side. "You go ahead in and start pulling boxes."

Pulling boxes? Had he heard her correctly?

"Yous tell me vhat is in dem and Buff writes it down, okay?"

Sure. Why don't I do it from here? Let's see . . . well, in box number one, we have a hoard of cluster flies. Oh, and over here the skeletal remains of a house cat. Wait, wait, there's more—are you getting all this, Buff? Don't forget the frigging bushel of spiders. Would you like me to identify the individuals, or will we just label the carton ARACHNIDS and let it go at that? My, you're a feisty gentleman, aren't you? Scarab? I believe so. Billy took a tentative step forward.

"Oooooo. Oooooo." Buff moaned ghost style and shoved him on. "Into the lion's den, Daniel."

Lions? No, no. Nothing nearly that ordinary. Billy approached the first box, tapping it with a finger. He waited, listening for an answer, and when none came slowly pried the lid open. Bedspreads. Lots of them.

"Bedspreads," he said. "A box of bedspreads. White with lacy trim."

"Yah, okay. Ve don't care about dem," Andrea said.

Brought up short, I see. Billy toed another box. This one was heavier, and he thought he heard the tinkle of glass on glass. He touched the lid with his left hand. If something grabbed him, it would get his weaker arm.

"Vhat iz in dair?" Andrea asked.

Billy peeked inside. Mugs.

"Drinking glasses," he said. He held one up, a golden LB stenciled to the round bottom. LB. What was that? All Billy could think of were the personal ads he thumbed through from time to time in which LB stood for lesbian-bi. Oh, how he prayed the letters on the glass did not stand for that.

"Good. How many?"

"Twenty-five. Maybe thirty." Billy did the math in his head. "Twenty-eight, I think."

"Iz dair any more of dem?"

He nudged another box. "Sounds like it."

"Yah, vell . . . okay, yous set dem by da door, yah?"

Billy slid the boxes close to the door and looked longingly at the outside world while Buff pointed a finger at him and laughed silently. She seemed to be getting quite a charge out of him today. Nothing like a woman laughing at you to sap your manhood, he thought. Bit by bit I'm being drained of what little masculinity I cling to. Soon, my case will be as hopeless as a eunuch's. Here's Billy, the gentle ox.

The next three boxes all contained women's clothing. There was everything from long, ornate dresses to short—very short—skirts, to kitchen aprons, to a pair of nurse's outfits. Andrea had played plenty of roles, Billy thought. There were high-heeled shoes, and higher-heeled shoes, and a pair of delicate glass slippers that he showed Buff, hoping she might join him in a little game of Cinderella later. I can be Cinderella, and you can be the wicked stepmother, he thought.

Stacked against the wall opposite the driver's side of the Chevy were the boxes of wigs. Five of them. Andrea asked that he place them and the clothing near the door. She let him leave a box of ledgers where it was, but made him restack a couple of boxes containing table cloths. He noticed the same LB embroidered on them but didn't mention it.

Billy ran his hand along the hood of the Chevy on his way to the other side of the building. There was something almost erotic about its lustrous, well-waxed finish. Something that caused his hand to trail gently down the front fender on the passenger side, fingers caressing ever so delicately, eyes closing as he palmed the chrome strip on top of the wheel well.

"Vhat do you see?" Andrea snapped from behind him.

Buff spread-eagled and naked . . . no, not naked, but close . . . in a baby-doll negligee on the hood of the Chevy. The days of July printed in calendar form above her. That's what Billy saw.

"Iz dair some small boxes? I vant yous to open da small boxes now, pleaze."

Before Billy could open "da small boxes, pleaze," he had to open his eyes, an action he didn't particularly look forward to—in part because he didn't care to disrupt his nice picture of Buff, but also because he dreaded prying into the little cardboard containers he feared he'd see. A small box was just the sort of place a scorpion would feel at home.

"See how this individual has positioned itself," he whispered in his Discovery Channel narrator's accent. "Notice its use of barricade, structure on three sides, barbed tail pointed outward, a creature with capital defense strategy. I've got to be *very* careful now." Billy gingerly touched the lid of a shoe box. "One thrust with that tail, and it's all over." He imagined the spike ready and coiled, eager to flip catapult style toward an artery in his wrist, a superhighway for the venom to course into his nervous system, where it would slowly shut down all bodily functions, conscious and automatic alike. The fact that scorpions were not indigenous to Montana provided little comfort.

"Vell, ve iz vaiting."

No doubt. Waiting was a relatively easy thing to do in the light of day where there were no scorpions. Billy opened the lid away from him. Let whatever is inside exercise its flight option first, he decided. He tipped the box slightly, lowering it to the floor at a comfortable angle for something to slither out, even something with an aversion to heights. Whatever was inside seemed intent on staying there, and after a few seconds and a couple of whistled notes from the *Raiders of the Lost Ark* theme, he removed the lid and looked in. On a pillow of faded pink tissue paper lay a pair of fancy fountain pens, trimmed heavily with gold.

"Pens," Billy said, both surprised and relieved.

"Yah, bring dem to me."

More relief. Billy moved to the back of the Chevy, mindful not to let his guard down and overlook anything that could have taken up residence under the trunk. Outside, he handed the pens to Andrea and watched her twirl one of them through her fingers as expertly as a circus juggler.

"I love da veight of a good pen," she said. "Do yous use a computer for da writing?" She cracked a smile. "Or a pen?"

Buff was smiling, too. "When you write for the *New York Times*," she said matter-of-factly.

Billy said nothing. He turned back to the storage shed and disappeared inside. Never had he believed he would welcome its darkness. This time, as he passed the car he gave it a little nudge. Wake up, mamba, he thought. Wake up *green* mamba. Here's someone deserving of a bite. He lifted his pant leg to expose a strip of ankle.

The rest of the small boxes contained items as surprising as the pens. There were buttons, a sore disappointment to Billy, who was hoping for doubloons; long hat pins with glass beads every color of the rainbow; a frighteningly sharp letter opener shaped like a dragon; silk handkerchiefs; windup bedside clocks; a small first-aid kit; four pairs of handcuffs; twenty-one plaque-style OC-CUPIED signs attached to heavy, braided, gold rope—the sort of thing Andrea must have used for her dressing rooms; a pair of lovely cut-glass goblets—heavy, leaded crystal undoubtedly worth a fortune; candleholders of every shape and design; a mermaid paperweight; a china Cupid; money clips; and, in the last box, a pearl-handled derringer with a two-inch barrel and no trigger guard. Andrea asked for it and the goblets, and as Billy brought them to her, he wondered if she was planning his demise. Shoot the liar, then drink a toast. One less writer to kick around, he thought as he handed them over, even less at ease when it became apparent that Andrea knew her way around a pistol. She spun it in her hand as effortlessly as she had the pens, cocked and let down the hammer, then tucked it away in her purse.

"I played a cowgirl von time," she said, the smirk on her face and the sweat on Billy's neck appearing at the same time. "Now, ve take da car. I go home and yous two go have big fun. Must have something to talk about, yah?"

These weren't exactly the circumstances under which Billy had hoped to be alone with Buff in the Chevy. The bottoms of his feet itched, and a lump the size of a softball was creeping up his throat. A tumor? He looked at the front of his shirt, wishing now he hadn't opted for one so loose. Those growths had to be caught quickly and, beneath the ample folds of this T-shirt, might go unnoticed until it was too late.

"Big fun," Buff whispered in his ear. "Talk, too."

"Yous come back dis evening and maybe ve all have dinner, yah?"

"That sounds nice," Buff said.

"Ve have discussion together."

Andrea handed Billy the keys to the Chevy and waited for him to back it out of the storage building. The white leather did little to calm his nerves, and he drove back toward Andrea's with both hands on the wheel, his eyes fixed straight ahead, all the way to Excelsior. He had the fleeting realization that driving was better than walking, providing only momentary relief from the stress that had set in earlier in the day when he'd been privy to the recitation of his mother's thoughtful letter. That was an issue he knew he was going to have to address, and as Buff helped Andrea into her house, Billy's mind whirred faster than it ever had, excuses and explanations speeding by, none seeming adequate. Finally, he was left with only the truth, a route he knew would bring all this—the Chevy, the girlfriend, the high life—to an end. The truth is, I am destined to shuffle, he thought. Preordained to live as I have, a meager existence fraught with fear of landladies, domineering mothers, and dangerous insects.

"Go west, young man," Buff said as she vaulted into the passenger seat, not bothering to open her door. "The high dusty awaits."

And the low muddy soon follows, Billy thought, as he wheeled down Excelsior toward the interstate. And I shall mire down in it like a wood slug. He tried not to shudder at the thought of those soft and slimy creatures but was only partly successful. He simply wasn't ready to embrace one's existence. Well, in a few short hours . . .

Buff wanted to get off at the Anaconda exit. Maybe she'd checked Billy into the Stay Awhile portion of Pendergrast's office. How would that be?

"Where I can weave baskets all day long," Billy sang to himself. Well, three squares and a bed. It was more than his writing had afforded him. He was mildly disappointed when Buff didn't suggest stopping at the good doctor's.

They continued west through the pass between the Pintlar and Flint Mountains, the top down, the summer sun hot above them. Hot enough to mercifully keep the elk, moose, and deer—especially the males of these species—bedded down and out of sight. At Georgetown Lake, they turned south and rolled along a dirt road for ten miles to the East Fork Reservoir, the source of the fabled blue-ribbon trout stream, Rock Creek.

"Let's stop here," Buff said, pointing to a vacant fishing access overlooking the water, the steep granite cliffs of the Pintlars forming the horizon to the east.

Billy stared at the rock for a long time, wondering how it was possible to have so much sky beyond it.

"Come on, walk with me," she said.

Here it was. The take-you-by-the-hand talk about honesty and deception. The I-can't-be-with-a-man-like-you speech. Billy filled his lungs with what he hoped was enough air to keep him going until it was over. Unfortunately, Buff didn't say anything right away, and he was forced to take another breath. They walked to the edge of the reservoir, stepping on elk tracks from the previous night, to a smooth fir log stranded fifteen feet from the water. Buff pulled him into a sitting position on it next to her and, instead of talking, put her hand on his knee and watched the water, tiny waves whispering against the beach. After five minutes, Billy could stand it no longer. Let the ax fall, he told himself. Even if I am the one to wield it.

"I need to tell you . . ." He looked at the ground, a familiar place for his eyes lately. "I need to tell you something," he said slowly, straining hard to keep his voice from cracking.

"I don't think you do." Buff put her arm around him and squeezed.

This was terrible. Billy's whole body tensed, and even the fact that he felt good tone in his shoulders didn't help. Let it drop, he told himself. She's seen the letter from my mother and can make up her own mind. And her father? The dean? Billy sighed.

"I think you're trying too hard," Buff said.

That would be a first, Billy thought.

"Buff, there's something—some *things*, actually, that you need to know." He looked at the lake, the mountains reflected so perfectly on its surface that it was hard to tell where water ended and forest began. "Something in particular that may upset you."

"Try me. You might be surprised."

Billy stood up so he wouldn't feel the repulsion through her arm when he told her. That would be hard to take. Fingers digging, muscles contracting, holding on a few seconds out of obligation, then retreating as fast as a pit viper.

"Buff, I may not . . . no, I *am* not exactly who you think I am." Better to play it as though he hadn't found out about his mother's letter. This way it seems to come from the heart rather than from fear or embarrassment. "I . . ." This was the hard part.

"Shhh." Buff stood, put a finger to his lips, and shook her head. "Then don't spoil it for me," she said. "I like you for everything you want to be, regardless of who you think you are. And I'm a good judge of people. As long as you aren't going to tell me you're married—married or gay, that wouldn't be good either—then let me make up my own mind about who you are. I'm sure there are things about me you don't know, too. But isn't that half the fun? Getting to know not just the big things about people but the little things, too? Finding out what someone likes and doesn't like without being told? Learning to interpret expressions rather than words? I'm sure we could sit here and tell secrets about ourselves all day, but it isn't supposed to work like that. It can't always be planned that neatly. Besides, what if someday you realized you weren't quite who you thought you were? Words have a way of coming true sometimes, so be careful what you say about yourself. The aspirations and hopes we hold—they are *what* we are, if not who."

Billy turned away from her, the lump in his stomach growing larger, creeping toward his throat. Would it be all right to tell her he might have a tumor? He brushed at the corners of his eyes and faced her, his hands on her hips, eyes locked on hers. "There's still one thing—"

Buff cut him off. "Billy, I'm trying to tell you something here."

"What?" Anything to change the subject.

"Like I said, part of the thrill of getting to know someone is not having to be told all the time what they are feeling. I'm trying to tell you something, but you're going to have to figure out on your own what it is. If I told you, it wouldn't mean as much."

"One thing. I must tell you just one thing."

"Just one, then." Buff stepped back.

"It's about your father."

"Oh, spare me."

"He was—"

"Who cares?" Buff was growing annoyed. "Whatever he was, whatever he's done, it doesn't concern us, okay?"

Billy forced his eyes to remain on Buff. No more studying the ground, he told himself. "Please, just listen."

Buff folded her arms across her chest, and Billy didn't even think about what they rested on.

"Your father was the dean who recommended I be expelled from college."

"What? Dad?"

Billy nodded. "I had a bad semester. Partly my fault . . ." That stung to say. "And partly because I was young and away from home for the first time. I spent more time writing . . . really . . ." That was the truth. Billy remembered the nights in the library, afternoons on park benches, and cold winter mornings in the cafeteria with a mug of hot chocolate and his notebooks. He'd probably written more then than he had at any time since.

"Aren't you supposed to have a semester on probation to fix your grades?"

Billy shook his head. "That's an option your father wasn't in favor of. And, Buff, part of what—or who—I am is because of it."

"I don't wonder." There was a coldness in her eyes Billy hadn't seen before. Something as frigid as moonlight on deep January snow when the air is still and the ground glows light blue and spring is just something you faintly remember.

"I'm sorry, Buff." Now Billy could bow his head. Return his gaze to the ground his feet would forever shuffle along. No more thoughts of the high life. Not ever. Banish such foolish notions for good. In acceptance, there is peace.

"Well . . ." Buff bit her lip. "Well, now I have to tell you one thing."

Here it was. The coup d'état. Billy felt his body go slack, supported only by the wide stance of his feet. Soon he could crumble, and that would be good.

Buff stepped forward, put her hands behind his head—she could probably pull hard enough to do the job right—then kissed him on the lips, her mouth hot on his, her hair soft on his neck, her eyes as gentle as they'd been hard. This woman never ceased to amaze.

Billy looked at her, hardly daring to believe what he'd felt, then whispered, "That didn't feel like good-bye." It was a line he wanted to keep track of, one that might work its way into a novel sometime. A new novel.

"And if I'd had to tell you, it wouldn't have felt as good, would it?" Buff wound her hand into his T-shirt and pulled him back toward the car, thirty-eight high-steps away.

Billy let Buff drive on the way back to Butte, and an hour later as he lifted Andrea's brass door knocker, it seemed more than a lifetime ago that he'd let it smack his fingers.

Andrea let them in, the smirk still on her face, and pointed to the living room.

"Yous have big fun, yah?" Andrea asked.

"Yes, we did," Buff said.

"Good. Talk, too, yah?"

"Yes."

"And now we will all talk."

Billy's mouth dropped. Who had spoken? He'd seen Andrea's lips move, but he couldn't believe she'd said anything. The voice had been an old woman's, but not Andrea's. Who else was in the room? His eyes darted back and forth, found Buff's, took in her smile, then settled back on Andrea.

"I have a business proposition that I think will greatly interest the two of you. So humor an old lady and hear me out." She reached for Buff's hand. "I am certain you'll never regret it. I told you once, Billy, that I might have a story for you, didn't I?"

Billy crept down his apartment stairs, Jesus, Mary, and Joseph protesting minimally underfoot. There you have it, he thought, a fine, light bounce instead of the shuffle. Another perk of the high life. What other bonuses were in store? What wonderful things . . . things he could not yet begin to imagine? It was hard telling in what lovely ways respect and prestige would enhance his life. Difficult to guess how many high-steps would be taken, impossible to determine how many great sights his new vantage point, head held up, would afford him. At the front door, he flattened himself against the wall and side-stepped without shuffling to the keyhole, cupped his hands, and peered outside. And oh, there it was! Physical proof that he had finally turned the corner. He looked away, up the dim hallway toward his apartment, then back through the keyhole. Yes, the Chevy was still there. Not his for good, perhaps, but his for now.

Billy bolted out the door and climbed into the driver's seat, just as he had done an hour earlier. Just as he had done every hour since bringing the car home from Andrea's. He tugged at his T-shirt, polishing the glass over the gauges on the dash with the fabric, delighted by the way the chrome reflected his face. It is the face of a man on his way, he thought. A face that will in time relinquish the wrinkles of despair and hard luck. A face that will radiate success and inspire all those who gaze upon it. Billy reached for the wheel with one hand, hanging his other out the window.

"That's right," he said loudly. "Here comes Billy Bristol."

He sat in the car for the better part of twenty minutes, checking the rearview mirror frequently, hoping Helmsley would cruise by.

"Keep your hovel, woman," he would tell her. "I'm finished living in fear of you. Your town sheriff, too. Any man who attempts to remove my belongings will deal with someone of stature now." He liked the way that sounded. Maybe he should find a title to go with his name. Something like *sir* or *esquire.* Perhaps *laureate*?

Later that night, after the car had been put to sleep, its top tenderly pulled up, its door handles wiped free of fingerprints, Billy's living room window drawn open so there would be only air between the two of them, he stretched out on the sofa, stared at the open notebook on the coffee table in front of him, and grinned. Andrea's fine fountain pen felt good in his hand, a writing implement fitting for such a man, and as he outlined his notes, trying hard to remember every detail from the afternoon, he found himself once again thinking how strange the ways of Fate were. Who would have guessed that his lifeline was waiting at the end of his rope?

"To make one appreciate," he whispered. "And I will."

Billy closed his eyes to concentrate on what Andrea had told him. His uncluttered mind, no longer held fast by the jaws of a lowly existence, a life of change-hoarding, mother-dodging, and menial labor, a life attractive to the block, never far from being cut off, heard Andrea's words as clearly as he had earlier that afternoon. He listened to her voice, letting her story sink in, remembering every detail.

"I went to work for the Lincoln Brothel when I was seventeen," she'd said.

Billy wrote the number down and admired his penmanship.

"And before my first customer had his pants off, I knew someday I'd own it. That was nineteen twenty-nine."

Billy wrote that down, too. He liked thinking his book might have a time line inside the front cover. A golden bar across the page with bright blue stars on it calling attention to highlights. "Bright blue," he wrote.

"In nineteen twenty-nine, Butte was Butte. Probably just as well I can't see it anymore. From what I hear, it'd make me sick. Back then, men liked women, and women liked men, and I wasn't any exception. None of these gray areas that confuse things so much today. I liked men, I liked my work, and I had a nose for business. I'd have five, six, sometimes more customers a night. It was business, and it was pleasure, and I'm not ashamed to say I was good at it. By the time I was twenty-one, I was getting half a dozen marriage proposals a week and was visited regularly by the biggest names in Butte. Copper kings, politicians, friends of politicians—we were on a first-name basis. By the time I was thirty, I was one of the richest women in this city, and by the time I was thirty-two, I probably *was* the richest. Certainly the richest woman who'd *earned* her money. I bought the Lincoln Brothel a year later for a song, took my last paying customer a month after that—the governor himself—and began a serious profit-making enterprise. In a town of a hundred thousand men, hardworking, hard-living men, I sold what sold best."

Billy jotted that down word for word.

"For thirty years, through ups and downs in the copper market and a couple of wars, my services were always in demand. We kept our prices in pace with inflation, a step and a half behind sometimes if things slowed down, and we never put anything stale on the shelf—if you know what I mean. You can't attract customers in any business if you're not prepared to treat them well, and when the occasional girl would come along who, for whatever reason—I was never judgmental—wasn't cut out for the work, I'd see if there was a place for her behind the bar, on a cleanup crew, or helping out in the kitchen. All my girls lived in the house, so there was plenty to do that didn't involve men, and I suppose I had something of a reputation for not turning people away.

"But then in the sixties, things started changing. The *free* love frenzy took over, and the little indiscretions my customers were so fond of having behind closed doors—many of the men were married—weren't indiscretions anymore. Everybody started doing everybody, and hardly anyone needed to pay. And free love went hand in hand with love of your body. Lots of women decided they could sleep with whomever they chose, whenever they chose, but to take money for it was shameful and dirty. Never could figure that. To my way of thinking, if you've got the stuff, you might as well earn the dough, too."

That seemed logical to Billy. No more would he pedal his work to anything but the highest-paying periodicals. He made a note of that in the margin and circled it.

"Basically what I had left," he heard Andrea saying, "was a segment of society that couldn't get it anywhere else. And in nineteen sixty-five, if you had to pay, there was something the matter with you. I started seeing abuse. Not that there wasn't always a little of it, but it became common. There were biters and beaters and sometimes worse. New Year's Eve nineteen sixty-six, it all came to a head. I'd been paying the girls mostly out of my own pocket for two or three months . . . god knows I could well afford it, supplementing what little wages they earned, trying to keep them busy doing other things. Had a young gal working a Helena businessman that night, a *well-known* businessman, and when she started screaming, I could tell it wasn't part of the act. I busted in on her, and that son of a bitch had her tied up and was using a nightstick on her.

"Well, I was fifty-four years old and tough as nails. I'd seen most everything at one point or another, but I hadn't seen anything like this. That dickless bastard turned around and I put the barrel of my little pistol—and don't worry, I'm not talking about the one you saw today . . ."

Billy had breathed a sigh of relief.

"I put it against his forehead and snapped the trigger before I had time to think. And when I did, when I did have time, I never thought anything of it. Like killing a rabid coon or swatting a fly. If he hadn't been so highly thought of, there never would have been a problem. As it was, I had to skip town. And that wasn't such a bad thing. I'd played out the Butte scene. I paid a storage owner—a woman I could trust—enough to keep my car and a few other things safe, went overseas, and changed my name. Germany was starting to get back on its feet after the war, and my profession was, well, more highly regarded there. Three months after I left Butte, I was up to my elbows in it again, and it was just like old times.

"Stayed there almost thirty-four years. Invested in all sorts of things. Not everything made money, but what did made lots of it. My sight finally went a little over a year ago, and I decided to come home. I figured I could retire, but I can't. This town owes me a little something, I think. One final hurrah. I know it won't tolerate a house of—what the hell do they call them anymore?— ill repute? But I think the powers that be will accept a dance club. It will get me back to working with girls, and it will put a little spark into uptown Butte. A little flare-up before everything dies out.

"So I need a bartender. Someone who knows Chuck's and someone who knows Butte. And I need someone who's good with people. Good at helping them find work. I've got sixteen dancers coming in from the Stardust in Missoula, and at least that many on their way from Idaho and Nevada. I want them employed around Butte at jobs that will begin to take them somewhere. Further than the dance stage. If you're interested, you'll be well compensated. Extremely well compensated. What do you say?"

Billy nodded his head, just as he had done eight hours ago, then remembered Andrea's final words.

"What I have told you is for your ears only. If it makes its way into a story sometime, Billy, see that you tell it well.

"Now, if ve iz ready, ve goes into business, yah? Da story iz not end."

And that was that. Billy looked into his bedroom, where Buff had the light on waiting for him. How had all of this fallen into place? he wondered. Like stones that begin rolling down a steep mountain at the same time, yet far apart, and somehow converge at the bottom. He closed his notebook and quietly high-stepped to his room, his knees rising well above his waist. In time, they will touch my chest, he thought.

Buff took the Chevy in the morning. She had to give Job Services her notice, then begin looking for apartments for the girls. Billy stood on the front steps and watched her drive away, her kiss lingering on his lips. It didn't feel so bad to get up before noon. He waited for the car to disappear past Main Street, then turned quickly up the steps before any feral cats crossed the street. All he needed was a lanky black cat to pass in front of him to get him wondering if it was all a dream. He snuck back inside, tiptoed up the stairs, acknowledging Jesus, Mary, and Joseph with a whisper to each, then crept into his apartment. He had to look in his bed and make sure. Be certain he wasn't lying in there dead. It hurt when he pinched himself, so he didn't think he was, but he'd learned not to take too much for granted. Ten minutes later, when he worked up the courage to check, he found the bed empty and sighed heavily. By god, he had turned the corner.

But Billy's heart still pounded when his phone rang, actions of reflex hard to overcome. Massaging his chest, he picked it up and calmly said, "Hello."

I can deal with Mother. I can deal with an editor. I can deal with . . .

"Hell-ooo, Bill-y."

I can deal with Petie, too. "Hello."

"Auc-tion day is com-ing. Are you hang-ing in there?"

"Yes." Nice to see Petie so concerned.

"Thoughts on fath-er dean?"

"No."

"Ly-ing, Bill-y. Bad to de-ny."

"Not many thoughts." Why was honesty suddenly so important to people? A dose of it now and then was acceptable, but it wasn't a pattern Billy particularly wanted to fall into. They didn't call it the cold hard truth for nothing.

"Pe-tie is ready."

Billy said nothing.

"Yes, Billy, we're in your corner," Pendergrast said.

"Pe-tie is ready, and Pe-tie is talking," the puppet warned. "Want to in-ter-rupt?"

"No. No, I don't," the doctor said earnestly.

"Re-mem-ber in-ter-rup-tion talk? Pe-tie taught less-on."

"Oh, yes, I remember. I remember."

"Good. Now, Bill-y, dean will be at the auc-tion, right?"

"Yes," Billy said.

"Makes Pe-tie ver-y happ-y. Peo-ple-hurt-ers must pay. Bye, bye."

Billy hung up the phone and stared at his notebook from the night before. Buff had drawn a smiley face near the top of the page and written, "Me this morning," beside it.

"Thank god," he sighed. The high life seemed to have improved him in many ways. Billy flipped the page and lifted his pen, admiring again what a beautiful thing it was. Wonderful, too, how the desire to write, that elusive lust to create, had not left him during the night. He doodled a curlicue design in the margin, then began outlining the story. *Crossing Montana* would have to wait.

Billy paused an hour later as the thought that he might be in possession of a magical pen crossed his mind. Something from a Brothers Grimm tale. Never before had he been at it this long. Not without a break. He held the pen in his open hand and stared hard. Perhaps he could get it to move. Telekinesis would be a perk of the high life that he could make great use of.

Buff came back in the early afternoon with a big bag of take-out Chinese food. Billy wouldn't have minded seeing a bottle of Heineken in it, too, but she would learn those things in time.

Hadn't she said something about that being half the fun? Picking through his carton of sweet-and-sour pork, he debated telling her about Petie. Where could he begin? Billy decided he'd let her find out on her own about him, too. Instead, now seemed to be the right time to ask her about Andrea.

"When did you know?" he said.

"About what?" Buff pulled a hunk of deep-fried chicken off a toothpick in a way that made Billy sigh.

"About Andrea."

"Just recently."

She seemed to be telling the truth, and Billy was relieved. He was happy—more than happy, really, with the way things were working out, but to learn he'd been a pawn in a great conspiracy would have been troubling. What other schemes might he unwittingly blunder into? If it happened once, he'd forever be wary of women. The victim of a cabal was not a title he wished to wear.

"I always knew there was more to her than met the eye, but I wouldn't have guessed what. Not in a million years," Buff said.

"Me, either. You believe her?"

"Yes, don't you?"

"Yes."

"And is that what you're working on now? Her story?" She pointed to his notebook with the toothpick.

Billy had filled nine pages. "In a way, it is. I suppose in a way it's all our stories. I'm just waiting . . ." He picked up the pen and notebook. "I'm wondering what the ending will be like."

"Happy." Buff pulled the book from his hands and pushed him backward onto the couch, sitting on his chest. "And you know what they say, all work and no play makes Billy a *very* dull boy." She began to unbutton his shirt, and Billy tightened his stomach as much as he could. Firm, he thought. Not toned yet, but that's coming. Everything in time in the high life.

Time itself in the high life seemed to pass quickly. Days moved from morning to noon to evening in a blur of writing, passionate interludes with Buff, and Discovery Channel programs on everything from the great Greenland sharks that swim under the polar ice cap to a new species of tarantula in the Amazon jungle. Billy made it through that entire segment, Buff's arms wrapped around him beneath the blanket on the couch, and when it was over he'd looked at her and said, "You make *everything* better."

Buff had been touched by the comment, and they'd fallen together there on the couch. Billy didn't mind missing the next program, even though he'd always wondered about the Asian taimen
fish and whether it was possible that's what had eaten the rat he
and his mother saw at the Warm Springs pond. He didn't mind
many things anymore, and when auction day arrived, he and Buff
and Andrea making their way to Chuck's together in the Chevy,
high-stepping into the bar early in the morning, it was hard for
him to believe his feet had ever shuffled.

The trio took a table in the back, quite near the spot where
Billy and Buff sat after she'd broken the rum bottle over Leslie
Booth's head. Why did that seem so long ago? It was more than
Billy putting thoughts of the Cow Camp out of his head. It was an
entire reversal in fortune that made everything he'd done in his
life seem foreign. It simply wasn't who he was anymore. Step
aside, shuffler, here comes a man with standing. He imagined
himself swaggering up Main Street. It was a method of movement
he would have to work on.

Old Stan came in fifteen minutes later, his Armani pressed for
the occasion, smelling as if he'd bathed in cologne.

"My most favorite clients," he said, putting his arms around
Buff and Andrea. "My own cheering section."

For a moment, Billy felt bad for him. Then he remembered the
hundred thousand.

"Mind if I sit with you?" Stan asked.

"Yah, yous go right ahead. Ve help you out. Vait and see."

Stan snuggled in beside Andrea, running his tie up into his
chin, pulling at the knot with gusto.

"I look okay?" he whispered to Buff.

"Very handsome," she said.

He shrugged his shoulders and settled into his chair, greatly
pleased with her response. Stan was a man who could swagger,
Billy thought. He'd ask him about it later. Find out where he
bought the suit, too.

The door was blocked open with a brick, allowing the morning sun to filter in, cutting a bright beam through the permanent
cigarette smoke inside, silhouetting anyone who came in so that
Billy couldn't tell who they were until they stepped out of the
light. Chuck was there, the grand patriarch, sitting behind the bar
with two well-dressed gentlemen—liquor inspectors or other

state agents, Billy figured. Leslie Booth and Lilly Four-Toes had on matching blue dresses—probably the only ones that came in their size—and had taken seats near the door. No one spoke, and there was something in the atmosphere that reminded Billy of an empty church. A place no one *should* speak. He stared at the wooden pillars in the middle of the floor, reading the names whittled into them.

TIE ONE ON, someone had carved in June 1960. DJ LOVES AN MAY 1977. Billy wondered who DJ and AN were and if they were still in love? He reached for Buff's hand, wishing he could have slipped in earlier and carved something she'd see. Not the large DRUNK that appeared to have been engraved with a wood chisel, either. Below it, in smaller letters, was the word ALWAYS. It had probably been part of something more once, but right now it was enough. He squeezed Buff's hand and said it to himself. Always.

Billy's mother came in next. A flowered dress, matching parasol, and shiny high heels to boot. Like something from a 1920s time machine. Her purse looked especially bulky, and she had most of its strap looped up in her hand. She spotted Billy immediately and made straight for the table.

"Come to watch your mommy," she said. It was a statement, not a question. "Very nice, honey." She stared at Buff and smiled. "Got someone you want to introduce me to, baby?"

Billy's skin began to crawl. Here was a creature that could pull him from the high life.

"You'll have to excuse Billy," she said, swinging her parasol dangerously close to Andrea. Andrea didn't notice. "I have taught him manners, but sometimes he forgets. I'm Gloria Bristol, his mother."

"Hi," Buff extended her hand. "I'm . . ."

"And you're Buff Austin, Billy's girl." She shook her hand, then turned slowly to her son. "Mommy wrote her a nice letter. Wouldn't hurt to thank me sometime." She poked him with the end of the umbrella. "You be sure Billy brings you by on Spaghetti Day," she said as she clacked off toward Chuck. "You be sure he does that."

"Wow!" Stan hopped his chair close to Billy. "She really your mom?"

Billy nodded.

"Son of a bitch! She's . . . Jesus . . ."

That would be odd, Billy thought.

"She's the woman from my dream about the lottery. The one from the perfume shop. And no ring on her hand? Son of a bitch!"

Buff began to laugh, little giggles she tried to hide by putting a hand to her mouth.

Billy saw no humor in it. An awful vision of Old Stan and his mother walking down the aisle came to mind, a bright yellow cab decorated with shaving cream and strings of cans waiting in front of the church. The fact that Stan was interested bore out all Billy's previous suspicions that he was severely limited, and he pulled away from him before something rubbed off. Some infectious, incurable disease that would put a damper on the high life.

"Got her number?" Stan found a semiclean handkerchief in a front pocket and asked Andrea for a pen. "No, on second thought . . ." He wadded the handkerchief back into his pants. "Maybe I'll just go sit with her. Figure she'd mind?"

"No, iz good idea," Andrea said.

As he bowed, turned his back, and swaggered away, Buff whispered, "Daddy," in Billy's ear. The woman had no control.

There was no clock in Chuck's. Not one that worked. The hands on the one above the bar, a glossy piece of juniper shaped like Oklahoma, stood still at five after two and had for as long as Billy could remember. He looked at the watch on Buff's wrist, a brown leather band studded with German silver buttons that held a delicate timepiece with a mother-of-pearl face. She had no control, but she did have taste. It was nine-thirty, half an hour to go.

Pendergrast drifted in next, the lean man wafting through the door like the smoke that slowly flowed from the bar. He was wearing a long duster, weathered leather that hung well past his knees, unbuttoned its entire length, his hands in its pockets, his eyes shifting from one person to the next, his face as pale as morning mist. With longer hair he could have been Wild Bill. He motioned to Billy with a jerk of his head and floated out the door.

"Excuse me," Billy said. "I'll be right back."

On the sidewalk, Pendergrast looked more himself. "How are you?" he asked earnestly. "Are you coping?"

"I believe so," Billy said.

"Oh, that's so good. It's so very, very good." He patted Billy on the back. "These are trying times for you, I know."

Where was Petie? Billy studied him, a cop looking for a concealed weapon. There. Pendergrast's left front pocket. A noticeable bulge.

"We're proud of you, you know." His hand disappeared into the pocket, Pendergrast looked up and down Main Street, then Petie emerged and yawned.

"Hell-ooo, Bill-y." The little fellow waved, then burrowed out of sight under the duster.

"He's so anxious to meet the dean," Pendergrast whispered. "It's been all I could do to hold him back these last few days."

Petie's head poked from the coat and turned slowly up to face the doctor. "Talk-ing about Pe-tie?" he asked.

"No, no," Pendergrast replied.

"Bett-er not." Petie disappeared.

Billy had watched the doctor's mouth very closely the last time Petie spoke, and hadn't seen so much as a twitch. As Pendergrast would say, very, very unnerving. He turned his eyes up the street, then over to the East Ridge and Mary, who he felt was surely not impressed with Pendergrast or his puppet. Or him.

The black BMW pulled up to the curb a moment later, arriving soundlessly, and Billy nodded.

"Here he is," he said.

"It's okay, Billy. Do you want to hold my hand?" Pendergrast offered it to him. "We're right here with you."

Petie struck the inside of the duster hard. "Not yet, not yet," the doctor whispered, pulling the coat tight to his chest. "It's so hard to keep him back."

Carl and Susan Austin stepped out together, the woman dressed elegantly, the man extravagantly. He wore a green vest and carried a cane—blackthorn, unless Billy was mistaken.

Petie began thumping around under the coat in good shape, bubbling the leather, trying hard to find an exit. Pendergrast turned his back to the dean and cooed softly, his chin tucked into his collar. This seemed to mollify Petie. The thumping didn't stop, but it slowed down.

"Billy." Susan smiled. "I'm glad you could make it. And Buff? She inside?"

"Yes." Billy pointed to the door.

"Billy, aye?" The dean cast a critical eye on him. It wasn't the first time. "I say . . ." He tapped his cane on the sidewalk, looking him up and down the way one examines a horse he doesn't really want to buy. *Ta-ta-ta-tap, ta-ta-ta-tap.*

Billy began to shake.

"My wife has told me you are a man of some standing." The dean sneered. "Published."

Billy said nothing. It was so hard to look at him.

"I am also published. Extensively and well. Are you familiar with any of the academic journals?"

Billy raised his eyebrows. It wasn't a yes, and it wasn't a no.

"I see." The dean smacked his lips. "You would do well to peruse them. I am a frequent contributor to half a dozen of the best . . ." He looked back at the BMW. "In fact, just a moment." He popped the trunk with a button on his key chain and it rose slowly, a coffin lid opening all by itself. The dean walked deliberately to the back of the car, bent slightly, and came up with a sheet of paper. "Let's have a look-see at this," he said.

It was a copy of a short article, the dean's byline at the end. He should know better than that, Billy thought. Billy would never see his name anywhere other than the top. In bold letters, in a different font from the text. What had the dean written? His eyes scanned the article, as much so they wouldn't meet Carl's as anything.

We have before us an acute threat to our universities. Confronted with sloth and indifference within our student bodies, more and more of us are lowering our own standards—once lofty—to the level of these unmotivated, poorly prepared, aloof pupils, thus shackling our own intellect, imprisoning our minds in the cells of mediocrity, satisfied too easily, challenged very seldom. I must denounce our increasing conversion to academic sloppiness. It is an ugly word, but it is an ugly pattern.

We are the nation's great thinkers, the deep reservoir of knowledge that men all over the world draw upon for reasoning. And I say to you, my fellow peers, let us not allow this reservoir to become polluted. Let us begin a concerted purification effort. Let us begin once more to hold ourselves to the very highest standards: to weed from the barrel all bad apples, students and faculty alike. Let our halls echo the sounds of clapping hands for our achievements and our study walls proudly sport our accolades. Let us sleep well at night, knowing we are men of great learning and that we continue to learn. Let us keep the flame of knowledge burning bright and strong, at least within our own community. Let us read, let us write, let us publish, and let us not become stagnant, worn down by a culture in which average is acceptable.

"*Harvard Review,* 1977," the dean said when Billy finished. "A fine example of how good writing doesn't fade through the years. Here you go." He fished a pen, a fancy, gold-leaf Parker, from his shirt pocket and wrote, "For Billy: May he apply these words to everything he does."

Billy took the paper, his hands trembling.

"Well, then, Billy . . . Billy . . . You seem familiar," Carl said. "It will come to me. Now I'm going in to buy this establishment. What Butte needs is some culture. And I'm just the man to lend it some," he said as he walked away, the cane striking the sidewalk with authority.

Down the street twenty yards, Pendergrast was wrestling with Petie. It appeared that the puppet was winning, biting him savagely along the rib cage. Billy followed the dean inside rather than stay and witness a murder.

Back in Chuck's, Carl was talking with his wife, scratching his head, still trying to think where he'd seen Billy before.

Billy hurried back to his table and handed the article to Buff.

"Jesus Christ," she said as she crumpled it up.

"Okay, folks, I guess it's time." Chuck stood up behind the bar. "Glad to see some familiar faces out there." He pointed to one of the men beside him. "He'll explain what all goes, then we can get under way."

The man rose and stumbled through a legal description of the property to be auctioned.

"No surprises there, I hope," Chuck said. "I'm not an auctioneer, so don't expect no fast talking." He waited for laughter but none came. This was serious business. "Okay, we'll start at twenty thousand."

Billy's mother instantly put her hand up.

"Damn her for keeping it from me," Billy mumbled.

"Twenty-five?" Chuck looked around the room. A man Billy didn't recognize raised his hand.

"Thirty?"

"All mine," Stan said, standing up.

"Thirty-five?"

The dean nodded solemnly.

"Forty?"

Billy's mother raised her hand again. Just how much money did she have?

"Forty-five?"

The dean smiled and nodded.

"Fifty thousand. Anyone for fifty?"

Old Stan raised his hand, but he acted as if he wasn't sure. Billy's mother stared bitterly at the dean. He'd bid her out.

"Sixty thousand," Carl Austin said calmly. Susan looked worried. She bit at her nails and shifted in her seat.

"Yah, den ve goes seventy." Andrea stood up.

Chuck coughed. "Would you mind identifying yourself, ma'am?"

"My name iz Andrea Kauffman."

"And you understand the bid is sixty thousand?"

"Da bid iz seventy thousand," she said.

Chuck cleared his throat. "We have seventy thousand. Do I hear any more?"

Susan was saying something to her husband, trying to hold his hand. He pulled away from her, stood up, and said, "Seventy-five." She leaned onto the table.

"Jerk," Buff whispered.

"There is a bid of seventy-five thousand," Chuck said. "That's going once, going twice, three times. Any more bids?"

"Yah, okay, ve goes one hundred. Iz good deal. You vant a hundred thousand?" Andrea smiled in Chuck's direction.

The dean sat down.

Chuck choked reciting her bid, but no one opposed it. Andrea Kauffman bought the bar.

Billy's mother stood up and walked fast to the door, Old Stan one step behind, pleading with her about something Billy was just as glad he couldn't hear. It would probably make him ill.

Susan had her arms around the dean, rocking him against her chest, probably as much in relief as condolence. He let her hold him for a few moments, then shucked her off and headed for Andrea.

"Congratulations," he said wryly.

"Yah, tank you." Andrea smiled.

The dean looked at Buff, then at Billy. Behind him, close to the door, Pendergrast lurked in the shadows. "Tell me about him," Carl said, and he didn't seem to be asking out of curiosity. It sounded like a command.

"About who, Dad? Billy?"

"Yes, Billy." His face was growing red.

"Something from his past?" Buff said. "A little tale from college, perhaps?"

"Anything."

"Very well. Billy went to an eastern university."

"Ivy League?" the dean asked hopefully.

"Almost. A good school."

"And he majored in?"

Billy was growing very uncomfortable. The bottoms of his feet itched, and he was sure dean boils were not far behind.

"Literature," Buff said. "He wanted to be a writer."

"I saw lots of such students. Idealistic and without direction, for the most part."

"Is that what you told Billy?" Buff hadn't blinked since she began speaking.

"What?" The dean looked at him, the surprise evident on his face.

"Is that what you told Billy Bristol when you recommended he be expelled?"

"Bristol? You said Bristol?" The dean staggered backward, catching hold of a pillar before falling. Susan rushed to his side.

"Are you all right? What's going on? Honey, are you okay?"

The dean pointed a finger at Billy. "Bristol," he croaked. "Letter writer."

Billy nodded, beginning to find his strength. "Still going," he said.

Carl Austin clapped his hands to his heart.

He did that very well, Billy thought. Perhaps he *was* a writer.

"No, no, no, no," he moaned. "A lout. A vagabond. Illiterate and incorrigible. Oh, the halls, the halls." He slipped to his knees. "Not for you, Buff. Please, please. Think of the institute," he begged.

"I love him, Dad." She said it proudly. "Very much."

Her father let his cane clatter to the floor and pitched onto his face.

"Help him!" Susan screamed. "Somebody help him. Find a doctor!"

Pendergrast materialized beside her, his left hand still under the duster. "A doctor is here, ma'am," he said. "Please stand back." He knelt beside the dean, pushed his face close, and whispered, "I can make you all better, people-hurter."

The dean gasped and quivered. "Not Bristol," he said.

"Dis man needs hospital?" Andrea asked, her smile still present.

"Yes, yes he does," Pendergrast said. "But we'll take care of him now." He hooked his right arm around the dean and helped him to his feet.

Shuffle, Billy thought. Let me see him shuffle. He began breathing fast, eyes fixed on the dean's feet. They scuffed toward the door.

Just before stepping out, Pendergrast turned around. He moved so fast that if Billy hadn't been watching closely, he wouldn't have seen it. Petie sprang from the coat, clicked his heels, and Pendergrast mouthed, "Stay a while." Then the puppet melted into the sunlight coming through the open door, and the doctor and the dean disappeared.

· 18 ·

The thinnest sliver of October moon was visible over Mary's right shoulder. Billy stared at it through the cold night air, on the sidewalk in front of Chuck's, its new neon sign flashing above him. Outside, he couldn't smell the varnish or heady scent of wood from the stage that he liked so much, but it wasn't as loud. He waited until the music ended before he went back in. There was one more dance, and then it would be time to go home. He swung open the door, the painting of the miner replaced by one of a lewd-looking woman in a nurse's outfit that he liked much better.

The two bouncers, Leslie Booth and Lilly Four-Toes, stepped aside to let him pass. No one underage ever got in, and in two months there hadn't been a single fight. Billy nodded at them, and Lilly slapped his behind.

Most of the customers had gone, leaving Hector and Doug and a couple of truck drivers lined up along the stage, their stacks of dollar bills much depleted. Billy slid in behind the bar and looked expectantly at the blue velvet curtain that separated the women's dressing rooms from the stage. The redhead always danced last, and she was his favorite. He loved everything about her. He opened the drawer of the cash register and grinned. It had been another big night. They were all big nights. That was part of the high life, he figured.

The wall of speakers along the stage came to life with heavy bass, thumping hard off everything in the bar. Billy folded the last of the big bills into the night-deposit bag and settled onto his stool just as the woman burst from the curtain. How did she spin on the poles that way? And that smile . . . my god.

"Gorgeous," Billy whispered. He didn't even mind the way she teased Hector. With Leslie and Lilly, no customer ever reached for a dancer. Not ever.

The music came faster, and the stripper's clothes began falling off onto the stage, her naked body gleaming in the black lights set into the ceiling above her. She winked at Billy. Because she knows it drives me wild, he thought. He watched her long red hair fall between her legs as she did a split inches from a truck driver, and grinned as the open-mouthed man shoved bills at her. She kissed him on the forehead and rolled away, closer to Billy, and winked again. Why did he find her so irresistible?

The song ended too soon, and the redhead only worked one dance. That was her trademark, and partly why Billy liked watching her so much. As the bar emptied, customers herded out by Leslie and Lilly, he pictured her in the dressing room, all alone in front of those lovely mirrors.

"Do my most favorite employers need a ride home tonight?" Old Stan asked, one foot inside the door, his Armani suit neatly pressed, the front corner of a limousine visible behind him near the curb.

"No thanks," Billy said. "Not tonight."

"Then I'll call it a night."

Stan started to let the door close, then pushed it open. "Okay to pick your mother up on Thursday?"

Andrea let her cook spaghetti for the girls on Thursdays, and Stan had been itching to pick her up in the limousine since Chuck's reopened.

Billy nodded. Why not? "If she'll ride with you," he said.

Old Stan clapped his hands together and said something Billy didn't quite catch. Sounded like, "Ain't love great." He was thinking about it when the redhead came out of the dressing rooms, her sequin-covered dress sparkling like the stars Billy had seen outside.

"Ready?" he asked.

"You bet." She followed him to the door.

Billy clicked the lights off and stepped outside, feeling the woman snuggle against him as he locked the door. The Chevy was parked in back, and he wished it was warm enough to put the top down. He opened her door, then took his time getting to the driver's side. Billy still liked admiring the car.

"Well?" he asked when he got in.

The woman ran her hand through her hair, bent forward, and pulled the wig into her lap. Buff looked pretty damn good without it. "Not tired, are you?" she said as they pulled onto Main Street.

"Not too." Billy reached for her hand, and she squeezed, his entire body warming instantly.

"Chapter eight tomorrow?"

"I think so." Billy was making good headway, approaching the midpoint of his book. "And tonight?"

Buff laughed and moved closer to him. "Wonderful things," she whispered as she put her hand on his thigh and smiled.

In the rearview mirror, Billy could see Mary watching. He couldn't believe even she disapproved.